"Kate Carlisle dazzles and delights readers."
—Fresh Fiction

"Laugh-out-loud hysterical . . . with many twists and turns. . . . This is a great tale of who *didn't* do it!"
—RT Book Reviews

LITTLE BLACK BOOK

A Bibliophile Mystery

Kate Carlisle

BERKLEY PRIME CRIME
New York

BERKLEY PRIME CRIME
Published by Berkley
An imprint of Penguin Random House LLC
penguinrandomhouse.com

ISBN: 9780593201459

Berkley Prime Crime hardcover edition / June 2021
Berkley Prime Crime mass-market edition / June 2022

Printed in the United States of America
1   3   5   7   9   10   8   6   4   2

*This book is dedicated to my handsome,
valiant husband, Don,
who kept me laughing and kept me going
when I wasn't sure I'd make it through this year,
let alone this book.
But yay, we made it through both!
Next year in Scotland!*

Chapter 1

The black book arrived in the mail on a quiet Saturday afternoon.

My husband Derek walked into my workshop balancing a large bundle of letters and parcels in his arms. "We've quite a backlog of mail, darling."

I glanced up and smiled at him. We had been married less than a year so I could forgive myself for wanting to sigh dreamily. I would never grow tired of looking at his ruggedly handsome face with those dark blue eyes and dangerous smile. I simply loved everything about him, even the way he occasionally aimed one inquisitive, raised eyebrow in my direction—how did he do that?—or the way his voice could go all cold and upper-class Brit when dealing with some knucklehead trying to pull a fast one over on him. Of course, that same voice turned rich and warm when he was talking only to me. He was tall and lean and tough and sexy. And he made me laugh every day, which made him even sexier in my book. He was just plain perfect for me.

And somehow, he felt the same way about me.

"Darling?"

I blinked. "Oh." Whew, what brought that on? "Um,

yeah, looks like the mail really piled up while we were gone."

Late last night Derek and I had returned home to San Francisco from Dharma, where we had spent the last ten days enjoying the wine country, visiting our parents and friends, and checking on the final phase of construction on our new home away from home. It was no wonder we had so much mail.

And so much work to catch up on, I added mentally, staring at the fractured copy of *The Adventures of Tom Sawyer* spread out in pieces in front of me.

He was still staring at me, his lips twisted in a wry grin. "Are you sure you're all right?"

"Oh yeah, I'm dandy." But I had to take a quick breath and let it out slowly. Sometimes it hit me just how much I loved this guy. And what made it even better was that he loved me right back. I'd probably get used to it in a few hundred years or so. "I guess I'm still a little tired from the trip. And now I've got to finish this book before I do anything else."

"You'll get it done." He kissed the top of my head and we leaned into each other for a brief moment. Then he stepped away and I shook my head to clear my errant thoughts. It was time to concentrate on my work.

I carefully separated the ragged covers of the old *Tom Sawyer* copy I'd been asked to restore. I planned to replace the faded cloth cover and spine with a sturdy new cloth in deep forest green and then add new endpapers to the inside front and back. The textblock itself was remarkably undamaged, the pages still crisp and clean. Clearly the book had been lucky enough to have escaped the ravages of any children who, in general, had an overwhelming tendency to love their favorite books to death.

With a sturdy new outer shell and a little help from me, these pages might last a few hundred more years.

Derek walked around to the opposite end of my worktable and set the piles of mail down. Then he proceeded to sort them into smaller piles.

"Lots of bills," he muttered. "And plenty of junk. Ah, here's a postcard from Douglas and Delia. They're in Santorini."

"I hope they're having fun," I said. Douglas was Derek's oldest brother and a general in the British Army. His wife Delia was lovely and had a wonderful dry wit.

"It seems they are," he said, giving the card a quick scan.

"I'm glad."

"Alex is doing well, by the way," he said, speaking of our down-the-hall neighbor. "She promises she'll be by shortly with cupcakes in honor of our homecoming."

That got my attention. "Cupcakes? For real?"

"I saw them with my own eyes."

Alex Monroe had offered to collect our mail while we were gone and also to keep an eye on our place. As a former CIA operative, she was handy when it came to security issues. She was also the high-powered head of her own company and enjoyed baking cupcakes to relax. She really was the best kind of neighbor in every way.

Derek set the postcard down on one of the piles he'd created and continued perusing the stack. "Someone sent you a book."

He walked around to my end of the table and placed the excessively taped and padded manila envelope down in front of me.

"A book for me?" I grinned. "Why would anyone send me a book?"

He chuckled because I was joking, of course. I'm a bookbinder specializing in rare book restoration. I received books in the mail from clients all the time.

I was thankful the envelope was padded because the back was scuffed and dirty and slightly dented from traveling. I turned it over to see who it was from, but there was no individual's name on the return address. Just a company, Gwyneth Antiquities, located in Oddlochen, Scotland.

Scotland? "Where's Oddlochen?"

Derek whipped out his phone, tapped a few icons. "It's a village near Inverness."

Then I focused in on the addressee. "Derek, this isn't for me. It's addressed to you."

"Me?" It was his turn to frown. "How odd. I didn't even look. I could tell it was a book and naturally assumed it was for you."

"I did, too." I held out the package. "But it's got your name on it."

He took it and glanced around for some way to cut through the layers of packing tape.

"Scissors in the top drawer," I said helpfully, pointing toward my desk.

"Of course." Once he had it opened, he slid the book out onto the worktable. Looking at the title, he said, "Now I'm doubly sure it was meant for you."

I picked up the book. The cloth cover was a stark black. The only thing on the front of the book was the one-word title printed in faded gold and slanted in the upper left-hand corner: *Rebecca*.

"*Rebecca*." I flashed him a bright smile. "One of my favorites." I had always been a sucker for gothic novels. The plucky heroine doomed to live a life of drudgery, rescued by the handsome stranger—or is he a killer?

Dark and moody, romantic and suspenseful. I had spent my preteen years gobbling them up.

I chuckled at my own thoughts, then naturally turned to the book itself to examine the condition of the front and back covers. That's my job, after all, so it was second nature for me to check out the spine, which showed the same elegantly styled title and the author's name below in simple block letters. I ran my hand along it. The cloth covers of old books had a tendency to separate and sag away from the stiff material underneath, but this spine was still firm and smooth.

I turned the book over again. "Outer corners are slightly rubbed. Spine has a bit of wear at the bottom edge." I pointed out the discoloration.

"I see," Derek murmured.

"The binding is tight, though," I added, standing the book upright on the table. "No wobbling, see?"

"I do, and it thrills me." He leaned over and kissed my cheek.

I laughed. "You need to get out more."

He picked up the book and studied the cover. "Can you fix the discoloration?"

"Of course. But I won't do anything until we find out who sent it to you and why."

"Yes." He handed the book back to me. "Why, indeed."

"Do you know anyone named Gwyneth?"

"I do, yes. Someone I worked with years ago. But why would she . . . well, it doesn't make sense."

Opening the book to the title page, I studied the information written there. "Derek, it's a British first edition. First printing, 1938." I turned the page. "And look. It's signed by Daphne du Maurier." I looked up at him. "Wow."

"That is impressive," he said with a nod.

"I'll go through it more closely later, but overall the book appears to be in very good condition. And that signature raises its value significantly." I smiled. "Someone must like you a lot."

"I'm a likable fellow." But his eyes narrowed slightly and that wonderful mouth turned grim as he pondered where the book had come from. He pushed the sleeves of his navy sweater up to his elbows and leaned against the table. "Is there a card or something inside the book that indicates who sent it? And why?"

"Good question."

While Derek studied the front of the manila envelope, I carefully leafed through the book, then held it upside down, gently fanning the pages open so that anything that might've been slipped inside would fall out. But there was nothing. "Is there anything else inside the envelope?"

He checked it thoroughly. "Nothing."

"So it's a mystery," I said.

He raised an eyebrow. "Just what we need. Another mystery."

"It's been months since the book festival," I said with a shrug. "We're about due, don't you think?"

"Bite your tongue, darling."

The Dharma Book Festival last October had been a huge success and garnered lots of publicity, no thanks to the two murders that had taken place only days before it all began. Happily, though, the killer had been caught before a third murder could be committed, and eventually all of our lives had settled back down to normal. Or as normal as we could ever be, given my tendency to attract evil killers and their ilk.

So yes, mysteries and murderous intentions did seem to follow us wherever we went, but it wasn't all my fault. My dear husband was one of the world's top security experts and, after all, the book had been sent to him. So for once, this little puzzle was on him. Which was, no doubt, why he was staring at the mysterious book with such a thoughtful expression.

The doorbell rang and we stared at each other.

"Cupcakes?" I wondered.

"Let's hope so."

He took my hand and we walked over to the door.

"Welcome home," Alex declared, and strolled in carrying a large, sturdy, plastic cupcake carrier. She looked ridiculously elegant in simple black leggings, black-and-white sneakers, and a sage-green tunic. Setting the carrier on the kitchen island, she turned and grabbed me in a fierce hug. "So glad you guys are home."

"We are, too," I said. "Thanks so much for taking care of Charlie and for holding our mail. And for cupcakes and for everything else you always do. We really appreciate it."

"It's no prob." She glanced around. "Charlie was right behind me."

"Charlie?" I called.

Hearing her name, our little beast dashed through the door and immediately began winding herself around my ankles and mewing loudly.

"Aww. Hello, sweetie," I said, and picked up the cat. Charlie gave my cheek a light headbutt. "So good to see you."

Alex smiled. "I think she missed you."

"I missed her, too." I rubbed my cheek against her soft fur, enjoying the sound of her contented purring.

After another minute of cuddling, I set Charlie on the floor and got down to business. "Now, about these cupcakes."

She laughed. "Twelve of them. Three different flavors."

Derek joined us. Reaching down, he lifted the pretty white-and-orange cat into his arms, much to Charlie's delight. "Alex, honestly. We should be the ones bringing you cupcakes. We owe you."

"Don't be silly." She reached over to scratch Charlie's neck. "I got to play with Charlie for ten whole days, so that's more than a fair trade. Besides, you know I'm compelled to bake. I can't seem to help myself. So if I didn't give some of them to you, I'd have to eat them all by myself."

"So we're doing you a favor?" I said.

She grinned. "Exactly."

"Well, then, how can we refuse?" I glanced up at Derek. "Guess we should have a cupcake."

"It's about time." For a sophisticated international man of mystery, he pretty much turned to putty when it came to cupcakes.

The three of us clustered around the cupcake carrier and Alex snapped off the lid.

"Wow," I said.

"My thoughts exactly," Derek said.

I recognized her red velvet cakes with their tall swirl of cream cheese frosting. The chocolate chip cupcakes were slathered in glistening white icing with tiny chocolate chips scattered on top. The third row looked like a yellow cake with white frosting of some kind. I desperately wanted them all, but didn't say it out loud.

Pointing to each row of cupcakes, Alex said, "You've had the red velvet and the chocolate chip before, but this one is something I've been experimenting with. I think you'll love it."

"Of course we will," Derek said, examining the new treat. "What is it? Some sort of yellow cake?"

"It's a lemon meringue cupcake."

"Oh," I whispered in awe. "I've heard you talk about this."

"I didn't want anyone to try it until I'd perfected it." She wiggled her eyebrows gleefully. "And now I have."

"They're so pretty." The frosting was a towering swirl of shiny white with tiny sprigs of lemon and lime zest sprinkled on top.

"They taste even better than they look," she assured us.

I glanced at Derek. "We could split one. For starters, I mean."

"That works for me."

We both took a bite and discovered a surprise. Inside the cake was a pocket of rich, lemony curd, sweet and slightly tart. The meringue icing was light and fluffy and melted in my mouth.

"This is heavenly," I said, when I could speak again. "It's like eating lemon meringue pie."

"Only it's cake. Moist and delicious." Derek surreptitiously brushed a crumb off his sweater. "I believe your talents are wasted running that silly corporation of yours."

Delighted, Alex laughed and tossed back her long, dark, silky hair. "Thanks."

"It's true," I insisted. "Why sell your soul to high finance when you could be selling cupcakes out on the street?"

The three of us spent a few more minutes laughing and talking and gossiping. After she'd agreed to come over for dinner the next night, Alex headed back home.

Derek went to his office to return some phone calls and I went back to work on the *Tom Sawyer*. Even knowing that Derek was just down the hall, it was easy for me to become consumed by my work. Books—especially old, decrepit books—had always been a major part of my life and I looked at each one like a dedicated surgeon beheld a suffering patient. *How can I make you whole again? How can I improve your life?*

The interior pages of the *Tom Sawyer* were actually in pretty good shape, except for some tears and mild foxing in various sections of the book. I went ahead and separated the cover from the textblock in order to clean the gutters thoroughly and eventually resew the pages with a stronger new thread.

As usual, I got lost in my work and it wasn't until several hours later that I emerged, ready to call it a day. I straightened my work space and laid a white cloth over the separated sections of the old book to protect them from any dust particles or gusts of wind that might come through the room.

I hadn't realized that Derek had left the copy of *Rebecca* on my worktable, but now I saw it and a dozen questions popped into my head. Who had sent it to Derek and why? Why no return address? Was it from someone who simply wanted their book to be refurbished? What was this all about? Maybe they knew that Derek's wife was a bookbinder but didn't know my name.

But things were never that simple, were they? Then again, was I making too much of this little mystery? I had been involved in so many mysteries over the past few years that I might've been letting my imagination run away with me. Still, it would be smart to slip the *Rebecca* into our safe, just to be cautious.

Back in the 1920s when this six-story loft-apartment

building was a corset factory, my closet had actually served as a dumbwaiter with its rope and pulley system moving supplies up and down between the factory floors. It had a metal floor panel that slid back to reveal a shallow space where I would hide my important papers and any rare books I was working on.

When Derek moved in, he decided that my rare book hiding place needed to be upgraded so we had added a seriously well-built, steel-lined fireproof safe to the closet. Then he had his guys paper the walls of the closet with a thick fire barrier wrap normally used to encase air ducts. Over the wrap he put two layers of fireproof drywall. Drywall mud was applied to the seams and when that was dry, the surface was sanded and painted with a fire-resistant paint. And voilà! Our closet safe was effectively fireproofed.

Derek also installed a state-of-the-art security lock that was impossible to pick and set off an alarm if someone tried to open it.

That might've sounded like overkill, but our home had been turned into a crime scene more than a few times and it always seemed to revolve around a rare book. Needless to say, we no longer took chances.

No matter how valuable the *Rebecca* might turn out to be, it would be safe and secure for now.

I joined Derek in the kitchen, where he had just poured two glasses of red wine.

"You read my mind," I said, and pulled a box of crackers from the pantry. I found the round of cheese in the cooler drawer and remembered the little jar of fig and apple compote that my mother had given us, which would be perfect for spreading on the cheese and crackers. Then I filled a small bowl with olives and another with almonds and placed everything on a serving tray.

Derek handed me a glass and touched his to mine. "Cheers, darling. Welcome home."

"It's good to be home." I studied the rich color of the estate-bottled Cabernet Sauvignon we had brought home. "We were smart to bring all these goodies back from Dharma."

He wisely hid a grin. "Now we won't have to settle for takeaway on our first official night back in town."

It was a well-known fact that I didn't cook. Although, to be fair, lately I had been experimenting with a few simple meals. And since neither of us had come down with food poisoning yet, I considered that a real accomplishment.

I started to take a sip when the doorbell rang. I checked the kitchen clock and saw that it was just after five o'clock. It was still light outside, but not for long. "That's the downstairs doorbell."

"Yes. Let's see who it is." Derek's voice was calm. His posture was deceptively relaxed, but I knew he had gone on full alert. As he was the owner of a multinational security firm and a former MI6 operative, it was pretty close to his natural state.

I followed him over to the corner of the kitchen counter where our nifty television monitor and security system were set up. After we survived several disturbing break-ins in the past, our building security had been upgraded last year. The monitor screen would give us a good view of whoever was standing outside our building's front door, six floors down from our apartment.

An attractive woman stood on the sidewalk. She had dark red hair and I guessed she was in her early thirties. She wore a navy-blue anorak over a thick cable-knit sweater with faded jeans and sturdy ankle boots, an outfit similar to that worn by thousands of San Francisco women in the chilly month of May. Her shoulders were hunched and she held her arms tightly across her chest as though she were freezing from the cold.

And she looked vaguely familiar.

"Yes, hello?" Derek spoke into the microphone.

The woman glanced around as if she might be trying to figure out where that voice was coming from.

"Hello, good afternoon?" Her own voice held a hint of a British accent—was that a brogue? She continued looking around, then noticed the camera up above the door. "Oh, right. Hello. My name is Claire Quinn. I apologize for interrupting your afternoon, but I wonder, if you wouldn't mind, that is, can you tell me, please. Are you Derek Stone? And did you recently receive a package from Scotland?"

Derek and I turned and stared at each other. Then I glanced back at the woman on the monitor. I moved closer to the screen and took a good, long look. Gazing at Derek, I pressed my finger over my lips in the universal symbol to be quiet.

He leaned into the microphone and said clearly, "Just a moment, please, Ms. Quinn." He pushed the mute button so the woman wouldn't be able to hear our conversation.

"I know her," I said in a hushed tone.

"I thought she looked familiar, as well."

"She and I worked together on *This Old Attic.*"

"Ah, yes." He nodded, connecting the dots.

The popular television show traveled around the country and invited local people to bring their treasured family heirlooms and antiques in to be appraised on camera. When the production company came to San

Francisco a few years ago, I was hired to be their book expert for two weeks. I recognized the woman on the monitor as one of the other experts on the show.

"Claire," I said to Derek. "We were friendly. Do you remember her?"

It was Derek's turn to study the screen more carefully. "Wasn't she the weapons expert?"

I beamed. "Good memory. Yes, she specialized in antique weaponry."

"I watched her discuss various weapons," he said. "She did a very good job of bringing them to life. But I never had the opportunity to meet her."

"Things were a little hectic, I guess."

He lifted an eyebrow. "To say the least."

Being chased by a cold-blooded killer could hardly be called "hectic," but Derek let that go.

"She was a big reader," I explained. "So she and I bonded over books. She brought in some of her favorite old books and asked me if they might be worth anything."

"Were they?"

"Oh yeah." They were mostly gothic novels, I realized now. And wasn't that interesting? "I remember an amazing copy of *The Castle of Otranto* that was published in 1765. She could've easily sold it for ten thousand dollars, but apparently it had sentimental value." I waved my hands impatiently. "But that's not important. The package she's referring to is obviously the *Rebecca*."

"Yes." He frowned. "And apparently she has no idea that you live here."

"That hit me, too." I frowned. "She asked for you. Weird, don't you think?"

"I do indeed. Have you any idea where she's from?"

"I'm not sure. I always thought she was English, but since she mentioned Scotland, I'm going to bet she's from somewhere near Inverness."

Derek's eyes narrowed. "Just like the package."

I glanced at the monitor. "We shouldn't leave her standing out there in the cold. Let's buzz her in and find out what this mysterious book is all about."

"I'd rather not buzz her in," Derek said. "I'll go down and bring her up."

He knew his security stuff. Instead of allowing Claire to wander upstairs on her own, he would escort her from the lobby straight to our front door. "Much better idea."

Derek gave me a nod and a quick hug. "And then we'll figure out what in blazes is going on."

He switched off the mute button and said into the microphone, "Sorry to keep you waiting, Ms. Quinn. Did you send the package?"

She pressed her lips together and her eyes narrowed. In frustration? Anger?

I studied the woman for a few long seconds. She wore her thick red hair pulled back in a ponytail and she was very pretty, with a rosy complexion and clear blue eyes. Her leather bag had extra straps that she'd fashioned into a backpack. And despite her warm clothing, she looked chilled to the bone.

I noticed that her shoulders were stiff and her arms were tightly crossed. She was more than just cold. She glanced around nervously and I wondered if she thought someone might be watching her. Or worse. Did she have a partner out of camera range who would attempt to jump Derek? Was this a setup? Would the two of them attack him and rush into our building lobby? Would they race upstairs and break into our apartment?

I confess I have an active imagination. It comes from being confronted one too many times by vicious killers.

And if I were thinking more clearly, I would've remembered that it was next to impossible for anyone to get the jump on Derek.

After a long moment Claire admitted, "No, I didn't send it. I believe my aunt sent it. And now she's missing."

Derek and I exchanged a speculative glance and then nodded in unison. He said into the mic, "Please wait a moment. I'll be right there to let you in."

He jogged down the hall to his office. A minute later he returned wearing his black leather bomber jacket. He stopped at the console table by the front door to grab his keys and when he turned, I caught sight of him tucking a deadly-looking gun into his inside jacket pocket.

"I'm going with you," I said, pulling on the sweater I'd draped over a dining room chair. It was springtime in San Francisco and with the sun going down, it was growing colder. But that had nothing to do with the chills I felt sprinting across my shoulders.

He eyed me warily. "I'd prefer you to stay here."

"No way." I followed him as he hurried across the living room and through the alcove, into my office workshop, where he took a quick glance out the front window. This room had the only street view to the south.

"It looks safe enough out there," he reasoned. "I'll only be gone a few minutes."

"I'm still going with you."

He gave me a half smile. "Are you worried about me?"

"After everything we've been through? You're darned right I'm worried."

"And you think you can protect me?"

"I always do."

With a quick, fierce laugh, he grabbed my hand. "Then let's go."

Chapter 2

Rather than wait for the ancient, rumbling elevator to inch its way up to our floor, we both moved quickly to the stairs and dashed down the six flights. All the way, my mind flashed on old scenes of Claire and me at the television studio: laughing over something silly the floor director had whispered; grabbing a bite to eat during a lull in the show's taping; poring over old books together. Despite my being tormented by a killer, plus the added presence of a stalker on the set, Claire and I had quickly become good friends. And then, after two long weeks, I never saw her again.

What was she really doing here? I couldn't help but be suspicious. Were we being played? She hadn't said anything about the book, *Rebecca*. She had only mentioned that a package had been sent to Derek by her aunt . . . who was now missing.

But whatever mysterious reason she had for showing up here out of the blue, one thing was certain: It was all about the book. Anytime Derek and I had been dragged into something secretive or dangerous, it had always been connected to a book. It was my business, after all. Rare, often priceless books. It was amazing how much treachery they could produce in people. Claire hadn't mentioned a book, though. Just a *package*. Didn't she know what was in the package? Hadn't her aunt told her? *Maybe the contents of the package didn't matter to Claire*, I thought. But it certainly mattered to me.

We reached the lobby level and jogged across the hardwood floor toward the locked glass double doors. I could see Claire standing just outside the doors with her back to us. Before I could get too close, Derek held up his hand. "Stand back, love."

"I think I should go out there first. She knows me."

He gently took hold of my arm. "Let's think about this. She doesn't know you in this context. She's not expecting to see a familiar face. It might confuse her."

I took a few quick seconds to run that possibility through my head. "I hate to admit it, but you're probably right. She looked really nervous on the monitor. I don't want to shock her into running away." I glanced around the spacious lobby and walked over to the elegant entry table along the inside wall. "I'll wait here. I can still hear your conversation, but she won't see me until she comes through the door."

"All right, love."

I could see Claire huddled in the corner where the doors met the inset wall of the building. It provided a bit of a windbreak, but she still had to be cold. Was she also scared? I wondered.

She was facing the street and continued to take quick looks up and down the sidewalk. The glass doors were treated so she couldn't see that we had reached the lobby. When Derek tapped lightly on the glass to let her know we were here, she jolted and whipped around. Her eyes were wide as she stared at him through the glass.

He unlocked the door and opened it a few inches. "Ms. Quinn?"

"Yes. I'm Claire Quinn." She slowly took in Derek's tall frame. "And you are Derek Stone?"

"Yes, I am." He paused, watching her. "I'm still baffled as to why you've come here."

Claire hesitated, and cast another glance over her shoulder. "I'll be glad to tell you everything, but may I please come inside? It's quite chilly. And, well, I'd just like to get off the street."

I saw Derek's hand press against his jacket pocket as if to assure himself that his weapon was still there. "Are you in danger, Ms. Quinn?"

"I'm afraid I might be," she whispered.

Derek pushed the door all the way open. "Please come in. We'll talk upstairs."

As she walked inside, Derek took the opportunity to step outside and check the area for himself. Then he quickly stepped back inside and locked the doors securely.

Once in the lobby, Claire stood at the glass doors and continued to peer out at the sidewalk, stretching her neck to get a better look both ways down the street.

She turned finally and rubbed her arms briskly against the cold. And that's when she noticed me. "Oh."

"Hello, Claire," I said. "Do you remember me?"

Her eyes darted from me to Derek and back to me. She frowned, then blinked. "Brooklyn?" She blinked again. "My goodness. Of course I remember you. We worked together on *This Old Attic*. But what are you doing here?"

"I live here." I touched Derek's shoulder. "Derek is my husband."

"Your husband." She regarded Derek. "This is quite

odd. But that's why you look so familiar. I must've seen you when you visited the set."

"Yes," he agreed. "I was there quite a bit."

He certainly was, I recalled, because we'd been plagued with both a stalker and a killer on our set. Derek had appointed himself my guardian.

She gaped at me for another long moment, then squeezed her eyes shut and rubbed her forehead. "I confess I'm quite confused. And I'm very tired so I'm probably not going to make a lot of sense. But I need information." She glanced around the lobby, then back to Derek. "You said something about going upstairs?"

"Yes." Derek turned and headed across the lobby to the elevator, where he pressed the "up" button. As the door slowly opened, he said, "Here we go."

She gulped, as though she wasn't sure whether we were leading her into a trap or not. Then she firmed her jaw, adjusted the bag strapped to her shoulders, and bravely followed him into the spacious, old-fashioned elevator.

We were silent on the ride up to the sixth floor, where the elevator grumbled to a stop. We led her down the wide hall to our front door, where Derek unlocked it and ushered us both inside.

"We were just about to have a glass of wine," I said matter-of-factly. "Would you like one?"

She gazed at me as though I'd just rescued her puppy. "I would so love a glass of wine. Thank you." But she continued to wring her hands together, clearly anxious. "And perhaps a glass of water, if it's not too much trouble."

"No trouble at all." Her anxiety was rubbing off on me, but I tried to smile as I gestured toward our living room area. "Why don't you take your jacket off and sit down, Claire? We'll have some wine and a little something to eat, and then we can try to solve this mystery."

Her smile was wobbly as she sat down in the big red Polynesian-print chair. "You're being very kind."

Derek walked out of the kitchen carrying two wineglasses. He handed one to Claire. "Here you are."

"Thank you. I'm grateful."

"And here's yours, love." He handed me the second glass.

"Thanks." I touched his hand. "And Claire would like a glass of water, too, if you wouldn't mind."

"Not at all," he said with a nod, clearly understanding that one of us needed to stay in the room with Claire. It was nice to know that he could read my mind.

Derek walked back into the kitchen. A moment later he returned with the snack tray I'd prepared earlier, Claire's water, and his own glass of wine. He set the tray on the coffee table and then joined me on the couch. Lifting his wineglass, he said, "Cheers."

Claire looked ready to weep. "You're both being so kind and you don't even know me."

"I know you." I raised my glass and waited for her to do the same. "That is, I don't know you *well*, but we were friendly for a little while a few years ago. Right?"

"Yes, we were," she said, and leaned forward, resting her elbows on her thighs. "I wish we had kept in touch, but I was out of the country for quite a while, and when I returned to San Francisco, I went straight back to work. I was so busy traveling with the show that I let things slide. I'm sorry."

I smiled. "Don't worry about it. It's just good to see you now."

"Yes," she said slowly. "Yes, it is. Even though this entire situation is making my head spin."

"It's pretty weird, all right." I reached for a cracker and a small hunk of cheese. "So you're living in the city?"

"That's right. I have a flat in Noe Valley."

"I love that area."

"It's quite pleasant."

And weren't we being polite, I thought. "Please help yourself to some cheese and crackers."

"Um, okay. Thank you." But she glanced at her wristwatch.

"Do you have to be somewhere?" Derek asked.

"Not specifically. But I don't want to take up too much of your time."

"We're fine," I said lightly. "Just enjoying some wine and goodies."

But she was practically squirming in her chair and she wasn't making eye contact with either of us. Her anxiety level was looking to hit blast-off, so Derek took the hint. He set down his wineglass on the coffee table and sat forward. "Can you tell us why you decided to contact me?"

"You mentioned something about your aunt," I added softly. "She's missing, you said."

"Yes, she is." Claire's distress was obvious and real. "I know that she sent you . . . something . . . by *mistake*." She emphasized the word. "And I've come here to, um, retrieve it."

"So you know what's in the package," Derek said pleasantly.

She pressed her lips together in a scowl. "No."

"No?" I sat back, shocked. "You don't know what's in the package?"

She bared her teeth in frustration. "All I saw was the postal receipt. It had your name and address and the date and, well, that's all, really."

"Where did you see this postal receipt?"

"In my aunt's apartment."

"Does she live nearby?" Derek asked, his tone casual. But he already knew the answer. We both knew that the package had come from Scotland. Obviously, Derek was testing Claire's honesty. I felt a twinge of guilt for making her jump through a hoop or two, but it was important to verify that she wasn't trying to deceive us. Better safe than sorry, as my mother always said.

She sighed. "My aunt lives in Scotland."

"But you're here," I said, stating the obvious. "How do you know she's missing?"

"Because a few days ago I flew to Scotland to see her and when I got to her flat, she was gone. Vanished. And her place had been torn apart. It was awful. Drawers were pulled out and her bookshelf was upended. A few of the cupboards had their contents flung to the floor. There was obviously foul play."

"Did you contact the local authorities?" Derek asked.

"Of course I did."

"What did they do?"

"Basically, nothing. Oh, they took my statement and they promised to look into it. But I couldn't tell them that anything specific was missing. There was no blood or any sign of assault. It was simply a big mess. I persisted, but I was told that my aunt was a free spirit and she would turn up one of these days with an explanation of some sort."

"That's outrageous," I said.

"I think so, too. But it's a small town, you see. They know my aunt and her eccentricities. They claimed that she was probably off on one of her rambles."

I frowned. "Why would they say that when her place was obviously ransacked?"

"Exactly!" She looked ready to cry. "But they just claimed it was par for the course when it came to crazy Aunt Gwyneth. She can be a bit . . . unconventional, you see."

"Even if that's true, it's no excuse to ignore the fact that she could be in danger."

"Thank you!" she said. "And if they really knew her, they had to know that she would never leave her home in such a disheveled state. She's neat as a pin. And she was expecting me to visit. She wouldn't take off and frighten me like this." She rubbed her temples, and it looked as if she had one heck of a headache. "But I couldn't make the constable realize that something was dreadfully wrong. He flicked me off like a piece of lint."

"That must've been infuriating," I said, feeling her pain.

"Oh, it was." Her hands were bunched up in fists of frustration. "So what could I do? I searched her place, trying to find a clue as to who might've caused such a mess and perhaps figure out her whereabouts. It became clear that whoever was responsible for the mess had been looking for something. What could it be? I looked everywhere and finally found the postal receipt tucked inside a book." She curled her lip in derision. "Naturally, whoever was searching the place wasn't clever enough to look inside a book."

I bit back a smile. "Naturally."

"The date on the slip was only a few days ago," she continued, "and as I said, it had your name on it."

"Yes," Derek murmured. "So you said."

"So I took a chance and flew back here to track down whatever it was that she sent." She gave Derek a meaningful look. "And to find out who you were. I realized that you had to know my aunt. Otherwise, why would she send you anything? I thought you might be able to provide a clue as to her whereabouts."

"I'm afraid I have no idea if I know your aunt or not," Derek said. "What is her name?"

"Gwyneth Quinn."

If I didn't know Derek as well as I did, I probably wouldn't have noticed the minute change in his expression. It was mainly his eyebrow that quirked, just barely. Generally, the man defined the term *poker face*, but in this case, I was certain that he knew Gwyneth Quinn. I was equally certain that he didn't want to alert Claire to that fact. I would have to corner him at some point to find out what the story was.

I had a feeling that Gwyneth Quinn must've worked with him at MI6, the British equivalent of our CIA. Was she another spy? Or a handler? Maybe it wasn't as dramatic as that. She could've been a simple office worker. But I somehow doubted it.

Derek would have no way of knowing whether Claire was aware that her aunt had worked for the spy agency, so he would choose to be discreet for the time being. At least, that was what I surmised from the quirked eyebrow.

"I don't believe I know her," Derek said.

Claire's shoulders slumped. "I was so hoping that you knew her. I can't imagine her sending a package halfway across the world to someone she doesn't know." She sighed and grabbed her wineglass. "But there could be another reason for her sending it to you."

Derek's tone was stoic. "Perhaps she knows one of my brothers still living in Britain. We'll have to figure out what that connection might be."

But he already knew, I thought. And even if they did

know each other, why would a former MI6 friend of
Derek be sending him a rare copy of *Rebecca* out of the
blue? Was it connected to her disappearance?

Meanwhile, even though Derek knew Claire's aunt,
there were a few big, gaping holes in her story. "I'm still
confused. You flew all the way from here to Scotland
only to discover that your aunt was missing. The police
weren't helpful so you searched her home and found the
postal receipt. And then you flew back here on the off
chance that you might knock on the door of a person
you've never met in hopes of learning her whereabouts."

She winced. "I'll admit it does sound a bit bizarre."

"I don't mean to imply that I'm doubting you, but I
think we need a few more details. For instance, why did
you go to Scotland in the first place? Was it just for a
visit? Did your aunt specifically ask you to come? Did
she mention that she worried about something? And
once you discovered she was missing, did you talk to
anyone else about it? She must have friends in town. Did
you ask any of them if they knew where she went? Did
anyone see something suspicious? Did one of them
come across as nervous or guilty?"

She stared at me. "You're very good at this." She
took a big sip from her wineglass. And then she looked
at Derek. "I suppose I'd better tell you the whole story."

"That would be helpful," Derek said agreeably.

"Yes, very helpful," I said. "And also, you mentioned
that you might be in danger, too. Why do you think so?"

"I'll try to explain." But instead she reached for two
small hunks of cheese and a few crackers and set them
neatly on her cocktail napkin. "I just don't know where
to start."

"Start with why you think you're in danger," Derek

suggested. "That's something we might be able to help with. After that, we can discuss some ways to track down your aunt."

Derek had contacts at Interpol, MI5, and MI6, along with numerous police and security agencies around the world that interacted with his own security company. He would be able to put people to work tracking down Gwyneth. But the more immediate issue was to figure out if Claire herself was truly in danger.

At that moment our cat Charlie stalked across the room, stopped, and then jumped into Claire's lap.

"Well, hello, lovely," she said cheerfully, and ran her hand along the cat's sleek back. "What's your name?"

"That's Charlie," I said, smiling. "She's very sweet and friendly. I hope you're not allergic."

"Not at all. I have a tuxedo cat of my own. A boy." She shifted in the chair to make room for Charlie, then took a quick bite of cheese and cracker. I noted that one arm was still wrapped securely around Charlie and I figured the cat was already working to help soothe her nerves.

After a long moment and a few deep breaths, she said, "In the last week I've experienced two possible attempts on my life. I've had some creepy hang-up phone calls and one very scary car chase." She gazed down at Charlie and said under her breath, "I'm afraid that my past is catching up to me."

"What do you mean by that?" I demanded.

Derek gave my back a subtle pat. "Before we go there, let's hear more about those two attempts on your life. What happened?"

Derek was pragmatic as always. The life-and-death stuff needed our immediate attention. We could delve into her past life later.

Claire took another deep breath and let it out quietly. "The most recent attempt happened two nights ago when I got home from the airport. I was unpacking my suitcase and washing my face and, you know, puttering, sorting out the laundry, and just unwinding from a long, exhausting day of travel. I was in my bedroom and I suddenly heard a scuffling sound coming from my closet."

Uh-oh, I thought, but kept quiet.

She continued. "I confess that at that moment I was quite tired and feeling jet-lagged. I honestly wasn't thinking and simply figured that it was my cat making that ruckus."

"But it wasn't," I guessed.

"No. My cat's not even home." She waved her hands in frustration. "My veterinarian's assistant was taking care of him while I was away. But as I said, I wasn't thinking straight."

"So what did you do?" I was sitting on the edge of my seat.

"I walked over to the closet and made the usual cooing sounds I make when I'm talking to my cat, and pushed open the sliding door, expecting to see Mr. D pop out. Mr. D is my cat, short for Mr. de Winter," she explained. "But instead, I stared into the eyes of a strange, rather brutish man. I screamed and managed to run out of the apartment and down the stairs. Some of my neighbors came outside to see what was wrong."

"Did any of them go after the guy?"

"No." She scowled. "Although two of the men were good enough to go through the house with me to make sure he was gone. I have a back door in the kitchen that leads downstairs to a tiny yard. I'm certain he got out that way."

"Does the yard exit onto a street?" Derek asked.

"No. It's one of those tiny, boxed-in yards that San Francisco is famous for. It's surrounded on all sides by buildings, so he would've had to climb from the stairway onto the roof of our garage and then jump down to the alley."

"It doesn't sound like he would've been able to come in that way."

"No." She frowned in confusion. "He probably came in through the front door. Although I'm not sure how."

"Were there signs of a break-in?"

Still frowning, she shook her head. "No."

I glanced at Derek and knew what he was thinking. For the intruder to have escaped so quickly, he had to have been inside her apartment before. Probably snuck in once or twice to get the lay of the land before she arrived home.

"Did you call the police?" Derek asked.

"I did, but since the intruder was already gone, they didn't see an urgent need to come out until this morning. They took some fingerprints around the closet door and checked the front and back door locks. Nothing was taken so there wasn't much for them to go on. But they wrote a report and I have a copy. For all the good that will do me."

None of us spoke for a moment. It was entirely possible that this man had known she would be coming home that night. Perhaps he'd had an accomplice who'd followed her from the airport and called the intruder to let him know she would be home soon. They had probably stolen her key right out of her purse, made a copy, and returned it within minutes. That could've happened a few weeks earlier.

Anything was possible and all of the various scenarios were frightening. Still, I couldn't help myself; I had to ask. "On a semi-unrelated topic, did you really name your cat Mr. de Winter?"

It was the first time I'd seen her smile since she walked into our apartment.

"Yes. I'm a big fan of the book," she exclaimed, and I noticed that her light Scottish brogue became more pronounced when she was excited.

"Me, too," I admitted. Maxim de Winter was the name of the husband in Daphne du Maurier's *Rebecca*. There were way too many coincidences circling around this situation with Claire and I had to wonder again, did she really not know that her aunt had sent Derek a copy of that particular book?

"I don't know if you remember," I continued, "but we used to talk about books a lot while we were working together on the show."

"Of course I remember," she said with a fond smile. "I probably drove you crazy with my incessant chattering about my beloved gothic novels."

"You didn't, I promise."

"That's kind of you, but I've been known to put people to sleep with my dissertation on the pros and cons of Heathcliff versus Mr. Rochester."

I laughed. "I would love to hear that."

"No, you wouldn't." She waved her hands in protest. "But you did help make those two weeks quite bearable. Oh, and I should mention that since my cat is just as arrogant and condescending as the original Mr. D in the book, the name suits him to a T." She gave Charlie a hug. "Not like this little angel."

"She's a good girl," Derek said, causing my heart to pitter-patter. Yes, I was a sap. But how could I not be? Not only had Derek given me Charlie as a gift a few years ago, but he also adored the little creature as much as I did.

Have I mentioned how much I love my husband?

"I'm sorry I veered off topic," I said after taking a sip of wine. "You were telling us about this break-in. You didn't recognize the brutish man, did you?"

"No. That is, I recognized the type, but not this particular fellow."

"What do you mean, the type?" Derek asked.

"He quite reminds me of the men who were part of my father's gang while I was growing up."

"Your father was in a gang?" I asked.

She seemed to catch herself. "*Gang* isn't quite the right term, but he did have a number of rather tough fellows working for him, doing odd jobs, cleaning up messes, and that sort of thing. I'm sure you know the type." She twisted her lips in a grimace. "It's not important."

I had a feeling it might be *really* important, and one look at Derek told me he agreed. We would circle back around to that detail later, I thought.

"Can you tell us about the other attempt on your life?" Derek asked, judiciously changing the subject.

"Yes. That one was a little less frightening, but still disconcerting. It happened the very next night. That is, it was just last night." She shook her head. "Sorry. I'm still a little foggy from jet lag. Anyway, last night someone came to my door claiming that I had ordered a pizza."

"That's a clever tactic," I said. "Who wouldn't be tempted to open the door to a pizza?"

"Exactly," Claire said, with a quick nod. "But I hadn't ordered a pizza so I refused to open the door, especially after I got a look at him through the peephole. He didn't look like any pizza deliveryman I've ever seen. So I simply yelled out that he should try another door because it wasn't my pizza."

"Did he go away?"

"Not at first. He tried to argue with me, then tried cajoling me into taking the pizza anyway. He claimed he would lose money if I didn't take it. It was a silly argument and I told him to go away."

"I'm glad," I said. "Did anyone else in the area see him?"

"My upstairs neighbor, Paul, came out of his flat to see who was making all the noise. He told me later that when the guy was walking out of our building, Paul offered to take the pizza off his hands and the guy threw the box at him."

"What a jerk," I said.

"He really was," she said. "And what's worse, Paul said that the box was empty!"

"Now, that's a bummer," I said. "You could've at least snagged a free piece of pizza for your trouble."

Claire gave a rueful laugh. "It's so stupid, isn't it? But once I realized that the real motive was to get me to open my door, I began shaking like a leaf. And beyond my own concerns, I realized that Paul might've been hurt badly. It scared me silly."

"You were smart not to buy in to his deception," Derek said. "Your instincts are good. Keep listening to them and you'll be all right."

"I hope so," she whispered. "Thank you."

"I don't blame you for being scared," I said. "Was the man in the closet the same man who delivered the pizza? Or rather, the *empty* pizza box?"

"No. Two different men." She shivered visibly. "But both were hefty and broad-shouldered. And brutish. No smiles on either of them."

"And you have no idea what they wanted or what they were looking for?"

"Not a clue."

I stared at her directly. "You said that the one man resembles someone who works for your father."

She stared right back at me. "That was in the past. My father is dead."

I pressed my hand over my mouth. "I'm sorry."

She sighed. "That's all right. But I didn't want you to think that my own father would put one of his men up to this. It's got to be connected to something else entirely."

I wanted to hear more about Claire's father, along with the car chase and those phone hang-ups she'd mentioned. But at that moment, our doorbell rang. It wasn't the outside bell so it had to be one of our neighbors stopping by to say hello.

Derek stood, immediately on alert. "I'll see who that is." He scanned the room, then met my gaze. "Stay here."

"All righty." I turned to Claire and gave her a sunny smile, hoping she hadn't picked up on Derek's vibe. "I'm going to have another glass of wine. Would you like one?"

"Maybe a half glass."

I walked out to the kitchen and grabbed the bottle. At that moment Derek walked in with our neighbor Alex and came straight to where I stood. "I've got to run downstairs to get something out of my car for Alex. We'll just be a minute."

"What's wrong?" I asked immediately.

"Possibly nothing," Derek said quietly, in a futile attempt to calm me down.

"I went to the store a few minutes ago," Alex said, "and happened to notice someone hanging around the front door of our building. When I got back, the same guy was inside the garage."

"*Inside* the garage," I echoed, feeling a trickle of fear along my spine. I took a deep breath and exhaled slowly. "Was he following you?"

"No."

"Do we have any new neighbors?"

Alex shook her head. "Nope. I didn't recognize the guy. But he was standing by Derek's car, looking in the windows."

I looked from Alex to Derek. "Your car?"

"Yeah," Alex said. "He ducked out of sight when he saw me."

"Derek's car is really nice," I said, a little desperately. "Maybe the guy just likes cars."

"He wasn't a car aficionado," she said dryly.

"Can you describe him?" Derek asked.

"Big, burly, thinning black hair. He wore a heavy down jacket and funky old work boots. Had a rough look about him."

I felt the hairs on my skin rise and stared at Derek. "You'll be careful."

"Of course, love." Derek wrapped his arm around my shoulder. "Alex and I will go down and check it out. It's probably nothing."

Alex was ex-CIA, a sixth-degree black belt in tae kwon do, and an expert in Krav Maga. She was almost as dangerous as Derek. They would keep each other safe.

Derek shot a careful glance toward the living room and whispered, "We don't want to alarm our guest."

"Of course not."

He glanced at Alex. "Are you armed?"

"Naturally."

I felt my heart rate spike. Even growing up in rural

Sonoma County, I'd never been much for guns. But these two were professionals. If the guy in the garage was the same one who'd broken into Claire's apartment, then they were going up against a really bad guy and needed to be prepared for the worst. "Before you go I need to ask you one quick question."

"What is it?"

I whispered, "Do you know Gwyneth Quinn?"

He gazed at me. "Yes."

"From MI6?"

He nodded and rubbed my arm. "Yes, but let's talk about it later."

"Okay. Be careful out there."

"I love you," he said.

I smiled. "Back at ya."

He moved quickly down the hall to his office and I knew he was retrieving his weapon. When he and Alex left the apartment, I walked into the living room with the wine bottle, trying to be casual. It wasn't working. I'd been told I was a bad liar and this attempt at cheeriness was right up there with lying.

"Don't pretend nothing's wrong," Claire insisted, standing. "I've lived with chaos before. I recognize the warning signs."

"No worries," I said, waving her words away. "They're just checking something out in the garage. Probably nothing."

"Then let's go find out."

"That's not a good idea," I said.

"Brooklyn, please." She grabbed my arm. "If one of those horrible men followed me here, I don't want your husband or your friend getting hurt on my account."

She had a point. "They both know what they're doing."

"So do I," she insisted. "You can wait here, but I'm going. I don't want anyone else fighting my battles for me." She glanced around for her jacket and pulled it off the dining room chair.

I stopped her. "Look, I'll say it again. It's probably nothing, but—"

"If it's nothing," she interrupted, "then we'll all have a good laugh about it later."

"Fine," I said, exasperated. But I wasn't going to let her go alone. I grabbed my keys and sweater and we walked out. After locking the door, I quickly led the way to the stairs. "You might've noticed, the elevator's slow and very noisy."

"The stairs are fine," she said, and followed me down. "Brooklyn, have you got a weapon on you?"

"What?" I stared at her over my shoulder. "No. Of course not."

"That's all right." She slipped her hand into her jacket pocket and pulled out a vicious-looking antique jeweled dagger. "I do."

Chapter 3

As Claire and I rushed downstairs, I couldn't help but hear my mother's voice in my head, warning us kids about running with scissors. It was all because Claire had flashed that deadly sharp knife she'd kept hidden in her pocket this whole time. What if she tripped and fell on me and what if that knife . . . well, someone could get hurt, was all I could think.

To my great relief, we made it all the way down to the basement level without any accidental stabbing incidents.

"This way," I said, and jogged down the short hall to the heavy fire door that led into the garage. The lights down here on this level were normally dimmer than the resident floors, but Derek and his security crew had installed motion sensors last year. If anyone stepped one foot into the area, the lights would flash on instantly.

Sure enough, with my first step off the stairs, the entire space was illuminated and I had to give a silent cheer. No more scary dark shadows.

I took a quick peek through the small wired window in the fire door and saw Derek and Alex standing on the far side of the garage next to his gorgeous black Bentley.

They appeared to be having an intense conversation and my shoulders relaxed at the sight of the two of them together and out of danger. There was no sign of the stranger Alex had seen earlier.

"They're in there," I said to Claire. "And they're not pointing their weapons at anyone. I guess that guy must've gotten away."

"I suppose that's for the best," Claire said.

But she didn't sound too happy and I couldn't blame her. If the guy was able to get away, it meant that he might show up at her house again.

"Anyway, doesn't look like you'll need your dagger," I said. "At least, not right now."

She patted her pocket. "It's safely sheathed inside my pocket."

I nodded, then turned the handle and shoved the heavy door open, instantly alerting Derek and Alex of our arrival.

The garage was well lit also so it was easy to see most of the cars that were in for the night. The automatic rolling grille gate was down and except for the fire door we'd just come through, the grille gate was the only way out of the garage.

Had the guy been able to escape before Derek and Alex got down here? This fire door required a four-digit code to enter into the stairwell so I had to wonder how he'd done it. Maybe another car had come into the building and he had escaped while the grille gate was up. Or maybe he had somehow acquired the code to the door and had previously come inside our building to case the joint. And that particular thought brought a whole new set of chills to my spine. I tried to stop thinking about the possibility, but unfortunately, the phrase *case the joint* continued to circle inside my head. I had to wonder which old gangster movie we'd been watching when I heard that old line.

"Brooklyn, you might want to stay where you are," Derek said loudly when we'd crossed halfway.

I automatically stopped in my tracks, then frowned. "Why?" But within a nanosecond I realized why. "Is the guy still in here?"

"Yes," Derek said starkly, and glanced down. What was he looking at? But I already knew. Ugh.

"Is he dead?" I asked.

"He is, yes. And there's quite a bit of blood."

"Ah." I swallowed carefully. "Okay, thanks for the warning."

Alex walked toward us. "You really don't want to go over there, Brooklyn."

"I'm getting that feeling." And yes, everyone in the world knew about my little phobia.

She grimaced. "There's a lot of blood."

"That's what I hear." I had to hold up my hand to stop her from saying another word. I took a deep breath and let it out with a *whoosh*. "Did Derek kill him?"

"Oh no, sweetie," she insisted, touching my arm for support.

I reached out and grabbed her wrist. "Did you?"

The question surprised her enough that she gave a quick laugh. "No."

"Okay." I exhaled with relief. "Well then, what happened? What's going on?"

She scowled. "He was already dead when we got down here."

I could feel my mouth drop open. "Are you kidding me?"

"Nope."

"You're saying that between the time you came

upstairs to tell Derek and the time you both came back down here, somebody killed him?"

"That sums it up."

"I want to see him," Claire said abruptly.

I jolted. She had been so quiet, I'd almost forgotten she was still with me. "Are you sure?"

"Yes, I'm sure. He might be the fellow that was waiting in the closet for me. And if he's dead, whoever killed him might be after me, as well. I need to know."

I winced. "Oh my God, Claire."

Alex stepped closer to Claire and held out her hand. "I'm Alex, by the way. I live down the hall from Brooklyn and Derek."

I jumped in. "I'm sorry. Alex, this is Claire. She's an expert in antique weaponry. Claire, this is Alex, our good friend who's a black belt and a super-warrior and she makes cupcakes."

"My goodness," Claire said as they shook hands.

"You're both awesome," I added. "You should be friends with each other."

Alex grinned at me, then turned to Claire. "Derek was telling me you've had a few run-ins with some dodgy characters lately."

"Dodgy is putting it mildly," Claire muttered. "But yes. It's all quite unsettling."

"Sorry to hear it." Alex glanced over her shoulder. "Well then, come and take a look at this one." She turned and started back across the wide space of the garage.

Claire followed right behind her. I figured if Claire was brave enough to look at a dead guy who might've been tormenting her, then so was I. Maybe there wasn't as much blood as I was imagining.

"It's a crime scene, obviously," Alex warned us. "So I don't want you getting too close. Just watch where you're stepping, take a quick look, and let us know if he's familiar to you."

"Do you want me to call Inspector Lee?" I asked.

"Derek took care of it," Alex said, with a wry smile. "Apparently he's got her number programmed on his phone."

I shrugged lightly. "I do, too. Because, you know, she's our friend. Sort of."

"Sort of friends?"

"Well, you know, we've invited her to some of our parties and we like her a lot. But then sometimes it gets awkward."

She chuckled. "Like those times when there's a dead body involved?"

"Yeah, those times." It was a well-known fact that Derek and I had an alarming tendency to come across dead bodies, so it helped to have a top-notch murder cop on speed dial.

"Brooklyn, love," Derek called out as we got closer to the Bentley. "You might want to stay on that side of the car." He gave me a look that was pure sympathy, knowing I had this stupid phobia where I tended to faint at the sight of blood.

"I would like to get a look at the guy," I said, even though I was already feeling shaky, damn it.

"How about if I take a photo?" he suggested.

"That's a great idea." I smiled, then immediately frowned. Why was I smiling? Whoever he was, the guy was dead and it was nothing to smile about. And that was when I decided I needed to take just one good look at the guy. I would do it for Claire. I only needed to see his face. I would simply ignore the blood.

Derek gave me a quick smile, then looked at Claire.

"Are you squeamish about blood, Claire? There's no shame in it."

"I'm fine," she said briskly. "I want to see him." She straightened her shoulders and walked around to the other side of the car until she could see the body. I followed her, standing one step behind her. She stared for a long moment, then took another small step closer and so did I. She cocked her head for a better look. Then she sucked in a breath.

Derek watched her. "Do you recognize him, Claire?"

She nodded. "It's the pizza man."

The uniformed police arrived ten minutes later. Derek used his garage door opener to give them access, then introduced himself and showed them where the body was.

I had been sitting in my car, trying to breathe after having insisted on getting a good look at the victim. Despite my best efforts, I had taken one look at all that blood draining from his neck and nearly fainted. Before I could hit the ground, Derek had swooped me up and carried me over to my car, which was parked right next to his.

"Thank you," I whispered, feeling completely foolish.

"Shall I take you upstairs?" he asked, touching my cheek.

"I'll be fine. See? I'm standing up straight, with barely a wobble."

"You may wobble all you want."

"Thank you. That's very kind of you."

He grinned and I wondered, for the ten-thousandth time, how did I get so lucky? "I'm just going to sit in my car for a few minutes, rest my head on the steering wheel, and bask in humiliation."

"Bask away. I'll be right over here if you need me."

He left me to bask. It gave me a few minutes to think about the disturbing sight I had just seen. Despite my shamefully bad reaction, I had noticed that the victim's death was the result of a vicious knife attack. In fact, the knife was still sticking out of his throat.

Even with its deadly purpose, the weapon was quite beautiful, with an elegant mother-of-pearl handle and a thick, hammered-steel cross guard. It was undoubtedly an antique.

Claire must have noticed it, as well.

Eventually the uniformed officers ushered all of us over to the fire door while they cordoned off the crime scene. They took our names and other personal information and got a basic idea of the timeline and the fact that we lived upstairs. Before they could ask us anything else, Inspector Lee strolled into our garage. Tall and lean, with straight black hair worn in a simple ponytail down her back, she was impressive, to say the least. She greeted her officers first and gave them some instructions, then took a quick look at the body before walking over to talk to us.

With a grin, she shook her head at me. "Brooklyn Wainwright. Of all the crime scenes in all the land, you had to show up in mine."

I had to smile. "Inspector Lee, it's good to see you."

"Yeah. You, too. It's been a while, thank God."

"How are you doing? You look great." I tried not to be jealous of her gorgeous new trench coat, but it wasn't easy. It was a buttery light beige and it skimmed her calves, showing off her short, chunky brown boots and skinny black pants. The woman had the best wardrobe.

"I'm doing a helluva lot better than that guy." She jerked her thumb in the direction of the dead man. "What about you, Brooklyn? Derek? How're you two lovebirds doing? You're both looking good. Happy."

Derek slipped his arm through mine. "We're doing quite well."

I grinned. "Did you miss us?"

She chuckled. "You know I did." Her gaze shifted. "And how are you, Alex?"

"I'm well," Alex said. "Nice to see you again, Inspector. Great coat."

"Thanks. I'm kind of coveting your Chuck Taylors."

Alex glanced down at her black low-rise tennis shoes. "I wear heels all day long so these are the first things I reach for when I get home."

"Don't blame you." Inspector Lee turned to Claire. "Hello. And who are you?"

Claire's eyes widened. "I'm Claire. Claire Quinn."

"Claire is my friend," I said quickly, knowing how intimidating Inspector Lee could be. "You're going to want to talk to her because that dead guy over there is the same one who showed up at her house last night and tried to convince her to open the door."

"Is that a fact?" Inspector Lee frowned at the news and dug in her coat pocket for a small notebook and pen. "That must've been frightening for you."

"It was," Claire said, rubbing her arms to fight off the chill.

"Do you know the guy?"

"Heavens, no," Claire said. "I've never seen him before in my life. Well, that is, until last night."

Inspector Lee was taking fast notes now. "Think he followed you over here?"

"I think he must have." Her voice was beginning to quaver and I couldn't blame her for being freaked out. "How else can I explain him being here?"

"Good point." Inspector Lee slipped the pad and pen into her pocket. "Okay, Claire. Hang in there. I'm going to want to talk to you some more."

"Yes. All right."

The inspector signaled to Derek. "Commander, may I have a word with you?"

"Of course."

From the first time we all met, she had referred to Derek as the Commander. It was an honorific title since he was no longer in the British Royal Navy, but she still used it as a sign of respect—which made me like her even more than I normally would have.

The two of them walked halfway across the garage toward the crime scene. Because of the acoustics in this cavernous space, I could hear every word she said. It probably helped that I took a few steps closer to eavesdrop.

"I've sent my uniforms around to knock on doors," she told him. "We'll see if anyone else in the building got a look at this guy."

"Very good," Derek said.

"As soon as the medical examiner and my crime scene guys show up, I'd like to come upstairs and talk to you all."

"Shall I stick around down here while you wait for them?"

"Not necessary," she said, checking her wristwatch. "My guys left the station about the same time I did so they'll be here any minute."

"All right, then. What else can I do for you?"

"Keep everyone at your place, will you? Makes it easier."

"No problem."

She shoved her hands into her coat pockets. "Did you see who killed him?"

"Unfortunately, no."

"It wasn't you or Alex," she said.

Derek looked right at her. "No, it wasn't. He was already dead when we arrived in the garage."

"So there's someone else out there."

"Yes."

She nodded slowly, then glanced over at our little group. Her eyes narrowed. "I'm going to want to hear the whole story when I get upstairs."

"That's fine."

"I'll be up shortly."

Derek gave her a brief nod. "We'll be there waiting."

"Appreciate it."

I walked over quickly. "Can we send down a cup of coffee for you?"

She turned and grinned. "That would be awesome, but don't go to any trouble."

"It's no trouble at all."

Once everyone was settled around our dining room table, Derek opened another bottle of wine and I started a pot of coffee. Claire and Alex chatted quietly and Derek got on the phone with Pietro's down the street. This night definitely called for pizza.

I pulled a large thermos down from the shelf, grabbed six heavy-duty cardboard cups, and packed them up with some cocktail napkins. I hoped they all liked their coffee black.

As soon as Derek ended the call, I quietly pounced on him. "We only have a minute to talk. Tell me about Aunt Gwyneth."

He chuckled at my insistence. "All right, but just the basics. We worked together closely for several years on various projects."

"Are you going to tell Claire?"

"I'll tell her as soon as I can be certain I'm not committing a national security breach. Gwyneth might've wished to keep her job a secret."

"But she needs to know."

"I agree, darling," he murmured. "But more importantly, I need to know who these two men are and why this phony pizza deliveryman followed her to our home. She's clearly in danger and she's inadvertently brought the danger to our doorstep."

I cringed. "I know you're right but I really didn't want to hear it."

He wrapped his arms around me. "I didn't want to say it. But we've got to figure it out. Meanwhile, it's not my place to 'out' Gwyneth as an espionage professional before I know how much Claire knows."

I gazed up at him. "How well do you know her aunt?"

I could tell he was considering whether to tell me or not, but then he relented. "I knew her quite well. But then, everyone who worked with Gwyneth knew her and liked her very much. She wasn't just nice and smart. She was brilliant. Her mind was like a computer. And she's funny. She was practically a legend by the time I got there." He smiled. "The infamous Gwyn Quinn."

"Gwyn Quinn. That's pretty cute. But infamous?"

"She was quite formidable. Knew where all the bodies were buried."

"Ah." I poured the hot coffee into the thermos and tightened the lid. "So she was a spy?"

"An analyst. But, frankly, she was so familiar with

many of the cases that she often wound up being sent on missions all on her own."

I frowned. "And now she's missing. Do you think she's alive?"

"I do. But I'll make some phone calls tonight to make sure. And to find out what's really going on with her sudden disappearance."

"Who are you going to call?"

"Oh, you know. People." He smiled, leaned down, and kissed me. "I love you, darling."

"Which means you're not ready to tell me." But I knew he would eventually. "Never mind. I love you, too."

He reached for the thermos. "I'll take the coffee downstairs to Inspector Lee and her crew."

An hour later, Derek was off to pick up our pizzas and antipasto salads. By the time he returned, Inspector Lee was just arriving.

"You'll have a piece of pizza, right?" I asked.

She shook her head. "No."

"You need to eat," I said, ignoring her answer. "I'll make up a plate for you."

"Pushy."

I smiled. "When I need to be."

"Are you still on duty?" I asked. "Do you want a glass of wine?"

"Since I'm here to question you all about a murder that just happened in your garage, I'd have to say I'm on duty."

"Oh, yeah." I frowned, then relaxed. "Okay. We've got cola, water, juice, and milk. What sounds good?"

"Seriously? Milk? Juice? With pizza? What's wrong with you?"

I laughed. "I'll get you a bottle of water."

"Thanks."

"And if you want to talk to any of us alone, you can use my workshop."

"Cool." She hesitated, then walked with me back to the kitchen. "I'm going to want to talk to you about your friend."

"Claire?"

"Yeah. But let's go ahead and enjoy the pizza first."

I wasn't sure I could enjoy much of anything, knowing that Inspector Lee was suspicious of Claire. But why wouldn't she be? Claire was a stranger to Inspector Lee. And to me and Derek as well, to be honest. We had both been suspicious, too, at first.

One thing was certain, though, and it filled me with relief. Claire had been upstairs with me when the guy in the garage was killed.

It didn't take long before we were all feasting on pizza and salad and wine. And water, of course. We were chatting about every little thing and laughing and enjoying one another's company.

At one point Derek got up to get Inspector Lee another bottle of water.

"Thanks, Commander," she said with a smile.

Alex grilled me about the self-defense classes I'd been taking while I was in Dharma and we talked about Keith, the instructor, who was a friend of hers.

I asked the inspector about her mother and she let me know that she was doing well. She was still living in her Chinatown apartment and was currently involved in a big mah-jongg tournament. Inspector Lee was first-generation American and her mother was constantly trying to set her up with suitable Asian men. "She still talks about that book you made for her. She's got it displayed right out on the coffee table for everyone to see."

"I'm glad it makes her happy," I said.

But as soon as Claire took her last bite of pizza, Inspector Lee turned serious. "Claire, if you're ready, I'd like you to tell me about the man who came to your door the other night."

"Oh. Oh dear. Yes, of course." Claire dabbed her mouth with her napkin, then took a quick drink of water. She was clearly nervous, but finally settled herself in her chair. "Yes. Right. It was about eight o'clock last night. There was a hard pounding on my door. I checked the peephole and knew I'd never seen the man before. He said he had a pizza delivery for me."

"But you hadn't ordered a pizza." Inspector Lee had her notepad open and her pen in her hand.

"No," Claire said. "Although the minute he said the words, I suddenly craved pizza. Isn't that awful?" She shook her head and waved that thought away. "But I guess it's normal."

"It is," Alex agreed.

Claire smiled. "I quickly came to my senses and refused to open my door."

She continued to tell Inspector Lee the same story she had told us earlier, ending with her neighbor Paul stopping the guy and getting the empty box thrown at him.

"So the guy just kept insisting that you open the door and pay for the pizza."

"Yes."

Inspector Lee continued taking notes. "And all he did to your neighbor was throw the box at him? He didn't threaten him or pull a gun or anything?"

"That's right. He just threw the pizza box and stormed off."

I gasped. "Oh wow, Claire. I just realized that you might not want pizza tonight after all that happened."

There was complete silence for a long moment, then Claire started laughing. Inspector Lee joined her, and then everyone else did, too.

"You're so funny, Brooklyn," Claire said, followed by another little chuckle. "And very sweet."

I frowned. "I should've been more sensitive. I'm failing right and left tonight."

"You didn't fail." She grabbed my hand and squeezed. "I love pizza, even after the trauma of the empty box. It was the best possible thing you could've done for me."

I nodded slowly, then smiled brightly. "So it's kind of like falling off a horse, then."

Claire's eyebrows furrowed in confusion. "I . . . suppose so."

"I'm sure that made sense inside Brooklyn's mind," Inspector Lee said with a grin.

I took a quick sip of wine. "Look, if you're upset by a pizza box, the best thing to do is order another pizza. And get right back on that pizza horse, so to speak." I frowned. "Right?"

"Absolutely," Alex said, beaming at me.

"Makes perfect sense to me," I said.

"And to me," Derek insisted, with a wink. He stood up and went around the table filling wineglasses. I followed behind him, picking up dishes and clearing the table. I stacked everything by the sink and then remembered the cupcakes Alex had brought over earlier. Had it really only been a few hours ago? It felt like five days had gone by.

I took a minute to put them on a platter and then carried them out to the table. "We have cupcakes, courtesy of Alex."

"Oh Alex, that's so lovely," Claire said.

"They go well with pizza," she reasoned.

I laughed. "They go well with anything."

"There are three flavors," Alex said. "Red velvet, chocolate chip, and lemon meringue."

"They're all fantastic," I said.

"Man, you guys are killing me," Inspector Lee said with a groan. But she reached for a red velvet cupcake anyway.

"Does anyone want coffee?" I asked.

"Wine is still working for me," Alex said.

"Inspector?"

"No, I'll stick with water. I need to get through a few questions tonight and then maybe do some follow-ups tomorrow."

"You've been very patient, Inspector," Derek said. "We appreciate it."

"Hey, I got rewarded with pizza and a cupcake. Not a bad deal." But then she sobered, scanned our faces, and met our gazes one by one. Then she focused in on Claire. "Let's talk about how and why your pizza man turned up dead in the garage downstairs."

Her words were the equivalent of ice water tossed on our happy evening, but I was secretly glad she did it. It was time for all of us to face the truth and stop ignoring the glaring fact that a cold-blooded murder had occurred on our own turf earlier tonight.

One thing was certain. Claire Quinn was in serious jeopardy.

And now I had to wonder if Derek and I were in danger, too.

Chapter 4

"Claire, if you'd rather talk in another room, we can move." Inspector Lee sipped her water.

Claire stared at the inspector and then glanced nervously around the table at me, then Derek, and finally Alex. "I've already told Brooklyn and Derek everything. And I feel comfortable enough with Alex. So I think I'd rather stay here. Do you mind?"

"Not a bit," the inspector said.

I was relieved that Claire wanted to stay here at the table, mainly because I wanted to hear everything she said to the inspector. Yes, I was concerned that Claire might need our moral support, but mostly it was because I'm nosy.

Derek came out from the kitchen carrying five small water bottles that he set down in the middle of the table.

"Thanks, Commander," Inspector Lee said, reaching for one of the bottles. "Okay, let's continue."

"Wait," Claire said abruptly. "I beg your pardon, but why do you call him that?"

"What?" Inspector Lee looked puzzled.

"I've heard you call him *Commander* several times now. Why?" But rather than wait for Inspector Lee's answer, she turned and stared intently at Derek. "Who are you?"

Derek seemed ready for the question. "It doesn't mean anything. The title is a bit of a private joke."

"It's not a joke," Inspector Lee insisted. "I use that title because I want to show respect."

Surprised, Derek stared at her. "Why, thank you, Inspector." Then he turned to Claire. "I was with the British Royal Navy for a number of years before going to work for the government."

"The government." Now her eyes narrowed. "You worked for MI6. The Circus. Tell me the truth."

"Yes, I was with MI6." Then he frowned. "We've never actually called it the Circus, though. That's an affectation invented by a British novelist of spy fiction."

"So you *do* know my aunt," Claire said, cutting right to the chase.

He continued to gaze at Claire, taking his time to answer. "Yes, Claire. I know Gwyneth. And you must understand that I didn't say anything earlier because, frankly, I don't know you well and I couldn't be certain that you knew your aunt's history with MI6."

Claire sat up straighter. "Well, I do know. I've lived with her for half of my life, including the time she was working in London. I'm aware that she was responsible for unmasking several traitors to the Crown five years ago. I know that her antiques shop in a village outside of Inverness is a cover for her espionage activities." Her voice continued to rise. "And I know that she's been kidnapped and nobody will help me find her."

Derek held up a hand to stop her. "I told you I would help you, and I am."

"How?"

"I've made a few phone calls, which I'll go over with

you later. Right now Inspector Lee needs to finish her questioning."

Claire frowned and then seemed to realize we were all still sitting here, watching her. With her chin held high, she met each of our gazes head-on. "You needn't worry. I don't believe I've let go of any national secrets."

"You haven't," Derek said coolly, speaking with all the authority of his former office. "And as I've said, I'll be happy to talk to you about your aunt. Later."

"So there *is* more to tell. Do you know who took her?"

"Later." He said it bluntly, putting an end to the discussion. For now.

She looked at me. "He's very stubborn. How do you put up with it?"

"It's a constant battle." I gave Derek a sweet smile. He rolled his eyes, but looked relieved that Claire's anger seemed to have been defused.

Claire turned to Inspector Lee and nodded regally. "You may go ahead and ask me anything."

From the moment she had revealed the deadly dagger she carried in her pocket, I'd been watching her transform from shy girl to warrior queen. I had to admit I was liking this more spirited side of her.

"Okey-dokey." Inspector Lee was a tough, cynical cop, but she had good instincts and she was fair. That wouldn't keep me from fretting like a mama bear over her cub being interrogated, though. I tried to calm myself by taking slow, even breaths.

The inspector glanced at her notepad. "I understand you had another confrontation the other night with a completely different man than our victim in the garage."

"Yes. It was two nights ago, just after I arrived home from Scotland." Claire related the story of finding the guy in the closet and how she ran screaming out of the house. She described him as well as she could, then said, "When I thought about it more this afternoon, I remembered something else about him."

"Did you?" I asked. "That's good." I shot a quick glance at Inspector Lee. "Sorry. Go ahead."

Inspector Lee twisted her lips in a wry smile. "Thanks." She turned to Claire. "What did you remember?"

"I remember that he smelled like peppermint."

"Peppermint." Inspector Lee sat back in her chair. "Was he chewing gum?"

"I don't think so. It was more of a heavy perfume or cologne smell. It might've been the deodorant he was wearing. Or perhaps he was wearing one of those patches that you apply to achy muscles. It was quite intense."

"That could be helpful." The inspector wrote it down.

Claire frowned. "I can't imagine it's helpful, but it's something."

"Yes, it is." Inspector Lee's phone pinged and she checked the screen, then glanced up at Claire. "The dead man's name is Reggie MacDougall. Sound familiar?"

Sounds Scottish was my first thought. Just like Aunt Gwyneth. And Claire. Coincidence? But I stayed silent.

"I've never heard of him." Claire looked thoughtful as she took a sip of water. "My father had a good friend named Reggie, but obviously it's not the same fellow." With a sudden groan of frustration, she said, "Honestly, I don't know why I mentioned my father. I seem to be grasping at straws."

"Maybe not," Inspector Lee said deliberately. "Maybe there's something about your father's friend Reggie that reminds you of the dead man."

Claire pressed her lips together, then said, "Well, they are of a similar type, as I told Derek and Brooklyn."

"Tell me," the inspector said.

She told her about her father's buddies, the ones who were around a lot, helping him with the various jobs that came up.

I said, "I remember you mentioned that the guy in the closet was hefty with broad shoulders."

"And brutish," Derek added.

"Yes, that's right," Claire said. "And the pizza man was similar. Both were rather brutish. Heavyset, unshaven." She grimaced. "I'm certainly not saying that my father hired brutes. But they were humble men, used to doing hard work and getting their hands dirty."

"All right." Inspector Lee nodded. "Let's go back to Reggie for a minute. I was told that you saw his body in the parking garage earlier this evening."

"Yes, I did. I wanted to see his face. I needed to know who it was."

"And you recognized him as the one you call the pizza man?"

"Yes."

"Did you happen to recognize the weapon that killed him?"

The question surprised her. "Why would I . . . what are you asking?"

The inspector actually smiled. "Claire, I've been told that you're considered an expert in antique weaponry. The weapon used to kill Mr. MacDougall was definitely unusual and quite possibly an antique. Did you see it?"

"Yes, I saw it."

"Can you describe it?"

Claire's forehead wrinkled in a sure sign of worry. But then she seemed to gather the strength to calm herself. She gave a quick nod. "Yes, of course."

"Okay."

Claire closed her eyes. "Dagger. Stiletto blade, most likely English, circa 1865. Mother-of-pearl handle with some carved embellishments, although I didn't get a close enough look to describe the design or pattern. This type of weapon is what was once called a 'garter dagger' or a 'prostitute's dagger,' because it's quite small, only about seven inches long, and can easily be tucked into a woman's garter for protection."

I met Inspector Lee's gaze. "Girl knows her stuff."

"Looks that way."

After Inspector Lee left, I made a pot of tea for Claire and then cleaned up the kitchen. Derek, Alex, and Claire sat around the island directly across from me, chatting about the day and sharing various theories.

After the last dish was put away, I turned to Claire. "I don't think you should stay at your place tonight. We have two extra guest rooms that you're welcome to use until you feel safe going home."

"Oh, Brooklyn, you're being too kind. I've taken up your entire day and put you in danger. And despite all that, you still don't really know me."

"But we know you may be in jeopardy," Derek said.

I frowned. "We just don't know *why*."

"Neither do I," Claire muttered.

Alex pushed her stool away from the island and stood. Walking over to Claire, she grabbed Claire's shoulders for a quick massage. "Jeez, your muscles are tight enough to snap off." She gave her a few more light squeezes. "I know you've had a hell of a day, but try to relax for now. Remember, Inspector Lee is on the case and she's the best. And you've got Derek and Brooklyn on your side. And me, of course. How can you lose?"

"How can I?" Claire's eyes were shut, but she was smiling.

"You can't," Alex continued. "Trust me, we are all rock stars. You're in good hands. We're going to figure out this whole mess in no time."

I jumped in. "And we all agree that you can't go home alone."

"Absolutely not." Alex gave Claire's shoulder a couple of final pats, then grabbed her wineglass and carried it over to the sink. "Now, speaking of home, I've got to go. I have an early-morning conference call and I still have to look over some notes."

"It was lovely meeting you," Claire said.

Alex gave her a hug. "You, too. Stay safe."

There were hugs all around and then Alex left.

Once she was gone, Claire tried to convince Derek and me that she would be perfectly safe at home alone.

"My house is pretty secure. And my neighbors are all close by."

"Close enough to hear your screams?" I said pointedly.

She winced. "It shouldn't come to that."

"The closet guy was waiting inside your house when you got home," I said. "Do you really think you'll be able to sleep knowing that he probably has a key to your front door?"

With that, she lost some steam. "Well, when you put it that way."

"We're going to drive you home," Derek said with

finality. "We'll wait while you pack a few things. You can spend the night here and then tomorrow we'll put our heads together and get to the bottom of whatever has occurred with your aunt."

"I'm not certain we'll be able to find out without being there, in Scotland," she said.

"Neither am I, frankly. But as I told you, I made a call earlier to an old friend at Interpol. I asked him to contact the local constable in your aunt's village and he assured me he would do so right away. But now it's the middle of the night in England so I can't check up on him until the morning. By then we might have some answers."

She blinked, clearly on the verge of tears. After sniffling a few times, she said, "Thank you."

"You're welcome." He glanced at me. "I also intend to call Douglas and Duncan to explore a few other angles."

"Those are two of his brothers," I explained. "He has four altogether and they're all superheroes. If they can't help you, nobody can."

"I'm quite overwhelmed by your generosity." She chewed on her lower lip and fiddled nervously with her ponytail.

"We don't want you to get hurt."

"Thank you." She sniffed one last time and then straightened up. "I'm determined to be more positive, starting now."

"Good," Derek said. "Let's drive over to your place and pick up what you'll need."

"Thank you again." She rolled her eyes, then smiled sheepishly. "I feel quite like a gothic heroine, always depending on the kindness of strangers."

I gave her a look. "That's Tennessee Williams."

She smiled. "Right. Southern Gothic."

I laughed. "You've got me there."

We took my car because it had more room for people and baggage than Derek's Bentley. I headed for Dolores Street and drove through the Mission District, past the beautiful Mission Dolores Park.

"You can take Dolores all the way up to Valley Street and turn right," Claire said.

"Okay," I said.

When I made the turn on Valley, she said, "I'm the ninth house on the right, just opposite the church."

"Got it." I slowed down to count the houses.

"Sorry," she said with a chuckle. "You don't really have to count. I'll show you where to turn into the driveway. It's fine to park there since I won't be long."

I pulled into the narrow driveway in front of an attractive, Marina-style three-story house with a traditional decorated stucco façade and wide bay windows. It was classic San Francisco, with a shared garage on the ground floor and two roomy apartments—or flats—above.

"Do you own this place?" So many of these two-family buildings had been turned into condominiums that I had to ask.

"Yes, I own the first-floor flat and Paul is upstairs."

"And you have a little backyard, you said."

"That's right. I love it here."

"Was it painted like this when you moved in?"

"No, Paul did all the exterior painting. Isn't it fabulous?"

"Yes." The house was painted a light grayish blue with a darker blue trim around the windows, as well as the decorative flourishes and cornices. "It looks so elegant."

"He would love to hear you say that."

As we walked to the front stairs, I noticed that her upscale street was quiet, although there was plenty of activity going on a few blocks over on 24th Street, where restaurants and clubs were still open.

I recalled that I'd once thought I might want to live around here, near one of my favorite bookstores in the city and close to the amazing views of Twin Peaks. But over the past few years Noe Valley had become a haven for families and now there were always pregnant moms and baby strollers on the sidewalks and in the fancy shops. Not that there was anything wrong with that, unless you happened to get your ankle clipped by one of those strollers. It could leave a mark. Trust me, I knew what I was talking about.

Anyway, now I was perfectly happy living with Derek in our loft apartment in SOMA across the street from another favorite bookshop and close to a ton of other shops and restaurants. And we were walking distance from the Giants' stadium overlooking the Bay. On any sunny afternoon we could easily walk a few blocks and take in a baseball game.

We followed Claire up the stairs and when we reached the landing, she turned the key. "Here we are." She pushed open her front door and gasped. "No!"

"What is it?"

Then she screamed, "Oh my God!"

Without hesitation, Derek grabbed her arms and gently moved her aside to take a look inside her house. Immediately he turned and looked directly at me. "Wait right here." He drew his gun and walked into the house.

"Oh, crap. All right, but be careful." I wanted to follow right behind him, but knew I couldn't help. As soon as he verified that it was safe, I'd be right there. For now I pulled Claire close and she rocked against me.

I had caught a glimpse of what she had seen. Her front room was a complete shambles. Her couch and two chairs were overturned and pillows were slashed, their foam and cotton innards scattered across the floor. A large bookshelf had been toppled and dozens of books lay every which way, their pages torn and tattered. For that alone I couldn't blame her for screaming.

"I have to get inside," she said as her whole body shuddered in fear and disbelief.

"Just give it a minute. Derek wants to make sure there's nobody hiding in there."

She fell back against the wall of the stairwell. It seemed like she had reached the limit of her patience. I knew how she felt.

"It's going to be all right," I said, trying to soothe her.

"How?" she demanded. "How will anything ever be all right?"

Good question. I wasn't exactly sure, but I had to give it a shot. "If you'd been home, you could've been badly hurt. Or worse."

"Maybe. I suppose." She buried her face in both hands. "Oh God. Why is this happening?"

"We'll find out," I insisted, but inside I felt helpless. She had asked a good question. I tried to work the puzzle, put some pieces together while we waited to hear Derek say everything was okay. Things had started to go badly for Claire, first in Scotland when she found out her aunt was missing. And then as soon as she returned home, those two thugs had showed up to frighten the hell out of her. Why?

Claire suddenly gasped again and her eyes were wide with dread. "Mr. D! I need to make sure he's all right."

It took me a few seconds. "Your cat."

"Yes. I picked him up from the vet's this morning so

he's been home all day. He was here when this happened. Oh God, what if they hurt him?"

That settled it. "Derek," I called. "We're coming in."

"All right," he said from somewhere down the hall. "There's nobody here. But be careful. Don't trip over anything."

"We need to find Claire's cat."

"Ah, yes. Of course." A moment later he called back, "The cat is hiding under your bed, Claire."

"Oh, thank goodness." She was breathless. "I'm coming to get him." She tiptoed across the living room, but as she made her way through the mess, weaving and dodging, she suddenly uttered what could only be called a quiet shriek. "Oh no."

"What is it? What's wrong?" I asked.

She bent over and picked up a thick book that had fallen from the shelf. *Mistress of Mellyn*. She held up the front cover that had almost broken off completely. Happily, though, it was still holding on by a few threads. "It's one of my favorite Victoria Holts. And now it's ruined."

"Give it to me. I'll fix it."

"Oh God," she whispered. "Thank you, Brooklyn." She handed me the tattered book and without another word, she disappeared down the hall.

Glancing down at the floor, I spied the book's dustcover splayed open and ripped along the fold. Picking it up and folding it around the book itself, I followed in Claire's footsteps, creeped out with every step. What were we going to find down the hall? Around the corner? Under the bed? Even though Derek had already covered that ground, I still had my active imagination to deal with.

"Derek?" I called. "Where are you?"

"I'm here in the second bedroom."

I passed one door on the left and saw Claire on her hands and knees next to a queen-sized bed, trying to coax the cat to come out from under it. The door on the right was the bathroom. When I got to the second door on the left, I found Derek standing by Claire's desk, staring down at something. The floor around him was littered with dozens of papers that had obviously been swept off the desk.

"This is a mess," I said. "The entire place has been ripped apart."

He glanced at me, his eyes narrowed. "And unless she has her laptop locked up somewhere, it's missing."

"How can you tell?"

"They threw the power cord across the room and took a knife to the mousepad."

"Well, hell. Who would do this? And more importantly, why?"

"Yes, the 'why' is definitely the key to this puzzle. Does she keep a diary on there? Did they want her calendar? Or a contact list? Maybe she keeps photos and details of her weapons collection."

I stared up at him, then turned and called out, "Claire?"

"Yes?" Her voice was muffled and I assumed she was still trying to coax Mr. D out from under the bed.

"Do you have a computer?"

"I do, yes. It's right here in my backpack."

I let out a quiet breath and looked at Derek.

He nodded. "It appears they were frustrated when they couldn't find it."

"Good." I glanced around the room again, mentally ticking off the most affected areas of the intruder's wrath. Papers, bills, and letters thrown off the desk; even more damaged books scattered across the floor; a small ottoman in the corner torn apart with stuffing floating everywhere.

"It wasn't Reggie MacDougall who did this," I reasoned, "because he was following Claire and now he's dead. But it could've been the other guy. The closet guy. Mr. Peppermint."

He raised an eyebrow. "Mr. Peppermint. That's what we're going with?"

"It's as good a nickname as any, don't you think?"

"Absolutely."

I smiled, but just as quickly sobered. "So it's got to be him. Mr. Peppermint, I mean. And maybe he has another accomplice or two. But what do they want from Claire? What are they looking for?"

"Darling, think about the timing," he said, and I realized he had already figured it out. "Claire returns from Scotland, where she discovered her aunt missing. Within minutes of being home, those goons show up to threaten her. Soon after that, Claire arrives at our house."

I grabbed his arm. "Right after we received the package from Aunt Gwyneth."

"Exactly."

"But wait," I said, quickly following the timeline in my head.

"I'll wait." He watched me as I began to figure it out.

"Oh crap. Oh no." I started pounding my fist against his arm. "Derek, they're not after Claire. They're after the book. They're after *Rebecca*."

Chapter 5

"I should've known," I whispered. "The minute Claire showed up, I should've known it was all about the book."

"But we *did* know." Derek gently but firmly wrapped his hand around my fist to keep me from slugging him again. "And now, just a few hours later, we know so much more than we did before. That book is the key to everything. We just need to track down a few more puzzle pieces."

"And then maybe we can figure out what in the holy heck is so important about that book."

The plain fact was that whenever Derek and I had been confronted by a dead body, there was invariably a book involved. It was one of the golden rules of our lives. Books can kill.

"Darling, perhaps Claire has a clue."

"Maybe." I leaned back in his arms and gazed up at him. "You're right. When we first saw the book, we realized that there was a mystery to solve. We just didn't consider that the mystery would lead to murder."

"Perhaps we should have."

I nodded heartily. "Absolutely. From now on, whenever we see a new book, we need to think, *murder!*"

"Excellent plan."

Despite everything, his words made me smile. He gave me one last quick squeeze, and we walked down the hall to find Claire.

She sat on her bed, cradling her cat in her arms.

"You rescued your cat," I said.

"Yes. It was a struggle. He's quite traumatized."

"I'm so sorry."

"If you don't mind, I'll put him in his crate and bring him with me."

"Of course," Derek said. "He's more than welcome."

"Thank you," she said softly, and buried her face in Mr. D's furry neck. Abruptly, she looked up at me. "I'm so sorry for going crazy on you earlier. The damage they did to my house was horrible, and then I saw that book and simply flipped out."

"It's one of your favorites, you said."

"Yes. It's a classic. But that doesn't mean you have to take it home and fix it." Dismayed, she shook her head. "I'm becoming quite the melodrama queen."

"You have every right," I insisted. "Please don't give it another thought. Besides, I love working on books."

"I owe you."

"Okay, maybe you'll show me how to throw a knife."

She perked up. "I can do that."

Derek was pulling out his phone. "We should call Inspector Lee."

"Good idea." I was relieved that he had thought of it because the last thing I wanted to do was wake her up. No, I'd let the *Commander* do it.

Inspector Lee was still awake, thank goodness. Derek put her on speaker so Claire and I could hear the conversation.

"No one is injured?" she asked.

"No," Derek said. "Just a lot of damage to her property."

"I'll send a pair of uniformed officers over there right now to do some preliminary work and cordon off the scene. Then I'll come by first thing tomorrow morning."

"We'll wait here for the officers."

"Appreciate it. Claire, you're staying elsewhere tonight, right?"

"Yes," she said. "I'll be at Brooklyn's place."

"Good," Inspector Lee said. "I've got your number so I'll text in the morning to let you know when I'll be at your house."

Claire said, "I'll meet you there anytime."

"Good. Commander, can you be there as well?"

"Of course."

"You, too, Brooklyn," she added, and I could hear the wryness in her voice.

I flashed a happy smile. "Naturally."

"See you all then. Hey, if anything else occurs, call me."

"Oh, we will," I said.

"And, Claire," she said. "Hang in there. We'll get this taken care of."

"Thank you."

It was close to midnight when we finally got home. Claire was exhausted so we put off any conversations until the morning. After making sure that she and Mr. D had everything they needed, we said good night.

Once we were in our bedroom, Derek said, "I'm going to set the alarm."

"I'll do it." I sat on the edge of the bed. "What time do you want to wake up?"

"Early, but I'm not talking about the alarm clock."

"Oh." He was talking about the security alarm. But we set that every night so I wasn't sure why he'd even mentioned it. But then it hit me. "You're worried about Claire?"

"Aren't you?"

"Yes, I am. But probably for different reasons."

"My reason is simple," he stated. "I'm concerned that she might either leave in the middle of the night . . ."

"Or?"

"She might open the door to allow someone else to enter our home."

I stared at him, almost afraid to ask the next question. "Did you run her?"

He gazed at me for a long moment. "I beg your pardon?"

"You heard me," I insisted. "You ran her name through your system, didn't you? That system of yours. The international security background-check gizmo you use for your work. I forget what you call it."

"Good." He scowled. "I prefer that you not remember the name and never bring it up again."

I couldn't help but laugh. "Okay, fine. So you ran her name through your system. What did you find out?"

He was still scowling as he pulled off his sweater. "Not much of anything."

I tried to hide my smile. "So she's not a vicious criminal."

He inhaled deeply, then exhaled slowly. "It's hard to say."

"What's that supposed to mean?"

"It means that she's a blank slate. She has a passport and a driver's license and that's it."

"So she's not an international crime boss?"

"It's hard to say."

"Stop it," I said, laughing. "Look, a driver's license and passport are all I have, too. So what exactly are you saying?"

"It's suspicious, that's all."

I frowned at him. "Why?"

"What if her records have been deliberately wiped clean?"

That shocked me into silence. For a few seconds anyway. "Are you serious? How does that even happen?"

"I have a few theories. I imagine you could probably come up with one or two yourself."

I thought about it for a moment while I slipped into a nightshirt. "I suppose her aunt Gwyneth could've taken care of it."

"Perhaps."

"Wait." My eyes widened. "Do you think Claire is actually an agent herself?"

"No."

That was succinct, I thought. "Okay, good. It's true that she seems to be an expert in weapons of all kinds. That kind of skill could come in handy in your line of work."

"It certainly could." He put his wallet and wristwatch on top of the dresser. "Look, let's forget all the intrigue for now and get back to my original question. You know the woman better than I do. Would she try to sneak out of here in the middle of the night?"

I thought about it briefly. "I doubt it. She's genuinely frightened. Besides, where would she go? She can't go home right away after her place was ransacked. And don't forget, she's got her cat with her."

He mulled over my answer, then nodded. "Makes sense. All right. Now tell me your reasons for worrying about Claire."

"Three reasons. One, I worry that this thug, Mr. Peppermint, will really try to hurt her." I moved into the bathroom and began to brush my hair. "Two, I worry about her aunt. Where can she be?"

"My people will track down her aunt."

"I hope so." Then I sighed heavily. "And three, I worry that we're going to wind up getting very involved in Claire's troubles."

"Darling." He leaned against the doorjamb and watched me brush my hair. "We were involved the moment we opened that package from Aunt Gwyneth."

Dismayed, I shook my head. "Why did it have to be a book?"

"Because you are who you are."

"And so are you."

"Yes. And from this moment on, you must be very careful."

I put down my brush, walked over to him, and wrapped my arms around his waist. "And so must you."

He held on to me. "I always am."

I savored the feeling of being held by him. Finally I gazed up. "I don't believe Claire will try to leave in the middle of the night. But on the off chance that she did, it would only be because she felt guilty for bringing murder to our doorstep."

Derek scoffed. "If she only knew how often that happens."

"If only." I turned back to the counter, picked up my brush, and put it away in the drawer. "Tomorrow we should tell her that I'm a murder magnet. She'll feel less guilty."

He chuckled. "So now *you* feel guilty that she feels guilty?"

"Well, yeah."

He kissed me. "Darling, if you must carry the weight of the world on your shoulders, then so be it. But I don't like you calling yourself a *murder magnet*."

"Really? I think it has a ring."

"If you say so," he said with a laugh. "Oh, and there's one more thing we must do tomorrow."

"Yes. We must tell Claire about the book."

I woke up at 6 a.m., shocked and grateful to realize that I'd slept straight through the night. I hadn't been sure I would, given all the anxiety-inducing events we'd been a part of last night.

I stretched, then rolled over to greet Derek—and found his side of the bed empty. That wasn't unusual; Derek was normally an early riser and could often be found at the crack of dawn in his office, chatting on the phone with one of his partners in Europe or Asia or with his brothers in England. The time zones could be tricky so early mornings were usually best for him.

I jumped out of bed and rushed to wash my face and brush my teeth. I applied some moisturizer and lip balm, then brushed my hair back and threw on a comfy sweatshirt and leggings.

I found Derek and Claire in the kitchen, drinking coffee and chatting. I went straight to the coffeemaker, poured a tall cup, took my first sip, and almost moaned, it was so good. I had always added half-and-half to my coffee until our honeymoon in Paris, where I'd started to drink it black. I was still in that zone.

"Good morning," I said, setting my cup on the island and sliding onto the stool on the kitchen side.

"She doesn't speak until she gets that first hit of caffeine," Derek explained, his eyes twinkling with humor.

"I understand completely," Claire said. She seemed

to be in a pretty good mood, considering how her life had come crashing down in the last few days.

"How did you sleep?" I asked her.

"Much to my surprise, I slept quite well. Your guest room is lovely. And I hope you don't mind, but I took Mr. D out of his crate last night. I needed some creature comfort, I suppose."

"It's no problem at all," Derek said.

"Of course it's fine," I said. "And he must've helped because you look well rested."

"I feel well rested." She held her coffee mug with both hands for warmth. "And I want to thank you again. I'm so grateful for your kindness and generosity."

"You're welcome," I said, and added with a short laugh, "and that's the last time you have to thank us. You've been through hell, so we're more than happy to help."

"I should tell you that I received a text from Inspector Lee a while ago. She wishes to meet me at my place around nine a.m."

"Oh, good to know." I opened the refrigerator and pulled out a basket of fresh strawberries. "That gives us time to have some breakfast and talk."

She stood. "I insist on helping you with something."

"You can set the table."

Over breakfast at the dining room table, I brought up a touchy subject.

"Claire, what are we going to do about Mr. Peppermint?"

"Who?" she asked.

Derek chuckled. "Mr. Peppermint is the man who was hiding in your closet. Brooklyn often nicknames the evildoers who come into our lives. It makes them seem more easily vanquished."

"It works for me," I said with a shrug, ignoring Claire's look of surprise at Derek's comment on all those evil-doers. "So have you given the situation much thought?"

She set down her fork. "I have, a bit. But first, I honestly don't know what I did to trigger such a bizarre set of occurrences." She gazed at Derek. "First Aunt Gwyneth disappears, her home is left a shambles, and then I fly back home and these horrible men show up. One breaks into my house and scares the life out of me and the other one follows me over here to your building and winds up dead in your garage. And then I go back home to find my own place ransacked. It's like something out of a horror story. I'm not sure I can take much more."

"I'm so sorry," I said. "We're going to try and figure it out."

"But that's another thing," she said. "I shouldn't even be involving you in my problems."

"But we are involved," I insisted. "And it's not your fault. We're involved because your aunt Gwyneth sent Derek a package."

She blinked, completely stunned. "Good heavens, Brooklyn! I forgot all about the package." She rubbed her forehead thoughtfully. "But of course. That's why I came over here in the first place. And that fellow Reggie followed me here and wound up getting killed in your garage." She gaped at me. "Oh my God. Of course that's the connection. I feel so stupid for not thinking of it sooner."

"You've had a lot on your mind," I said with a sympathetic smile.

"That excuse is getting old." She inhaled and let her breath out slowly, trying to regain some of the steadiness she'd shown before. Looking at Derek, she asked,

"So Aunt Gwyneth sent you the package and then she disappeared. And then I flew home and suddenly these awful men are chasing me. Do you think the men are connected to Aunt Gwyneth's disappearance in Scotland? It's the only thing that makes sense, and yet, it makes no sense at all."

"I believe there is a connection," Derek said.

"But how did her kidnappers get from the Scottish Highlands all the way over here to San Francisco?"

"I'm not saying the men who are tormenting you are the same ones responsible for Gwyneth's disappearance. But I do believe that they're all connected."

She frowned. "My mind must be a muddle. I'm afraid I'm barely understanding you."

I sat forward, smiling. "That's because this whole thing is a convoluted mess."

"It is, isn't it?" Claire seemed relieved by my statement. But her expression quickly turned pensive. "I wonder if I've been on their radar for a while now. Those bad men, I mean. Perhaps they were watching me even before Gwyneth was taken?"

Derek and I exchanged a quick look. "No," I said slowly. "Again, we think it all started when Gwyneth sent the package to Derek. You wouldn't have been on their radar before that."

Claire stamped her foot in frustration. "I keep forgetting about that package! Why?"

"Easy, Claire," I said. "It's understandable. You've got a lot on your mind."

"There's that excuse again." She took another breath and visibly tried to chill her temper. With a rueful smile she said, "Honestly, please believe me. I'm usually not so flaky."

"Never apologize for being a flake," I said. "That's my go-to state of mind most days."

"I just don't know why these men want to hurt me. It feels very personal."

"Of course it feels personal," I said. "One of them was actually hiding inside your house. That's not just personal. It's terrifying."

"I suppose if we gave them the package," Derek said, "they might leave you alone."

"No," she said stubbornly. "Aunt Gwyneth sent the package to you. They don't get to have it."

"I have no intention of giving it to them," Derek said. "I just wanted to hear you say it."

"Even if you gave them the book, they would still want to hurt Claire," I said matter-of-factly. Then I winced. "Sorry, Claire. I don't mean to bum you out, but you know, they're bad guys. It comes with the territory."

To my surprise, Claire laughed. "I'm well beyond being bummed out. But I find it's actually cheering me up to know it's not all about me. I can blame it on that stupid package."

"That's right," Derek said. "Nevertheless, I agree with Brooklyn's point. You're still very much in danger."

And with that cheerful thought, I decided it was time to tell Claire what was in the package. But she chose that moment to check her watch and groaned. "I've got to get going or I'll be late meeting Inspector Lee."

"We'll take you," Derek said. "Let's go."

On the ride over to Claire's place, Derek told us about the crack-of-dawn telephone conversation he'd had with his good friend Harold, who worked at Interpol, the international criminal police organization.

"He spoke to your local constabulary and got the

same runaround that you did regarding your aunt's disappearance."

"Was he able to convince them to take action?" I asked.

Derek smiled. "Of course. Harold is nothing if not persistent. He threatened to call out the big guns in Edinburgh if the guys didn't get busy finding Gwyneth."

I turned to look at Claire, who was sitting in the back seat. "Harold is great. He was able to cut through some major red tape in another investigation we were involved in a while ago."

Claire gave my shoulder a friendly pat. "You sound like a detective, Brooklyn."

"Sometimes I feel like one," I admitted. I glanced at Derek, expecting to see him rolling his eyes, but instead, he winked at me. It warmed me right down to my socks.

We arrived at Claire's place and saw Inspector Lee waiting by the stairs that led up to the apartment. We joined her and she explained what she wanted to do. "I'm going to ask you two to wait outside while I go through the place with Claire."

"That's fine," I said, figuring it would only take a few minutes before we would be able to join them upstairs.

"Then I've got my crime scene guys showing up in a little while." The inspector glanced at Claire. "I'll want to go through your place with them, too, and get them started in the areas that were most affected by the intruders."

"The whole place was affected," Claire grumbled. "They didn't leave much of anything undamaged."

Inspector Lee nodded somberly. "My guys will be very thorough."

"Okay," Claire said. "That's good, I guess."

If Claire thought the place was a mess now, then she

would be unpleasantly surprised when the crime scene guys were finished. They would go through everything in her house, searching for fingerprints, and there would be black powder residue left everywhere. Having gone through a similar experience myself more than once, I made a mental note to recommend my friend Tom to Claire. Tom was a great guy who owned and operated an excellent crime scene cleanup service. Because that's what friends were for.

"I'm also going to want to talk to your neighbor," Inspector Lee was saying as she glanced through her notes. "Paul, right?"

"Yes, Paul. He lives upstairs."

"The officers who were here last night were able to speak to him briefly, but I'd like to talk to him as well. It would be helpful if you'd introduce him to me."

"Oh, of course," Claire said, willing to do whatever it took to help the inspector get answers.

I slipped my arm through Derek's. "We'll take a walk while you guys assess the damage."

Derek looked at his watch. "We'll be back in forty-five minutes, if that works for you."

"Perfect," Inspector Lee said.

"That was very brave of you," Derek said as we walked up to Church and turned left.

I shook my head, dejected. "I really wanted to hang out and watch the crime scene guys, but I saw the writing on the wall. There was no way Inspector Lee would go for it."

"No way in the world," he said, biting back a grin. "And now I have a chance to take a lovely morning walk with my beautiful wife."

If that was his way of perking up my spirits, I'd have to say it was pretty good.

"Let's find a bookshop," he suggested. "That will cheer you up."

"True." I wasn't always the most patient person, but I could linger for hours inside a bookshop. So we strolled a few blocks to Omnivore Books, which specialized in all kinds of cookbooks and books about food. It had a fine selection of vintage and antiquarian books on the subject, too, so I was always excited to peruse their latest acquisitions. This was also the perfect store to shop for my sister Savannah, who was a professional chef.

I would've loved to find a vintage cookbook for Savannah, but I knew she would never care about it as much as I would. She wasn't a booklover. She just loved cooking. In fact, she loved it more than she loved eating. And that would never make sense to me.

We had agreed that we were officially just browsing today, not buying. But I did make a list of a few intriguing titles, including a gorgeous new cupcake cookbook for Alex. I would definitely be back soon.

We wandered over to Sanchez Street and walked another few blocks to Folio Books, which had an impressive collection of children's books as well as plenty of other genres. Derek spent time going through the latest nonfiction selections while I thumbed through some of the children's books, searching for birthday and Christmas ideas for my nieces and nephews. I wrote down a few titles that I would run past my sisters, since they always liked to know what eccentric gift I was giving their children. I didn't know when or how I had turned into the eccentric aunt, but I was okay with it.

Gazing at all these children's books, I was reminded that I had to finish my best friend Robin's baby gift. We planned to return to Dharma in two weeks for her baby shower.

I had designed a mobile made of several dozen small, colorful origami birds and hearts and butterflies attached to invisible fishing wire that descended from an open book. It was light and ethereal and gave the impression that the characters had come alive and flown out of the book. I knew Robin would love it.

I had already constructed the book itself and the handmade pages, too. The pages were pretty pastel colors with deckled edges that fanned out to go with the light and airy feel of the origami creatures. The origami was all I had left to do—and then assemble the different parts.

The book was attached to a smooth wooden hoop that could be hung from the ceiling over the crib so the birds and butterflies would flutter and sway above the baby. And as the baby grew, the mobile could be moved and used as a wall hanging.

It figured I would wind up fashioning a baby mobile out of a book. But that was me in a nutshell.

On the way back to Claire's we stopped at a charming tearoom where Derek got himself a to-go cup of very strong tea and I bought a selection of scones and teacakes that I thought Claire would enjoy.

It was a gorgeous late spring day and Noe Valley was hopping. The baby stroller mamas were out in force and I was determined to stay out of their way.

When we reached a sparsely populated stretch of sidewalk along 28th Street, I turned to Derek. "What are we going to do about Claire?"

"Do you mean today? Or ultimately?"

"I guess I mean both."

"Ultimately, everything will be fine and Claire and her aunt Gwyneth will live happily in a thug-free world."

I chuckled. "But what about today?"

"Today," he said, and frowned. "Well, first we should

insist that she stay with us as long as necessary to make sure she's safe."

"But when will she be safe?" I wondered.

"She'll be safe as soon as your Mr. Peppermint is behind bars."

I stopped to gaze at a storefront display of fascinating kitchen gadgets. "How can we arrange for that to happen quickly?"

"Perhaps he'll arrange it himself," he said darkly.

"And what about Aunt Gwyneth?"

Derek gritted his teeth. "I don't know yet. I'm waiting for Harold to confirm that things are getting straightened out on his end."

"So he'll find out who kidnapped her?"

He hesitated. "He'll have more information later today."

"Can you tell me more about your conversation with him?"

"Yes, of course." He was finished with his tea and he tossed the empty disposable cup into a recycling bin. Then he slipped his arm through mine and we ambled arm in arm toward Claire's street. "Harold confirmed what Claire told us, but there's more to the story."

"What's that?"

"The woman in charge of the area is on maternity leave and the fellow they left in charge is a bit of a git."

A "git," according to Derek, was an ignorant, immature jerk. The term was one of his favorites, but I hated to hear it being used to describe a police officer.

"That's not good," I said.

"No. But Harold also spoke to the area commander for Inverness and made her aware of exactly what had happened. She knows there's a problem with the local man."

"You mean, the git?"

"Yes," he said with a reluctant smile. "And she assured Harold that she knows who to contact for more information and would be sending two of her officers to investigate the aunt's disappearance."

"Okay. Harold comes through once again."

When we arrived back at Claire's, Inspector Lee was standing out in the driveway talking to a man I didn't recognize.

"Commander, Brooklyn," she said, "this is Claire's neighbor Paul."

Both Derek and I shook hands with him and I thanked him for looking out for Claire.

"She's a good neighbor," Paul said. "I would hate to have anything bad happen to her."

"We're going to do our best to make sure nothing does," Inspector Lee said.

Claire came downstairs at that moment, carrying a medium-sized duffel bag. "Oh, you're back. What lovely timing."

"I told Claire that she would need to find alternative housing," Inspector Lee explained. "So she packed a few extra items to tide her over."

"Yes, I was able to grab more clothing and necessities to get me through the next few days."

"Good," Derek said.

Claire set her bag down on the driveway. "Now, look. I'm perfectly happy to have you drop me off at a hotel. It can't be easy to have a houseguest when you least expect it. Especially a guest who brings her own perils with her. And a cat, for God's sake."

"You're welcome to stay with us for as long as it takes to clear up this situation," I said. "I don't want you to worry about it anymore." With a smile, I added, "And we like cats."

Paul kept his gaze on us as he draped his arm around Claire's shoulders and gave her a squeeze. "Thank you for taking care of my girl. I'm relieved to know that she has some good friends looking out for her."

"We heard you also had a run-in with one of the men," I said. "Are you all right?"

"Oh yes." He waved away my worries. "I just got a pizza box in my face for my trouble. But I'm fine. I have a friend coming over to stay with me for a few days."

"Good," the inspector said, and handed him her business card. "If you have any trouble or see anything suspicious, give me a call."

It was just after noon when we arrived back home. Being super-cautious, Derek advised us to stay in the car until the garage grille gate came all the way down and locked in place.

When it was safe, we scrambled out of the car and hurried over to the fire door. Derek was carrying Claire's duffel bag so I tapped in the code and we entered the basement elevator lobby.

When we were finally inside our house, we all gave a sigh of relief.

"I'm so sorry to bring all this tension into your world," Claire said.

I glared at her. "I warned you. No more apologies."

She managed to smile. "Yes, you did. Please forgive me."

I chuckled. "That's better. Look, why don't you take a few minutes to get settled and say hello to Mr. D?"

"I will, although I doubt he's even missed me. But he needs a treat and I need a hug."

"Take as long as you want. Then, as soon as you're ready, we have something to show you."

Her blue eyes grew wider when she realized I was talking about the *package*. She grabbed my arms and gave me an excited squeeze. "Yay! I'll only be a minute. I'm dying to see what all the madness is about."

Chapter 6

While Claire was in her room nuzzling her kitty and unpacking her duffel bag, I hurried to our closet safe and pulled out the *Rebecca*. I wasn't trying to be sneaky. Okay, maybe I was, but the safe in our hall closet was a pretty big secret, something that Derek and I rarely discussed with anyone but ourselves.

I brought the book into my workshop and set it atop a piece of clean white cloth on my table. When I was doing bookbinding work I always kept the various pieces of the book on a white cloth in order to easily see them as I took the book apart. Sometimes with a very old book, those pieces included chunks of old leather or wisps of thin tissue linings.

Without much thought, I took out my phone and started snapping photos of the front cover and spine from all sorts of angles. I opened the book and took another few pictures, mainly close-ups of the inner hinge or joint, which was fraying. The once-white endpapers were now light gray with age.

I had once read that *Rebecca* had never gone out of print. I believed it. The book had been wildly popular from day one and had always been considered a romance, despite the darkly sinister plot and all the horrors the narrator went through.

I turned when Derek walked into the room with Claire. "Here it is," I said, closing the cover. "This is what your aunt sent Derek."

She approached the worktable slowly, almost reverently. "It's the black book," she whispered.

"So you're familiar with it," Derek said, watching her expression from his spot on the opposite side of the table.

"Aye." She glanced up at him. "Aunt Gwyneth has had it for years. It's one of her favorite versions, mainly because it was signed by the author. She always called it her little black book."

"Do you know where she got it?" I asked.

Claire's lips twisted in thought. "It was a long time ago, but I think it's one of the books my father gave her."

"Your father?" I had to admit I was not expecting that answer.

"Yes," Claire said. "Gwyneth is his sister."

"Ah. They're brother and sister."

"Yes. I didn't mention it before?"

"No."

"Is it important?"

I glanced at Derek, who managed to conceal his surprise. "I have no idea."

I wasn't sure why we were so surprised. Her aunt Gwyneth had to have been related to either Claire's father or mother. Was it important? I wondered. It might be. After all, Gwyneth had sent the book to Derek and then Claire showed up, followed by big burly bad guys who seemed to want to hurt her and to get their hands on this book. Big burly guys who reminded her of the men who used to work for her father. So yeah, it might be important. Or maybe not. I made a mental note to ask her more about her father later.

"Aunt Gwyneth promised she would eventually give the book to me because it had come from my father." She idly ran her index finger along the shallow outer hinge of the front cover where it connected to the spine. "I was thrilled not only because it was from my father, but also because it's such a gorgeous edition. And because I was simply obsessed with gothic novels at the time. Well, I still am. And *Rebecca* is quite possibly my favorite book of all time."

"Gwyneth told you she was going to give you this book someday?" Derek asked.

"Yes."

"But it originally came from your father."

"That's right. When I was young, about eight or nine, Aunt Gwyneth used to read to me and I always loved this story in particular. Everyone is so elegant, aren't they?"

"Seriously?" I said. "You were reading *Rebecca* at age eight or nine? That's pretty young to be obsessed with gothic novels." Especially this one, I thought, with its dark, melodramatic twists and edgy malevolence.

She laughed. "Oh, aye. Quite inappropriate. But that was Aunt Gwyneth to a T." She gazed at the cover and smiled. "And I could so easily relate to the tragic heroine trope."

I smiled, imagining how Claire could picture herself in that role.

"I know I missed out on the psychological nuances of the story," she said. "And of course, the mystery itself went way over my head. But I loved the characters and the settings. So wonderfully odd and dramatic."

"They were that, for sure."

She sighed. "Then after a few years when I started reading on my own, I must confess I didn't enjoy reading this hardcover version because the pages and the cover were rather stiff. It was impossible to race through it without damaging it. I knew if I wasn't careful, I would ruin it. It was quite expensive, as I found out later."

"Kids can be pretty brutal with books."

"I know I was at that age."

"I'm still marveling at you reading gothic novels when you were so young."

She laughed lightly. "I learned to read in kindergarten and from then on, it seemed I always had a book in my hand. It didn't matter what the subject was. I was simply in love with reading. And when my father sent me to live with Gwyneth, I discovered that she loved books as well. Of course, soon after I arrived on her doorstep, she shipped me off to a local boarding school."

"Oh dear," I said.

Claire chuckled. "I'm not complaining. It was exciting to live with Aunt Gwyneth and the school she sent me to was quite simply the most beautiful place in the world. Surrounded by woods and rolling green hills and very close to the waters of the Moray Firth."

"Wasn't Gwyneth working in London at that time?" Derek asked.

"Aye, but she always came home on weekends." Claire smiled dreamily. "She would zip up to school in her fancy Triumph sports car on a Friday afternoon and off we'd go. We had plenty of adventures, but sometimes we would simply sit under a tree and read all day. Then every Monday morning she would deliver me back to school. She was the most amazing person." Her eyes clouded up. "She *is* the most amazing person. She's still with us. I know she is."

"And we will find her," Derek promised.

I gave a firm nod of agreement while crossing my fingers, hoping he was right. I decided to bring the conversation back to the book. "So you didn't take this copy of *Rebecca* with you when you moved away from Gwyneth."

"No. When I went away to university I left the black book with her. I had my own copy that was quite worn, but I was comfortable with it." She gazed up at me. "She promised she would take good care of the black book for me."

"She did," I said with a smile. "It's in very good condition."

"Of course you would recognize its condition," she said, grinning. Her smile turned a bit vague then, as though she were caught up in memories.

"What other books did the two of you read together?" I asked, just to keep her talking. If she was talking, she wasn't worrying about the fate of Aunt Gwyneth.

"Well, *Rebecca* had a good long run. Back in those days I thought the story was terribly romantic. Of course, as I grew older, I came to the stunning realization that Mr. de Winter was a bit of a cad."

"You might say that," I said with a laugh. "He did murder his wife, after all."

"But he never cheated on her," she insisted, laughing with me. "But he was careless and rather selfish with his time, don't you think? And good grief, that horrible housekeeper of his was a demon. I felt he just didn't take very good care of his new wife." She laughed again. "That was my learned opinion by age ten or so. Aunt Gwyneth and I used to debate his qualities—and lack thereof—rather vigorously."

I could tell that Derek was getting antsy with the

subject of gothic heroes and heroines because he began strolling around the workshop. When he reached the far end, he casually stared out the front window. After a long moment, he turned and smiled at me, but it wasn't a happy smile. Claire didn't notice because she was still talking about her favorite books.

"Pardon the interruption, but I need to make a phone call," he announced. "Be back in just a moment."

I caught his gaze. "What is it?"

"It's nothing." But his smile didn't quite reach his eyes and while most people might not notice the tension at the corners of his mouth, I definitely did.

"All righty," I said a little too cheerfully, not wanting to alert Claire. "We'll be here."

"Tell me some of your favorite books," Claire asked when Derek was out of the room.

I didn't even have to think. "My all-time favorite when I was eight years old was *The Secret Garden*."

"Oh, that is a wonderful book."

I told her the story of how my brothers stole my copy of the beloved book and took it outside, where they tossed it back and forth until it fell in the dirt. Then they flung it across the fields to see who could throw it the farthest. When they were done, the cover was barely hanging on. My mother suggested that in lieu of murdering both of my brothers, I should take the book to the commune bookbinder and see if he could rescue it.

I realized too late that I had mentioned the commune. Claire immediately asked me what that was like. I gave her a brief explanation of my upbringing, as though growing up in the commune was the most natural thing in the world.

"And the rest is history," I said, with a short laugh.

"And that's how you got interested in bookbinding. How wonderful. You must know so much about books."

"I know quite a bit, but there's always something new to learn." I reached for the *Rebecca* and opened it to the title page.

"Tell me about this book," she said.

I smiled, turning the book over in my hands. "It's still in great shape. As you probably know, it's a signed first edition and I would guess that it's worth several thousand dollars."

"Honestly?"

"I'd have to look it up to be sure, but Gwyneth kept it in fine condition." I paged through, checking for foxing and any worn pages or tears. "Excellent condition," I amended, using the preferred bookseller term. "Just a bit of rubbing on the spine, and that can easily be repaired." I continued turning pages. "Do you know if it came with a dustcover?"

"That's a good question. I believe it did, but we must've lost it somewhere along the way. Aunt Gwyneth might still have it in her bookshelf."

"That would increase the value," I said nonchalantly, then noticed a tiny tear at the top of one page. *Easily fixed*, I noted, and continued on to the next page, silently admiring the beauty of a well-made book.

But when I got to page 87, I stopped and stared. Almost to myself, I asked, "What are these marks?"

"What marks?" Claire asked, and leaned in closer to see what I was referring to.

I angled the book toward her.

"Is it dirt?" Claire asked.

"I doubt it." I went to my desk and took my microscope out of the drawer, then returned to the worktable to examine the page more closely. "Looks like pencil marks. They've marked every few letters, but it doesn't seem to be a discernible pattern."

"That's odd," Claire said. "I don't ever remember seeing that."

"You did say you've never read this copy."

"Oh, but I have. I've read it several times. Gwyneth has read it, too. Often. I was always very careful with it, which is why I preferred to read my trusty old used paperback copy. With that one, I could leave it open or toss it on the nightstand. I didn't have to worry about treating it gently."

"I understand." I turned the page and noticed there were pencil marks there, too. All in all, the marks continued for four pages. "So you've never seen these markings?"

"No."

I glanced up. "Do you think they could've been here all along and you just didn't happen to notice them?"

Claire shook her head. "I notice everything, Brooklyn. I can be a little neurotic about things like that. Trust me, if those marks had been there when I was reading the book, I would've had to erase them before I could even start on that page."

"Really?"

"Yes, really. I'm what you might call a neat freak."

"I'm sort of that way, too." I nodded. "Everything in its place, you know."

"Exactly."

It was no wonder the mess in Claire's apartment had driven her so crazy. But then, that kind of destruction would've driven anyone over the edge.

I pulled a piece of scratch paper from my printer cabinet and began to write down the letters that were marked.

"What are you doing?" she asked.

"Writing down the struck-out letters. It might be a code of some kind," I muttered, almost to myself.

Claire perked up. "That would be amazing. You know the book was the basis for some secret enemy codes used in World War II."

I gaped at her. "Are you serious?"

"Yes. Did you ever read *The Key to Rebecca*?"

"Ken Follett, right? I like his books. But no, I've never read that one." *But I would have to now*, I thought. "Wasn't it a movie, too?"

"Yes."

"I'll have to watch it."

"If you must. But the book is much better."

I was still shaking my head at the possibility of secret codes when Derek walked back into the workshop.

I pounced. "Who were you talking to?"

He gritted his teeth and I knew something was wrong.

"He's out there?" I said, before he could utter a word. I jumped down off my stool and walked quickly over to the window.

He scowled. "Get away from that window."

"Who's out there?" Claire demanded. "Is it the same man?"

"Perhaps you'll tell us," Derek said carefully, "since we've never seen your closet man."

She hurried to the window and carefully peeked out. After a long moment, she ducked her head back and stood with her eyes squeezed shut. "It's him. I recognize his barrel chest. And his hair. It's quite bushy."

She was practically shaking so I slung my arm around her shoulders and gave her a light squeeze. "You're going to be all right."

"I'm fine." She took another quick look out the window, then began to pace up and down along the work-table. "No, I'm not fine. What am I going to do?"

Derek stepped in front of her to interrupt her nervous pacing. "I've called the police and they're on their way. I'm going down to meet them."

"I'll go with you," I said. "We can hold him until the cops come."

"Oh, Brooklyn," Claire cried, "you can't."

"Thank you," Derek said to her, then turned and grabbed my arm. "You'll stay right here. Claire needs you. I'll be back soon."

"But . . ." He was already on the run and seconds later, I heard the door slam shut. "Damn it," I whispered. "Be careful."

"That horrible brute," Claire said, staring at the window with her teeth clenched in anger. "Now he's ruining *your* lives. How can we stop him?"

"Derek will stop him. And so will the police."

She huffed out a breath. "I can't keep letting you two fight my battles for me."

"In case you haven't noticed, it's our battle, too. We're in this with you." *It was true*, I thought. We had been involved from the minute we opened Aunt Gwyneth's package.

"Where are the police?" she wondered as she stared out the window.

As if on cue, I heard the faint sound of police sirens. "They're close by."

But then I groaned. "Oh no, he's starting to run up the street."

"He's getting away," Claire cried.

I scowled and pounded my fist against the wall. "Derek's going to be too late."

But just then, Derek came tearing out of our building and began racing down the street after the guy. They were on opposite sides of Brannan running east toward the Bay. Derek stayed on the north side of the street until he saw a break in the traffic and dashed across. I could see his phone in his hand and thought he might be talking to Inspector Lee.

The thug had a good head start, but Derek was fast. And the sirens were even closer now.

Seconds later, two black-and-white cop cars came screaming down the street. The bad guy had already turned south on a side street.

"He's headed toward Mission Creek," I said. "He could get lost in that area." *Damn it*, I thought. Was he familiar with the neighborhood? That would add a whole new level of creepiness.

If they lost him, it might be another day or two before he would dare to show himself again. Or maybe not. Maybe he would take his chances and try to break into our house. Did he have a gun? What if he started taking potshots at us?

That thought did not sit well.

Was he actually after Aunt Gwyneth's copy of the *Rebecca*? Or did he want to hurt Claire? In moments like this, I couldn't be sure what his target was. But either way, I had to wonder, *Why*? What was going on?

I recognized Inspector Lee's department-issued green sedan racing down the street. It slowed down, then turned onto the same side street the other cops had taken. I imagined Derek was still running after the guy and I silently urged him to catch the creep.

I realized I was starting to pace back and forth in front of the wide window so I forced myself to stand still. "I'm not really good at waiting patiently," I admitted, trying to tamp down my frustration at having stayed behind. "I should be out there."

Claire took a peek out the window. "If I wasn't here, would you really be out there chasing that man?"

"I would try," I said, then grinned. "I'm sure Inspector Lee would give me all kinds of grief for interfering. But honestly, don't you just hate being left out of all the fun?"

Claire stared at me as if I had two heads. "First, I question your use of the word *fun*. And second, do you recall that I told you I'm quite like a gothic heroine? I grew up alone with no brothers or sisters. I was the grown-up in the house by the age of five since my father was always concocting some scheme."

I was dying to ask her more about her father, but my cell phone buzzed just then. "It's Derek."

I answered and immediately asked, "Did you get him?"

"No," he groused. "He got away from us. Damn fool raced across the BART tracks just as one of the cars came barreling down. I wasn't sure he made it until the car passed. By then, the man was gone."

"Damn," I muttered.

"My thoughts exactly."

"Are you on your way home?"

"I'll be out here for another few minutes commiserating with Inspector Lee. Then I'll come home."

"All right, love."

"Tell Claire I'm sorry we didn't get him. But we will. He'll be back and we'll nail him."

"I'll tell her."

We ended the call and I gave Claire the message from Derek.

"I'll hold him to it," she said.

"We'll get him," I promised. I told her about the train line and how he was able to dash across while the BART car was speeding toward him.

"Bad luck for our side," she said.

"Yeah."

She sat down at the worktable. "He could be anywhere by now."

"He's still in town and you know he'll be back."

"Aye, he'll bide his time until he can attack me again." She threw up her hands in disgust. "This is maddening. I refuse to sit around waiting to be a victim to this creep."

"Now that's a good attitude," I said. "You're not a victim. And he's just a low-life thug. The cops will get him and he'll spend his life in jail."

She stared at me. "Brooklyn, you are quite the fighter. A real inspiration."

I laughed, feeling embarrassed and gratified at the same time. "Actually, I was always more of a lover than a fighter. Comes from growing up in a commune surrounded by all those peace and love vibes."

"That may be true, but I still see the fighter instinct in you."

I thought about it. I'd faced down a dozen or more killers in the last few years so maybe she was right. "I'm feisty when I have to be. And so are you. When you pulled that knife out yesterday, I was so shocked I thought I might fall down the stairs."

She started to laugh, then shook her head. "Is this situation insane or what?"

The sound of her laughter brought a smile to my face. "Totally insane."

I was starting to wonder where Derek was so I looked out the window to check. He and Inspector Lee were across the street talking to each other. But now there was a small crowd gathered around them. Had these people seen Derek running? Were they trying to help? Were they just lookie-loos or did they have information to give Inspector Lee?

I chuckled to myself because one of the guys in the group had a bright blue L.A. Dodgers baseball cap pulled down low to protect his eyes from the bright sunlight.

A Dodgers cap! Didn't he know that our Giants had just crushed the visiting L.A. team last weekend? He was either clueless or a diehard fan, but either way, I hoped he and the rest of the group would be helpful. Otherwise, they needed to break it up soon. I wanted Derek to come home. Call me a wimp, but it just wasn't safe out there.

I forced myself to walk away from the window and sat down to chat some more with Claire.

Fifteen minutes later, Derek walked in and I almost melted with relief. I ran and grabbed him in a hug and then kissed him. He kissed me back. "Not sure I deserve that since we didn't catch your intruder."

"I'm just glad you're back."

"Yes, so am I."

"I noticed you and the inspector attracted a little crowd out there."

"They were mainly tourists enjoying one of our rare sunny afternoons. Inspector Lee questioned them all but none of them saw anything."

"That's too bad."

"Yes." He pulled out his phone and began to send a text. "I thought of something on the way upstairs, though."

I watched him for a few seconds, then asked, "What are you thinking?"

He took another few seconds to finish his tapping,

then looked up. "I believe I have a temporary solution to our problem."

"I'd like to hear it," Claire declared immediately. She had been paging through the black book, but set it back down on the white cloth and gave Derek her attention.

"Good," he said. "I suggest we each pack a few things. We're going on a short trip. Might be gone two or three days."

"A trip?" She gave him a quizzical look. "May I bring Mr. D?"

Derek winced. "No, sorry. Alex will look after him. And Charlie, too, of course."

I stared at Derek. "You already talked to Alex?"

"Yes." He reached for my hand and held it as he spoke. "While I was talking to Inspector Lee out there, we came up with a plan. So I called Alex to get her input and she's completely on board with it."

"And what's the plan?"

"We all agree that the best thing to do in the short run is get Claire out of danger, which means we should leave town for a few days. Alex will watch our place and take care of the cats. She's agreed to work from home in order to keep an eye out for our intruder. She'll stay in contact with Inspector Lee, who's arranged for a drive-by every hour for the next three days."

"Wow," I said, taken aback. "Guess you've taken care of everything."

He picked up on my tone immediately. "I'm sorry, darling. I should've included you in the phone calls."

Yeah, he should've, I thought. I wasn't about to get snippy, though, because getting out of town was a good idea.

He rushed on. "I told Alex that we wouldn't make any moves without first getting your input."

I squeezed his arm because I could tell he felt bad. "I would've liked to have been included in the planning, but I understand I'm just a civilian."

"You're *my* civilian," he whispered, and pressed his lips to mine.

I smiled. "Pretty good save."

"Thank you, darling."

I rolled my eyes. "Okay, the plan sounds good. So where are we going?" I was always willing to take an unplanned trip with Derek, but it would be nice to know our destination, along with a few dozen other details.

Derek was all business as he stared at his phone again. Then he looked up at me and smiled. "We're going back to Dharma."

Chapter 7

"Are you ready to go?"

I looked up to see Alex standing at my bedroom door.

"Almost," I said, thankful that I always kept a bag half packed with essentials since we traveled to Dharma so regularly. I had already packed up my bookbinding tools and supplies in a separate case, along with Claire's broken book and my origami papers. I'd slipped the *Rebecca* into my backpack, so that I could keep it with me at all times, just to be safe. The *Tom Sawyer* would have to stay home but I promised myself I would finish it as soon as I got back from Dharma.

Now I tucked my workout gear and an extra pair of socks into my bag, then nodded. "That's it. I'm ready."

"It's best to leave right away," she said. "Before Mr. Peppermint gets a clue that you're gone."

Since we last saw him running to get away from Derek and the cops, I doubted he would be back today. I glanced up at Alex. "He'll probably show up tomorrow."

"And I'll be here to greet him. And as soon as I make the call, Inspector Lee will be here, too."

"Just be careful, please. He might bring friends."

"If he has any friends, the inspector and I will take care of them, too."

I managed a smile. "Yeah, you will. Two badass women."

She grinned. "You got that right."

Claire walked in. "I'm ready to go." She clutched Alex's arm. "Are you sure you're okay watching the cats?"

Alex smiled. "The cats are the best part of this gig. I love Charlie. And Mr. D and I will get along famously."

"He can be quite snooty," Claire said. "He might simply ignore you."

"That'll break my heart." Alex chuckled. "But I promise I'll still feed him."

Derek, meanwhile, was conducting a walk-through of our apartment, stopping at every window to make sure it was locked, then going back to texting from his phone. He ran upstairs to check on the door to our rooftop patio. When I heard his footsteps coming down, I knew we were safe from anyone trying to come in from that direction.

I'd never seen him do so much texting, but I figured he had a lot of moving parts to wrangle in order to make this trip happen. He had to alert his assistant Corinne and his business partners, along with a bunch of people in Dharma who would need to know we were coming. And I had to assume he was still in touch with Harold at Interpol.

Finally he walked into our bedroom, where I was talking to Claire and Alex.

"Alex," he said, "I've decided to assign several members of my security team to watch the building while we're gone. One of their cars will be parked across the street at all times, twenty-four/seven. I'll get you their license plate numbers as soon as Corinne emails me back."

"That'll be helpful," Alex admitted. "And text me Corinne's number, too."

"Will do."

"I'll be working from home," she said, "but I may have to go into the office once in a while. I'll let your people know when I'm coming or going."

"Good. Let me know, too. Call me or text." He seemed to remember that Alex wasn't one of his employees. "I mean, if you have a minute. I'd appreciate it."

She grinned. "Don't worry about it, Commander. I'm happy to do whatever it takes to make sure this guy gets caught."

"He might have associates," Derek warned.

"Hey, I just said the same thing," I said.

"Except you called them *friends*," Alex said, smirking. "Either way, I'll watch for anyone else working with him."

Derek gave me a quick kiss. "I'm willing to bet that Mr. Peppermint's so-called friends would just as soon stab him in the back as share a meal."

"I wouldn't take that bet," I said.

Derek winked at me, then glanced at Alex. "I'm depending on you to kick anyone's ass who comes near this place."

"That's how I roll," she assured him, then turned and gave me a saccharine smile. "Be sure to let me know how your sessions go with Keith."

I frowned back at her. "We might not be in Dharma long enough for me to take a class."

Her eyes narrowed. "Make time."

"All right, all right."

"Who's Keith?" Claire asked.

"He runs the Dharma Dojo," I said. "And he's a good friend of Alex's."

"Is he nice?" Claire asked, her voice hopeful.

"He kicks my butt," I muttered.

Alex quickly added, "He's a great guy and an awesome teacher."

"Well then," Claire said, "I would love to take a class, too."

"That would be great." It would be nice to have company. And also nice to have someone who was less experienced than me.

Alex flashed me a big, wide smile. "There you go. No more excuses."

I glanced at Derek. "I forgot to ask. Where are we staying?"

Derek maneuvered through crosstown traffic on our way to the Golden Gate Bridge after wisely checking the rush-hour traffic situation on Highway 80 and determining that this route was quicker.

I couldn't believe I hadn't asked about our accommodations earlier, but my mind had been occupied with other details, such as, would my husband be able to catch the big ugly brute who was staking out our building and tormenting Claire?

But now I wanted to know. We had stayed at his parents' home on our most recent visit, but they were expected to return any day now. *It was too bad our own home wasn't ready yet*, I thought. We had started building seven months ago and while it was close to being finished, it wasn't quite ready for prime time yet.

"We're welcome to stay at my parents' house again since they've decided to remain in England for another month." He glanced at me. "Unless you'd rather stay with your parents?"

"You're kidding, right?" I said with a quick laugh. I

loved my parents and would undoubtedly be spending time with them anyway, but the idea of having a spacious house all to ourselves was infinitely more desirable. Derek's parents had a charming Craftsman-style home at the top of a ridge with beautiful views of the vineyards and Dharma Creek. There was plenty of room for the three of us for as long as we needed to stay.

"I vote to stay at your parents' house," I said firmly.

"Me, too." He reached over, took my hand, and brought it to his lips.

As we approached the Golden Gate, I glanced over my shoulder. "How are you doing, Claire?"

"I'm doing well," she said. "You know, Brooklyn, in spite of those horrible men, I'm actually having a lovely time. It's so nice getting to know you two. And Alex has been wonderful. And Inspector Lee as well." She smiled, then turned to look out the window. "This is such an interesting city, isn't it?"

"I love it," I said. "How long have you lived here?"

"It's complicated," she said, with a self-deprecating smile. "I came to Berkeley to pursue a PhD in history and fell in love with the area. But afterward I got a job and was traveling for a few years. I finally moved to the city when *This Old Attic* hired me for the show."

"I was only on the show for those two weeks when they were in San Francisco." I turned in my seat to meet her gaze. "But you stayed on for a few years, didn't you?"

"They didn't have many options when it came to antique weapons experts, so they had me working on almost every show."

"People do like to collect weapons."

"They do. I was very lucky."

"It wasn't just luck," I said. "You know more about weaponry of all kinds than anyone I've ever seen."

"That's kind of you," she said modestly. "I do tend to soak up information wherever I go."

"It must've been fun to travel with the show."

"It was, for a few years. After a while, though, I did get tired of living in hotel rooms."

"Are you still doing anything with them?"

"I was, off and on. But then last month they let me go. Frankly, I was surprised, but that's the way it goes." She said it so casually that I wondered what the real story was.

"What's next for you?" I sounded as if I were conducting an interview, but I was honestly curious. Claire had led such an odd and interesting life so far.

She sighed. "I'm starting to look for a new job, but I'm being very picky. I want something wonderful."

"I don't blame you for that."

"It would be nice, wouldn't it?" Her smile faded. "But just as I was starting my job search, I suddenly heard from Aunt Gwyneth, who beseeched me to come to Scotland. And when I arrived, I found that she was missing."

"And here we are," I murmured.

She clutched her hands together, clearly worried. "Yes, indeed."

Her mention of Aunt Gwyneth reminded me of something and I turned to Derek. "I forgot to tell you. While you were chasing down Claire's intruder, she and I took a closer look at the copy of *Rebecca* that Gwyneth sent you. There are marks in the book."

"Marks? What sort of marks?"

"They're pencil marks. Someone struck off certain letters on at least four pages that I've found so far. I haven't checked the entire book yet so there could be more."

"Can you tell if they mean anything?"

"Not yet. Claire insists that they're new. She's read

the book before and never saw them. And she assured me that she would've noticed."

"I should think so," he mused.

"I started writing down the letters, but so far they don't make sense. I'll continue working on them once we're settled at your parents' house."

"You brought the book with you?" he asked, then gave a short chuckle. "Of course you brought the book."

I smiled. "Of course."

"I'll want to have a look at those pages." Derek thought for a moment, then asked, "Are you thinking it spells out something?"

"I don't know. After working with Dalton on the old cookbook, nothing would surprise me. Maybe it's some kind of secret message. That would be fun, wouldn't it?"

"Fun," he muttered, shaking his head.

"It'll probably turn out to be nothing, but for now it's a mystery."

"It's a mystery for certain," he said, then his brows furrowed. "And I doubt it's nothing. After all, there must be some reason the book was sent to me. And unless we're well off the mark, the book seems to have become the focus of some dangerous people's attention. So we'll check it out with Dalton tomorrow."

I turned around to Claire. "Dalton is Derek's brother. He's a cryptographer."

"He likes to solve puzzles," Derek added, with a cynical grin.

"Real-life puzzles," I explained. "He works for a super-secret department that tracks down conspiracy theories and communications between terrorist cells."

"My goodness," Claire said. "I can't believe those simple pencil markings would be important enough for him to bother with."

"Oh, he'll bother with it," Derek assured her. "He won't be able to help himself."

I nodded. "Especially when we tell him what your intruders have put you through, theoretically, in pursuit of the book."

Derek glanced in the rearview mirror and made eye contact with Claire. "Dalton was acquainted with your aunt Gwyneth."

"Was he?" I asked. That was news to me.

"Is that so?" Claire's eyebrows rose. "Perhaps having that connection will help arouse his interest."

We were silent after that and I took a moment to mentally make a list of everything I wanted to do while we were back in Dharma. Show Dalton the book, of course. And then I had to stop by Keith's dojo to sign up for some classes. I would introduce him to Claire to make sure she was comfortable with him. And I needed to check on Robin, who was almost ready to have a baby.

And speaking of the baby, I hoped I would have some free time to work on the mobile for Robin's baby shower.

Derek, meanwhile, would want to dig deeper into Mr. Peppermint's background to see what his connection was to Aunt Gwyneth. And that reminded me that we really had to come up with a more appropriate nickname for him.

"Do you think we'll be safe up here?" Claire asked, breaking the silence.

Again Derek made eye contact with her in the rearview mirror. "We'll be safe for a few days, but I still don't want to take any chances. Peppermint appears to be a professional and if he does enough checking, he might just figure out that Brooklyn and I have a strong connection to Dharma."

I turned in time to see Claire's reaction to that

possibility. It was as though she'd been punched in the gut and had the wind knocked out of her.

"Don't worry," I said quickly. "We'll be safe for a few days and that should give Alex and Inspector Lee enough time to corner him."

"I hope so." Claire scowled. "I wish I'd never mentioned that he smells like peppermint. It's much too pleasant a name for him. I'd rather call him Fish Face or something that makes him sound ugly and disgusting."

I glanced at Derek. "Does Fish Face work for you?"

"Much better." He grinned at Claire.

She gave a brisk nod. "Fish Face it is."

The drive to Dharma took slightly longer than usual, a full hour and a half thanks to some unusual wine country traffic on Highway 121. As we drove closer to town, we started seeing billboards announcing the Spring Wine and Cheese Festival.

"I forgot all about the festival," I admitted, although I should've known there would be something going on. Dharma and the surrounding towns invariably had some sort of festival or event planned for every month of the year.

"That's why there's so much traffic," Derek said. "Today's the first day."

"But it's late enough in the day that I would think the heavy traffic would be gone."

"Perhaps they've scheduled some evening events," Derek guessed.

"I remember hearing that some of the local restaurants were offering dinner specials." I considered. "Maybe Arugula is doing something."

Arugula was my sister Savannah's award-winning restaurant in the center of town.

"Claire, you might enjoy spending time at the festival," Derek said, then glanced over at me. "I imagine we'll find your father and your brothers taking part in the festivities."

"Pretty sure they wouldn't miss it," I said, smiling at the thought of my brothers and father serving up wine and lively conversation, as always.

We approached the center of town and stopped at a red light on Montana Ridge Road. Derek quickly checked his phone, which had been beeping on and off for the last few minutes.

"Text from my mother," he said, and read the screen. "'You'll use the master bedroom as before. I want you to be comfortable.'" He glanced at Claire. "She says you're to use the larger guest room with the spa bath."

"My goodness," she said. "How can I refuse?"

"You really can't," I said with a laugh.

Derek's lips twisted into a frown. "I'll just say it. There's a bit of a creep factor connected to the idea of sleeping in one's parents' bed."

"I get that," I said. "But it's got those French doors with that beautiful deck overlooking the green hills beyond the canyon. And I bet the sheets are all laundered and you know the rooms are spotless, so it'll be like sleeping in a hotel."

He chuckled. "You're as smart as you are beautiful."

"And so are you." I blew him a kiss.

"You two are so funny," Claire said from the back seat. "I want to say that I'm perfectly happy to sleep on a sofa or a pullout. I don't want you to go to any trouble."

Derek glanced over his shoulder. "You don't understand. My mother has spoken."

"Don't worry about it," I added with a smile. "There are two guest bedrooms and the master bedroom so we'll all have an actual bed to sleep in. And it's no trouble at all."

We were settled within minutes. As predicted, Derek's parents' room was impeccably neat and clean and the sheets were newly laundered.

Claire was very happy with her room that had a cozy window seat with a view of the hillside. And as promised, there was a large spa tub in the adjoining bathroom. "Oh my goodness, I'm in heaven."

I grinned. "I'm glad you're happy."

"Thank you, I am," she said. "I can't wait to luxuriate in this gorgeous tub."

Derek nodded as he brought in the last suitcase. "I think we'll do just fine."

"It's getting close to happy hour," I said. "Shall we open a bottle of wine?"

"Absolutely, and I'll take care of it." He wandered down the hall into the kitchen, where his parents had a well-stocked wine refrigerator.

We had remembered to bring all the cheese and crackers and various munchies we had at home, so I prepared a platter of snacks to serve with the wine. "We can sit outside and watch the sunset. It's not too cold yet."

Derek handed us our wineglasses. "You both go ahead. I'm going to give Gabriel a call."

I gave him a grateful look. "Thank you."

As Claire and I walked out to the deck, she whispered, "Who is Gabriel?"

"He's a great friend of ours. Another security expert. And he's also Alex's boyfriend."

"She has a boyfriend living all the way up here?"

"They make it work," I said. "Gabriel's got several

massive satellite dishes on his property that can track anyone and anything within a thousand miles of Dharma. Everything is hooked up to this sophisticated surveillance system that allows him to monitor communications between people whose activities are suspected to be dangerous or unlawful."

"He sounds like someone you want on your side."

"Oh, absolutely." *And we could use all the help we could get*, I thought.

Derek was on the phone for barely a minute, then hung up and walked outside to the deck. "He'll be here in twenty minutes."

As soon as Gabriel arrived, we moved everything inside. The sun had set and the air was already turning chilly.

I introduced him to Claire and he said, "Good to meet you, Claire. I spoke to Alex a little while ago and she gave me a quick rundown of your circumstances."

"She was very kind to me," Claire said.

He nodded. "She's pretty special."

We congregated at the kitchen table and spent the next half hour giving Gabriel more details on Claire's situation and the mystery of Aunt Gwyneth's disappearance. We talked about the package arriving for Derek and the disturbing appearances of Fish Face and the dead guy, aka Pizza Man.

"You were smart to come up here for a few days," Gabriel said to Claire. "We run a pretty tight security operation here. Plus, chances are good that Alex and the cops will scoop up this guy in a day or two and throw him in jail."

"I hope so." Claire was wringing her hands, suddenly nervous again.

"Now, what are we doing about your aunt?" Gabriel asked.

Claire swallowed, then looked at Derek. "You know more about that than I do."

"I'm in touch with my man at Interpol," Derek said. "He's got the local authorities working on the case. There are some snags, but we can talk about it later."

"Snags?" Claire said immediately.

"Just some thorny local politics," Derek said with a light shrug. "Nothing to do with your aunt, and nothing to worry about."

Gabriel sat forward, resting his elbows on his knees. "So what can I do to help?"

Derek smiled. "It may be a lot to ask, but I wonder if you might be able to monitor every car license plate that comes into Dharma in the next two days."

"No problem."

"And do you have the capability to do a deep dive on any male driver between the ages of thirty and forty-five?"

"Piece of cake." Gabriel sipped his wine. "But why? You really think this clown will follow you out here?"

"I think when our car doesn't return to our garage after twenty-four hours, he'll be smart enough to do some research on Brooklyn and me. I imagine he'll put two and two together and figure we've headed to Dharma."

Gabriel nodded slowly, then cracked that roguish smile of his. "Don't you just hate it when the bad guys are smart like that?"

"Yeah, and here's the problem," I said. "If this smart guy does his own deep dive, he might just come up with my parents' address."

Gabriel took out his phone and started typing with

his thumbs. It was shaming to realize that he was faster with those two thumbs than I was with all ten of my fingers. "Okay," he said. "I'll have one of my guys monitor your folks' house for a few days."

I nodded slowly. He was pretty good at the whole security game. "Um, okay. That works. Thanks."

"Out of an abundance of caution," he continued, "we'll expand our net a little."

"How do we do that?" I wondered.

He smiled at me. "Low tech, babe. You call your brothers and alert them. I'll call Robson and let him know we might have trouble."

Robson Benedict was the head of the commune, a wonderful leader and a good man to call in a crisis.

While growing up, my siblings and I had called him Guru Bob. Not to his face, of course, but somehow he seemed to know. Actually, he seemed to know everything that happened around here. Always. It was weird.

"I'll call my brother Dalton," Derek said.

"He'll make sure that Savannah is safe," I said. "And I'll call my other sisters, just to cover our bases."

"I hate to be the cause of all this trouble," Claire groaned.

I leaned over and looked straight at her. "You are not the cause of this trouble. Fish Face and Pizza Man are the cause. Don't forget it."

Gabriel grinned at Claire. "Might as well accept that you're part of the family now."

She inhaled, a little shakily, and exhaled slowly. "I may never get used to it, but I'm unspeakably grateful."

Once the real business was finished, Derek stood and walked over to the refrigerator to survey its contents. "We should eat something more substantial than cheese."

Claire rubbed her stomach. "I ate so much cheese and crackers, I'm stuffed."

Derek was already on his phone again, tapping out another text.

"I could eat," I admitted. This was no surprise to anyone who knew me.

After a minute, Derek came back and sat down at the table. "There's spaghetti and tomato sauce in the freezer. Because I'm a good son, I texted my mother and she insisted that we eat it."

Gabriel laughed. "Meg comes through."

"Please tell her we love her," I said.

"I already did," Derek said, patting my knee.

"And tomorrow we'll go shopping and replenish everything."

"She won't care, darling. But we'll do that anyway."

"Well, since it's spaghetti," Claire began, "I might be able to choke down a small portion."

I had to laugh. "Good. And we'll all sleep better tonight."

I did sleep better. When I woke up, I was surprised to see Derek still sound asleep beside me. That almost never happened. He had been wiped out from the day before and I didn't want to wake him up, knowing he could use an extra few minutes of rest.

I silently tossed back the covers and climbed out of bed. I rummaged through my suitcase and found a clean pair of jeans and a top, then pulled on my sweater that I'd folded neatly on the nearby chair. After washing my face, brushing my teeth, and combing my hair, I quietly snuck out to the kitchen to start a pot of coffee.

It was a shock to find Claire already at the table, drinking a cup of coffee that smelled like heaven. She was dressed in another one of her fisherman's knit sweaters, this one a gorgeous baby blue, with rainbow-knit socks peeking out from her skinny black jeans. Her thick, dark red hair was brushed back from her face and tamed with a sturdy barrette.

"You made coffee," I whispered in awe.

Her shoulders jerked and she quickly closed her laptop.

"Sorry," I said. "I didn't mean to sneak up on you."

She patted her chest to calm down. "That's okay. I was a million miles away and didn't realize anyone else was awake."

"We're both usually up around this time. Thanks for starting the coffee."

She glanced up at me. "I hope it's all right."

"As long as it's strong, it'll be fine."

"I like it strong," she said with a shy smile.

I grabbed a mug from the cupboard and filled it up, then took one long sip. "Oh yeah. Perfect. Thanks."

"Did you sleep all right?" she asked.

"Yes." I sighed contentedly as I came and sat at the table. "After the day we had yesterday, I wasn't sure I would. But I fell right out and slept all night. How about you?"

"I had dreams of Aunt Gwyneth." She stared at me through stricken eyes. "She's still alive; I'm sure of it."

"Then so am I," I said with a firm nod of solidarity.

She gazed at some vague point on the wall. "I tossed and turned and finally dozed off, but then woke up at dawn with a deep desire to get started on a new project."

"What's the new project?" I asked. I noticed that she had six pens and three pencils lined up in precise order next to her laptop. Each pencil was sharpened to a pin-point and each of the pens had its clip turned in the same position. She had called herself a neat freak and I figured that was accurate.

"I'm organizing my weapons collections, starting with my knives." She opened her laptop again. "I already have them listed in chronological order, of course, and by country of origin. But I think it'll be useful to also list them by size, type, weight, material, and color. Then I can create a cross-referencing document that will be helpful in the future."

"Now, that's what I call getting organized," I said, chuckling, then rushed to add, "in a good way."

"Aye, it's definitely a good thing."

I sat back in my chair. "It sounds like you're creating an inventory. Are you planning on selling your weapons?"

"Oh, I'm not sure I could ever sell them," she said, shaking her head. "To be honest, I'll mainly use it to keep the details and particulars of each weapon straight in my mind."

I was trying to relate. "I've done that sort of organizing when it comes to the books and binding materials in my workshop. I have a master list of hundreds of items and procedures and refer to it all the time when I'm about to start a new project or when it comes time to order supplies."

Her eyes gleamed and she nodded enthusiastically. "That's exactly what I'm talking about. The organizing I'm doing right now will help me when I start writing my book."

"You're writing a book?"

"I plan to try. It's going to be a book about weapons."

"I figured," I said with a quick smile. "You know more about that subject than anyone I've ever met."

She laughed lightly. "I'm hoping it will be more of an

art book than an educational treatise. It'll have photographs of my jeweled knives and crossbows, of course, and I hope to include some of my more unusual pieces, as well."

"Ooh, like what?"

"I have a Lochaber axe from the sixteenth century that is spectacular."

"Lochaber," I repeated. "It sounds Scottish."

"Aye, it is," she said, beaming. "And I am proud to say so. The Lochaber region is a beautiful part of the Highlands, near Fort William."

"I love that area." And I was delighted to hear her brogue become stronger as she spoke with pride of her homegrown weapon. "How small is the axe?"

"Oh, not small at all. It's actually quite large." She stood to demonstrate. "It consists of a deadly chopping blade attached by brackets to one end of a five-foot shaft of thick, sturdy wood. The blade itself is about a foot and a half long and very sharp. And there's a vicious hook attached above the blade, for good measure."

I pictured the weapon in my mind. "It sounds scary. And too big to be carried easily."

"You carry it as you would a large staff. Like this." She held her arm out and tightened her fist to simulate holding the long handle. "Both ends can be used for fighting and slicing. And the hook—it's called a *cleek*— can easily catch a rider's jacket and pull him off his horse."

She mimicked grasping the long handle with both hands, lashing out with the blade end and then striking with the other. "There." She grinned. "I sliced his stomach open with the axe and then bludgeoned him with the blunt end."

"Ouch," I said, wincing. "You're very good with that."

She shrugged lightly. "It's easy when it's imaginary."

"Still, I got the picture." I took a bracing sip of coffee. "It's definitely deadly. I take it that one's going in the book."

"Absolutely. It's a colorful weapon and fun to describe." She sat back down. "With each photograph I'll have a short description of the weapon's use and its origin."

"I can already picture it. Very upscale and classy, right?"

"Yes. The photos I've already taken are quite pretty." She grinned at me. "Some of the smaller throwing weapons are so lovely. Especially the axes. I'm a big fan of throwing axes."

"Like the ones they show on TV?"

"Yes, they've become quite popular in pubs back home."

I shook my head. "Darts weren't dangerous enough?"

She laughed. "Guess not. Anyway, I've also got several beautiful broadswords and basket swords." She waved her hands. "I should stop talking. I'm starting to sound quite manic."

"You sound excited and I don't blame you." I took a sip of coffee. "What is a basket sword?"

"It's a classic Highlander broadsword and the basket, or cage, wraps around your hand and provides protection. They're often quite ornate."

"I think I know what you're talking about."

"I'll show you the ones in my collection when we get back to the city."

"I'd love to see them. And I can't wait to see the book when it's finished. It sounds fascinating."

"I hope it will be. I've given so many lectures over the years and spent so much time on *This Old Attic*, I'm hopeful that some of the people I've met along the way will be interested." She gulped in air and slowly exhaled. "I still get nervous talking about it."

"I understand, but you're a world-renowned expert. It should be a bestseller."

She waved away the compliment. "It's sweet of you to say so."

I chuckled. "I'm not that sweet. I think you've got a really good idea there."

We sipped our coffees in silence for a minute. Then I said, "Where do you keep your collection of weapons?"

"In my home," she said simply.

I had to let that sink in. "Wait. They're in your home? The place that was ransacked? Oh my God, was anything stolen?"

"No. Thank goodness. I built a hiding place underneath my kitchen cabinets that's fairly undetectable. And it worked. This time, anyway. I probably need to come up with a better solution for the future."

"I would say so." I had a niggling thought that the bad guys might really be after her priceless collection of antique weapons instead of the *Rebecca*.

"I'll probably transfer everything to a bank vault once I'm able to go back home." She shook her head, unsure of her feelings. "I hate to do it because I like having my weapons nearby. That sounds odd, but you know, they're like old friends. I'll often take a piece out of the safe and study it for a day or so, then switch it for another one." She laughed ruefully. "I sound like that sad little gothic heroine we were talking about."

I chuckled. "No, you just sound like someone who's serious about her collection."

"That's a better way to look at it," she said.

"Well, I hope you consider moving most of them to a

more secure place, because many of them are not only priceless, but also dangerous. Especially if they fall into the wrong hands." I stopped abruptly. "Sorry for the lecture."

"Don't be sorry," she said, reaching across to squeeze my hand. "I appreciate it. Because it's true. They're deadly, for sure."

"Exactly *what* is deadly?" a quiet voice asked from the doorway.

Chapter 8

This time I jolted even more than Claire had. I'd been so focused on my lecture that I hadn't heard or seen the person walk into the kitchen. And when I saw who it was, I was even more shaken.

"Robson!" I stared at him for a few seconds, then shook myself out of it. Pushing my chair back, I rushed over to give him a hug. "It's so good to see you."

"Hello, gracious," he said softly. "It is always a pleasure to see you."

As he took another step into the kitchen, I noticed Derek waiting behind him.

"Hey," I said, and reached for his hand.

"Good morning, love. I was on my way downstairs and saw Robson coming up the walk."

"That's good timing." I gave him a quick kiss, then turned back to Robson. "Robson, I'd like to introduce you to my friend Claire Quinn. Claire, this is Robson Benedict."

Robson preferred to be introduced in the simplest way possible, so I tried never to mention that he was the spiritual leader of my parents' commune, otherwise known as the Fellowship for Spiritual Enlightenment and Higher Artistic Consciousness. My parents considered him a highly evolved conscious being and that was the main reason they had dragged my five siblings and me from civilization in San Francisco to rural Sonoma County all those years ago.

Like many other followers, we had spent a year living out of an old Airstream RV and a couple of tents while we built a house and planted grapevines. I had been pretty cranky about it when I was eight years old, but I quickly grew to love it. And I still did.

Claire stood politely to greet Robson and they shook hands.

"I understand you have had some trouble," Robson said, still clasping her hand. "I hope that you find the peace and sanctuary you need here in Dharma."

"I'm quite overwhelmed by all the help I've received," she said. "I appreciate everyone's concern."

"You have a brogue," he said, surprised. "Are you Scottish?"

"Aye, I am."

I had come to the conclusion that Americans loved British accents of all kinds, and a Scottish brogue was near the top of the list of favorites.

"How lovely," he said. "It is a beautiful country and we are delighted to have you visiting our corner of the world."

"That's a nice thing to say. It's beautiful here, too."

Robson gazed at me and Derek, then back at Claire. "I hope to assure you that these are good people. They will make sure you are safe."

"Thank you. I agree, they're lovely."

He beamed at her.

She took a deep breath, then said, "I hope to keep them safe as well."

"Ah." He turned and grinned at me. "Like you, she is a quiet warrior."

Thinking of all those deadly weapons, I wouldn't have called Claire a *quiet* warrior. But I smiled at him. "She's no pushover, that's for sure."

Surprised, Claire glanced from Robson to me. "Thank you."

Derek moved into the kitchen and headed for the coffeemaker. "Coffee, Robson?"

"No thank you, gracious."

Robson often used that endearment in the hope that it might influence the person to show some grace. Sometimes it worked.

"Claire?" Derek said, holding the coffeepot. "A touch more?"

"Oh yes, please." She held out her coffee mug. "And good morning to you, Derek."

"Good morning," he said jovially, then glanced at me. "I was explaining to Robson the reason we returned to Dharma so soon."

"It's my fault," Claire began, but I quickly stopped her. "No."

She looked ready to pout, but then smiled reluctantly.

Turning to Robson, I said, "There are a couple of bad characters that came after us because of a certain book that fell into our hands."

"Ah, of course." He nodded solemnly. "It is always about a book."

I gave a tight smile. Robson was familiar with my history with books—and with all the dead bodies that had come along with those books. It was a subject on which he had counseled me more than once.

"They ransacked my house," Claire said, then looked shocked that she'd actually spoken up.

"I am so sorry," Robson said.

"I wasn't home, wasn't injured. I'm alive, so I'm grateful for that much."

"Still, it hurts," he said. "I understand the pain. We all do." After a moment, he turned to Derek. "There was a fatality."

"Yes," Derek said. "It occurred in our parking garage, but we have very few clues as to who killed him."

I added, "But we're fairly certain his death is related to that book I mentioned."

Robson pursed his lips in thought. "It would seem so."

"Alex Monroe is watching our place," I continued. "She'll let us know if the remaining thug shows up again. And if he does, the police will catch him. We hope."

"Gabriel mentioned that Alex was holding down the fort, as he put it." Robson pushed away from the counter. "I will think good, strong thoughts of her. And of the three of you as well."

"Thank you, Robson," I said.

"I wish you all a safe visit here. It was lovely to meet you, Claire."

She smiled shyly. "Thank you. And the same to you."

Claire and I sat silently while Derek walked Robson to the door. Within a minute, he returned. "Robson is concerned that the guy might try to show his face in Dharma." He turned to Claire. "His *Fish* Face, that is."

Claire laughed. "Very good."

I grinned at him as I opened the refrigerator and pulled out two apples and a banana that I'd brought from home. I sliced up both of them and laid the pieces out on a plate and set it in the middle of the table.

"I'll make us some toast, too. I hope that'll be enough to eat until we get to the market." I grabbed a half loaf of whole wheat bread from the freezer and popped two slices into the toaster. "Or we can stop at a restaurant for a real meal. Or we can beg for scraps from my parents when we stop there."

"Your mother always has excellent scraps," Derek said, and found a half stick of butter inside the fridge. "I'll take care of the toast."

"Thanks. Hey, we still have some cheese left." I cut the remaining cheese into small chunks and placed it on the fruit platter. Stepping back from the cutting board, I brushed against Derek's back. He glanced over his shoulder, then leaned in and kissed me. "Good morning."

"Hi." I had to remember to breathe and wondered when I would ever get used to looking at the man without losing brain cells.

He must've read my mind because he aimed his smile directly at me and whispered, "Toast is almost ready."

It was sort of like poetry, right? I was still smiling a few minutes later when we all sat down with fresh cups of coffee and our light breakfast fare, and made a plan for the day.

Derek had his phone open as he reached for an apple slice. "Brooklyn, I know you have a list of things you want to get done, so let's hear it."

"Okay." I held up my hand and ticked the items off on my fingers. "First, I'm going to call Robin and see how she's doing. I can do that anywhere, by the way. And second, you know we need to see Dalton and show him the book." I glanced around the table. "That could take some time."

"At least an hour," Derek muttered as he typed it into his calendar app. "Probably two."

I took a quick moment to peruse my mental list. "Third, we should stop by my parents' to say hello and let them know we're here for a few days. And I would love to introduce them to you, Claire."

"That would be lovely," she said.

"Fourth, I need to run by the dojo and see if Keith can fit us into his schedule today or tomorrow."

Claire nodded enthusiastically. "I definitely want to do that with you, if possible."

"Absolutely." I took a quick sip of coffee. "I've got one more item." I frowned, then brightened. "Oh yeah. Fifth. Since we're here, don't you think we should stop by our new house and see how it's going?"

Derek was still staring at his phone, but nodded. "That's on my list, too."

"I thought it might be."

He glanced up. "Anything else?"

"Yes. We have to stop at the market on the way home."

"Can't forget that." He gazed at his phone screen. "The items on your list are going to fill up most of our day."

"Sorry about that."

"No worries."

"What's on your list?" I asked.

"Let's see." Again, he perused his phone screen. "I should check in with Alex. And then I may have to drop you two off at one of your stops because I'll need to drive over to see Gabriel. It won't take long, but I want to give him some names and also try to get a sense of what his surveillance equipment can do for us."

"Good idea." I looked at Claire. "Do you have something you'd like to do, Claire?"

"Besides staying alive?" But she smiled when she said it.

"We'll make sure that happens," Derek said determinedly.

"Anything you'd like to do for fun?" I asked.

She hesitated, then said, "Perhaps we might visit a winery?"

"Now you're talking," I said, giving her a thumbs-up.

"That can definitely be arranged," Derek said with a big grin, and typed it into his schedule.

After cleaning up the kitchen, Derek and I were back in our bedroom getting ready to leave for the day.

"I want to run something by you," I said, as I checked to make sure I had moved everything I would need for the day from my purse to my backpack. Including the copy of *Rebecca*.

"What is it?" he asked.

"You weren't in the kitchen earlier when Claire was talking about her weapons. Hey, you know, she's writing a book."

"About the weapons?"

"Yeah. She's a real expert. I mean, I knew that before, but she has amassed quite a collection of deadly objects."

"That's an interesting way to put it."

"Well, anyway, she was describing some of them and then she described where she keeps them in her house." I told him about Claire's makeshift hiding place under her kitchen cabinets.

"She has a cache of weapons in her kitchen cabinet?"

"Yes. I know it sounds odd, but I guess it works for her. Anyway, I was thinking of suggesting that we ask Alex to move them to a safer place while we're out of town."

He only thought about it for a few seconds. "I don't think Claire would go along with that."

I grimaced. "Hearing myself say it out loud, it's not such a good idea."

He ran a quick brush through his hair, then washed and dried his hands. "I might have a better one."

We were stopped at the red light at the bottom of the hill. Derek glanced into the rearview mirror and met Claire's gaze. "Brooklyn was telling me about some of your amazing weapons."

"I have a rather eclectic collection," she said with a modest smile.

"She also mentioned that your hiding place isn't the most ideal."

"Oh. Um, well." Her cheeks puffed out and she exhaled heavily. "No. But I plan to move everything to a safer spot when we return to the city."

The light turned green and Derek crossed the road and made a left on Abbey Lane.

I turned around in the passenger seat. "Derek has an idea for you to think about."

He looked at her in the mirror. "I would be happy to arrange for one of my security team to watch your home while we're away. They won't go inside, but they'll keep a close eye on things in case someone tries to break in."

"You can do that?" she asked, her eyes wide.

"He can do that," I said.

She frowned. "I would hate to trouble you."

"It's no trouble," Derek insisted. "Frankly, we'll all breathe easier if we know your collection is safe."

"They won't go inside? You promise?"

"They won't go inside. I promise."

She nodded, then closed her eyes and breathed in and out. "Then yes. Okay. That would be awesome."

"Good," I said with a big smile.

"Consider it done." Derek glanced at his phone, but didn't reach for it because we were driving in traffic. "As soon as we stop I'll call and arrange to have three of my people take shifts over the next twenty-four hours. After that, we'll regroup. Who knows? We might be able to return to the city in a day or two if all goes well."

"That would be nice," Claire murmured.

"As soon as it's set up, I'll call Alex and Inspector Lee to let them know what we're doing."

"Good thinking," I said. "We don't want anyone to get bent out of shape."

"Exactly."

A moment later, Claire cleared her throat. "I think your Inspector Lee is a lovely person and quite capable, but I'd rather not alert her to the fact that I have dozens of dangerous weapons in my house."

"Dozens?" Derek asked.

She simply nodded. "Aye, dozens."

A few minutes later Derek pulled into my sister's driveway and parked. Derek had spoken briefly to his brother Dalton the night before so he was expecting us.

"Before we go in, I need to make those phone calls," Derek said.

"Okay," I said. "I'm going to call Robin." I looked at Claire. "Do you mind?"

"Not at all. This is a charming neighborhood. I'm going to walk up the hill and look at the view."

"Okay, we'll be right here and we'll only be a few minutes." And I planned on keeping an eye on Claire the whole time.

Derek stayed in the car to make his calls so I stood outside and called my oldest best friend Robin.

"Hey, kiddo," I said when she answered.

"Brooklyn? Hi. Are you back in the city?"

"No, we're here in Dharma. We drove back last night.

We've got a few things to take care of, one of which is you. I wanted to check in. How are you?"

"I'm . . . fat," she grumbled.

"It's not fat," I said cheerily. "It's baby."

"Well, whatever it is, it's keeping me awake at night."

I chuckled. "So I take it you're tired."

"Yes, I'm tired and my back hurts and—oh my God." She took a deep breath and exhaled. "I'm sick of hearing myself whine."

Was she as exhausted as she sounded? "You need to book a massage. Someone to come to your house and give you the full spa treatment."

"Your mother offered, but I couldn't take her up on it."

"Why not? She loves you and she's good at it."

"I love her, too. But Brooklyn, she's your mother." She lowered her voice. "More importantly, she's *Austin's* mother. I can't have her giving me massages. It's just weird."

"Well, fine. But there's got to be a few thousand masseuses in Dharma. We're like the spa capital of the universe. Call someone."

"It's too much trouble." She groaned. "Oh God, Brooklyn. Do you remember when I was fun?"

"I do." I was laughing again. "You were the original party girl." She really was. Robin was short and curvy with dark, curly hair, almond eyes, and a fun personality. She loved to dress up and party down, while I, on the other hand, had always been more serious, blond, and tall. I used to complain that while Robin had men begging her to dance, I had men begging me to reveal my groundbreaking technique for waxing thread to sew books.

I knew at age eight that we would be friends when I saw her clutching her bald-headed Barbie doll. She was still my dearest friend.

These days, she was married to the man she had loved since fourth grade. My brother Austin. I couldn't believe she was about to become a mother. Sometimes it felt as though life was whooshing by in nanoseconds.

"Was I really fun once?" she asked again. "I can't remember."

"You were always fun. Much more fun than I ever was."

"Oh, I like that. Keep going. This is working for me."

"I'll try to stop by later just to say hi."

"That would be nice." She groaned again. "Ouch. That was a rough one."

"Robin, are you going into labor?"

"No, no. Don't worry. I've still got two weeks before this little one is fully cooked."

I frowned. "Okay. Is Austin home?"

"He had to run over to the winery for a few hours. They've got the festival going on so everyone's working like crazy."

Hmm. "Okay, I'll stop by in a few hours."

"Can't wait to see you. Hey, I'm going to try and take a nap in a little while so just let yourself in if I don't answer the door."

"Call me if you need anything in the meantime. I can be there in ten minutes."

"I will," she said, sounding grateful. "Thanks, girlfriend."

"Love you, honey."

"Love you back."

I ended the call and stared at my phone for a moment.

"Is she all right?" Derek asked. I hadn't heard him get out of the car.

I looked at him. "I guess so."

"I heard you mention the 'L' word."

I gave him a puzzled look. "The what?"

"'L' word. *Labor*," he explained.

I smiled. "Oh. She says it's not that. But her back is hurting. And she groaned a couple of times so I asked her if she was going into labor."

"What did she say?"

"She insisted she wasn't, said the baby wasn't due for another two weeks. But that's just a date on a calendar. The baby's going to come whenever he or she is ready."

He reached for my hand. "Do you want to call Austin?"

I thought about it. "No, he's wrapped up in all that festival business. What I'd like to do is stop by my parents' after we finish with Dalton and ask Mom what she thinks."

"An excellent idea."

Claire was just walking up the driveway. "Are we ready?"

"Yes. Did you have a nice walk?"

"Oh yes. It's so lovely here. Everywhere I look is a photograph."

I smiled at her. "That's very true."

"I spoke to my security coordinator," Derek said. "She's setting up a team to watch your house. The first man should be there in about an hour."

She gazed up at him. "Oh, that's fast, isn't it?"

"It's often necessary to respond to a situation immediately. My people are ready to go at a moment's notice."

"I'm very impressed." She gave him a look. "Did you speak with Inspector Lee?"

"I did. She's relieved to know that we've got people watching your place. She had planned to schedule a regular drive-by team, but her guys would only be able to show up every few hours."

"I like your plan better."

"Me, too," I said.

"Were you planning to stand out here all day?"

We all whipped around and looked up at the front porch to see Dalton Stone glaring at us. For one quick second, it was as if I was looking at Derek. All of his brothers were tall and lean with dark hair and dark blue eyes. They all had an air of danger that was both attractive and intimidating. And oh my God, I loved them all.

"Dalton." Laughing, I ran up the steps to grab him in a hug.

He hugged me back. "I'm glad somebody's showing the proper reaction to my presence."

"You're still an ass," Derek said as he climbed the steps, but he grabbed him and they gave each other man-hugs, complete with back slaps and shoulder punches. It was the natural result of having five boys in the family.

"This is my friend Claire," I said as soon as the hugs were over and done with. "Claire, this is Dalton Stone, Derek's brother."

"Youngest brother," Derek murmured.

"Best-looking brother," Dalton countered. "Nice to meet you, Claire. Is it your book we'll be looking at?"

"Actually, it's my aunt's book."

"Ah, yes," he remembered. "Your aunt. The incomparable Gwyn Quinn."

"Yes."

"Well, let's go inside."

We followed him into the house and down a short hallway to a room that was obviously his office. Watching him walk reminded me of Derek again. The Stone men walked like the most dangerous jungle cats, prowling, always on guard, and ready to pounce in an instant.

I almost laughed out loud at where my imagination

had suddenly taken me. Instead, I came back down to earth and asked, "Is Savannah home?"

"No. Your sister's at the restaurant, prepping for a big night of hungry festivalgoers."

"I suppose her place is completely booked," I said, disappointed.

"They could probably squeeze us in," Dalton said. "You know she usually sets aside a table in case your parents or mine or some family member wants to come in."

"What?" I was shocked and delighted. "Dalton, I think you've just revealed a closely guarded secret. She's never mentioned that to me before."

He grinned. "Ah well, she and I will have it out later." Then he frowned. "Problem is, she carries a full set of knives."

"We'll protect you." I glanced from Derek to Claire and back. "Shall we have dinner at Arugula? It's vegetarian," I added for Claire's sake.

"Sounds marvelous," Derek said.

Claire nodded happily. "Yes, please."

"I might join you," Dalton said casually.

"That would be great," I said, squeezing his arm.

"Oh now, we should talk about this," Derek grumbled, but I knew he was teasing his brother.

Dalton's eyes narrowed. "In that case, I'll be there."

"Good." I pulled out my phone. "I'll call Savannah."

"Now that we've wasted enough time," Dalton said, sitting down at his desk, "let's see the book."

Chapter 9

I pulled the black book out of my backpack as Dalton powered up his laptop.

"Bring a chair over," he muttered, and jerked his head toward a couple of folding chairs leaning against the wall.

"Always the perfect host," Derek said with a brotherly sneer, and retrieved two chairs. "Sit here, love."

"Thanks."

He unfolded the second chair and indicated to Claire that she should sit.

"Thank you, Derek." She sat down and stared avidly at Dalton's computer screen, which currently displayed a blank page.

I turned to Dalton. "I don't know how much Derek has told you."

"Not much," Derek said.

"Good." I held up the book. "The book is *Rebecca*, by Daphne du Maurier. It's a signed first edition so it's very valuable. It showed up in our mail the other day when we got back from Dharma. Apparently it was sent to Derek by Gwyneth Quinn."

"Does that have any bearing on our ability to break the code?" Dalton asked.

"Probably not, but you should know what's at stake. Claire has been terrorized by two men for the past few days, ever since she returned from Scotland. And it's probably related to the fact that while she was in Scotland, her aunt went missing."

He glanced at Claire. "That's a lot of trauma in a short time."

Claire's shell-shocked expression said it all, so I jumped in. "It hasn't been a picnic."

"Aye, for sure not," she managed to add. "I'm beside myself with worry for my aunt."

I picked up the story. "When Claire went through her aunt's ransacked apartment in Inverness, she happened to find a postage slip and discovered that her aunt had shipped a package the day before to Derek. Thinking it might be a clue as to her aunt's whereabouts, Claire flew back to town and tracked down Derek."

Dalton gave Claire an approving nod. "Very clever of you."

But Claire looked miserable. "Now one of those men following me has been murdered."

"That's right," I said, "and we're fairly certain that they were looking for this book. I mean, what else could they be after?"

Dalton held up both hands. "So what you're saying is, *Don't screw this up, Dalton.*"

"Exactly," Derek said darkly.

"I just wanted to give you some background," I said. "My point is that both Claire and her aunt Gwyneth appear to be in real danger."

Dalton turned to Claire. "And you believe this book

may be the catalyst for the disappearance of your aunt and the danger now surrounding you."

Claire nodded. "Aye. I do."

"Got it," he said. "So let's get to it."

"Okay." I opened the book to page 87 and showed it to him. "Starting on this page and going on for four more pages, there are letters that have been stricken with a pencil mark."

"Let me see." He reached for the book but I stopped him.

"Wait a sec." Still gripping the book, I reached down to lift my backpack off the floor. Unzipping the main compartment, I pulled out a single sheet of paper. "I wrote down the letters. I only got through the first two pages, but it's a start."

"Okay, fine," he said, taking the sheet of paper and setting it down on the desk. "Now let me see the book."

I handed him the book.

He stared at page 87 for several long moments. Then he gazed at my written notes. "I think we can work this out."

"Really? Yay!" I wanted to jump for joy but settled for lifting one fist in victory. "You're the most brilliant cryptographer ever."

"That's true, of course." He humbly bowed his head, then went back to studying page 87. "Technically, though, this is not an example of cryptography."

I leaned over and stared at the pages. "It's not? What are we looking at?"

"Let me explain some basics to you. A cryptographic puzzle is one that would at first appear to be unreadable. In this unreadable state it is known as cipher text. You might see symbols or circles or stars, or whatever the originator wishes to use. It means nothing unless the receiver of the message obtains a key to decipher the code so that it can be read."

"Like in the cookbook," I said.

Dalton smiled at me. "Yes, grasshopper."

The old cookbook we were referring to was an American Revolutionary War–era book that I had been asked to refurbish. In the margins of many of the pages someone had written lots of strange symbols. At first I thought the owner had been doodling. There were stars and crescent moons, circles with dots in the middle, eyeballs, astrological signs, triangles, and all sorts of little drawings. They looked like hieroglyphics, but they turned out to be much more than that.

"So if this isn't a cryptograph, what is it?" I asked. "Why are these specific letters scratched out?"

He frowned. "This is closer to being an example of what we call steganography."

"Stega . . . what?"

"Steganography. It's an even more ancient practice that involves hiding messages in plain sight. When done properly, no one should be able to tell that there is any hidden communication taking place."

"But with the pencil marks, it's not very well hidden."

"Right, and that's why this isn't a crystal clear example of steganography." He thought for a moment. "Let me give you a better one. If someone wanted to send a message using this book, a better example of steganography would be to take a piece of paper and cut out a template so that when you laid it down on this page, you would actually read certain words that made up the clue."

"Oh, I get it. So you'd never know by looking at the book itself that there's a hidden message in there."

"Exactly."

I scanned the page again. "I guess this technique is pretty lame."

"Not lame," he insisted. "I would call it unsophisticated. Still, it's clearly a code of some kind." He reached for my page of letters. "These letters don't spell out any words that I recognize. So we have to go down a layer."

"How do you go down a layer?"

"By assigning these letters to other letters in the alphabet. And there are vast ways to go about it."

"Oh," Claire said. "So like, the letter 'A' equals 'Z,' 'B' equals 'Y,' and so on through the alphabet?"

He frowned at Claire. "Trying to steal my job?"

"Aye, sure." She laughed. "But my example is too simple."

"It still works in a pinch." He looked back and forth from my list of letters to the book itself for a full minute while we all stayed perfectly quiet.

Genius at work, I thought. It was fascinating to watch him simply stare at the page, knowing his mind was turning and twisting things over and around and trying to make them fit.

He set aside my page of letters. "This was a good effort, Brooklyn, but I'd rather refer to the book itself."

"Probably for the best," I admitted.

A moment later, Dalton began to murmur under his breath and I tried to make out what he was saying.

"The first ten letters don't spell any words known in the English language."

"How can you know that after a few seconds?" I asked. "Don't you have to try every different letter code you can think of?"

He smirked. "I suppose I could go through each and every one of them. Starting with 'A' equals 'Z.'"

"Right. And then you could try to split the alphabet

in half or in quarters, so you'd start with 'A' equals 'N' and so on through 'M' equals 'Z.'"

Claire leaned forward. "What about A-B-C-D-E equals P-Q-R-S-T?"

"Good one, Claire." I held up my palm and she laughingly gave me a high five.

"Yes, very clever," Dalton said drolly. "You all get a participation ribbon."

"Don't be a twit," Derek said, and gave Dalton's head a light smack.

"Hey," Dalton complained, and rubbed his head. But I saw that he was grinning. "All right, all right. If you'll allow me to call on my years of study and research, I'll tell you what I think this is."

"What is it?" I demanded.

"Yes," Claire said, "tell us what you think."

Dalton rewarded her with a benevolent smile. "I think it may be a foreign language."

Frustrated, I asked, "So now what do we do?" I glanced around at each of them. "Do any of you speak a foreign language? Oh wait. What am I thinking? Derek, you speak twenty-seven different languages, right?"

"Not quite that many, darling. But I can certainly curse in most of them."

"Class act, bro," Dalton said.

Claire giggled, and it was the most upbeat sound I'd heard from her since we'd first seen her shivering outside our building. I thought again how glad I was that we had managed to get her out of town for a few days.

Dalton reached over and pulled a few pages of clean paper from the stack next to his printer. Handing a sheet and a pencil to each of us, he said, "Here. Everyone can play."

"Okay." I was getting the gist of what he had in mind.

"I'll read off all the marked letters and we can each try to figure it out. Ready?"

"Go," Dalton said.

I stared at page 87. "A-F-A-L-A-C-H-A-N-N-S-A-N-T-U-R-C-L-A-G-C-O-I-M-H-E-A-D-F-O-N-P-H-L-A-N-C-F-I-O-D-H-A." I glanced around. "Does somebody want to read that back to me, just to be certain?"

"I'll do it," Claire said, and proceeded to repeat the same letters in the same order.

"That's right," Dalton said. "Now let's see what we've got."

"That is like no foreign language I've ever seen," Derek murmured.

"Me, either," Dalton admitted. "Perhaps at this point we ought to go through the work of assigning letters again."

Claire coughed to clear her throat. "Um, those last six letters? *F-I-O-D-H-A*. That sounds Gaelic."

I felt my eyes widen. "Really?"

"Do you know what the word means, Claire?" Derek was rubbing the back of his neck. Was he as anxious as I felt?

"No, sorry," she said quickly. "My Gaelic is quite rusty. But I do remember hearing my father speaking to my aunt in the old language, probably in the hope that I wouldn't understand what they were saying." She splayed her hands. "I didn't, of course. Still, that word looks like something similar to what I've seen written on signs around town."

"There's a way to find out," Dalton said. "But it's tricky and I wouldn't suggest trying this at home."

"We won't," I promised. "Just do it."

"All right," he said. "Here we go. Now, watch carefully." He clicked on a browser and brought up Google. There he typed out *FIODHA TRANSLATE*.

"You can't be serious," Derek said derisively. "You're using Google Translate?"

"You're cheating," I cried.

"Every chance I get." He laughed. "Now, watch and learn." He clicked his mouse and a new screen popped up. I recognized the Google Translate page. In the "Scottish" box was the word *fiodha*. And in the "English" box was the word *wood*.

"*Fiodha* means *wood*," I murmured.

Dalton turned in his chair and flashed a grin that managed to be both smug and adorable at the same time. "It's Gaelic indeed, children. More specifically, Scottish Gaelic."

"I could've figured it out," I grumbled on the drive back through town.

Derek laughed out loud. "But my brother is a highly trained professional. And a twit, lest we forget."

"He can be a twit, but he's still pretty good at his job."

"Which is why we keep him around," Derek said.

Claire sat forward to join the conversation. "I'm not sure we ever would've broken the code without him."

"Unfortunately I agree," I muttered. "Still, it makes me feel like a dolt." Now that I'd seen him Google the information, I was rolling my eyes at my own shortsightedness.

But in fairness to all of us, we hadn't had a minute to concentrate on those marked pages since we'd first seen them. After all, we only discovered them soon after we found the dead body in our garage. A few minutes after that, we'd spied Fish Face stalking our building. Then

Derek took off running after him and the next thing I knew, we were driving off to Dharma.

I sighed. "I'm just glad he was able to figure it out."

"It was quite exciting to watch him work," Claire said from the back seat.

I had to admit she was right. Dalton was amazing at his job, even if he had sneakily taken the easy way out this time. It had been fun, I realized, to figure out how to turn all of those letters into different words and phrases. Like an intricate game or a really complicated puzzle.

We'd started with the chain of marked letters in this order: A-F-A-L-A-C-H-A-N-N-S-A-N-T-U-R-C-L-A-G-A-N-I-A-R-C-O-I-M-H-E-A-D-F-O-N-P-H-L-A-N-C-F-I-O-D-H-A.

Eventually we fumbled our way, trying one thing or another, as we clumped them together to form words. And that was when we were finally able to translate the words into English.

A 'falach anns an tùr clag an iar translated to *Hiding in the west bell tower*. But what was hiding? I wondered. Or *who*?

Coimhead fon phlanc fiodha translated to *Look under the wooden plank*. At least, that's what Google told us it all meant.

I had never verified the accuracy of any online translator program. But this result seemed close enough for now.

I turned around and faced Claire. "We still don't know what it means, though. What are we looking for under a wooden plank? And the western bell tower? Was there an eastern bell tower?"

"I haven't a clue," she said.

I thought about it. "Does Gwyneth's village have a bell tower?"

"Well, yes," she said. "We have the church, and it does indeed have a bell tower."

"Maybe something's hidden up there."

"And then there's the castle," Claire added.

I felt my eyes light up. "You have a castle in the village?"

"Aye," she said eagerly. "Well, it's outside of the village. A good walk through the woods, now that you mention it. But it's close enough and it supports many of the townspeople, as castles tend to do."

I had no idea what castles tended to do, but it was intriguing to think about. "Did your aunt grow up in the village?"

"Yes, she and my father were born and raised in Oddlochen."

I smiled. "Oddlochen is the name of the village?"

"Yes. It's a lovely little town on the banks of Loch Ness."

"Were you born there?" I asked.

"Oh no. I was born in Florida."

"Florida?" I repeated in amazement. "There must be a story there."

"Aye, there is," she said with a grin. "My father came to the States to make his fortune and that's where he met my mother."

"In Florida?"

"Aye. At Disney World."

"You're kidding," I said with a laugh.

"It's true." Her smile softened. "Mum was Sleeping Beauty in the Main Street Parade. Dad saw her and fell in love at first sight."

"That's fascinating. So you grew up in Florida?"

"Until I was almost seven. Then my father sent me to

live with Aunt Gwyneth. I remember him telling me that I would benefit from being raised by a woman." Her smile faded. "I think he never got over my mother dying."

"That would take a toll on a man," Derek said.

"Yes. He loved her very much. And he kept her memory alive for me. He told me stories and gave me some of her things. She was beautiful."

"I'm sure she was," I said.

"That was good of him to keep her things for you," Derek remarked.

"Dad was a lovely man. A bit of a scoundrel, I suppose, but a wonderful father."

"Why do you think he sent you to Scotland?"

She pressed her lips together. "I told you that he was always scheming to make money, and that his buddies weren't the brightest or the nicest fellows."

"Yes, you said something about that."

"Right. Well, to be blunt, I think he sent me away to protect me from those buddies of his."

"Do you think they meant to do you harm?"

"I never felt afraid of any of them." She sighed. "My father was a handsome devil of a man who used his charm and good looks to get ahead in life. His friends weren't as charming, but they didn't seem violent or scary. Not at first, anyway," she added.

"Did something happen to cause him to send you away?"

She thought for a minute. "There was one thing. A big thing, really. It's a rather long story."

"We're all ears," I said, trying not to sound too eager. I loved hearing stories about other families.

She smiled. "My father didn't go in for the nine-to-five lifestyle, but he and Mum managed to run an antiques shop for a few years when I was still a baby. Once she died, he lost interest in the shop, even though the antiques business was in his blood."

"Is that how you got interested in antique weaponry?"

"Aye." She chuckled. "That's a whole different story."

"Well, I want to hear more about what happened with your father."

"I do, too," Derek said. "If you don't mind telling us."

"I don't mind at all. It feels right to be talking about it, somehow." We were stopped at a red light so she unbuckled her seatbelt, adjusted her position on the seat to get more comfortable, and then buckled up. "So if you're familiar with Florida, you might know that every year, dozens of items fall out of small planes and land in the Everglades. And one day my father's good friend Bill witnessed a large bale fall out of the sky. He thought it had to be drugs. Cocaine, perhaps."

Maybe I shouldn't have been surprised, but I was. "A bale of cocaine fell out of the sky?"

"Yes. It wasn't the first or last time a pilot flying up from Mexico had dumped his cargo over the Everglades."

"In the hope of going back and retrieving it?"

"Yes. The pilots were afraid of having their planes searched when they landed at one of the local airports, so they would drop their load of drugs and then venture into the Everglades and pick them up."

Derek shook his head. "Plenty of people have died that way."

"Oh yes," she said. "The alligators are quite hungry."

"So your father's friend Bill decided to find the drugs before the pilot got them?"

"Exactly. Bill brought my father and two more of

their friends in on the deal and the four of them went on an expedition into the swampland."

"Did they know who they were going up against?" Derek asked.

She smiled ruefully. "They didn't think they'd get caught."

I winced. "Oh dear."

"But here's the thing," Claire said. "They *didn't* get caught. They actually found their treasure, this ridiculously large bale filled with cocaine, or so they thought. It was wrapped in layers and layers of cotton gauze, then covered in thick cardboard and wrapped in wire. They didn't open it right then but hid it in our garage for two years. Their plan was to lie low and then after two years they would slowly start dividing up the bounty and selling it off, bit by bit. No one would be the wiser."

"How'd that work out?" Derek wondered. He was just as involved in the story as I was.

"To make a long story short," she said, "when they finally broke into the bale, it was empty. Just a bunch of stuffing and wires with nothing at all inside. I was supposed to be asleep that night, but I heard them arguing. Bill was yelling. He said they wouldn't be able to buy the guns now and insisted that he wasn't going to take the blame. He said that 'he' was going to be very angry."

"He was going to be very angry? Who's he?" I asked.

"I don't know."

"Did your father say anything?"

"He was disgusted that their stuff had been stolen out from under them. All of the men were."

"So what happened?" I asked.

"They began to fight among themselves," Claire said. "Here they had managed to wait for two long years, only to come up with nothing. Bill blamed my father because they had hidden their stuff in our garage. And of course they claimed that it had been Dad's idea to lie low all that time before starting to peddle the drugs—or whatever they thought they'd found. Dad told Bill he should've been out looking for a job in the meantime instead of sitting around on his *bahoochie* waiting for the big payoff."

"I beg your pardon?" Derek said.

I laughed. "I'm going to take a wild guess that it means he was sitting on his behind."

"Yes, exactly. Sorry." But she smiled as she said it. "It's Scottish slang. My dad and his friends used to say it a lot."

Something occurred to me. "So the other men were Scottish?"

She blinked. "Oh. Well, yes. Of course. Dad had met them at a local Scottish pub when he first moved to Florida and they'd become fast friends."

I exchanged a glance with Derek, but said nothing.

"So Bill blamed your father," Derek said. "Did the other men blame him as well?"

"At first they blamed Bill, and rightly so, but then Bill convinced them that my father must have stolen the drugs—or whatever was inside the bale—and sold them himself."

I stared at her. "Would your father have done that?"

"I don't think so. He was awfully smart—which makes me think he did go into the garage and check out the bundle—but he was also loyal to his mates. So," she said, shrugging, "it's a mystery."

"Do you remember anything else about that night?"

"Yes. I thought they were all getting ready to leave. I had to get up and use the bathroom, and as I tiptoed down the hall, one of the men saw me. It wasn't one of Dad's usual mates. I didn't recognize him."

I rubbed my arms from the sudden chill. "What did you do?"

"I scurried to the bathroom and locked the door. I waited until I heard them all leave, then I went back to bed."

"Did you tell your father about it?"

"No. He was quite distracted after that so I didn't want to upset him."

I remembered Claire saying she'd been the grown-up in the house, so here was another example of that.

"And then what happened?" Derek asked.

She took a deep breath. "A few days later, Dad was walking me to school when a car drove up beside us. The passenger rolled down the window and said, 'Pretty little girl.'"

I gasped. "Oh no."

"Yes."

Derek stared at her in the rearview mirror. "Did you recognize him?"

"It was the man I saw that night. I remember he had a big head. He was a big man. I'd never seen him before that night and I've never seen him since."

"Your father must've been scared to death."

"Apparently so, because we didn't go to school that day. Dad spent the day packing up my things and we flew to Scotland soon after. He dropped me off at my aunt Gwyneth's house and then disappeared."

I frowned at her. "What do you mean, disappeared?"

She shook her head. "He simply disappeared."

"For how long?"

She swallowed carefully, obviously upset. "I never saw him again."

I turned in my seat and gazed at her. "You said your father was dead."

"Is he dead, Claire?" Derek asked quietly.

She used both hands to brush her hair back from her face. "I honestly have no idea. But since I haven't seen him in over twenty-five years, he might as well be dead."

Derek came to a stop and turned off the engine. And I realized we were parked at the top of my parents' driveway. I turned again to face Claire. "This is my parents' house and I just have to spend a few minutes with them. If you'd rather not come in, I'll just tell them you're, um, not feeling well."

"No, no, don't be silly. I'm fine. Just . . . reliving old times is not as entertaining as it's cracked up to be."

"That's for sure," I said with a sympathetic smile. Opening the car door, I stood and stretched. "I don't know about you, but I'm getting hungry."

Now Claire smiled. "I could eat something."

"Seriously, we'll only stay for a few minutes," I said. "I just want to let my parents know that we're in town for a day or two."

"I'm looking forward to meeting them," Claire said politely.

"They'll love you," I assured her, and linked my arm with hers. I had already begun to feel like we were friends and right now she was obviously hurting after telling us about her father.

Derek gave Claire an encouraging smile. "They're lovely people."

Claire didn't respond. She wrapped her arms around herself and seemed to have reverted to her old nervousness. Was she embarrassed about her father? She shouldn't have been. I'd found the story fascinating and I knew Derek had, too. But I had to wonder: Was the man dead or not?

We had barely stepped out of the car when my mother

ran out of the house and down the front steps, waving madly. She wore an adorable pair of yellow denim overalls with a tie-dyed T-shirt underneath. *Once a Deadhead, always a Deadhead*, I thought fondly.

"You left for the city two days ago," she said as she wrapped me in a tight hug. "What are you doing back here?"

"We have a friend visiting and decided to bring her here for a little wine country fun." I had always been a terrible liar, but I thought that line sounded completely sincere.

"I wish your father was home, but he's at the winery helping out with the festival crowd."

"We'll stop by the winery later and say hello." I angled Mom toward Claire. "Mom, this is our friend, Claire."

"Hello, Claire," she said with her usual sunny smile and extended her hand to shake Claire's.

"It's lovely to meet you, Mrs. Wainwright," Claire said.

"Now, you call me Becky." Mom clutched Claire's hand and after staring at her for a few seconds she frowned and narrowed her eyes. "You look familiar, Claire." She glanced at me and then back at Claire. "You were on that show with Brooklyn."

My eyebrows shot up. "Wow, good memory, Mom."

"I recall seeing you talk about a . . . was it a Civil War sword?" Mom said. "Yes, that's it. It was fascinating."

Claire's smile lit up her eyes. "Oh yes. It was a Virginia artillery saber. Quite rare and in remarkable condition. Curved, single-edged blade. Manufactured in 1806, I believe." She frowned, thought about it, and then nodded. "Yes, that's right, 1806."

"I just remember that the curved blade made it look very dangerous."

Claire nodded. "In the hands of the right soldier it could be."

Mom grinned. "Gave me chills." She finally let go of Claire's hand but continued questioning her. "Do you ever get any vibes about the weapons' owners?"

Claire was taken aback, but recovered quickly. "Nobody's ever asked me that question. But the answer is yes."

A gleam appeared in Mom's eyes. "We'll have to sit down and have a long talk about that."

"But not right now," I added quickly, smiling brightly.

"No, of course not." She gave me a look. "I think Brooklyn gets those same vibes about books, don't you, sweetie pie?"

"Uh, yes. I guess I do."

"Oh, I'm that way about books, too," Claire declared. "That's how Brooklyn and I got to know each other. Over books."

One glance at Claire and I could see that she'd lost the haunted look she'd worn after talking about her father.

My mother was someone who got vibes over every little thing wherever she went, but I was still impressed that she was able to zone in on Claire's favorite topic and then take it one level deeper.

"Are you kids getting hungry?" Mom asked, and patted Derek's arm. "Can you stay for lunch? I've got leftover fried chicken and I just made a batch of my crazy delicious apple crisp."

"We'll stay," Derek said instantly. He was a big fan of my mother's crazy delicious apple crisp. Her chicken wasn't bad, either.

*   *   *

Halfway through lunch I asked Mom about Robin. "I spoke with her about an hour ago and she sounded like she might be going into labor."

"She's been having backaches," Mom said. "But that's normal at this late date. She still has a few weeks to go and Austin's been keeping a close eye on her. He calls me a couple of times every day just to see what I think. It's cute."

Because when it came to babies, my mother had given birth to six of us. She was the local expert, for sure. But still, I was concerned about my friend.

"Robin told me that Austin's at the winery today."

"Oh, shoot." Mom was frowning now. "Of course he is. In that case, let's give her a call after lunch."

"Good idea. Thanks."

But we had barely made it through lunch when the phone rang. Mom dashed into the kitchen to pick it up. Less than thirty seconds later, she hung up. "Speak of the devil. That was Austin letting us know that Robin's water broke. They're on their way to the hospital."

Two hours later I sat in the waiting room of Sonoma Valley Hospital surrounded by my family and half the town of Dharma. That's what it felt like, anyway.

Every time a nurse came into the room to give us their bubbly, gushing update—"Another half centimeter!" or "She's a feisty one!"—they made it clear, laughingly, that we had hours to go before the actual baby would show up.

I had years of memories of just how "feisty" Robin could be, so all I could do was send thoughts and prayers to Austin. And Robin, of course.

Every few minutes, Austin would come in and give

his own quickie report. At one point he waved me over. "She wants to see you."

"Me? Is anything wrong?"

"Wrong?" He slung his arm across my shoulders in a brotherly gesture as we walked out of the waiting room. "No, nothing's wrong. Just the usual intermittent screaming labor pains with her suddenly cursing me to the depths of hell and swearing like she's acting out a scene from *The Exorcist*. And she's been squeezing my hands until my fingers are numb, raw stumps, but other than that, it's going great."

"And you love it," I said with a laugh.

"She's amazing," he admitted, with love shining in his eyes. "I don't know how, but she's hanging in there."

"Good."

"But look, we shouldn't keep her waiting, so let's go."

We walked down the wide hall and through a set of double doors marked BIRTHING CENTER.

"She's in the first room." He gave me a little push toward the open door.

"Wait. Anything I should know before I go in there?"

"Yeah," he said, sounding a little desperate. "She decided to go for the epidural and the nurse just gave it to her. I figure you've got about ten more minutes of dealing with Godzilla before she chills out."

"Good to know." I watched him walk away, then stepped into the room. "Wow, this is deluxe."

The space was larger than any hospital room I'd ever seen. The hospital bed took center stage and next to it was a crib outfitted with all the same electronic monitoring gadgets that the regular bed had. Across the room was a bathtub that resembled my in-laws' spa tub, and I admit I wondered what that was all about. The walls were a soothing pale blue with touches of light gray. There was a sitting area with a couch and chairs and a small dining room table and more chairs nearby. It was like a junior suite at a really nice hotel—except for the afore-mentioned electronic monitoring gadgets everywhere.

"You can come closer," Robin said. "I probably won't bite your head off as long as you don't tell me how pretty I am when I know I look like a sweating bull moose with a bad attitude."

"You look more beautiful than anything I've ever seen."

She started to laugh, but then moaned, "Don't make me laugh."

"Sorry. Are you in pain?"

"Yeah, but it's okay. I'm waiting for the epidural to kick in."

I glanced at my wristwatch. "Any minute now."

She smiled wearily. "Yeah."

I glanced around. "This is a nice place."

"Oh yeah. They've got mood lighting and I can cus-tomize my musical playlist."

"Seriously?"

"Uh-huh. And once I pop this critter out, I can join in a yoga class down the hall."

"That sounds . . . awful?"

She sighed and closed her eyes. "Thank you. I knew you'd understand."

I moved closer to the side of the bed and reached for her hand. "What can I get for you?"

Her eyes opened. "A margarita."

"Salt?"

"Yes." Her smile was beatific. "On the rocks."

"Of course."

She turned her hand over and squeezed mine. "I like you better than Austin."

"I warned you not to marry him."

She sighed. "Teach me to listen to you."

I stayed with her for about five minutes, until another contraction started. "Oh no, oh no, here it comes." Her back arched up and she cried, "Get Austin!"

"He's right here," my brother shouted and rushed into the room.

"Oo-kay," I said, tiptoeing toward the door. "Hang in there, sweetie."

"Easy for you to say," Robin growled in mid-groan.

"I was talking to Austin," I said. "But I love you, Robin."

She tried to laugh but the pain took over. I walked backward out of the room. Hopefully the epidural would start to do its job soon. Once I was safely outside in the hallway, I blew out a breath of pure relief.

When I got back to the waiting room, I found Claire and asked, "How are you doing?"

"I'm doing fine. Your family is so nice."

"Yeah, they are." I sat down next to her. "But you know, we're all going to be here for hours still, so I was thinking you might like to go home and chill out. You can watch TV or read a book and drink a glass of wine in peace and quiet."

Claire gazed around the room at all these people she'd never met until today and her lips twisted in a rueful smile. "It's been fun meeting everyone, but the thought of a good book and a glass of wine is tempting. Would you mind?"

"Of course not," I said. "You've had a pretty miserable few days. You deserve to relax and do your own thing for a while."

"I must confess, for the last hour I've been imagining myself floating away in that beautiful spa tub."

"Doesn't that sound great?" I looked around and found Derek chatting quietly with my brother Jackson. I caught his eye and a few seconds later, he strolled over to me.

"What is it, love?"

"Claire would like to go home and take it easy for a while. I'll drive her there and come right back."

He pondered it for a long moment. "Why don't you stay here in case Robin needs you? I'll drive Claire home."

"I guess that makes more sense." Then I grimaced. "We never made it to the market so we don't have much to eat."

"I'll make a quick stop at the store and pick up some things."

"I wish I'd thought to bring some apple crisp with us."

He was instantly on alert. "How can we get some of that?"

I grinned. "We'll have to wait until tomorrow morning. But it makes a really good breakfast treat."

"Don't I know it." He leaned over and kissed me. "Okay. I'll be back as soon as I can get here."

"Be careful. I love you."

"Love you back."

I reached out and touched Claire's arm. "Please just relax and enjoy the quiet."

"Aye. Thank you, Brooklyn. Please give my best wishes to your friend for a happy, healthy new baby."

"That's nice. I'll tell her you said so."

She scanned the room. "Your family is so warm and welcoming. I appreciate you inviting me to join them today."

"They enjoyed having you here." It was true. My

mother had been completely charmed by Claire, who had easily won over everyone else with her quiet humor and self-effacing style. But as she followed Derek out of the waiting room, I wondered what they would say if they ever got a glimpse of her wielding that kick-ass Lochaber axe. I guess we'd never know.

Twenty minutes later, Gabriel stalked into the waiting room. As usual, he was dressed in black from head to toe. Black baseball cap, black leather jacket, black jeans, black T-shirt, black high-tops. And as usual, he looked sexier than any man had a right to look. Except Derek, of course.

He took a quick look around, then came over, sat down next to me, and said, "Babe."

"Hey," I said. "Didn't expect to see you here."

He shrugged. "Got to put my name in the baby pool."

I smiled. "There're only a few spots left. Jackson's taking bets."

"Yeah, I'll get to that. There's something else."

"I figured," I said, and stood up. "What's going on?"

"Your buddy just arrived in town. What are we calling him? Fish Face? He's here."

"Oh my God." I grabbed his jacket. "Derek. I've got to get to him." I took two steps forward, then turned around and found Gabriel right behind me. He gripped my arms. "Chill, babe."

"But Derek just took Claire home. He was going to stop at the grocery store."

He pulled me out of the waiting room and into the deserted hallway. "Don't worry about Derek. I just spoke to him. He asked me to swing by here and pick you up."

Instinctively I clutched my small backpack that held the copy of *Rebecca* to my chest. I tried to rub my arms to get rid of the sudden chills, but it wasn't working. "What about my family?"

He tilted his head to get a look at the crowded waiting room. "Looks like most of them are here."

"But they'll be going home eventually."

He met my gaze. "Babe, listen to me. I've got people assigned to everyone in your family."

"Are you sure?" I frowned. "I didn't see anyone outside my mom's house earlier."

He snorted. "You're not supposed to be able to see them."

"Oh." I had to think. "What about Savannah?"

"Dalton is at the restaurant, hanging out in the kitchen. And I've got a second guy sitting at the bar, watching the door in case your Fish Face pal shows up."

I took in a deep breath, let it out slowly. "Okay. Thank you. I hate to leave Robin, but she's got the whole gang here and apparently it's going to be a few hours before the baby will be ready to greet the world."

"Earlier today I spoke to both Jackson and Austin. They're on top of things here. Nobody's going to get hurt while they're on the case."

I nodded. He really did seem prepared for anything. "Okay, where's the best place for me to be?"

"With Derek, of course. I'll take you home and my plan is to stay there with you guys overnight."

"Thanks. That's a really good idea."

"Yeah, I thought so." He grinned again. "So do you need to tell your mom or anyone else that you're leaving?"

"Oh yeah. Guess I'd better." But what excuse could I make? I had to think about this.

"Tell you what, babe." He used his typical laid-back tone and I knew he was doing it to calm me down. "You go talk to your mom, I'll put a few bucks in the Baby Wainwright betting pool, and then we'll make like a banana and split."

Chapter 10

"What kind of car does he drive?" I asked Gabriel on the ride home. I wanted to find that car, find that thug who had invaded our town.

Gabriel was still in his calm-and-cool mode as he watched the road ahead. "He drives a silver truck. Late-model Dodge Ram pickup."

"That's really specific," I said, and snuck a peek down the side streets and driveways we passed in hopes of finding the truck. "Does your satellite system give you that much information?"

"It can." He easily passed a car driving too slow in the fast lane. "But this time I happened to catch a shot of him on the traffic camera at Montana Ridge and Old Oak Road."

"Seriously? That was lucky."

"Plenty of luck involved, but it was also a matter of perseverance. I spent most of the afternoon download-ing camera shots and texting them to Alex. She finally nailed him."

"Alex found him?" I felt a ray of hope. "That's great. You were smart to involve her since she's actually seen his face."

"Right? Always pays to bring Alex in on a case."

"You guys are the best." So why couldn't I stop shivering?

He gave me a sideways glance. "You okay?"

"A little nervous." It was more than a little. I was actually shaking like crazy, worrying about Derek.

"Hang on. We'll be home in another minute."

"But what if the guy followed them home and he managed to get inside the house? What if he brought a couple of thug friends with him?"

"He was alone in the truck," Gabriel said. "Now, whether he had one of his buddies follow him up here, we can't say for certain. But for now I'm going with the probability that he's acting alone."

"He's really big and dangerous," I whispered, then wanted to bite my tongue. I sounded like some kind of silly damsel in distress and that just wasn't me. Besides, Gabriel and Derek and my brothers were big and dangerous, too. They could handle one big, hairy thug. And so could Claire, for that matter. She knew how to handle weapons. So why was I being such a worrywart?

Gabriel turned right on Whitman Way and headed up the hill.

The closer we got, the more I shivered. What would we find when we arrived at the house? I might've moaned out loud.

Gabriel shot me a look of concern. "Gotta say, Brooklyn, I've never seen you like this before."

"Like what?"

"Like, you know, shaky. Fretful. Freaking out. Used to be, if there was any sign of trouble, you were the first one charging out the door."

Really? That was me? I would have to think about it.

For now I just said, "I'm happily married now and I don't want anything to ruin that."

"I hear you, babe."

I held up my hand. "No. That was lame. I don't know what's wrong with me. Maybe it's because we found that other guy dead in our garage and this guy has already terrorized Claire in town and now he's followed us up here. That means he has a way of digging into our personal information and at this point, he could attack anyone in my family."

"It won't happen." He reached over and squeezed my hand. "We'll get this guy, Brooklyn. I promise you."

"I know we will," I said, hoping it was true. "Did you call the police?"

"No local cops yet," he said flatly. "My people can handle this guy."

If this were San Francisco I would've argued with him. But here in Dharma? The fact was that I had trusted Gabriel with my life on more than a few occasions and he had always come through for me. So why would I stop trusting now? Besides, Dharma had only recently hired a small police force to keep pace with the growing population. There was exactly *one* detective in charge of the office and the four young uniformed officers who kept the peace.

Who knew if they could handle a truly bad guy like Fish Face?

I patted Gabriel's shoulder. "I have full confidence in you and your team. I know you'll make sure we're all safe."

"We will. Never doubt it." He held up his finger. "And we'll have a little help from Derek and Dalton and your brothers."

I grinned. "Okay, that's a pretty formidable group."

"And by the way," he added, "Alex is on her way up here."

"Ah." I smiled. "Now I know for sure we'll beat that fool."

He smiled. "My girl is a real fighter."

I had seen Alex in action and had no doubt of her courage and ability in a fight. "She'll kick his ass."

"That about sums it up," Gabriel said.

Much to my relief, we made it to Derek's parents' house without incident. Gabriel took precautions to bring the car all the way into the driveway and before he got out of the car, he pulled a seriously scary-looking gun from a locked box in the driver's side door.

"Oo-kay, then," I said, and tried to rub away the chills that had returned to my shoulders.

He took his phone out and pressed a number. "We're here," he murmured into the phone, paused to listen, then said, "Okay, boss."

"Who was that?" Gabriel didn't have a boss. Unless he was talking to Robson.

"Derek," he said. "Now, here's the deal. We don't know where this guy is, so just to be safe, I want you to get out of the car and walk straight to the front door. I'll be right behind you keeping an eye out for anyone wanting to ambush us."

I breathed in and out. "Oh God. Okay. Let's do it."

"I'll get out first and come around to meet you."

"Got it." My heart was beating a few hundred miles an hour, but I followed his plan. I exited the car and he slammed the door behind me. I put one foot in front of the other and before I knew it we were safe inside the house.

Derek was waiting at the door and grabbed me in his arms. "Are you all right?"

I hugged him tightly. "A little numb. Petrified, really. But I'll be fine."

"You did great," Gabriel said.

"Sure. And now I can collapse." But I didn't. Instead, Claire walked over and I gave her a hug.

"You okay?" I asked.

"Aye. Though I didn't get to take my bath yet, but I did have a glass of wine so I'm doing quite well." She studied my face. "Better than you, I think. How are you feeling?"

"Much better now that we're all home."

"Good." She bumped her fist against mine. "You might try a glass of wine. It tends to smooth away the rough edges."

I managed another smile. "That's a good way to put it."

Gabriel's phone rang and again he answered and just listened, then said, "Okay."

He swore under his breath, then ended the call and looked straight at me. "Don't freak out."

"Uh, too late. What happened?"

"The Fish Man tried to break into your parents' house."

"Oh no," Claire said. "Fish Face?"

"Yeah, that guy." His teeth were clenched tightly and I'd heard him cursing so I knew there was something else going on.

"Did someone get hurt?" I asked.

"No. Nobody was home."

"They must still be at the hospital."

"Yeah. So my two guys were able to keep him from getting inside."

"But?" I said. Because Gabriel didn't look happy.

He scowled. "They spooked him and he was able to run off. They went after him but he managed to slip away in the trees."

"That's pretty easy to do," I admitted, picturing the beautiful thicket of evergreens across from my parents' house.

"A half a minute later, they heard a truck engine start up on the next street over. Pretty sure it was him."

I huffed out a breath. "Damn it."

"He probably won't return to your parents' house tonight, but they'll keep watch anyway." He glanced from me to Derek. "Sorry."

"It's not your fault or your team's fault," I said. "The guy's a professional bad guy."

I knew Derek was fuming inside although he stood perfectly still next to me. It was his bunched-up fists that gave him away. "Brooklyn's right," he said tightly. "Your team is not at fault. This guy's been lucky so far, but that won't last."

"No, it won't," Gabriel promised.

Derek said, "So now we wait and watch."

"Eventually he'll come here," I said.

Gabriel nodded. "Sometime tonight is my guess."

"And we'll be ready for him," Derek said.

It was close to eleven o'clock that night and I was starting to doze off when my mother called.

"It's a boy!"

It took me a few seconds to register her words. "Oh, the baby? He's here?"

"He's here, he's beautiful, and he's healthy as a little horse. His mom and dad are doing just fine. They're exhausted, but completely besotted by their little miracle."

"Oh Mom, that's wonderful," I said, feeling the sting of tears. "Thank you so much for calling to let us know."

"I thought you'd come back to the hospital," she said, and sounded a little worried.

"I'm sorry. I thought so, too, but we ran into a little trouble."

"Oh sweetie, are you all right?"

I thought briefly about telling her about the attempted break-in, but I knew there would be people watching her house and knew that she and Dad would be safe. So I decided not to alarm her. Not tonight, anyway.

"We're fine," I quickly assured her. "We'll come by the hospital first thing in the morning to meet our beautiful new nephew. Does he have a name yet?"

"They went traditional with *James Robert*."

I sniffed and felt the first teardrop tickle my cheek. "They named him after Dad. That's so sweet."

"Yes, and they chose the name Robert after Robson."

"Oh." I couldn't hold back the tears.

"Robin picked the names to honor them both. She said that Jim and Robson were the two men in her life who had always been there for her. Like real fathers."

Oh boy. Where were the tissues? Robin had grown up without a father of her own and her mother hadn't been there for her, either. "That's pretty awesome."

"Isn't it?" She was crying now, too, and when we both stopped to blow our noses, it started a short laughing jag.

"Congratulations, Gammy," I said finally.

She sniffled again. When her first grandchild was born, Mom informed us that she'd decided she wanted everyone to call her Gammy. "Grandma makes me sound like an old lady," she said. "But don't tell anyone I said so."

We kids all thought of our very own grandma, her mother, and promised we would never say a word.

"Now get to sleep," she said, "and we'll see you in the morning."

"Yes, Gammy."

I thought I heard another sniffle. "I'm so happy. Good night, sweetie."

"Oh wait, Mom. Who won the pool?"

She made a *tsk-tsk* sound. "Gabriel. That scoundrel. He was the last one in the pool and he won the whole pot."

"He really is a scoundrel," I said, and ended the call.

I managed to sleep fitfully and woke up early the next morning, wishing I could stay in bed for another hour or two. I'd had an awful dream in the middle of the night involving Fish Face and his mate, Reggie MacDougall, the dead guy we'd found in the garage. They were both alive in my dream and skulking around the hospital. I woke up trembling with fear that they might sneak down to Robin's room and hurt the baby.

After the dream woke me, I couldn't go back to sleep. I finally got out of bed and pulled the stack of origami papers from my supplies bag. For the next hour, I folded and twisted and transformed the colorful paper into birds and butterflies and flowers. It was a fascinating art form and almost meditative, I thought. I was so relaxed, finally, that I almost fell asleep on the loveseat across from where Derek slept. I managed to make it over to the bed and was asleep in minutes.

                              *   *   *

Derek walked into the bedroom just as I threw back
the covers and sat on the edge of the bed. It was barely
6 a.m. and I was still getting my bearings.

"Good morning," he said, and came over and kissed
the top of my head.

"Hi. Have you already been up for a while?"

"I was downstairs talking to Gabriel. I didn't want to
wake you."

"Thanks. I didn't sleep too well."

"I know, love."

"So what's going on?"

"Everything is fine downstairs. I was about to call
Harold to check on the situation with Aunt Gwyneth."
He glanced at his watch. "But I also want to call one of
my contacts at MI5."

"Oh." I jumped off the bed. "I could call Harold while
you talk to MI5." Harold and I had become friendly recently when he helped us track down an international
killer.

Derek stared at me for a moment. "I suppose you and
Harold know each other well enough."

I gaped at him, then threw my arms around him.
"Thank you."

"For what?"

"For trusting me."

"Darling, I trust you with my life."

I squeezed a little harder, then gazed up at him. "I
feel exactly the same way about you."

"Good." He smiled. "Make the call. Take notes."

"Got it."

It was fun talking to Harold, a charming British
agent with an encyclopedic mind and a good sense of

humor. I spent fifteen minutes on the phone and when I
hung up, Derek handed me a cup of coffee.

"You are the best person in the world," I uttered,
gripping the cup and taking a long sip.

He sat down next to me on the loveseat. "Now, what
did Harold tell you?"

I stared at my notes. "Well, first he warned me not to
get my hopes up. Gwyneth is still missing, but Harold
seems to think there's something odd about her
disappearance."

"Something odd in Oddlochen?" Derek said.

I had to smile, but sobered up quickly. "He said it's
hard to tell exactly what's going on without being there.
But he did mention that there's a new major player on
the scene."

"Ah, the major *player*," Derek said. "According to my
source, that major player is Cameron MacKinnon."

I frowned at the name. "Darn it. I was just about to
tell you that."

He grinned. "Sorry, love. You go ahead."

"Well, I'm sure you already know this, but Cameron
MacKinnon is the new laird of the castle."

"I heard that somewhere," he said wryly.

I had realized while talking to Harold that I had no
idea what the social and political ramifications of having a new laird might mean. But I would figure all that
out eventually. Right now I had another concern.

"Here's my question," I said. "What happened to the
old laird?"

"Now, that is the right question to ask."

"Thank you." I smiled at him. "Do you know the answer?" As we talked, I pulled on a pair of black leggings
and topped them with a warm, wine-red tunic.

"I believe I do." He stared out the window of one of the French doors. "Now, let me first say that this information comes through my MI5 source, who obtained it from the local constable."

I grabbed my notes. "Harold did tell me that the git he talked to earlier is no longer in charge."

"Thank God," Derek said. "The woman who left on maternity leave is back at work and quite helpful, according to my man."

"That's one good thing, anyway."

"Yes. So apparently the old laird grew up with Gwyneth and her brother. They were all of an age, you see."

I had to work out the math in my mind and realized that those three were approximately the same age as my own mother and father. "That makes sense."

I set my notes down and slipped into comfortable black flats, but decided to stick my white sneakers and a pair of socks in my backpack in case I had to do any running. But halfway across the room, I stopped and turned. "So Claire's father grew up with the laird of the castle."

"The *old* laird."

"Right."

"And according to my fellow at MI5, they were great friends."

"That's interesting. I'm not sure what it means, but it's interesting."

"Interesting indeed," he said. "Unfortunately, though, over the years the old laird had been running the castle into the ground. He owed thousands of dollars in gambling debts to some dangerous people, so apparently, just recently, he . . . 'disappeared.'"

"What? You're kidding." I felt hopelessly confused. "At the same time Gwyneth went missing?"

"No," Derek said. "It was about six months ago. Reportedly he left the country and is said to be somewhere in the States. Again, according to MI5. And by the way, he left the castle in an even more horrible state than previously thought. Rumor has it the old place is still beautiful, but the neglect is beginning to show."

I blew out a breath. "I need to try and work this out in my head." I walked into the bathroom to brush my hair. "First, Claire's father disappeared twenty-five years ago."

"That's what she told us," Derek said.

"And his friend, the old laird, ran away six months ago. He just vanished, according to Harold."

"Right. That happened a month or two before the constable left on maternity leave."

"And Gwyneth disappeared less than a week ago."

"Again, that's what Claire told us."

"And the castle needs a lot of work," I said. "Which is why the new laird took over. Well, that, and the fact that the old laird has done a runner."

"By George, darling, I believe you've got it exactly right."

I glanced at him and knew he was teasing me. I set my brush down and applied a touch of lip balm. "The info about the new laird is fascinating, and I'm sorry about the condition of the castle. But let's get serious. When will we get more info on Gwyneth? Where the heck is she? Harold indicated that they'd just recently hit a wall as far as getting answers from these people."

Scowling, Derek shook his head. "My MI5 contact only knows what the constable told him, namely that the new laird has put himself in charge of the law in Oddlochen."

"Well, that's annoying." I thought for a moment.

"But Harold did tell me that he put in a call to the new laird."

"Maybe he'll get more information than my contact did."

I walked to the French doors and opened them up to the morning air and the gorgeous view. "I feel so helpless. We can't do anything from here. And Claire must be going out of her mind, although she's putting up a good front, isn't she?"

"Yes," he agreed, coming up behind me. "She's been quite the good soldier."

"Can one of our contacts send someone up to Oddlochen to investigate more thoroughly? Maybe someone from MI6. I can't imagine your old firm would be happy to hear that one of their well-respected former employees has disappeared."

He reached for my hand. "Let's go downstairs."

We locked the French doors and walked out the bedroom door and down the stairs. "The only way we'll get to the bottom of this mystery is for Harold or your guy to send their own person to Oddlochen."

"That was the gist of my conversation. I intend to check back to see if they follow through."

"Good." I leaned closer. "We need to tell Claire what's going on."

"Yes, of course. I know she's frustrated and so am I." He pursed his lips in thought. "I just think . . ."

"You think we should go there," I said. "To Scotland."

He stared at me. "Are you reading my mind now?"

"I know you," I said with a smile. "And I was thinking the same thing. If we were there, we could search for Gwyneth and get answers for ourselves."

"And I would know exactly who to trust," Derek added.

I gazed up at him. "Who?"

"Myself."

"Ah. Right. Would you be able to trust any of these other players?"

"I rarely trust players."

I chuckled and slipped my arm through his. Halfway down the stairs I remembered that Alex had driven out here last night. And as soon as we walked into the living room, I saw her sitting on the couch with Gabriel. They both had coffee cups in their hands.

"You're here," I said. "I'm so glad."

"Hey, you two." She got up from the couch and met us halfway, grabbing both of us in a bear hug. "You guys doing okay?"

"Not too bad," I said. "We had some excitement yesterday."

"So I heard."

"There's a lot going on," Derek said.

We were all talking in understatements.

Gabriel was still sitting on the couch so I turned and asked, "Did you sleep well?"

"Yeah. This sofa makes a pretty good bed." He pulled off the old, torn sweatshirt that he'd obviously slept in, revealing his signature tight black T-shirt. His hair was mussed up from sleep, but he wore a clean pair of khaki cargo pants so he must've had time to pack an overnight bag before he picked me up the night before.

I looked at Alex. "Did you sleep here last night?"

"No, I slept at Gabriel's place." She grinned. "I wanted to bake."

"You baked last night?"

"Yeah. There are cupcakes in the kitchen."

"You are an angel," Derek said.

I checked my wristwatch. It was a quarter to seven. "Has anyone been outside yet?"

"I did a perimeter check at four fifteen," Gabriel said.

"Good man," Derek said.

"And I did another one when I got here at five thirty," Alex said.

"Thanks," I said, feeling safer already.

"You do seem a little calmer this morning," Gabriel said.

Alex rubbed my back. "Did you have a rough time?"

"I was pretty shaken last night," I admitted. "Knowing that Fish Face had found us, and then worrying that he might come after Derek or my family." I rubbed my arms. "Creepy. And we still don't know who he is."

Gabriel leaned forward and rested his elbows on his knees. "But the good news is that we have his photograph from the traffic cam."

Alex said, "Gabriel is running it through his sources and has contacted Interpol as well."

Derek nodded. "We'll find out who he is."

"That was a really lucky catch," I said.

"Sure was." She smiled. "And I heard about the new baby."

"Isn't it great?" I managed to grin back at her. "But you might not have heard that Gabriel won the baby pool."

Gabriel raised his fist in victory. "Yes!"

I laughed. "We're going to go see the baby later this morning." I glanced up at Derek. "But coffee and cupcakes first."

"Absolutely," he said, leading the way into the kitchen. "And maybe a little something else besides cupcakes."

I smacked my forehead. "I forgot to ask. Did you stop at the market last night?"

He shook his head. "I didn't want to take a chance after finding out that Fish Face was in town."

"That was smart." I opened the refrigerator. "We still have some cheese and fruit from yesterday."

"I stopped on the way and picked up some things, too," Alex said, following us into the kitchen.

"You're a lifesaver," I said, and started another pot of coffee. The four of us stood around the kitchen island waiting for the coffeemaker to do its thing. "Have you seen Claire this morning?"

"No," Gabriel said. "But I heard the bathwater running earlier."

"Ah, good," I said. "Guess she finally got her spa experience."

"That sounds intriguing," Alex said.

I chuckled. "The guest bathroom has a big spa tub. She was dying to try it out."

"Good for her," she said. "She could probably use some relaxation time."

At that moment, I heard footsteps on the stairs. "That sounds like Claire now."

A minute later she appeared. "Good morning," she said. "Oh, Alex." She gave her a hug. "So good to see you. But . . . are the cats all right?"

Alex grinned. "Yes, they're fine. Vinnie and Suzie are watching them."

Claire flashed me a look of alarm.

"No worries," I said immediately. "Vinnie and Suzie live right across the hall from me and Derek. They have two cats of their own and they've taken care of Charlie before. So I can promise they'll take good care of Mr. D."

She exhaled. "Okay."

Alex changed topics. "How was your spa experience?"

Claire closed her eyes. "Heaven." Her eyes opened and she laughed. "I feel renewed."

"You look renewed," I said with a grin as I pulled mugs down from the cupboard.

"Yeah, you look great," Alex said.

"Thank you." Her cheeks turned pink from the kind words, but it was all true. Her hair curled down around her shoulders and she looked pretty in a forest-green sweater and blue jeans.

"Coffee's ready," I said.

Everyone grabbed mugs and Derek reached for his phone to text someone about something.

"I'm going to step outside for a few minutes," I said. "The air is so fresh up here. I want to take advantage of it."

"I'll go with you," Claire said. "It's such a beautiful view at the top of the hill."

"Don't go too far," Derek said.

"No worries." We walked out to the front porch.

"I hope they find Fish Face soon," she said quietly. "I can't stand feeling afraid all the time."

"I'm sure they'll catch him today," I said, taking a careful survey of the quiet street, looking for a silver pickup truck and not seeing one. "He's bound to show up at one of our houses and Gabriel's men will trap him."

She gazed around the neighborhood, then pointed. "I love the English garden they've planted on the side of that house."

"That's the Sutherlands' house," I said. "Priscilla Sutherland is English and her garden is her pride and joy. Do you want to go see it?"

"Do you think it's safe?"

I glanced around some more, then poked my head inside the front door. "We're just going over to the Sutherlands' for a minute."

"Be careful," Derek said.

"We will."

"I'll join you on the porch," Alex said. She walked out and sat on the porch swing. "This is nice."

I turned and looked at Claire. "Let's go." But I continued looking every which way as we walked. Claire did the same.

After a few minutes of flower gazing, we strolled back toward the house. Instead of taking the walkway, I headed up the driveway.

"Did you hear that we have a new baby?" I said.

"No, I didn't. That's wonderful."

"It's a little boy. We're going to visit later and you're welcome to come along or stay here and just veg out."

"I'd love to see your family again."

"Okay, we can . . ." My voice faded and I couldn't look away from what I'd just seen.

Claire glanced at me. "What's wrong?" She followed my gaze and saw what I was looking at. "Oh no. Oh God."

She screamed and the sound was deafening, sending more chills up my spine to join the ones that were already living there rent-free. I grabbed her arm. "Let's go. Come on. We're getting out of here."

She buried her face in her hands and trembled uncontrollably.

Alex was already across the lawn and jumping over the trim rosemary hedges onto the driveway.

The body was lying on the driveway in between the passenger side of Derek's elegant black Bentley and the hedges that lined the lawn.

It was the thug we'd been calling Fish Face. Even from this far away I could see the knife stuck deep in his throat and the blood dripping down and forming a small red pool on the concrete. By all indications, this guy was dead.

Chapter 11

It probably wasn't the best thing to obsess over in that moment, but I couldn't help but notice that Derek's Bentley had attracted its share of dead bodies lately.

First there had been Reggie MacDougall lying dead in our parking garage at home. And now Fish Face, bleeding out on the driveway of his parents' home in Dharma. Both of them found next to Derek's flashy black car.

It was weird to keep calling him Fish Face, but that was better than Mr. Peppermint. Finding out his real name would have to wait until the police identified him.

Derek and Gabriel had dashed out to the porch at the sound of Claire's screams.

"What is it? What happened?" Derek demanded.

Alex was leading Claire down the driveway and onto the lawn.

"Are you hurt?" Derek asked her.

"She'll be okay," Alex said.

I realized he couldn't see the body from the porch or the lawn because of the short rosemary hedges.

"Over here," I shouted, and pointed at the body lying

on the driveway. "Fish Face. Dead." At least, I was pretty
sure he was dead.

Gabriel and Derek both ran to the hedges.

"I'll call the police," Gabriel said, and pulled out his
phone. He scanned the area intently as he spoke to the
dispatcher.

Derek stepped over to me and stared into my eyes.
"Are you all right?"

"Yeah. Claire got a little woozy, but I'm okay." It was
weird to see someone else react to blood and death the
way I usually did. I hadn't expected it, not after seeing
the way she'd acted in our parking garage. She had
toughed it out and walked right over to look at Reggie
MacDougall's body. But now she was scared witless.

"I'm fine," she whispered. "Just a wee bit shocky."

I watched Alex help Claire sit down on the porch
swing. Was there something about Fish Face that had
caused Claire to freak out? Maybe she had simply hit a
wall. One dead body was acceptable, but two? Her mind
might've simply had to shut down.

I knew the feeling. And the strange thing was, I
seemed to have had the opposite reaction. Freak out in
the parking garage the other day, but feel ready to get
up close and snap photos today.

Weird.

"It caught her off guard," I murmured to Derek. "We
were enjoying the flowers and next thing you know,
there's a body oozing blood." I rubbed my stomach.
"And hearing myself say those words? It makes my
stomach twist a little."

He rubbed my back. "Then don't say those words."

I smiled, despite feeling gloomy. "Good advice."

He glanced over at Claire, then back at me. "You

may not see it, darling, but the two of you have quite a bit in common."

I gazed up at him. "But she carries a knife. And she knows how to use it."

He raised an eyebrow. "And you've got an entire toolbox filled with instruments of torture."

"I only use my bookbinding tools for good."

As he laughed, I wrapped my arms around his waist and laid my head on his shoulder, just for a few seconds. I needed this moment. I couldn't believe we were once again standing by another dead body. And once again I had to assume that it was all about a book.

With one last squeeze, I let him go. "You need to see what's up with the dead guy before the police get here." I added, "I'd do it myself, but you know. Blood. Yuck."

He gave me a sympathetic smile and a quick kiss. "Why don't you go over and sit on the porch?"

"Good idea."

He glanced around and found Gabriel pacing where the driveway met the street, still on the phone. Derek stooped down to check out the body.

Instead of going directly to the porch, I took a few steps closer to the body to see what Derek was doing. And suddenly I had a perfect view of that knife sticking out of the man's neck. Talk about *yuck*. But I persevered.

I noticed the hilt of the knife glittering in the morning sunlight. It was similar to the antique weapon that had killed Reggie MacDougall.

Someone with a sick talent for knives must have killed both of the thugs who'd been tormenting Claire. Did she know who it was?

Without thinking, I moved even closer, pulled my

phone out of my tunic pocket, and took three different
shots of the knife hilt so I could show them to Claire.
And only then did I notice that the blood was beginning
to crust on the dead guy's neck. I quickly executed a
world-class moonwalk all the way down the driveway to
the street.

Gabriel looked up. "Hey, you okay?"

"Oh yeah," I said, in spite of my head beginning to
spin. "I'm groovy."

"Cops'll be here any minute."

"Good," I said. "I'll be waiting on the porch with
Alex and Claire."

He walked over to join Derek and they proceeded to
do a cursory examination of the body, apparently looking for any clues that might explain who this guy was
and who could've murdered him.

Who could've murdered him?

"Oh no," I said with a groan, stopping halfway up the
walk. "Who murdered him?"

"What's wrong, Brooklyn?" Alex called, and I realized she must've been watching me.

I hurried the rest of the way to join her and Claire.
"Who murdered him?"

"What?" Alex said, frowning.

"Who murdered him?" I repeated, and sat down on the
step. "At first I thought this guy, Fish Face, was the one
who killed Reggie MacDougall. You know, Pizza Man."

"Aye," Claire said. "That makes sense."

Alex nodded. "Sure."

I glanced from Alex to Claire. "Except, who killed
Fish Face?"

Claire stared at me for a long moment, then gazed
over at Derek and Gabriel, who were searching the dead
man's pockets. "Oh dear."

"Yeah," I said, nodding dramatically. "Oh dear."

Alex took a deep breath and let it out slowly. "I should've been way ahead of you on this one, but I've only had a few hours' sleep."

"Understood." I sat down on the top porch step.

She turned to check on Claire. "How are you doing?"

Claire, whose color had begun to return to her face, turned as pale as a ghost again. She took slow, even breaths, trying to calm down. "I'm worrying over the fact that someone just killed off the two men who were terrorizing me."

"Which means there's someone else out there," I murmured.

"Yes," Alex said.

Claire closed her eyes. "Seeing that body reminded me of that scene at the end of *The Castle of Otranto*, when Manfred mistakenly stabs his own daughter Matilda."

Alex cringed. "What?"

I remembered the book and could envision the horribly tragic climax. "What made you think of that scene?"

She leaned forward. "Do you remember it?"

"All I remember is that the whole book was convoluted and tragic. Didn't the father and mother go off at the end to become a monk and a nun?"

"Yes." She grinned suddenly. "Great fun. And quite grisly."

I bit back a laugh. "You are too much."

"Do real-life scenes often remind you of books?" Alex asked.

"Oh, aye." Her color was back and she nodded enthusiastically. "I wasn't close to a lot of girls my age growing up so I spent much of my time in the pages of books. So now when I see something or meet someone, it often reminds me of a scene or a character."

"You are fascinating," Alex said.

Claire laughed uncomfortably. "That's one way to put it."

"Alex, you said that you did a perimeter check when you arrived here at five thirty this morning."

"That's right."

I nodded. "So this guy and his killer must've snuck up here at some point after that."

Alex scowled. "That's right. I should've been keeping an eye out, but you know how it goes."

"Sure. We were all talking and catching up with one another." Something occurred to me and I turned to Claire. "Can you think of anyone who might be trying to protect you?"

"By killing people who are trying to hurt me, you mean?" she asked, her voice a bit shrill—and who could blame her?

I shrugged. "It's hard to explain otherwise."

"I suppose, but . . ." She didn't go on, just shivered.

Alex nudged my arm with her elbow. "Let's table this for now. We'll wait for the police to get here and do their thing. Then once they're gone, the five of us can talk this through."

"And plot our next move," I added.

As if we'd summoned them, we heard the sirens approach. Within seconds, a black-and-white cop car zoomed up the hill and parked in front of the house. A black SUV followed behind them and parked on the other side of the street.

At that moment I remembered something. "Claire, I took pictures of the knife. Do you want to see them before the police talk to us?"

"Oh yes," she said.

I handed my phone to her and she studied the photo. "It's mid-nineteenth century." She swiped her finger across the screen to look at the other pictures. "Yes. It's a style that was normally carried by a Scottish Highlands officer, although this one is rather elaborate so the fellow might've been a landowner. As you can see, the hilt is carved ebony with silver embellishments and an inlaid faceted glass stone on the pommel."

"That's amazing," Alex said, then watched as the officers approached. "Okay, here we go." She turned to Claire. "You ready for this?"

Her eyes were wide with concern. "Aye. I think."

"They're going to want to question all of us," Alex said. "Especially when they find out about the body we found in our parking garage."

Claire groaned. "Do we have to tell them?"

I totally understood her pain. "They'll find out whether we tell them or not."

"So it's better if we mention it up front," she said, and nodded. "Got it."

The two officers stopped to view the body, then continued toward us. We stood and walked down the walkway to meet them.

The driver of the SUV climbed out, slammed the door shut, and crossed the street.

"Stevie!" I called, then winced. "Sorry. Detective Willoughby. How are you?"

"Hey, Brooklyn," he said, walking up to the house. "Good to see you."

I had gone to grammar school with Stevie, but he had moved to Minnesota in high school. He had recently returned to Dharma after ten years with the Minneapolis police department, just in time to be offered the job of head cop of the newly formed Dharma Police Force. He was cute and blond and a star athlete. And he was very polite, which earned him extra points with my mother.

I gave him a quick hug and introduced him to Alex and Claire. Then Derek and Gabriel walked across the lawn to greet him. *One big happy family*, I thought. Except for the dead guy over there.

"Detective," Derek said as the two men shook hands. "Thanks for coming out."

"Looks like you've had some trouble," Stevie said. He nodded toward the dead guy, causing all of us to turn and stare at the body.

"This is the guy I told you about," Gabriel explained.

Last night Gabriel had said that he didn't want to involve the cops. So maybe he had told Stevie the situation when he called a few minutes ago. I thought he had called 911, but Gabriel knew everyone, so now I wondered if he had called Stevie directly.

"Looks like someone stopped him permanently," Stevie said.

"Yeah." Gabriel turned and stared at Detective Willoughby. "It wasn't any of my people."

"We don't think he's anyone local," Derek said. "I can't see anyone from Dharma being involved in his death."

"How can you say that?" Stevie asked, pulling out a small notebook and pen. Every cop I'd ever known used something very similar to take their notes.

Derek brought his full Commander status to the fore. "This man has been identified as a person of interest in several crimes that recently took place in San Francisco. Specifically, he and another fellow had been harassing our friend Claire for the past few days. The other fellow was killed two days ago in our parking garage in the city. If you want to follow up on that incident, you should contact Inspector Janice Lee at the Hall of Justice on Bryant Street. I have the number if you want it."

As the three men walked across the lawn to join us, Derek pulled out his phone and gave Stevie the number for Inspector Lee.

Stevie looked at Claire with sympathy. "I'm sorry to hear about your troubles. Are you all right?"

"Yes, thank you. I just wish I knew who was behind it all." She glanced at the body. "I thought it was that fellow, but now that someone has killed him, I honestly don't know what to think."

"Okay," Stevie said. "Why don't you all wait inside and my officers will speak to you one at a time."

Once the officers had finished with all of us, they left to go knock on the neighbors' doors to see if anyone had witnessed any unusual activity earlier that morning.

At some point, a team from the coroner's unit of the Sonoma County Sheriff's Department arrived and determined that Mr. Fish Face had indeed been murdered, and they were looking at a homicide. After emptying the contents of his pockets into evidence bags and removing the knife from his neck, they zipped him into a body bag and carried him to the van. Then they drove off to have the body autopsied.

Stevie came inside to talk to us one last time. "I'll contact you if I need to follow up on any issues. There is one more thing." He held up a plastic evidence bag that contained the antique knife. "Do any of you recognize this knife?"

"May I please see it?" Claire said.

Stevie's eyes narrowed as he brought the bag closer and lifted it up for her to get a better look.

"Claire is an expert in antique weaponry," I quickly explained. "She worked for a few years on *This Old Attic*, so she knows her stuff."

"Hey, I like that show," he said with a grin.

Claire studied the knife through the clear plastic and then told Stevie almost word for word what she had told Alex and me. She ended by saying, "The hilt is carved ebony with silver embellishments and an inlaid faceted glass stone on the pommel."

I realized that must've been what I saw glistening in the sunlight and asked, "What's the pommel?"

"It's the butt end of the hilt," Claire said, then looked back at Stevie. "The blade appears to have been sharpened recently."

"You do seem to know your stuff," Stevie said, and winked at me. "Have you seen this specific knife before?"

She seemed taken aback by the question but answered succinctly. "I've seen dirks and daggers very similar to this style, but I don't believe I've ever seen this particular weapon before."

"Okay, thanks. That was very educational. I might call you if I need more details."

She nodded. "I gave my contact information to Officer Perkins."

"Thank you."

"Oh, Detective," I said. "Were you able to identify the dead guy?"

"Yes." He pulled out his notebook and flipped back the pages. "His driver's license identifies him as Jerome Smith."

*   *   *

Stevie left a few minutes later and Derek and I began to put breakfast together. Claire, Alex, and Gabriel sat and drank coffee at the kitchen table while we set down a platter of pastries and a bowl filled with hard-boiled eggs, both courtesy of Alex. I cut up some strawberries and apples and arranged them on another platter with the leftover cheese. It wasn't your typical massive English breakfast, but it worked for us.

While I was searching the drawers for serving utensils, I leaned up close to Derek. "I saw you going through Fish Face's pockets. What did you find?"

"Some cash and coin," he said, not bothering to lower his voice.

I frowned at him. "Wait. You didn't take them, did you?"

Derek placed a butter dish and a small bowl of strawberry jam on the table. "I did. I pilfered a five-pound note and a 10p coin."

His easygoing answer made me laugh. "But why?"

"I wanted to show them to Claire."

"Oh yes," Claire said, perking up. "I do want to see them."

I put serving forks and spoons on each platter and glanced at Derek. "Let's sit down."

We sat, and Derek pulled the note and the coin from his pocket and handed them to her. "Tell me what you think."

"It's a Scottish five-pound note," she said, frowning. "You'd only use it in Scotland because they're not always accepted elsewhere. Most people carry British sterling because they're accepted all over, naturally."

She picked up the coin. "10p. It's British, of course, as you must know."

Derek nodded and continued, "You can use the coin anywhere in England and Scotland."

Claire looked at Derek. "That man was carrying these?"

"Yes."

"So . . ." She nodded, then swallowed nervously, her throat obviously dry. She reached for her water glass and took a big gulp. "So he followed me from Scotland." Her voice began to shake as the realization was setting in.

"I'm sorry," Derek said. "But I can't see any other reason he'd be walking around Dharma with Scottish money in his pocket unless he'd recently arrived from Scotland."

I asked, "Is the name Jerome Smith familiar to you?"

"I know any number of Smiths," she said. "Don't know any named Jerome."

"Smith is such a common name," Alex said.

"Aye," Claire said. "It's the most common name in Scotland. Because of the silversmiths and blacksmiths and all the other metalworkers over the centuries who supplied our soldiers with swords and dirks and jewelry and such."

"Same as here," Alex said, reaching for another egg.

Suddenly a look of sheer anguish came over Claire's face. "He might've been on my plane."

Gabriel frowned and pulled out his phone. "I'm going to give Willoughby a call." He pressed a button and waited for the detective to answer. "Hey, Detective, it's Gabriel."

He listened for a moment. "Yeah, you mentioned this guy's driver's license. Was it from California?" He listened for another moment, then grinned. "No kidding. Thanks a lot for your help."

He ended the call and looked at each of us. "Jerome Smith was carrying a Scottish driver's license."

"Now there's no doubt," Claire said with a sigh.

"He was definitely from Scotland." I set down my coffee mug. "And I'll bet his buddy Reggie MacDougall was, too. And whoever killed Fish Face, er, Jerome Smith, probably traveled here from Scotland, as well."

"So they had three men follow you all the way to San Francisco," Alex said, reaching out to squeeze Claire's hand. "They must consider you a formidable opponent."

I could tell that Derek's mind was working, trying to figure out what was really going on, but he said nothing.

"Were they following Claire?" I wondered. "Or were they looking for the book?"

"How could they think that Claire would lead them to the book?" Gabriel asked.

Claire made a sound of pure disgust. "But I did just that. I led them right to the book. And right to you." She looked at Derek and me. "And now your lives are in danger, too."

I shook my finger at her. "None of this is your fault."

"You keep saying that and I appreciate it, I do." She stood up to pace the room and I noticed her accent grew thicker as her fear level rose. "Och! I've been a radge bringin' ya naught but trooble."

I held up my hand to stop her. "Translation, please."

It seemed to bring her back because she laughed ruefully. "Sorry. I said I've been a dangerous fool and have brought you nothing but trouble."

"Don't be daft," I said.

Her laugh was lighter this time. "I do appreciate you, Brooklyn."

"I appreciate you, too." Then I turned to Derek. "So, are you thinking what I'm thinking?"

He studied my expression. "Always, love."

I smiled. "Good."

He inhaled sharply, then breathed out. I realized that he was angry, really angry as he glanced around the table. "It's time we tracked down the source of the trouble."

"High time," Gabriel agreed.

Derek managed to shake off the temper, gritted his teeth, and squared his shoulders. When he looked at me again he was smiling, but his eyes were narrowed and that gave me more of a chill than any scowl he could summon up. "We're going to take a little trip."

Chapter 12

Claire froze in mid-pace. "Where are you going?"

"To Scotland," I said, reading Derek's mind, as always.

"But . . ."

"You're coming with us, Claire," I added.

She heaved a sigh of relief. "I am?"

"We can't go without you." Derek's dark eyes gleamed. "I hear it's lovely there this time of year."

"But what if he follows me back there?" The tone of her voice quickly rose again, moving from fear straight into panic. I couldn't really blame her. "He could get on the same airplane with us. He could—"

"That won't happen," Derek said flatly.

"But we don't even know who he is," she cried. "Or what he looks like."

"It doesn't matter," Derek said softly. "We're taking a private jet."

Gabriel smirked. "Fancy."

"Oh yeah, it's fancy all right." I had to laugh. "Derek's sister-in-law owns the company." I glanced at Derek. "You called her?"

He nodded. "While you were taking your walk with Claire."

"I remember your sister-in-law Daphne," Alex said. "Married to Duncan, right?"

"That's right," I said. "You met them at our wedding."

"Sure did," she said. "We had a nice long talk over several glasses of champagne. She's a kick in the pants."

"I was hoping you two would hit it off." I reached for the empty platters and began to clear the table. "She purports to be a housewife and mother, but I'm pretty sure her security clearance is higher than anyone's in this room."

"That's true and it's quite lowering," Derek said.

I grinned. "Well, when your family supplies fighter jets to the Royal Air Force, it's got to come with some perks."

Derek turned to Gabriel. "If you're willing, I would appreciate it if you'd follow us back to the city."

"Whenever you're ready," he said easily.

"And I'll be right behind you," Alex said, standing and picking up the bowl that was now empty of hard-boiled eggs.

"And my guys will continue staking out your family's places here in Dharma until we get the word that the danger has passed."

"Thank you for that, and for everything else." My family would be safe, and Gabriel and Alex would provide extra security for Claire as we drove into the city. I wanted to hug them both.

Alex gave Claire a warm smile. "And once I'm back in the city, I'll take over the cat duty."

"Oh, thank you. I'm very grateful for everything. And so is Mr. D, even if he doesn't appear to appreciate your kindnesses."

Alex laughed. "We have an understanding."

"We can't leave Dharma right away," Derek said. "Brooklyn and I have to meet our new nephew first."

"Aw," Alex said. "That's sweet."

I totally agreed. Derek knew there was no way I could leave without first seeing our darling new baby, James Robert.

"Hey, I want to see the little guy, too," Gabriel said.

I scoffed. "You want to collect your winnings."

He grinned. "Damn straight."

"Claire," Derek said. "If you can think of a hotel or two in Oddlochen that might accommodate Brooklyn and myself on short notice, I would be very appreciative."

"We haven't any actual hotels in town, but there are some lovely B and B's."

Derek glanced at me and I shrugged. "We'll have to take what we can get." I looked at Claire. "We want to be right in town, if possible."

"I know just the place."

"I assumed that you usually stay at your aunt's apartment, but if you don't feel safe there, you should book a room in the same B and B where we'll be staying."

She thought about it. "I always felt perfectly safe until this last trip. I'll feel better staying at the B and B with you."

"Good," I said. "We'll watch out for each other."

We hurried upstairs to pack up our things and Derek made a phone call to his assistant Corinne to let her know our plans.

While Derek chatted on the phone, I packed the rest of our things and straightened up the bedroom and bathroom. I realized we would have to come back to Dharma before Derek's parents returned so we could wash all the sheets and towels and make the beds properly.

I couldn't imagine our trip to Scotland taking more than a week. We would get to town, find the bell tower, look under the wooden plank, and . . . then what? Abracadabra, Gwyneth appeared? Not likely. We needed a plan.

Derek ended the call with Corinne and checked his text messages. "Daphne says the plane will be waiting for us at the Executive Terminal at eight o'clock tonight."

I checked my watch. It was almost noon now. "How can it get there so fast? Isn't it coming from England?"

"It's coming down from British Columbia," he said. "A few of their executives are flying there for a conference and they're set to arrive in a few hours. Once the plane is cleaned up and restocked with all the best goodies, as Daphne said, the pilot will take off for San Francisco and pick us up on his way back to the UK."

"That was lucky."

"Yes." Derek zipped up his overnight bag. "I anticipated leaving sometime tomorrow, but this is perfect. We'll land at Inverness tomorrow in midafternoon and be in Oddlochen before dark."

"And hopefully be checked into the perfect B and B before nightfall."

"I'll let Claire know what time we're leaving tonight and our estimated time of arrival in Scotland."

We walked out to the hall. "We might as well see if she's still in her room." I knocked on Claire's bedroom door, but there was no answer.

I knocked again loudly and called, "Claire?"

"She must've gone downstairs already."

"Of course." When we reached the first floor, we didn't see anyone. Derek walked to the front door and opened it. "They're out here."

I didn't know why it made me nervous when Claire didn't answer my knock or when I didn't see anyone downstairs. But I figured I'd better get used to my nerves going wonky for the next few days.

Alex and Claire sat on the bottom porch steps and Gabriel stood talking to them. When we walked out, Gabriel said, "Hey, wanted to let you know I'll come by and scrub down the driveway as soon as Detective Steve gives me the high sign."

"That's so nice of you," I said.

"Thanks, mate," Derek said. "My parents will really appreciate it."

"They'll never have to know," Gabriel said. "I'll do it in the next few days, before the blood gets caked into the concrete."

"I appreciate it." Derek gave a short salute. "Above and beyond the call of duty."

"Thanks, Gabriel," I said, and gave him a hug. "You're the best."

"It's true," he said with a shrug.

I laughed, then turned to Claire. "Are you all packed?"

"Yes, but I'm afraid I'll need a few more things before we take off for Scotland. Would you mind if we stopped by my house? It won't take me more than five minutes."

"You can take longer," I said. "Derek and I have to pack, too. Mainly because we'll be gone for a while and I know it'll be colder in Inverness than it is here."

"It's always a bit chilly on the Loch," Claire said.

"I've never been much farther north than Edinburgh," I confessed.

"It can get up to ten degrees colder in Inverness."

"Do you think it might rain?"

"There's always a chance," she said. "Don't forget to pack your brolly and a mac."

"Thanks for the reminder." I'd always liked that an umbrella was called a "brolly" and a raincoat was a "mac," short for "mackintosh," in Great Britain. I pulled out my phone and started making a list of things to pack.

"You're the cutest little thing I've ever seen," I cooed. "Yes, you are. Yes, you are."

I sat in the rocking chair next to Robin's bed and gazed at the tiny baby in my arms. "I love how he just stares at me."

"He thinks you're pretty," Robin said.

"Right." I laughed, then looked down at the baby. "Your mommy is crazy. Yes, she is. Yes, she is."

Robin and Austin had decided to call the baby Jamie in order to differentiate him from my father Jim, especially since my mother often called him Jimmy.

"He can call himself whatever he wants to when he's older," Robin had said.

"Be careful. He might want to call himself Nimrod."

"And we'll love him just the same."

I snorted, but left it at that.

"Where did your friend go?" she asked, glancing around the spacious suite. The room had reached its capacity of nine people, but she didn't seem to mind the crowd as long as she could keep track of who was holding the baby.

"Claire? I think she went to the cafeteria with Alex."

"She's got the most gorgeous red hair," she said.

"I know. Hey, do you remember seeing her on *This Old Attic*?"

"Actually, I do. I thought she was wicked smart and

knew everything about the guns and swords they featured. It's almost like she was obsessed with them, but in a fun way."

I smiled. "She insists she's not obsessive, just kind of a freak about some things."

"That works for me," Robin said, then smiled at the baby. "How's my angel doing?"

"I think he's fallen asleep from the rocking."

"Oh, good. Let him sleep. Don't move a muscle."

"I won't. I love holding him."

"Do you really?" She grinned and wiggled her eyebrows suggestively. "Derek enjoyed holding him, too."

I could read her like a book. *When are you and Derek going to have a little one of your own?*

"Don't look at me like that," I said, shaking my head. "You of all people. Derek and I have a few years to go before we make any decisions like that."

"I didn't say a word." But her Cheshire cat smile said it all.

She closed her eyes and I realized she had to be exhausted. I cautiously checked my wristwatch and saw that we'd been here almost an hour. "We've got to be going pretty soon."

She slowly opened her eyes. "Do you know when you'll be back?"

"Probably in a few weeks," I said, keeping an eye on the little one, who was still sleeping. "I'm hoping the next time, we'll be able to stay in our own house."

"I'm so happy you decided to build a house. You'll be coming up a lot more now and you can watch Jamie grow up."

"The next time we visit, he'll already be much bigger."

"I hope he doesn't grow up too fast," she murmured.

"Well, don't feed him so much."

She laughed as I hoped she would since she looked like she'd been about to cry. I stopped rocking and looked around for my mother. I needn't have worried. Mom had been keeping an eagle eye out for me, waiting for her turn to hold the baby again. She hurried over to take little Jamie so I could stand up.

"Finally I get you all to myself, you little cutie," she said, and sat down in the rocker.

"He's adorable, isn't he?" I whispered.

"Absolutely precious," Mom said. "Hey, guess what. Gabriel got his winnings and promised me he was going to use it to open a savings account for Jamie."

"That's pretty great," I said, smiling.

"He's a good guy," Mom said. She had always had a soft spot for Gabriel and had even helped nurse him back to health when he ran into some deadly trouble a few years back.

I watched Jamie for another few seconds, then gave Mom a kiss on the cheek. "We'll be taking off soon so we'll see you in a few weeks."

"I love you, honey," she said.

"Love you, too, Mom." I brushed my hand across Jamie's tiny head. "Take care of this little bean for me."

"I'm on the case, sweetie pie."

I chuckled as I walked over and sat down on the edge of Robin's bed. "We've got to go. I'm sorry."

"That's okay." She took hold of my hand. "You'll be back."

"Of course. I can't wait. You stay healthy, okay?"

"I'm too healthy," she griped. "I want to lose this baby weight."

"We'll work out together when I come back."

She frowned. "Maybe don't hurry back, okay?"

We both laughed, then I said, "I really miss you."

She sniffed. "You're just trying to make me cry."

"Is it working?"

She bit back a smile. "Get out of here."

I leaned in and kissed her cheek. "I'll see you soon."

"Be careful," she said. "Stay safe."

"Always." But as I walked out of the room with Derek, I worried whether we'd actually be able to stay safe while some vicious killer was on our trail.

The drive back to San Francisco was uneventful, which was all I could hope it would be. No crazed murderer swerving behind us, trying to push us over the bridge. I'd had those thoughts the whole way home, thanks to my overactive imagination.

Claire actually snoozed for a short time, and that was amazing to me since she had spent a good part of the trip bouncing back and forth between frantic and hysterical. But who could blame her? At least she was calm for now. It wasn't until we approached Sausalito that she spoke. "We didn't make it to the dojo."

"No," I said. "And we didn't go wine tasting. It just means we'll have to come back in a few weeks."

"I would love to," she said wistfully.

"Our house will be finished by then. You'll stay with us."

She didn't say anything and after a minute, I turned around. "You okay?"

She sniffed. "I'm so lucky I met you two."

"You're not going to thank us again, are you?"

She laughed, as I'd hoped she would.

"We're lucky, too," Derek said.

I met Claire's glance and we both sighed happily at Derek's perfect response.

* * *

We hadn't told any of our family that we were taking off tonight. I didn't want to take the chance that some bad guy would get wind of our plans and hop on the next plane headed for Scotland. Our enemies would discover where we'd gone sooner or later.

While I packed a larger suitcase and Derek pulled our passports out of the safe, Claire played with Mr. D. Then Alex and Gabriel came by and there were hugs all around. Their plan while we were in Scotland was to stay at Alex's with the cats and watch the building for any sinister activity. But first Gabriel would drive us to the airport after a quick stop at Claire's house.

Claire didn't want to stay inside her ransacked house for more than a few minutes. She explained that she kept a lot of clothing at her aunt's place, so all she really needed were some toiletries and books and a few of her favorite knives. And within ten minutes we were on the road to the airport.

The private jet was waiting for us at the Executive Terminal less than a quarter mile from the main airport terminals. As far as I was concerned, this terminal was a million miles away in terms of luxury and tranquillity. I normally didn't mind traveling, but I had to face the fact that in the last few years, airports had become the epicenter of mass chaos.

As I walked up the stairs and stepped into the plane, I had to stop and soak it all in. "Wow, this is impressive."

"Absolutely deluxe," Derek agreed.

"We're going to owe Daphne for this," I whispered to Derek.

"She told me she'd take a week at our new place in Dharma in exchange for this trip."

"Really? We can do that. That's easy."

Claire was already on the plane and was simply walking around staring. When she saw me, her smile lit up. "I have chills and they're the good kind for once. This is heavenly."

"Yeah, it's really cool."

There were eight leather chairs spaced throughout the main cabin. Each was big and wide and comfortable. They reclined completely so that we could sleep when we wanted to. They also rotated so that we could face one another and talk easily. The wide tray tables swung out from the side panels and they, too, were much larger than what I was used to in a regular airplane.

I told myself I would simply enjoy this onetime experience and let it go at that. But I was afraid I was already spoiled, just having walked onto the plane.

I settled myself in my seat and pushed my hefty overnight bag into the side panel next to me. Since the flight would be more than ten hours long, I had brought my bookbinding tools and supplies with me, hoping I might be able to dedicate some time to my origami project or to Claire's *Mistress of Mellyn* that was in such sad need of repair.

I also had the *Rebecca* with me and hoped to find some time during the flight to page through it in case we had missed anything else that might be important. After all, I thought, Aunt Gwyneth had sent it to Derek for a very specific reason and I had to wonder if those marked letters were the only thing she'd wanted him to see.

The pilot, a tall, gray-haired man who could've played a pilot on TV with his straight shoulders and military bearing, walked into the cabin and introduced himself. "I'm Commander Frank Simpson and I'll be your pilot for this flight."

Derek stood. "Hello, Commander."

"You must be Derek Stone," he said, shaking Derek's hand and flashing a self-deprecating grin. "I figured that out all by myself when I saw you come aboard with two women."

"Well done," Derek said, chuckling.

Derek introduced him to Claire and me, and Commander Simpson shook our hands as well. "Mrs. Stone sends her regards and has advised me that you're in quite a hurry. So let me assure you that we'll get you to Inverness as quickly and safely as possible. We'll be making one fuel stop in Goose Bay on the east coast of Canada, and then it's straight on to Inverness. Enjoy your flight."

We all murmured our thanks and watched him return to the cockpit.

"So Daphne spoke directly to the pilot," I said. "She is a goddess."

Derek nodded. "She does carry some clout."

I grinned. "You can say that again."

Claire gazed at Derek and me. "Before we land and get swept up in all the madness that surely awaits us, I want to say something. And I don't want any back talk."

I blinked and glanced at Derek. "Okay."

She smiled. "I just want to thank you so much for including me on this flight. Honestly, I feel like Cinderella."

"I know what you mean," I said with a laugh. "It's totally freaking deluxe."

"Well put, darling," Derek said. "But, Claire, you're included on this flight because you're a vital part of this mission and we're determined to keep you safe. Got it?"

She stared at him for a few long seconds. "Aye. Got it."

"I'm not sure I'll be able to sleep but I'd like to," I said.

"If we can all get a few hours' sleep, it'll be helpful. We'll hit the ground running tomorrow and we'll need to be in top form."

As the plane taxied down the runway, Claire said, "I'm going to try to chill out and maybe sleep for a few hours myself."

"Okay, good luck," I said.

She mumbled her thanks and turned to face the window.

Derek took hold of my hand as the plane climbed into the air. I closed my eyes and my mind automatically drifted back to *Rebecca*. I told myself I needed to devote more time to figuring out what else was in the book besides those marked-off letters. I could flip through the pages, but I thought it might be better if I simply read the book in its entirety. I certainly had enough time. And after all, *Rebecca* was the reason why we were all flying off to Inverness in the middle of the night. That, and the fact that Aunt Gwyneth was still missing.

I pulled the book out of my overnight bag and began reading. Once the plane reached cruising altitude, the pilot indicated that it was safe for us to move around. Seconds later, a man walked into the cabin pushing a drink cart. "Good evening, I'm Shane, your flight attendant. Because of our late departure, we're serving appetizer-sized meals of Atlantic lobster with curried coconut sauce, tomato and cheese polenta, and peppered beef tenderloin with cranberries and spinach custard."

"Sounds wonderful," I murmured.

He placed a lovely plate of those three small servings on each of our linen-covered tray tables. They all looked good and smelled even better.

Claire sat up to check out the meal. All three of us asked for sparkling water, then Shane and his cart disappeared after wishing us *bon appétit*.

"I'm still going to try and sleep, but I must try these lovely little bites."

"Everything looks delicious."

Claire curled up in her chair and nibbled while reading a paperback novel. She looked wiped out and I would be surprised if she managed to stay awake through the meal.

I took a forkful of polenta. "This is really delicious."

"It truly is," Derek said. "I'll have to remember to tell Daphne how fabulous everything is."

I scooped up a small piece of lobster coated in sauce, took a bite, and wanted to moan. I systematically finished everything on my plate and sat back in my chair, happily stuffed. I glanced over at Claire, who appeared to be sleeping after taking a few small bites. *She must've been exhausted*, I thought.

I, on the other hand, seemed to have found my second wind. I pushed my plate aside and continued to read the *Rebecca*.

"What are you thinking you'll do with that?" Derek asked quietly.

"I thought I'd read the whole book. Maybe I'll notice something else that Gwyneth wanted us to see."

"I was wondering about that myself," he said. "Hoping we might find more clues inside the book besides the marked letters."

"Would you like to go through it before me?"

"No, you go ahead. You're better than I am at working out those small, vital details."

"Thank you, I think." I smiled up at him. "What are you going to be doing?"

"I'll stick with my strengths," he said cryptically.

"So you're going to shoot somebody?"

He smirked. "Very funny. No, I'm trying to come up with an overall plan of attack."

"Ah, the big picture stuff."

He hid a smile. "That's right."

"And how is your plan coming together?"

"It's not. We don't have enough pieces of the puzzle to really scope out a strategy. I think we'll have to wait until we arrive in Oddlochen."

"Makes sense." I sipped my water, then stared at the book. "I really want to know who's behind the men who came after Claire. You know they wanted this book. I'm just not sure if part of their plan was to kill Claire to get it."

"My guess is that, yes, they would've killed her to get the book. And what's more, I believe they'd be just as happy to kill you and me, as well."

"Pleasant thought," I muttered.

"Sorry, love."

"That's okay." I frowned. "I just wish I had more skills."

"Your skill as a book restoration expert is unparalleled."

I laughed lightly. "By skills, I meant martial arts. Or knife throwing. It would be fun to be able to throw a weapon and take someone down."

"You're already learning martial arts, and according to Alex, you're getting quite good."

"Did she tell you that?"

"She did. But as far as throwing knives or axes, you've only to look it up online. They have classes in everything."

"I know. But I never even considered learning to

throw a knife until Claire came along. You know she carries a knife wherever she goes."

"I'm aware."

I sipped my water. "It's kind of awesome."

"Perhaps she'll give you a lesson or two while we're in Scotland."

"That would be so cool."

"I'll be happy to," Claire mumbled, bringing her chair up to the full sitting position.

"Sorry, Claire," I said. "Did we wake you?"

"I wasn't really sleeping. Just trying to rest my eyes. But instead I was smelling the food and getting hungrier by the minute. And then I heard you talking and I had to join in." She took her first bite of polenta and her eyes grew wider. "Oh, this is fine, isn't it?"

"It is, for sure."

"So what were you talking about?"

I glanced up at Derek, then said, "I was wishing I had some skill like yours. Throwing knives seems like an excellent means of self-defense."

"I suppose it is, although I've never thrown a knife in self-defense."

"Really?" I said. "How did you first get interested in antique weapons? Was it because of your parents' antiques shop?"

"Yes. My father and my aunt grew up in the antiques business. My aunt still has her collectibles shop in Oddlochen."

"The one you said was a cover for her espionage activities?" I asked.

Embarrassed, she pressed a hand to her cheek. "I was being very rude," she admitted.

"I believe you felt a bit trapped," Derek said. "It's fine. Don't apologize."

"All right." She exhaled slowly. "The shop may have been a cover, but Aunt Gwyneth really does love to sell and trade antiques and old things. My father was more involved in the acquisition side of the business."

"So he bought weapons?"

She leaned her head back on the soft leather chair. "No. Actually, I'm not sure if he bought them or *stole* them." She sighed. "I was too young to really know. But I do know that he got himself into trouble more than once. Nevertheless, he was a wonderful father, funny, caring, supportive."

"Is he the one who taught you how to use a knife?"

"Oh, no. I was much too young at the time. But he influenced me. I wanted to be good at it because I knew that when he finally returned, he would be impressed. So I practiced with knives and a throwing axe." She frowned. "And a crossbow and a rifle. And other things."

"So this was in Scotland," I said. "Did you go out into the woods to do all that?"

She smiled. "Yes. And at school we had a shooting range and archery field. I became the top in my class. You might've noticed that when I get involved in something, I have a tendency to take it to the nth degree." She took a bite of beef and closed her eyes to savor it. After a moment she continued. "It was that way when I went to college, too. I'd find a field of study I enjoyed and I'd stay with it until I wound up with a degree."

"How many degrees did you end up with?"

"Four," she said, looking embarrassed.

"Four degrees?" I said, incredulous. "That settles it. I'm a total slacker."

"You're not a slacker." She studied her fork self-consciously. "Honestly, sometimes I think I just didn't have anything else to do, so I studied incessantly. And as far as knife throwing, I remember my father telling me that I would always be a petite little thing. Because of my mother, you see. And he was right. So knowing how to use different weapons is my way of leveling the playing field, as they say."

"Wow. Have many dates in high school?"

She threw back her head and laughed. "Most of them ended badly."

"I'm still getting over the fact that you have *four* degrees."

"Four postgraduate degrees," she admitted. "And a BA, of course. Undergraduate."

"Of course," I said.

She smiled. "I probably sound crazy to you."

"I'd only go so far as to say 'quirky,'" I said. "But that's okay. Some people think I'm quirky, too."

She laughed. "I do have little quirks, like I'll often check and recheck something over and over. A reservation, or directions, or a series of numbers. I absolutely must have order in my life. Everything in its place."

"I'm that way in my work," I said, trying to relate.

She shook her head. "People love to judge others with idiosyncrasies and special interests. I *am* proud to be a collector. I have hundreds of knives and axes and crossbows. I love crossbows. I also have a number of guns and rifles, too, although they don't interest me as much. My aunt insisted that I learn in order to protect myself. But now I avoid them except when it comes to pointing out historical features and for appraisal purposes."

"But you do have some guns in your collection?" Derek asked.

"Aye. Mostly antique pieces. Dueling pistols, of course. Several Colt handguns and two early versions of the Winchester rifle, the so-called 'gun that won the West.' A Buffalo rifle from 1864. Some old muskets."

Derek stared at her quizzically. "But guns scare you."

She smiled. "Believe it or not, they do. I've never cared for artillery fire. None of my guns are ever loaded. I don't own any bullets."

"Huh," I said. "Interesting."

"Interesting and maybe a little quirky, right? But I'm fine with that." She stretched her arms and shoulders. "The history and the details are what I love most. I suppose you could call weapons an obsession for me, but it's a good obsession because it's my job. And it makes me happy to know the facts about things."

"What are you most proficient at?" Derek asked.

She pressed her lips together, clearly hesitant to continue talking about herself. But then she gave in. "I'm quite skilled with knives and I do love throwing axes."

"Will you teach me to throw an axe?" I asked immediately.

She smiled. "Of course."

"Yay!" I said. "Thanks."

She laughed. "Okay. That's enough about me."

"No, it's not," I said. "I want to hear about those four degrees you have. You don't seem old enough to have earned four degrees."

"I'll tell you," she said. "But I want to hear about you first. How did you go about getting a degree in book-binding?"

I blew out a breath. It was late and I should've been exhausted, but I was having a good time chatting with Claire. "I've got a master's degree in library science, specializing in book arts, conservation, and authentication. Some people go the graphic arts route, especially if their interest is mainly in book arts. I was more interested in restoring old books, although these days I love creating books and paper art, too. But I'd have to say that my career is focused on rare book restoration."

"I remember you telling me that you also taught classes."

"Oh, I've been doing that for years. In San Francisco we have Bay Area Book Arts, which is a fabulous place where you can learn everything you ever wanted to know about creating new books or restoring old books. They have papermaking classes and typesetting classes and a hundred other courses."

"And you've taught them all?"

"Not quite, but I've taught a bunch of them." I stretched my back, almost ready to stand up and take a stroll around the cabin. "But let's get back to your four different fields of study."

"Oh, all right." She chuckled. "Mainly, I'm a historian. I have an MA in global history and international studies, an MA in English literature, an MA in art history, and a PhD in British history. My expertise is in eighteenth- and nineteenth-century British history and antiquities, specifically the weaponry, books, furniture, jewelry, and artwork of that era. Basically, I'm a total nerd."

I laughed. "I've always called myself a nerd."

"That's why we hit it off from the start."

I gazed at her for a long moment. "Your expertise was tailor-made for *This Old Attic*."

"Why did you leave the show?" Derek asked.

She waved his question away. "It's a sad, embarrassing story that would put you to sleep."

"No way," I insisted. "*Sad* and *embarrassing* are right up my alley." And just like that, I got my second—or third—wind.

Chapter 13

Claire's story wasn't sad and embarrassing at all. It was infuriating.

It started the day she was called into a meeting with the producer, Bob. "We're taking the show in a new direction, Claire."

She was mildly interested. "What does that mean?"

He sat forward in his chair, his expression deeply sincere. "It means that from now on, we're going to have 'real' people talking about the antiques."

"What do you mean by 'real' people?" Claire asked, feeling stupid for having to ask the question.

He held up his hands and sighed deeply. "Let's face it, Claire. You come across as a know-it-all. You're just too smart. Not that that's a bad thing! But you go into so much detail over the antiques that viewers get lost."

Claire was mystified. "I was told that the viewers love those details. Last year you said I was the most popular appraiser on the show. I thought the point of watching the show was to learn all those interesting facts about all sorts of things."

"Well, yeah, maybe, but . . . good grief, Claire." He

was angry now, as if Claire speaking for herself was un-acceptable. "You know too damn much."

It took her a minute to recover. "Have you already hired someone to take my place?"

He smiled brightly. "As a matter of fact, we've hired several fresh new faces to do the appraisals. I'm very excited about this innovative new format."

"Really, Bob?" It wasn't normally her style, but she couldn't keep the sarcasm from dripping off the words.

Bob frowned. "What's wrong with you, Claire? You've always been so agreeable."

"I guess I've never had to deal with someone who completely lied to my face before."

"I-I'm not lying."

"Yes, you are, Bob. You're lying. I don't like it. In fact, it sucks. Tell me the truth."

He mumbled and fumbled through an explanation, but the bottom line was the same and Claire was fired.

Claire's story fast-forwarded six weeks. She wasn't working anymore and it was depressing. She was still in her pajamas at four o'clock in the afternoon. She didn't know what to do with her life. She sat on her couch com-miserating with Mr. D, her cat, and in a moment of mas-ochistic pique, Claire cursed the world and turned on the television set. It was tuned to the network that aired *This Old Attic* and she couldn't look away. And within minutes, to her horror, she discovered that her replace-ment was none other than Bob's girlfriend, Mindy Marks.

Claire stared at the screen as the camera zoomed in on a lovingly restored sword displayed on its own stand.

"That's a beauty," Claire murmured to herself.

The camera panned over to Mindy, who looked

pretty and perky in a slinky pink cocktail dress and sky-high stilettos.

Claire thought the ensemble was a little odd, but maybe it went along with the show's "new direction."

Mindy stared at the antique weapon, looking terribly confused. She blinked, then gazed at the sword's owner and said in her baby doll voice, "Well, um, hello, sir. Tell us about this, er, thingie or whatever."

"Oh my God!" Claire shrieked. "It's not a *thingie*!" She jumped up from the couch and moved closer to the screen. "It's known as a *small sword*, you twit. Made of steel, with a silver hilt. Manufactured in England, probably in the 1740s."

The sword's owner spoke up. "I don't know a whole lot about it, but it's been in my family for generations and was originally owned by a Colonel Winslow, who gave it to Captain Farwell."

"Yes," Claire said triumphantly from her couch. "Which means it was quite possibly used by one of William Prescott's men against the British at the battle of Bunker Hill, you ignorant fool."

The sword's owner verified Claire's theory and she fell back on the couch, depleted of energy. "Ugh."

As another wave of depression threatened to overwhelm her, she heard Mindy say, "Well, it's shiny, I guess."

"That is horrifying!" I cried, after hearing her story. "How could they do that to you? What were they thinking?"

"Bob wasn't thinking," Claire said with a scowl. "At least, not with his big brain." She clapped her hand over her mouth. "Sorry, Derek."

Derek laughed. "No apologies necessary. Bob sounds like a right plonker."

Now I laughed. I knew that in British slang, the word

plonker meant *dimwit* or *idiot*. The term suited this Bob character to a T.

Claire knew exactly what the term meant and she laughed more joyfully than I'd heard her in a while.

It cleared away the sadness and the anger for the moment.

"Is Bob still working there?" I asked.

"No, he was fired last month."

"Can you get your old job back?"

She frowned. "The executive producer called me a week or so ago, but I was in the shower so it went to voicemail."

"Did you call him back?"

She frowned. "I listened to his message a few times and had to decide whether to return the call or not. I mean, the executive producer had backed up Bob's decision, so why would he suddenly be my champion?"

"Good point," Derek said.

"Thank you," Claire said.

"But he did call you," I reminded her.

"Yes, he did. And just when I'd decided I should call them back, I heard from Aunt Gwyneth and took off for Scotland. And that's when all the insanity began."

The three of us stared at one another for a moment, and then I said, "I'm so sorry, Claire."

"I'm sorry, too," she said, and yawned. "And I'm knackered. That story wore me out. Sorry to go on and on."

"Don't be sorry," I said. "I blame stupid Bob. What a jerk."

She laughed again. "Aye, Bob the plonker. He's to blame for everything."

Derek checked his wristwatch. "They'll stop for fuel in about two hours. Let's try to get some sleep and then regroup."

"Sounds good," I said, and slid my chair into the sleeping position. "Sleep well."

I managed to get almost four hours of sleep and woke up knowing I wouldn't be able to fall back to sleep until we landed. I pulled out the broken cover of Claire's *Mistress of Mellyn* and studied it in the light over my chair. I wouldn't be able to repair it here on the plane. The logistics were too unwieldy.

But checking out the book more thoroughly, I realized that it would be an easier fix than I'd thought. The textblock was intact and in good condition. And the front cover was indeed still attached, if only by a few thin cloth threads. It needed a new cover anyway, and I would be able to do that if I had two straight hours to do the job. The dried glue would have to be completely scraped off the spine and a new cover would have to be added, as well as new pastedowns and endpapers for the inside covers. And there was the dustcover to repair as well. That would be as simple as applying a clear strip of invisible archival tape.

"Piece of cake," I muttered, and closed my eyes for just a quick minute. And that was all I remembered before falling back into a deep sleep.

The jet landed in Inverness that afternoon. Local time was 3:30 p.m.

As the plane taxied toward the terminal, Claire said, "I must have been more exhausted than I realized because I completely forgot to tell you that we'll be staying at the castle."

I looked at Derek, then back at Claire. "Seriously?"

"Yes," Claire said. "I called several of the top B and B's in town and they're all full up for the weekend. I finally called my aunt's dearest old friend Mrs. Buchanan for advice. She's the head housekeeper at Castle MacKinnon and she insisted that we stay there. We'll have two lovely rooms in the east wing—which has been completely restored, according to Mrs. B. She assured me that she'll be happy to serve our meals as well, unless we decide to dine out."

I smiled at Derek. "I guess we won't have to worry about sneaking into the castle."

"No." But he didn't look happy. He looked wary. "What is the reason the B and B's are all full?"

"It's the Spring Bank Holiday and the town puts on their annual boat festival. It's become a big event that brings people in from all over the Highlands."

"Hmm," Derek said. "Perfect timing."

I leaned over and whispered to him, "We can get lost in the crowds."

Derek thought about it. "It could be a good thing."

I turned to Claire. "I've never slept in a castle before. It could be exciting."

"Oh, it's a lovely castle." She made a face. "Despite the shabby bits."

Just then Shane the flight attendant released the door and we watched it magically turn into a stairway leading down to the tarmac. We lugged our belongings off the plane and waited while each of us checked that we hadn't forgotten anything.

"Wait here just a moment," Derek said, and walked over to talk to the pilot.

Claire glanced around. "I usually take the bus from here down to Oddlochen, but there's also a water taxi if you'd prefer a more scenic route."

"I've taken care of it," Derek said, and less than three

minutes later a four-passenger electric shuttle cart
pulled up by the plane.

"You called for assistance?" the driver asked.

"Yes. Thank you." Derek put all of our luggage in the
back of the cart and we climbed in. "We're going to the
heliport."

"Yes, sir." The driver took off and drove for a few
minutes, then stopped at a small terminal on the far end
of the flight path. "Here you are. I'll wait right here with
your baggage until your ride arrives."

Derek touched my arm. "You can wait here. I'll only
be a moment."

"Okay."

He walked inside to speak to a woman at the counter
and returned two minutes later. "We're right over here."

"Do you need a ride, sir?"

Derek smiled. "Thank you, no. We can walk."

The driver got out and took our luggage out of the
cart and set everything on the ground.

Derek handed the man a folded bill and said, "Thank
you for your help."

"Thank you, sir." He tipped his cap, climbed back
into the cart, and took off. We walked around the building, where we saw a massive military helicopter parked
on the tarmac. It was big and black and powerful-
looking, like some futuristic stalking jungle cat.

"Derek?" I said, hesitating.

He laughed out loud. "Daphne comes through again."

"Seriously? That's for us?"

"My God, you people travel well," Claire said.

I laughed. "We really do, don't we?"

The interior of the helicopter was remarkably luxurious with white leather bucket seats behind the pilot,

whose name was Thomas. He studied his clipboard for a moment. "I'm to take you to Castle MacKinnon. It's just a few miles down the Loch, perhaps no more than twenty minutes."

"Yes," Derek said. "Thank you."

Thomas was a congenial host and handed out small bags of snack mix and mini water bottles for our quick trip south along the shores of Loch Ness. We were each given headsets to block out the noise and to enable us to ask him any questions we had along the way.

Thomas announced his flight plan to the air traffic control tower and then looked at us over his shoulder. "I'm about to start the rotors and we'll take off soon. Enjoy the flight."

If only I could, I thought, because the closer we got to Oddlochen, the more terrified I grew. And I didn't even know why, except that we could quite possibly confront a killer within a day or two.

Thomas opened up the throttle and we could hear the rotors starting, which activated the four-pronged blade on top and the smaller blade at the rear.

A mere three minutes later we were rising, leaving the ground and pivoting to the left. Then the pilot swooped up and began to gather speed. The airport disappeared as we quickly climbed higher and within minutes we were flying over the city of Inverness. Thomas took a moment to play tour guide, pointing out Inverness Castle and the Caledonian Canal down below.

I was surprised to see so much farmland as we flew east of the city. I mentioned it to Thomas and he said, "Aye, our farming industry has come back strong. And of course we've always had sheep and cattle farms in this area."

Sheep, of course, I thought. Scotland's wool products were famous around the world.

Thomas pointed off to his left. "We're close to the site of the infamous Battle of Culloden, where the Jacobites were kippered by the English in the bloody massacre of 1746 that killed over thirteen hundred Scotsmen."

Kippered? Good heavens. Thomas had a way of turning a phrase.

"It's a solemn place, Culloden," Claire whispered.

Thomas gave a grunt of assent. "It's said that most of the dead were buried in shallow graves." He paused, then added, "It's quite the lovely spot for contemplation."

"We'll have to try and get there," Derek said.

"Aye," Thomas said. "And if you've a fascination for standing stones and the like, you'll want to see the Clava Cairns, which are only a wee bit farther to the east."

"I've always wanted to see the Clava Cairns," Claire said. "And they're only a few miles from Cawdor Castle."

Cawdor Castle and its gardens were a well-known tourist destination close to Inverness.

I nodded. "I've heard Cawdor Castle is beautiful. Maybe we'll have a chance to visit there, too." I said it while at the same time realizing that we wouldn't have time for sightseeing. Not if we wanted to find Aunt Gwyneth and also figure out who had bumped off the two nasty thugs who'd threatened Claire.

After a few minutes, Thomas cleared his throat and said, "Sir."

Derek came to attention. "What is it, Thomas?"

"I've been informed that there's nae a helipad at Castle MacKinnon."

"No, I don't suppose there would be," he mused. "Is there an open field nearby?"

Thomas proceeded to carry on a short, incomprehensible conversation with his contact. Finally, Thomas said, "There is a lawn in front of the castle. Do I have your permission to land?"

"Is it flat land?" Derek asked.

"I believe so, but I'll double-check."

Derek frowned. "I'd rather not come down in the middle of a rose garden or a fountain."

"No, sir." He checked with his local contact and a few seconds later, he said, "I'm told it's mainly grass and scrub."

"Sounds good enough to me," Derek said.

We were flying over Loch Ness now and the hills in the distance were verdant from the spring rains. The Loch was a shimmering blue sea in the late afternoon sun.

Four minutes later the helicopter made a wide circle and swung out even farther over Loch Ness, then headed back to shore. I could see acres and acres of rich green forests covering the land right up to the shore.

Suddenly the trees fell away to reveal an astonishingly beautiful castle standing a mere hundred yards away from the water.

It faced Loch Ness and looked magnificent, surrounded by the evergreens and fronted by a wide green lawn lined with spring wildflowers.

The castle was huge with old stone walls tinged a pale coral in the light of the late afternoon sun. The grand edifice had a fairy-tale quality with its many incongruous sections and a roofline that was ridiculously erratic. There was a turret here and a circular tower there, parapets and battlements and then more turrets and towers, some with crenellated rooflines and in one case an oddly bulbous-shaped rooftop. One very tall, very thin round tower was topped by a light blue roof that resembled a witch's hat. There were a dozen balconies and at least ten chimneys, and like the towers, they were each configured differently.

I was instantly infatuated and wanted to explore them all. And yet, I had a sense of foreboding as though we were walking into danger. Or maybe I was just hungry. I hoped that was what this gnawing feeling in my stomach was all about.

In the interest of time I probably wouldn't explore everything. But I definitely wanted to find our way to the west tower as soon as possible. I couldn't imagine finding Aunt Gwyneth up there, but stranger things had happened. Maybe the tower was beautifully furnished with a nice little kitchenette for cooking. Maybe she was perfectly comfortable in her secret hiding place. Wherever we found her, I just wanted her to be alive.

The thought of the west tower gave me another little chill, but that wouldn't stop me from trying to get up there. We were here to find answers. To find Aunt Gwyneth. And maybe confront a killer.

The helicopter continued to hover about ten feet above the ground, then slowly settled down until it touched the grass. The wind whipped up by the blades caused the vegetation and flowers and nearby trees to be tossed back mercilessly and I worried that they would be damaged. But then Thomas turned off the engine and everything was calm again.

"That was a smooth flight and an excellent landing," Derek said as he climbed down from the back seat. "Thank you very much, Thomas."

"I appreciate it, sir. It's a pleasure." He pushed his door open. "I'll help you with your baggage."

Claire and I both took the time to thank him, too. And as we were collecting our luggage I noticed a woman approach from around the far left corner of the castle. The minute she saw us, she waved her arms in excitement and bustled over to greet us. "Claire, Claire!" she cried.

"Mrs. Buchanan!" Claire said, and waited as the woman threw her arms around her. "It's good to see you."

"I'm so glad you're here, child. Now we can get to the bottom of this puzzle." She held Claire at arm's length and took her time studying her. "Are you all right?"

"I'm fine, but I must know, have you received any word?" Claire asked anxiously.

Mrs. Buchanan glanced around. "We should talk inside."

"Of course." Claire took a deep breath and exhaled. "Let me introduce you to my friends. Brooklyn Wainwright and Commander Derek Stone, this is Mrs. Buchanan. She's my aunt Gwyneth's dearest friend."

I slid a glance toward Claire. Introducing Derek as the Commander had been a smart move, I thought. Smiling at the housekeeper, I said, "How do you do, Mrs. Buchanan? Thank you so much for accommodating us."

"As you'll see, we have more than a wee bit of room." She let out a hearty laugh as she shook hands with me. Then she turned to Derek. "Commander. It's so nice to have you here."

"Thank you." The two of them shook hands.

Mrs. Buchanan reached for one of the rolling bags while Derek turned back to Thomas and handed him a folded banknote.

Thomas gave a snappy salute. "Thank you, sir."

"We'd like to contact you for a ride back to the airport," Derek said. "But we're not yet sure of our departure time and date."

Thomas pulled out a business card and handed it to him. "Feel free to call me when you have the information. I'll be happy to pick you up and whisk you away."

Derek grinned. "Thank you."

Thomas hopped back into the pilot's seat. "You might want to head inside before I crank up the rotors."

"Excellent idea." Derek turned to the three of us and swept his arm toward the castle. "Shall we?"

Mrs. Buchanan chatted as we walked up to the castle. We turned and waved to Thomas as he started up the rotors. Even from this distance, the wind from the moving blades was punishing so we moved quickly around the side of the castle and then stopped in front of the main double doors.

On this side of the castle was a large, ornate fountain in the middle of a circular drive. In the distance was a parking area and what looked like a six-car garage with some sort of living quarters above it.

Mrs. Buchanan stopped at the doors. "Before we go inside, I want to warn you that the castle is not in tip-top shape. Due to no fault of my own, I hasten to add." She glanced at Claire. "As I told you, the former laird was quite profligate in his habits and he was not the tidiest of men. I was forced to leave his employ last year when he was no longer able to pay me."

"Oh, my aunt told me," Claire said. "What a terrible time for you."

"It wasn't easy," she admitted. "And while I was gone, the house wasn't kept up to my standards."

Claire gripped her arm. "Oh, Mrs. Buchanan. Why didn't you tell me?"

"You've had enough to worry about, lass." She patted Claire's cheek. "But I've been back now for several months and I'm making up for lost time. I can assure you, your bedrooms are pristine. The kitchen and dining rooms and most of the public areas are spotless. And I'm about to start on the main rooms of the west wing with help from the staff. You're free to walk around and see some of the beautiful artwork and furnishings, but please be careful. There are parts of the castle that have fallen into disrepair and I wouldn't want to see you get hurt."

She turned to push the door open, but stopped and glanced over her shoulder. "Also, the staff is in a bit of an uproar. The laird departed abruptly a few days ago and left no instructions for them." She waved her hands. "But that's not for you to worry about. Please come in and be at home."

I stared at Derek and he stared right back. "It's going to be an adventure."

"Yes, quite."

We followed Mrs. Buchanan through the doors and into a massive foyer. She had obviously cleaned and polished this space and it was beautiful. The elegant furniture and dark wood floors gleamed in the light of an elaborate crystal chandelier that hung from the ceiling.

"It's lovely," I said, gazing around at the flower arrangements on every table. "Do you arrange the flowers?"

"Oh, heavens no. The girl does it. Uh, that is, my kitchen assistant Treena does the flowers. She's so clever and really quite insistent that I refer to her as my *kitchen assistant*." She grinned. "She's a good girl so I play along." She pointed to a room to the left off the foyer. "This is the main dining room, where we'll serve your meals."

I glanced into the room and saw a table big enough to serve twenty people.

"It's very grand," Claire said, earning a big smile from the head housekeeper.

Mrs. Buchanan pointed straight ahead. "The great hall is just this way to the left, but I'll show you to your rooms first."

At the end of the massive foyer, she turned right and we saw the great staircase.

"Everything is quite impressive," Derek said.

Mrs. Buchanan preened at his words. "I'm happy you think so, Commander Stone." She turned and began to walk up the stairs.

"I appreciate your willingness to accommodate us," Derek said. "I understand that rooms are scarce this week because of your annual boat festival."

"Yes. I do hope you'll enjoy the festival. It's an extravaganza and brings in a lot of revenue for our little town."

"I'm sure we'll enjoy it," Derek murmured.

When we got to the top of the stairs, she led the way down a wide hallway. The carpeting was thicker and more luxurious than I would've expected based on her earlier warning and the artwork on the walls was remarkable. I thought maybe this wing had been refurbished recently.

"When do you expect Laird MacKinnon to return?" Derek asked, and I recognized the change in his voice. It was his upper-crust, lord-of-the-manor tone.

"He's been away for the past few days," she explained, "but we're expecting him back soon. Perhaps later tonight."

"I would very much like the chance to meet him and thank him personally for his kind hospitality."

Mrs. Buchanan's eyes popped open and she gulped. "I'll try to arrange an introduction."

"Thank you." Derek glanced at me and probably noticed my own eyes popping a bit, too. I had to wonder if Mrs. Buchanan had invited us to stay without first clearing it with the laird of the castle.

"Here we are," she said, opening a door and inviting Derek and me to go inside. "This will be your room and I hope you'll be comfortable."

I gave a quick glance inside and caught sight of a large picture window with gold draperies, a hunter-green carpet, and an enormous fireplace. The four-poster bed would require a stepstool for me to reach the top of the mattress. There was an elegant loveseat and matching chair at the far end of the room near another wide window. "It's gorgeous."

She beamed at me. "I happen to agree." She walked a few feet farther down the hall and stopped at the next door. "Here you are, Claire. Right next door."

"Oh, it's lovely, Mrs. Buchanan."

"I'm so pleased that you're all happy." Mrs. Buchanan checked her wristwatch. "We serve dinner at eight. Please let me know if I can bring you anything in the meantime. Or if you're feeling peckish, feel free to come down to the kitchen and forage on your own. We're quite informal here. And if you decide to go out for a meal, I would appreciate your letting me know."

"Of course," I said.

She reached into her pocket and pulled out two keys, each attached to different-colored ribbons. "These are your room keys. We rarely lock our rooms but since you're traveling, you might feel more comfortable locking your door."

We took hold of our keys and then she said, "When you next come downstairs, I'll introduce you to the staff."

"Wonderful," I said. It would be good to get to know the people who worked here on a regular basis.

As we were standing there, a black-and-white cat rushed down the hall and streaked into Claire's room.

"Oh, that blasted cat!" Mrs. Buchanan cried. "I was hoping he would stay downstairs."

"It's quite all right, Mrs. B," Claire said. "When he's ready to leave, I'll push him out the door."

"I thank you. And if you've a liking for the fiendish creature, you're free to keep him with you. He's actually a loving boy when he's not being the devil himself."

"I have a cat of my own at home," Claire said. "I would enjoy the company of this one. What's his name?"

"Robbie," she said, pronouncing it *Rabbie*.

"For Robert Burns?" I asked.

"Aye. You know our people's poet, then?"

I grinned. "I'm familiar with the man." And with his rabid followers, too, I thought. I had once been waylaid by a carful of Robert Burns Society members in Edinburgh. I would never forget their deep-seated devotion to their leader.

"There is just one more thing I should explain," Mrs. B said as her smile faded. "As Laird MacKinnon may be arriving later tonight, I would ask that you not wander into the north wing of the castle. That is where he resides and he doesn't appreciate uninvited guests."

"Perfectly reasonable," Derek said, which brought a smile back to her face.

We all thanked her for the hundredth time, then watched her dash off down the hall.

"We're going to unpack a few things," I said to Claire, "but feel free to come in and talk once you're settled."

"Aye, we should talk," she said. "We need a plan."

Derek said, "We do indeed."

"We'll leave the door unlocked," I said, "so just knock and come on in when you're ready."

"All right. Thanks."

We walked into our room and I was happy to see that the space was clean and bright. Not a cobweb or dirty window in sight. Even though Mrs. Buchanan had told us these rooms had been renovated, I had still worried. But this beautiful room was beyond my expectations. There was even a bookcase filled with enticing books. I promised myself some time to peruse the contents at some point in our visit.

After unpacking a few essentials and setting out my toiletries in the lovely, large bathroom, I walked out to talk to Derek and was surprised when he pulled me up close to whisper, "Claire needs to ask Mrs. Buchanan where the laird has been."

"Yes, all right. Let me tell her."

He pressed his index finger to his lips, signaling that I shouldn't speak. Did he think the room was bugged? It was possible.

As if to answer my silent question, Derek picked up my cell phone and turned it off. He did the same with his, then took a small piece of equipment from his pocket. He turned it on and walked slowly around the room, holding the device in front of him and moving it across the books in the bookcase. He walked over to the luggage stand that held my suitcase, then on to the nightstands on either side of our bed.

I trailed a few feet behind him, thoroughly intrigued by the process.

After a few moments, Derek moved over to the bathroom, where he scanned the towels on the rack and the jar of potpourri on the counter.

Finally he switched off the detector. "I didn't pick up anything."

"How does that work?" I asked, fascinated by the little gadget.

"I first had to turn off our cell phones because they emit frequencies that may interfere with the detector."

"Okay."

"If a bug has been planted in the room, it transmits a radio frequency signal to a receiving device. This detector will scan for all signals in the RF spectrum. And if it finds one, it will emit a beeping sound. Much like a Geiger counter does when it detects radiation."

"Cool."

"We're safe here for now," he said. "We should ask Claire to join us."

"I'll get her." I opened the door and walked into the hall. I was about to knock on Claire's door when another door opened at the end of the hall and a man stepped into view. He was tall and blond and very handsome, if you liked the tall, blond, handsome type. And what woman didn't?

He had sculpted cheekbones and clear blue eyes and hair that was a touch too long and curled just slightly. Not to put too fine a point on it, but the guy was adorable.

"Hello," he said. "I didn't realize anyone was up here."

"We just arrived," I said. "Are you staying here also?"

Claire leaned out of her doorway to see who was talking. Her eyes widened in surprise. "Allen?"

"Claire?" He was obviously taken aback, but quickly recovered and grinned. "What an excellent surprise."

She looked puzzled. "I didn't realize you were living here."

"I'm not," he said. "I'm only up here because the downstairs maid suggested I might find my hammer in one of these rooms. She thought Trevor or Billy had used it to hang some pictures."

"Did you find it?"

He held out his empty hands and grinned again. "No. I suppose it'll show up somewhere."

He was staring at Claire with real interest, enough to cause my matchmaker antennae to stand up and cheer. Which was weird, because I'd never had any matchmaker antennae before.

Derek walked out just then and gazed at Allen with curiosity. "Hello," he said with a smile.

Allen took a subtle step back, having clearly recognized the alpha dog.

Claire looked at me and Derek. "Allen is the estate manager for Castle MacKinnon."

I perked up. "That must be an interesting job."

"It's all I've ever done," he admitted with a sheepish smile. "All I've ever known, really. My father had the job before me, working with the old laird."

"Allen Brodie," Claire said. "These are friends of mine from San Francisco. Brooklyn Wainwright and Commander Stone."

We shook hands all around and he said, "Good to meet you."

"You, too," I said.

He glanced from Claire to me and Derek. "Are you all staying here?"

"Yes." Claire shrugged. "All the B and B's are filled up because of the boat festival so Mrs. Buchanan was kind enough to let us stay here."

His smile faded. "Aye, it makes sense that you wouldn't want to be staying at your aunt's."

"No, I wouldn't."

"Has there been any word yet, then?"

"Not yet." She quickly brushed aside the distress and said, "Well, we're going to get settled now, so perhaps we'll see you around town."

"Around town or around the castle," he said easily. "Say, if you've no plans, I'll be going to the pub tonight and I'd be happy to show you the way through the woods."

Claire glanced at me. "The pub is a good place to meet some of the local townspeople."

"We'd love to go with you," I said, after a quick look at Derek. "Thanks."

"Good." He gave us a nod and began walking toward the staircase. "I'll collect you in the foyer at seven."

"We'll need to let Mrs. B know that we're going out to dinner," Claire said.

"I'll let her know on my way out," Allen said.

"Would you? Thanks so much."

Allen gave her a thumbs-up and continued down the hall toward the stairs.

I looked at Derek. "Do you think he might help us find Gwyneth?"

"No. At least, not yet. I don't want to bring it up to him until I've done some digging first."

I stared at him. "You don't trust him."

"I don't trust anybody," he whispered. "Except you."

I would've given him a melting smile, but Claire started to go back to her room just then and Derek quickly stopped her. "Claire, before you get settled, we need to talk."

"All right." She followed us into our room and sat at

the small table in front of a picture window that looked out on the Loch.

"Isn't this view fabulous?" I said.

"It's better than a B and B, that's for sure," Claire said, then winced. "I hope I didn't twist your arm into going to the pub tonight."

"Absolutely not," Derek said. "Sounds perfect." He stood leaning against the fireplace mantel, looking darkly handsome and much more to my taste than the admittedly very cute Allen Brodie.

"Now, what do we need to do to find my aunt?" she asked.

I said, "First, we think it would be a good idea to find out where the laird is."

"The laird?" She frowned. "Mrs. B said that he'd probably be back tonight."

"I hope she's right," I said. "But don't you think it's strange that he's been gone a few days?"

She gave a shrug. "From what I hear, he goes off a lot."

Derek thought for a moment. "Is there any chance you'd be willing to query Mrs. Buchanan as to his exact whereabouts?"

Claire blinked in surprise at the odd request. "I suppose I could. But why?"

"Here's the thing," I said. "Derek's friends from Interpol and MI6 are the ones who've been investigating your aunt's disappearance. One of the local cops mentioned that she was running into roadblocks because apparently there's a new major player who recently came to town."

"A new major player?"

"Yes," Derek said. "That major player is the new laird."

"And we think it's a real coincidence that he's been

gone for a few days and he's supposed to be back tonight."

"Yes," Derek said. "Just in time for our arrival."

She glanced from Derek to me and shook her head. "I'm still not following you."

I leaned forward. "I'll put it this way. What if this so-called major player is the one who flew to San Francisco with Fish Face and Reggie?"

She gasped and smacked her hand over her mouth. "Oh my God."

"Yeah," I said. "Think it's possible?"

"Oh, you bet I do." She pushed away from the table and paced across the floor, her fist pounding against the palm of her hand. "So you want me to give Mrs. B the old third degree." She stopped at the window and took a deep breath. "I'll do it."

Chapter 14

The three of us were waiting for Allen in the foyer when Mrs. B came bustling around the corner carrying a small bouquet of flowers in a vase.

"Those are pretty," Claire said.

"And they're for you," Mrs. B said, wearing a wide smile. "Just arrived."

"For me?" Claire gave the spring bouquet a look of dark suspicion. "Who would send me flowers?"

"Who knows you're here?" Derek asked.

"Nobody," she said. "Except Mrs. B. And now Allen."

"Oh, but my entire staff is aware you're here, dear," Mrs. Buchanan said, then added, "I hope that's not a problem."

"Not at all," Claire rushed to assure her.

"Who are they from?" I asked.

"Och." Claire rolled her eyes. "It would help to know." She set the vase down on the center table under the chandelier, pulled out the small envelope, and opened it. She read the card and began to blink rapidly. "Oh." She backed away from the flowers. She clutched the card with both hands and pressed it to her chest. Tears sprang up and trickled down her cheeks.

"Oh, Claire," I said as my own eyes threatened to tear up. Nobody cried alone when I was around.

"Who's it from?" Derek demanded, and reached out to take the card from Claire. He read it aloud. "It says, '*My dearest Claire, don't worry about me.*'" He squinted to read the next line. "'*I am no bird; and no net ensnares me.*'"

"Why does that sound so familiar?" I asked, wracking my brain to remember my college literature classes.

Claire had to swallow to clear her throat. "It's a classic line from *Jane Eyre*, Aunt Gwyneth's favorite gothic novel."

Derek handed the card back to Claire. "She would know that you'd recognize the quote."

"Oh yes. We used to discuss the Brontë sisters all the time, comparing our favorite tortured heroes." She gazed at me. "I was Team Heathcliff while she adored Rochester."

I had to smile. "So you think the note's from her."

"I do. Yes." She closed her eyes and swayed a bit.

I grabbed her arm to steady her. "You're not going to faint."

"Oh no." She breathed in and out a few times. "No, I'm not. But how did she know I was here?"

"Good question," Derek said.

"Do you recognize the handwriting, Claire?" I asked.

"I—it looks like my aunt's writing."

"Let me see it," Mrs. Buchanan said. She stared long and hard at the small card. "It does look like Gwyn's writing." She held out the card and pointed. "See the way she makes the curlicue on the C in *Claire*? Gwyn always does that."

I had to wonder how many people in the village knew Gwyneth's signature style, but said nothing.

"How did the flowers arrive, Mrs. Buchanan?" Derek asked, keeping his tone calm. I knew he didn't want the housekeeper to freak out on us.

"A young man from the village brought them. Brian Page. He's a good lad. Works at one of the small inns on the other side of town."

"Did he come to the front door? Ring the doorbell?"

"No, no. He came around to the kitchen door and poked his head in. Most anyone who's delivering to the castle knows to come to my door."

"And you took the flowers?"

"Nooo," she said slowly. "Treena took the flowers. You see, she and young Brian, well, they fancy each other, so I let her spend a moment with him."

"Did Brian happen to say who sent the flowers?"

"Not to me, but he might've told Treena."

"Let's find Treena, shall we?" Derek ushered her into the empty dining room and we followed her to the kitchen door at the far end of the formal room.

Treena was standing at the stove wearing a long white apron. She appeared to be in her late twenties and looked sturdy and cheerful. She was stirring a rich, beefy stew in a large pot. It smelled delicious and made my mouth water.

Standing next to her was a pretty young woman in casual clothing, jeans, a flannel shirt, and sneakers. They were whispering together and giggling.

"Treena, dear," Mrs. Buchanan began, and waited for her assistant to turn. "Commander Stone would like a word with you."

The other girl's eyes grew wide and fearful. She stared at her friend as though she was about to be dragged off in chains. "I gotta go."

"No need to hurry off, Jenny," Mrs. Buchanan said. "Commander Stone only needs a moment of Treena's time."

But she was already rushing out the door.

"Text me later, Jenny," Treena cried, then turned to face the Commander, looking like she feared the worst.

"Hello, Treena," Derek said, his smile reassuring. "I'm Commander Stone. I just have a few questions for you."

"All right." She grabbed the nearest kitchen towel and dried her hands.

"A few minutes ago your friend Brian arrived with flowers for Ms. Quinn."

"Aye, that's right, sir." She looked slightly less terrified now that Derek had mentioned her boyfriend's name.

"Did Brian tell you who asked him to deliver the flowers?"

"He said his boss told him to take the flowers to the castle for the new guest."

"Who's his boss?" I asked. "Do you know?"

"It's Mr. Gordon, ma'am." She swallowed. "Well, and there's Mrs. Gordon. She's the boss as well."

Derek and I both glanced at Mrs. Buchanan, who spoke up. "Oliver and Harriet Gordon own the Manor House Hotel two blocks off the high street. They also own the antiques shop at the far end of the high street."

Derek nodded, then turned and flashed Treena a full-wattage smile. "Thank you, Treena. You've been very helpful."

Her eyes were still big and round. "You're welcome, sir."

I led the way out of the kitchen and crossed through

the dining room. At the arched doorway leading into the foyer, Derek said, "Mrs. Buchanan, perhaps tomorrow morning you could introduce us to the rest of your staff."

"Aye, I'd be pleased to do so."

"For now, though, would you mind giving me their names?" He pulled out his phone. "It would be helpful. First and last names, if possible."

"Of course. You just met Treena McHugh, the kitchen assistant. There's also Celia Turnbull, assistant housekeeper; Ida Maguire, the upstairs maid; Jenny MacDougall, the downstairs maid; Margaret Hastings, the cook; and Roy Turnbull, the laird's chauffeur. He's married to Celia, our assistant housekeeper. And finally, Silas Abernathy is our head of security."

Derek looked up. "You have a head of security?"

She rolled her eyes. "He calls himself that. Mainly functions as a bodyguard when the laird travels."

A bodyguard? Was the laird in danger of some kind? In any case, it was clear that Mrs. Buchanan was not impressed with the man.

Derek nodded as he continued typing all of the names into his scheduling app. "And that's it?"

"No, actually. The laird recently hired a small staff to help with a special project he began a few weeks ago. There's Billy, Stella, Trevor, and Diana. They're studying at the college in Inverness, but I believe they all live in the village. I'm afraid I haven't memorized their surnames yet, but I can get them for you."

Derek typed rapidly with one finger and then smiled. "Sometime in the morning is soon enough. Thank you very much."

"You're welcome." Then she looked at Claire. "I'm sorry, my dear. I've been a ninny. It only just occurred to me that with Gwyneth missing, you might be in danger as well. I should've alerted you right away so you could've spoken to young Brian."

Claire managed a smile. "It's all right, Mrs. B. It's not your fault."

The two women hugged each other, then Mrs. Buchanan turned and took hold of my arm and Derek's. "She's lucky to have you two looking out for her. You'll keep an eye out for trouble."

"We will," I said.

"I'll do the same," she said sternly, "now that I know there could be shenanigans."

I almost laughed at the word, but this situation was hardly a laughing matter. Shenanigans? Really? There had already been two murders. And despite Claire's affirmation, we couldn't be absolutely certain that the flowers and the card had come from Gwyneth herself or from some villainous creep intent on taunting Claire.

I wondered if maybe we should cancel our trip to the pub, but then realized that it might be the perfect place to run across a killer. And there was safety in numbers, after all, so we would just have to stick together.

At that moment, the double doors opened and Allen walked into the foyer. "Looks like you're ready."

"Aye, we are," Claire said, but quickly turned to Mrs. Buchanan and whispered, "May I leave the flowers here until I return?"

Mrs. B leaned in. "Why don't I put them in your room?"

"Oh yes, please. I would so appreciate it."

She patted Claire's cheek, then said to all of us, "Have a wonderful time. You all have your room keys so you can get back inside?"

"Yes, ma'am," I said, and Claire held hers up for the woman to see.

"Good." Mrs. B chuckled. "Off you go, then. Have fun. Ta."

"I'm really glad you offered to show us the way," I said to Allen. "It's so dark already."

"'Tis the trees that tend to block out the light," Allen explained. "It'll be lighter once we're out of the woods. But see here, as long as you stay on the path you'll be fine."

The path, such as it was, was barely two feet wide and covered in pine needles, which could be slippery if you didn't step just right. Other than that, no problem. I would have to remind myself to bring a flashlight next time.

As we strolled, Allen pointed the way toward a few good hiking trails and entertained us with a couple of funny stories about some of the locals. Then he mentioned that a ghost used to inhabit the castle tower.

"He was said to have occupied the west tower," Allen said with a laugh. "So you should be safe enough sleeping in the east wing."

Oh great, I thought. A ghost in the west tower. Not that I believed in such things, but really, why plant the scary seed in my brain? My imagination was already running rampant. I didn't need to add ghosts to the mix. Good grief.

Allen launched into another silly story and by the time we reached the edge of the village, we were all laughing and chatting together like old friends. The old-fashioned streetlights and storefronts had a Victorian flavor that made everything picturesque and inviting.

The high street was a popular area and there were plenty of people strolling from the pub to one of the other restaurants or into the shops that remained open to take advantage of the visiting festivalgoers. There was even a bookshop, I realized, and felt that special little zing that happened whenever I came in close contact with my favorite thing: books. I made a mental note to check the place out while we were here.

In the middle of the block, Claire stopped and stared at a pretty store window.

"What's up, Claire?" I asked.

"This is Aunt Gwyneth's shop."

I stared at the delightful shop with its Victorian style and wide, clean windows. The outside was painted blue with white trim on the window frames. A large white wooden sign hanging from a post and swinging over the sidewalk declared it to be GWYNETH ANTIQUITIES.

"It's charming," I said. Stepping closer to the window, I used my hands to shield the light so I could get a better look inside. "It looks really nice."

"She has beautiful things," Claire murmured.

Claire had called her aunt's store a "collectibles shop," but I'd never associated the word *collectibles* with the elegant antiques I was seeing here. I'd expected a curio shop filled with knickknacks and such, not this sophisticated store filled with such fine furnishings. I was itching to go inside and explore.

Claire added wistfully, "Aunt Gwyneth lives upstairs."

We all glanced up at the windows along the second floor. To my shock, a cat sat on the interior window ledge looking down at us.

"There's a cat," I said, in a "duh" moment.

"That's Heathcliff," Claire said. "Isn't he beautiful?"

"Yes."

"He's a longhaired Siamese cat and quite a darling thing."

From where I was standing the cat looked healthy and well loved. I turned to Claire. "You've got someone feeding him?"

"Yes, my friend Sophie stops by every day to feed him and spend time with him. But I know he misses Gwyneth."

It made me think of our cat, Charlie, and I hated to imagine what she would do without us. Even more wrenching was the thought of what *we* would do without *her*.

Claire took one more look upstairs. "I'll come by tomorrow morning to play with Heathcliff and see how the cleanup went. Sophie hired a cleaning company to put it back in order."

"That was nice." But I glanced at Derek and wondered if he was concerned that we might've lost out on a possible clue or two. On the other hand, it would've been unconscionable to leave the poor cat alone in a place that was a ransacked mess.

"We'll come with you tomorrow," Derek said.

I nodded in agreement. There was no way we were going to let Claire come into town—or go anywhere else—by herself. And besides, despite the cleanup, there might still be the possibility of finding clues to Gwyneth's disappearance.

We continued our slow walk, checking out the store windows and reading the menus posted outside the local restaurants. Once we'd reached the second block of stores, I looked at Allen. "Will you tell us a bit about the new laird?"

"Of course." He smiled at me. "Cameron's my oldest

friend so I probably know him better than anyone. He's amiable and can be very charming—when he wants to be."

"Do the townspeople like him?"

"Aye, they do. He's made it clear that he plans to devote himself to elevating the appeal of the castle with the goal of creating a more positive legacy for his family and for the village. He also has a passion for preserving the land and improving the village economy. We're hopeful that he can accomplish a lot of good."

"It sounds like he has to be part politician," I said with a smile.

"Aye." He shrugged. "You've got to have a bit of the politician in you if you want to appeal to the majority of people."

"So you've known him a long time?"

"Since we were both in nappies. As lads we rambled through the woods together, went fishing, and raced boats on the Loch. His father, the old laird, was a good man. He and my father were fast friends. But now the old laird is gone and my father . . . well, he passed away last year."

"I'm so sorry," Claire said.

"That must've been hard for you," I murmured.

"He'd been sick awhile. Dementia, you know."

"Oh, that's tragic," I said.

"Thank you." His smile was heartfelt. "But enough morbid talk. Back to Cameron, who is both fair and honest. Some even say he's a good-looking fellow." He grinned, but the smile soon faded. "I should warn you to have a care around him, because . . ." He stopped.

"Because what?" I asked.

Claire gave his arm a little swat. "Don't tease us, Allen."

Reluctantly, he said, "Some say he's a dangerous man."

Derek's eyes narrowed. "Dangerous in what way?"

"Ach, I should keep my mouth shut." Allen waved his hand as if he could brush the words away. "I don't set any store by rumors."

"Then why'd you say it?" Claire asked casually. It was clear to me that they'd known each other a long time.

He smiled sheepishly. "Well now, I can only blame it on the company. We were having some laughs and I was feeling comfortable with you. I forgot myself."

But I watched him silently grit his teeth and finally he blew out a throaty breath. "Och, fine. I might as well be the one to tell you because you'll hear the rumors eventually." He made eye contact with each of us. "They say that Cameron MacKinnon killed his wife. Drowned her in the Loch. It's not true, of course. Just silly, vicious rumors."

"Drowned her in the Loch?" Claire whispered.

I saw her face go pale and knew instantly what was going through her mind. I had to admit I was envisioning the same thing. It was a scene from *Rebecca*. I pictured the movie version, in which Mr. Maxim de Winter, played by Laurence Olivier, kills his first wife and puts her body in a small boat. He takes the boat out on the lake, dumps the body in the water, and sinks the boat.

I managed to shake myself out of the disturbing vision, but Claire was still trembling. Allen clutched her arm. "I'm sorry. So sorry. I've frightened you."

"A little," she admitted, and shook her head to get her wits back. "I'll be fine. I've never heard those rumors before."

"You haven't lived here for a long time, Claire," Allen pointed out.

"No, but I visit my aunt fairly regularly." She shook her head again. "Ah, well, I suppose she didn't want to upset me with any of your lurid local gossip." She managed to smile as she said it, and Allen seemed mollified.

"Let me make up for my bad manners by treating you all to dinner," he said.

"You don't have to do that," I protested.

"It's really not necessary," Derek said.

"I'm not talking about haute cuisine," Allen said, chuckling. "It's just the pub. Still, I'd be honored to have you as my guests on your first night in town."

The pub was crowded, but Allen managed to snag two seats at the bar. Claire and I sat down and Derek and Allen stood behind us. There was live music playing in one of the other rooms and it brought back memories of the last time I was in Edinburgh for their annual book festival. The memories weren't necessarily good ones because someone I cared for was killed while I was there. I shoved those thoughts away and tried to concentrate on the music, the laughter, the faces of the people, and the scent of dark, yeasty ales mixed with deep-fried fish and chips.

And that perked me right up.

"Well, now, what's this all about?" the bartender said as she approached us for our orders. She had long, dark hair that she'd pulled into a sexy, tousled twist on top of her head. She wore a plain long-sleeved white shirt tucked into skinny jeans and seriously thick-soled Doc Martens.

Claire grinned. "Hello, Sophie."

"Claire!" Sophie leaned across the bar and gave Claire's hand an affectionate squeeze. "I'll get a hug from you later."

"Aye, you will," Claire said.

Sophie winked at Allen, then said to Claire, "Who are your friends?"

"These are my friends from San Francisco." She introduced us to Sophie, who explained that her parents owned the pub and that she was the manager. I liked her immediately.

We ordered beers and continued to chat like old friends. Both Claire and Sophie introduced Derek and me to a few other Oddlochen residents as they passed by us.

From Sophie I found out a few things about the town that Claire hadn't mentioned before. Apparently there had been a BBC historical drama filmed in the area a few years back and since then, a regular stream of eager tourists continued to visit Oddlochen to tour the nearby abbey ruins, bike along the Caledonian Canal, fish in the Loch, and pray for a Nessie sighting. The BBC drama was a big reason why so many small inns and B and B establishments had proliferated in the area. One of them, the recently renovated Loch View Manor, right in the middle of the high street, was said to be haunted by the innkeeper who first opened the place in 1879. Apparently his wife had killed him after catching him in bed with a pretty barmaid.

"That reminds me that there used to be a popular ghost tour in the castle," Sophie said. "But the old laird shut it down."

"A ghost tour," I said, glancing at Derek, who raised his eyebrows in interest. It made sense because according to Allen, the castle had its very own ghost.

"Oh yes," Sophie continued as she dispensed an IPA for a nearby customer. "Complete with secret passages, odd sounds at night, and a chilly spot on the staircase. I was hoping the new laird would bring back the tour. It was a kick, you see, and I imagine a decent source of income as well."

I couldn't keep from wondering where those secret passages led to.

"It did bring in revenue," Allen said. "But the Mac-Kinnon isn't convinced it should be brought back. Thinks it might be in bad taste."

"Well, what's so wrong with that?" Sophie asked saucily, and cackled with laughter.

"I'll send him to talk to you," Allen said with a grin.

"Do that," Sophie said. "Now, wasn't there some talk of turning part of the castle into a museum?"

"That sounds interesting," I interjected, "and not in bad taste at all."

"Not a bit," Allen agreed. "Now, the laird isn't quite convinced that the castle should be open to the public again, but it is truly brimming with Scottish history. The cellar is fairly stuffed with old suits of armor and weaponry, odd pieces of furniture of all sorts, and books that belong in the library. We recently hired more staff to start an inventory and bring up some items he'd like to display in the foyer and the great hall."

"I'd love to see them," I said.

"I shall give you a personal tour." He took a hearty sip of his ale. "The library itself is impressive, too. Or it would be if not for the layers of dust and grime that would keep even the most ardent booklover from ever entering the room."

I met Claire's gaze. Allen had just checked off our two main interests: books and weaponry. What were the chances of that? Probably pretty high, I realized, since medieval castles in general would be rife with such items as books and weaponry. Still, how amazing would it be if we could actually convince the laird to turn the castle into a museum and library? We could help!

I laughed at myself. It was silly to even contemplate. Still, it would be awesome to have a hand in assisting the laird in planning out his new museum and library. If he did intend to open his home to the public, that is. And if he didn't turn out to be a vicious killer, of course.

"Can I draw you another lager?" Sophie asked. "Or would you rather get a table?"

Claire looked at the group. "Are you hungry?"

I rubbed my stomach. "I'm famished."

"I could sit down to dinner," Derek said.

"Right, then." Allen nodded. "We'll have a table, Sophie."

"I'll take care of it. And Claire, if you're interested, we've added four new axe-throwing lanes next door."

I stared at Sophie, then gave Claire a hopeful look. "Axe throwing right here in the bar."

"Well, not exactly in the bar," Sophie said, "but just next door. It's all the rage in Scotland now."

Claire smirked. "Might be due to all the men who fancy themselves mighty Highland warriors."

"I'd love to see it," I said.

"It's like darts on steroids," Sophie explained with a laugh.

"Have you ever thrown an axe, Brooklyn?" Allen asked.

"Um, no."

"Would you like to, then?"

I'd never shied away from a challenge and after begging Claire to teach me how to throw an axe, how could I say no? I glanced at Derek, who was grinning back at me in a clear signal that he was game for anything. "Sounds like fun, but first I need fish and chips."

* * *

We threw axes.

We paired up, with Derek and me composing one team against Allen and Claire on the other.

Plywood boards lined the target wall and floor of the well-lit space. In case the thrower missed his target, they didn't want the nice sharp edge of an axe to ruin the regular flooring or the paneled walls. Indoor-outdoor carpeting was laid down in the area where customers stood to aim and throw to prevent anyone from slipping or sliding with an axe in their hand.

The lanes were each about fifteen feet long with large wooden bull's-eye targets nailed to the far end. A wall of chicken wire separated each set of two lanes from the next two. The chicken wire was a brilliant idea because nobody wanted an axe to fly off and land in someone else's target a few lanes over.

The axes themselves were lighter weight and more well-balanced than the typical axe used to split wood.

I was given a quick lesson by the sprightly fellow in charge of the lanes. But still, my first few throws were wildly off target and probably would've landed in the next county if not for the chicken wire barrier. I started to get the hang of it, though, and was thrilled when my fourth throw placed the axe just millimeters away from the center ring on the bull's-eye.

It was no surprise to find that Claire was a certifiable expert at the sport. After a while I was happy to just stand on the sidelines and watch her throw.

Apparently there were a number of people who felt the same way and a small crowd grew to watch her demonstrate her talent.

Allen cheered her on and quickly began to act as her agent, lining up competitors to take a chance against her. We had a good time, even when a couple of men began placing bets on her ability to take down the next challenger. It was all in good fun, or so I thought.

After a while, Allen jogged over to us. "Sorry, but I've got to use the head. I won't be long. After that, we can go whenever you're ready."

"All right," Derek said. "We'll wait here with Claire."

"She's in a class by herself, isn't she?" Allen stared at her with admiration. "The crowd loves her."

The crowd had grown, I realized, and I casually surveyed the people watching Claire. It was a jovial scene with everyone smiling and having a good time—except for one guy who was scowling. *He must've been having a fight with his girlfriend*, I thought. I watched him for another minute and finally decided that he was alone. Maybe that was why he was scowling. But there was no explanation as to why his cranky mood seemed clearly aimed at Claire.

Was he jealous of her prowess? I sighed inwardly. Too bad he was so good-looking, I thought, because he definitely needed an attitude adjustment.

He was almost as tall as Derek, but slightly more muscular. His skin was fair and his hair was dark red, which matched his closely cropped beard. He was seriously gorgeous, with clear blue eyes that were currently cold and flat.

What was it about the British Isles that produced men so ridiculously handsome? For instance, there were my husband and his four brothers, all outrageously hunky. And for another instance, there was Allen Brodie. And now this guy, with his brooding good looks, who was staring at Claire as if he wanted to reach out and throttle her.

Was it because she was so good at axe throwing? Did he resent her for her skills?

I suddenly felt the familiar chills on my arms. Was this another guy who was out to get Claire? Or to steal the copy of *Rebecca*? We had come to Oddlochen to track down the bad guys, but I honestly hadn't expected to find one in the pub on our first night in town.

Then again, maybe his cranky mood was as simple as him having that fight with his girlfriend, as I'd first thought. Maybe my imagination was spinning tales again. Either way, I was going to keep my eye on this guy. His attitude was weird. And possibly dangerous.

I pulled out my camera and leaned into Derek. "Pretend I'm taking our picture," I whispered, but instead switched the camera around to take the broody guy's picture. I flashed a toothy smile, took four quick shots, and then kissed Derek on the cheek. "Thanks."

"Not that I'm complaining, but what was that for?"

"Don't look yet," I cautioned, "but that guy across from us with the really nice camel's hair trench coat in the middle of the group? He hasn't stopped glaring at Claire."

Derek gave me a warm smile, then casually turned to watch Claire throw another axe and hit the bull's-eye. The crowd cheered and Derek said, "I see him. Send me one of those photos and I'll run it through my facial recognition app. I'm not taking any chances with her."

"Coming right up." I went through the quick process of sending and seconds later I heard his phone beep.

"Got it," he said.

Less than a year ago, Derek would've been forced to send the photo to his assistant, who would run it through his company's program that accessed the worldwide system used to track down bad guys. But now there was an app for that.

Of course, Derek's wasn't just any app that anyone could download. This app had been developed by scientists employed by the international intelligence communities for those few individuals who possessed the highest security clearances on the planet.

Derek pressed a few buttons and swiped his screen once or twice while I went back to watching Claire. It was fascinating to see the change that came over her whenever she had a weapon in her hand. She became a different person. *A warrior princess*, I thought, and smiled.

"Brooklyn," Derek whispered in my ear.

"What is it?" I turned and saw his grim expression. "You got a match already?"

"See for yourself." He showed me his phone screen.

I stared at the screen, saw the name, and cursed silently. Gazing up at Derek, I said, "I don't believe it."

"Believe it, darling."

The man whose eyes had been shooting daggers at Claire was none other than laird Cameron MacKinnon.

Now I wondered why more of the townspeople hadn't noticed him or made a fuss over his presence. But then, that sharp glare of his had probably made them all think twice about approaching him.

I looked back at Derek and just shook my head. Then, because I couldn't help myself, I snuck another glance at the angry man—the angry laird, that is. But he was gone.

Derek and I waited on the sidelines until Claire won her next challenge. We continued to look around for Allen, but he never returned.

It worried me. And judging by Derek's expression, it

worried him, too. Where had Allen gone? And for that matter, where had laird Cameron MacKinnon slipped off to?

Claire finally finished off her last challenger and joined us. "Thanks for hanging in there while I shamelessly showed off." She was flushed and happy from her awesome axe-throwing performance and neither Derek nor I was willing to bum her out just yet.

"That was so much fun," I said. "You're just fantastic."

"Thanks." She glanced around. "Where'd Allen go?"

I fibbed a little. "I guess he had to meet someone. We thought he might come back, but it's getting late. He probably went home."

"Let's get back to the castle," Derek suggested. "We can talk in the privacy of our rooms."

"Sounds good," she said.

I slipped my arm through hers. "I hope you'll lower yourself to give me some pointers."

"I'll be happy to," she said with a laugh. "And thanks. It was really fun."

The three of us took off, following the village high street to Aunt Gwyneth's shop. Without a word, we all stopped and looked up at her apartment and saw Heathcliff the cat sitting on the ledge without a care in the world. For some reason, the sight relieved some anxiety in me.

"All is right with the world," Claire whispered.

"A calm cat is always a good sign," Derek murmured, making me smile.

We started to walk on, but I took a quick look back at the cat. And that was when I saw an odd light flashing in Gwyneth's shop. I blinked to make sure my eyes weren't playing tricks, then looked again. There were no flashes.

"What is it, Brooklyn?" Derek asked.

"It might be my imagination," I whispered, "but I thought I saw a light moving inside the shop. It might've been coming from a flashlight, but it's gone now."

"Wait here. I'll be right back." He ran to the first side street and disappeared around the corner.

"Do these stores have a back entrance?" I asked.

"Aye," Claire said. "The delivery entrance for the shop is in the back as well as the staircase leading up to the apartment."

If someone had been inside the shop, they had obviously broken in through the back way.

I took a few stealthy steps back to the front display window and snuck a peek inside the store. It took a moment for my eyes to adjust.

"What do you see?" Claire asked, her voice low.

I scowled. "Nothing. I was probably imagining it."

Claire linked her arm with mine. "Given all that we've been through, I'm perfectly willing to believe you saw exactly what you say you saw."

"Thanks." So at least one person thought I was sane. That was a hopeful sign.

It was another minute before Derek rounded the corner and jogged up to us.

"Did you find anything?" I asked.

He pulled me close. "Let's wait until we get to our rooms."

"All right," I said, but the tone of his voice was ominous.

We walked in silence through the woods. A slight breeze stirred the leaves and the rustling sounds gave me chills. I forgave myself for being freaked out, though, because it was so dark in these woods that I could barely see in front of my feet. At one point I had the creepiest feeling that we were being watched, but I knew I was imagining it. How could anyone see us in these pitch-dark surroundings?

"Boy, it gets dark in these woods," I said, trying to sound casual but hearing the tremor in my voice.

"Don't worry," Claire whispered. "I'm carrying a knife and I know how to use it."

"Yeah? Okay, that's good." Did she think someone was watching us, too? Or did I sound so rattled that she just wanted to reassure me?

Derek finally pulled out his phone and turned on the flashlight app.

"Genius," I said.

He shook his head. "I often forget I have this app, but it really comes in handy."

Somehow we made it back to the castle without incident and used our room key to open the main entry into the foyer. We locked the double doors and hurried upstairs to our rooms.

Claire opened her bedroom door, then jolted when the little black-and-white cat zoomed past her ankles and headed for the staircase. With a laugh she said, "Hello, Robbie. Are you here to welcome us home?"

"Take a few minutes to chill out," I said, "then come next door so we can talk."

"Sounds good," she said. "I'll just be a few minutes."

I closed our door and Derek wrapped his arms around me. After a long, comforting moment, I finally said, "I'm afraid to go to sleep."

He rubbed my back. "I'll be right here to keep you safe."

"My hero," I said, and smiled up at him. "I'll keep you safe, too."

"My heroine," he said, and planted a kiss on the top of my head.

He stepped away and began to move around the room, checking odd things like the doorknob and the magazine on the table and my suitcase zippers.

"You took precautions before we left?" I asked.

"Yes."

We'd stayed in hotel rooms before and I knew that Derek set little traps for any would-be intruder. "So what's the verdict?"

He gazed at me from where he stood in front of the pale gold drapes that we'd pulled across the picture window before we left. "Nobody entered our room."

I sank down onto the chair. "That's a relief."

"Yes, but not for long. Something is very wrong around here."

"But Claire is pretty sure her aunt is safe, based on the card that came with the flowers."

His glance said it all. "What do you think?"

"I'd like to think it's true, but why has Gwyneth gone missing all this time?"

"Perhaps she knew she was in danger and went into hiding on her own."

"And maybe she got word that Claire was back in town and didn't want to alarm her any more than she already was."

"Maybe." He joined me at the table. "We've got to get to the bottom of this."

"We have a few ways to go about it," I said. "We can check out the west tower first thing tomorrow. And we can swing by Gwyneth's place with Claire. We might find some answers there." I frowned and stared at Derek. "I just realized you didn't tell me what you saw when you checked out the back of Aunt Gwyneth's apartment."

"The store is locked up safe and sound. But the

apartment door was unlocked." His lips twisted into a frown.

"I can't imagine Sophie would leave the door unlocked when she came by to feed the cat."

"No."

"Someone was looking for something?"

"I believe so," he said. "Although there was no sign of ransacking. Everything looked nicely tucked away in their places."

"Maybe we scared him off before he could do any damage."

"Perhaps."

"Do you think our presence in town forced someone to take action?"

"Quite possibly." He scowled. "I locked the door, so if he comes back, he'll have to break in."

"Oh great." I shook my head. "I guess we're assuming an awful lot. Maybe it was just Sophie checking up on the cat."

"Maybe," he said with a rueful smile. "But you don't really think so."

"No, but assumptions and guesses are all we have right now."

We were both silent for a moment, then Derek changed the subject. "I don't know the significance of this yet, but I noticed that one of the castle staff has the same surname as one of our San Francisco victims."

That was news to me. "Really? I didn't catch that."

"I was typing them into my calendar and the name was unusual enough to catch my attention." He pulled out his phone, pressed open his calendar app, and stared at the screen. "Here. It's Jenny MacDougall, the downstairs maid. She could be a relative of Reggie MacDougall, formerly known as Pizza Man."

"Jenny was the name of the girl talking to Treena in the kitchen."

"Right," Derek said. "Good catch, darling."

I gave him a quick smile. "You know, MacDougall is a fairly common name in Scotland, although we don't see it much in the States."

He nodded. "Exactly."

"Let's talk to Jenny tomorrow morning." I grabbed my own phone, opened up my own calendar app. "I need to make a list of things to do." I added Gwyneth's apartment visit to my list, along with our goal to get a look at the west tower.

"Claire will be here any minute," he said.

"I'm ready." I left my phone open on the table. "So how do we break the news that our so-called major player appeared at the pub tonight and glared at her like some panther stalking his prey?"

"I wonder if she even saw him," Derek mused.

"I doubt it. If she'd seen him, his intensity would've screwed up her throwing arm."

"Then perhaps it's a good thing she didn't see him."

Chapter 15

"The new laird was at the pub?" Claire sank down into the chair. "Watching me throw axes?"

"Yes," I said, draping my jacket over a wingback chair before joining her at our small table. "I didn't know who he was, but his expression was irate enough that it worried me. So I took a photo and Derek ran it through his facial recognition app."

"What's his problem? Why would he be angry with me?"

"I don't know, but look." I pulled out my phone and showed her the photos. "You tell me what that's all about."

"He certainly doesn't look happy," she admitted after studying the pictures. "I wonder why."

"His mood might have nothing to do with you," Derek said. "He might've simply been off his dinner. Or ran into an acquaintance and got into a fight."

"Yeah," I said. "Maybe he was just in a bad mood. Maybe his girlfriend stood him up."

She continued to stare at the photos. "He looks so stern. Handsome, though." She rolled her eyes. "Oh God, what a stupid thing to say. As if his looks had anything to do with it."

"He is handsome," I agreed. "But even good-looking people can kill."

She winced.

"Sorry about that," I said quickly.

"No, no. You're right. Good-looking or not, somebody killed those two men who were after me." She slumped back in her chair. "I'm not sure the laird even knows who I am."

"I'm going to wager he does," Derek said.

"I've got to go with Derek on this one," I said.

She was close to wringing her hands. "But he looks so angry. What did I ever do to him?"

"I can't imagine you ever did anything to him." I exchanged a look with Derek. "But is it possible that Gwyneth did something?"

Claire looked at both of us. "What do you mean?"

"Oh, you know. Like, maybe she stole something from him. Or maybe she accused him of something." I snapped my fingers. "Or maybe she accused his father of something. They were all friends, right?"

Claire frowned at the thought. "Right. I suppose it's possible. But why would Gwyneth say anything to the MacKinnon about his father?"

I stood and began to pace. "Look, I'm just throwing out possibilities. The thing is, there could be something going on here that has nothing to do with you."

"Brooklyn." She tapped my phone screen for emphasis. "If it doesn't have anything to do with me, then why is he giving me dirty looks?"

"Hey, maybe he likes you," I said. "You know how a boy sometimes hits a girl with a stick because he likes her?"

Claire burst out laughing. "Perhaps if he's six years old."

I shrugged. "Some guys never grow up."

"Oh, Brooklyn." She reached across the table and squeezed my hands companionably. "Thank you for making me laugh."

Derek folded his arms across his chest. "Maybe we'll find out more at breakfast tomorrow."

"Oh dear," Claire said. "Do you think he'll be there?"

Derek glanced at me, then back at Claire. "I would bet he'll make a point of it."

Clearly concerned about the possibility, she took a moment to think about that. "We should go right up to the tower and see what's there."

"Right now?" I asked.

"No, no. Sorry, I'm already thinking about the morning. We should go right after breakfast."

Derek stood and moved around the room. I couldn't tell if he was antsy or if he just had something on his mind. "Breakfast is definitely first. We might meet some of the staff then."

"Good thinking," I said.

"The other agenda items can wait," he said. "But I've been thinking about the tower and my feeling is that it'll still be there whenever we're able to get to it. I think the first thing we should do after breakfast is go to your aunt's apartment."

"Oh. Well, I definitely wanted to go by Aunt Gwyneth's."

"Why are you making it a priority?" I asked.

Now that he'd stated his initial feelings to us, he was able to sit down and relax. "Your aunt sent me a book and thanks to Brooklyn's keen awareness, we were able to find the code and break it. I have a feeling she might've left some other messages around her house."

"That's a good point," I said.

"We worked together for many years. I think she used her knowledge of the job and of me to fashion a message that only I could interpret."

"You guys were master spies together."

The look he gave me was droll to the max. "I beg your pardon. We were intelligence officers."

I grinned back at him. "I like 'master spies.'"

"I'm perfectly happy to go to Aunt Gwyneth's first thing," Claire said. "I can visit with Heathcliff while you investigate and scrutinize."

"Then it's settled," I said. And having said it, I suddenly felt exhausted. But Claire looked troubled. "What is it, Claire?"

She pressed her lips together and then frowned. "Do you worry that our rooms are bugged?"

"No," Derek said.

"Derek already checked for bugs," I said. But I lowered my voice automatically.

"I didn't check your room yet," Derek said. "But I will."

She shrugged, then finally said, "Please do. I'll sleep a lot better that way."

Derek asked, "Have you had any conversations with anyone while you've been in your room?"

"No. I don't really have anyone to talk to. But it could happen."

He nodded. "I have a device that can detect bugs. I'll sweep your room tomorrow morning before we go downstairs to breakfast."

"Oh, that's great." She shook her hair back. "I'm afraid I'm becoming quite paranoid."

"It's perfectly normal," I said. "After all, someone may be trying to kill you."

She rolled her eyes. "Thanks a lot for that."

"The upside is that it's not just you," I said with a tight smile. "They may be trying to kill all of us."

It was still dark out when I woke up. Checking my phone, I was bummed to see that the local time was barely 4 a.m. I closed my eyes and tried to ease my way back into sleep, but it was useless. Jet lag had screwed up my circadian rhythms and now I was wide awake with nothing to do.

"You're a bookbinder. You always have something to do," I muttered irascibly, and carefully slipped out of bed so I wouldn't wake up Derek. He was the world's lightest sleeper so I was surprised to see him still zonked out.

I pulled my binding supplies and equipment from my suitcase, then sat down with *Mistress of Mellyn* and got to work.

As I arranged my things on the table, I did the math and realized that it was barely 9 p.m. in San Francisco. I typed out a quickie text to Alex and hit send. Three minutes later I had a response from her that trailed all the way down the screen. Lots of news, I thought, and it was all pretty good.

Now I'd be able to report to Claire that Mr. D was doing well. He and Charlie were new best friends and were enjoying daily visits not only from Alex, but also from our neighbors Vinnie and Suzie and their little girl Lily, and young Tyler Chung, who lived farther down the hall.

Alex further reported that according to Gabriel, things were quiet in Dharma. She also said that Inspector Lee had called off her drive-by team, which convinced me that the hubbub had died down the minute the three of us left town. That news also went a long way toward verifying our theory that whoever had accompanied Reggie and Jerome—and subsequently had killed them both—had fled San Francisco about the same time we did.

I would have to remember to ask Derek if his security team was still watching Claire's house. And ours, too, for that matter. Then I set my phone down and forgot about everything else but the book.

I splayed Claire's *Mistress of Mellyn*, cover side down, on one of my white cloths and carefully ran my X-Acto knife along the hinge between the back cover and the spine. I wanted to completely remove the cover from the textblock and go to work on scraping up the dried glue on the spine itself.

At this point I didn't have to worry that I was harming the old cloth cover because I would have to replace it anyway. The intruder had caused the front cover to break away from the spine except for a few weak threads.

Coincidentally, the cover of this book was black with the title gilded on the spine, similar to the *Rebecca*. On a whim, I picked up the textblock and turned to the title page of *Mistress of Mellyn*. It was published in 1960 and I wondered if it was a first edition. That probably wasn't something Claire cared much about, but I thought it would be interesting to know more about it.

I suddenly yearned for my bag of chocolate caramel Kisses and was disgusted to realize that I was a hapless victim of Pavlovian stimulus. In other words, whenever I start working on a book, I automatically begin to crave chocolate candy. Or maybe it was the caramel. Either way, I had to admit that scarfing down a dozen chocolate caramel Kisses at four in the morning was a bad decision.

With both covers separated from the spine, I picked

up the front cover and began to pry the pastedown—the paper that covered the interior—away from the heavy board beneath. The boards themselves were in fine shape, but they were smothered in so much old glue that they would have to be sanded before I could re-cover them smoothly with the new cloth.

If I'd wanted to salvage the old cloth cover, this could've been a precarious job. But that wasn't the case for this book and it actually felt good to simply run my knife under the edges of the endpapers and pry and tear as I went.

I couldn't wait to get out my file and sandpaper and scrub off that old dried glue from the boards and the spine.

"You're working on a book."

"Huh?" I looked up and saw Derek sitting up in bed and staring at me.

"You're up and working already."

"I am. Good morning." As usual, I had become so wrapped up in what I was doing that I hadn't realized how much time had passed. "I couldn't sleep so I decided to get some work done."

Sunlight was slipping through the edges of the heavy drapes so I knew that a couple hours must've passed while I'd worked. I started to reach for my phone to check the time, but Derek beat me to it. "It's just after six o'clock. What time did you wake up?"

"Around four. Jet lag. I'm glad I took the time to do some work because I've barely done anything with this book since we've been on the run."

He gave me a half smile. "On the run?"

"Doesn't it feel like that?"

He climbed out of bed and tossed the covers back over the pillows. "I suppose it would if we were sneaking through the forest, eating berries, and hiding under tree limbs."

"You've never been on the run like that," I said, laughing.

He gave me the raised eyebrow, but said nothing.

"Are you saying you've eaten berries on the run in the forest?"

"I've never had to resort to picking berries, but I've had a few close calls."

I walked over and hugged him. "You'll never have to do that again."

"I'm determined to avoid it at all costs," he said, and stroked my hair. "But you're right that we're being kind of sneaky."

"I guess that was my point."

After a moment, he patted my back. "Help me make the bed."

"Okay." I walked over to my side of the bed and fluffed the pillows and straightened the quilted bedcover. I supposed that Mrs. Buchanan had someone on her staff who took care of such chores, but I hated to depend on them. This wasn't exactly a hotel.

I reached for my phone. "I'm going to text Claire to see if she's awake."

He opened the drapes and gazed out at Loch Ness. "That is beautiful."

I set down my phone and joined him, and we held on to each other. "I wish we had more time to enjoy it."

"We'll be here a few more days," he said, and smiled as he stroked my hair. "There might be an opportunity to explore the area."

"Maybe. But first things first."

His expression hardened. "Yes. It's important that

we confront the MacKinnon before we leave the house today."

I bit my lower lip, a sure sign that I was worried. "Do you honestly think it'll be a confrontation? Not just a happy little tête-à-tête?"

He pursed his lips to keep from laughing. "I have no idea what to expect so I'll expect the worst and see what happens. Perhaps I'll be pleasantly surprised."

Encouraged, I smiled. "Will you know by looking in his eyes if he's the one who sent the men to San Francisco?"

He gave that a light snort. "I doubt it. But it's possible we'll be able to determine by his answers whether he's lying or not."

I wrapped up the pieces of the book in the white cloth and then began to pack up my bookbinding tools, sliding them into their individual slots inside my canvas tool holder. Folding and rolling up the holder, I said, "We'll talk to Claire. We've got to be on the same page when we come face-to-face with the laird."

"Exactly right."

"So what questions do you have in mind for the laird?"

"Simple ones," Derek said, crossing the room to open his suitcase. "I want to get him to tell us where he's been for the past few days."

"You could keep it light and say something like, 'Mrs. Buchanan told us that you only returned last night. Were you out of town?'"

"Something like that." Derek pulled on a pair of blue jeans as we talked. "Except a question like that only requires a yes or no answer. Better to phrase it, 'Where did you go?'"

"I wouldn't have the nerve to be that straightforward."

He smirked at me. "Oh, I think you would if you had to."

"Maybe." I took in a breath. "But from what I saw of him last night, he's an intimidating guy."

"You might've been intimidated because you felt protective of Claire. But I refuse to believe that you'll be scared off once you meet him face-to-face."

"I appreciate your faith in me. I guess we'll have to see what happens." I combed through the clothes I'd brought with me, then looked back at Derek. "I could always ask him some other kinds of questions."

He grabbed a denim shirt to wear over his black T-shirt, and sat down to tie his hiking boots. "Maybe something particular about the castle or the town."

"Oh, yeah." I perked up. "I could ask about that ghost tour they used to have."

"There you go."

"And I could request to see the library."

"You're perfect, darling."

"I love you, too." I slipped into black jeans and pulled a dark gray sweater on over my head. "And then once the laird's gone off to his quarters, we slip out of here and check out Gwyneth's pad for secret messages."

Derek grinned. "Piece of cake, as you would say."

I snorted politely. "And fat chance, as you would say."

Before heading downstairs for breakfast, we knocked on Claire's door. When she opened, the cat dashed out into the hall and disappeared down the stairs. I quickly handed Claire a note that read: *We want to sweep your room for possible bugs.*

She stepped out into the hall and closed the door behind her. "How can I help?" she whispered.

"You'll have to turn off all of your wireless devices," Derek said. "Laptop, tablet, smartphone."

"I left my laptop with my neighbor Paul so I only have my phone with me." She had her phone in her hand and switched it off. "Can you tell me why?"

"Yes, of course," Derek said. "They emit frequencies that may interfere with this." He pulled the same cell-phone-sized radio frequency detector from his pocket and held it up for her to see. "This device will pick up the presence of any bugs that have been planted in your room."

"I see."

Derek gave her the same basic information he'd given to me. "A bug transmits a radio frequency signal to a receiving device. This detector will scan for all signals in the RF spectrum. And if it finds one, it will emit a beeping sound."

"Like a Geiger counter does when it detects radiation," I finished for him, and grinned proudly.

"Fascinating," Claire said, slipping her phone into her pocket. "I'm ready."

"Then let's go."

We walked into Claire's room and I shut the door and locked it. "I'm turning off my phone, too."

"Good." He turned on the detector and walked slowly around the room as he'd done in our room, holding the device in front of him. He hit the bookcase and then walked over to check out Claire's suitcase. Then he moved to the nightstands on either side of her bed.

Claire and I couldn't help but trail a few feet behind him.

After a few moments, Derek moved over to the bathroom. We followed and watched him scan her toiletries case and her bathrobe. He came out a minute later and moved right up to Claire and scanned her up and down, front and back. He held the device over the purse she wore like a backpack.

Finally he switched off the detector. "I didn't pick up anything."

"That's great," I said. "I'm so impressed."

Claire looked relieved. "Thank you so much."

"But I'm not quite finished." Derek pulled a high-powered mini-flashlight out of his jacket pocket, turned it on, and walked around the room again, shining the light into every little nook and cranny he could find. He shone it into the bookcase, and ran it up and down and over and in between the books. He aimed the beam up into the corners of the room and along the plate rail wainscoting that ran all the way around the room.

"Okay," he said, and slipped the flashlight into his pocket. "I think we're safe for now."

"What was that for?" I asked.

"I was concerned that they might've hardwired a camera in here."

"Oh, yuck," I said.

He shrugged. "It could be an attempt to monitor theft, but it's the wrong way to do it and offensive as well. But thankfully, I didn't find any cameras, either."

"How do you find them with a flashlight?"

"The light beam reflects off the lens."

"Oh." I squeezed his arm, impressed. "That's so clever."

He grinned. "Fairly low tech, but it works."

"How marvelous that you know all this intriguing stuff," Claire said. "Thank you. I feel much safer now."

"I'm glad," he said. "We'll be out for most of the day, which could give someone another chance to sneak in here and plant a device. So I'll sweep again this evening, just to be sure."

"Thank you again," Claire said. "I'm not sure I could deal with all of this without you two."

"We'll deal with it," Derek said resolutely. "And we'll find your aunt."

"Damn straight we will," I said, and gave Derek a big kiss.

On our way downstairs, I said, "Oh, before we go in to eat, I'd like to get a quick look at the great hall."

"I'm eager to see it, as well," Claire said.

Derek pointed the way. "Let's go."

At the bottom of the stairs we crossed the foyer and turned right. And stared in awe at the truly impressive room.

I had only one frame of reference to compare this room to and that was the great hall at Edinburgh Castle. Castle MacKinnon's hall was smaller, but not by much. It was probably about fifty feet long by thirty feet wide.

Claire gazed up at the ceiling. "Wow."

"My thoughts exactly." The entire ceiling was constructed of thick dark wood beams crosshatched to create a wide archway. Hanging from five of the beams were three-feet-wide chandeliers fashioned from hammered wrought iron with ten sturdy candleholders.

At the far end of the room was an enormous fireplace that I imagined was once used for grilling huge hunks of meat for serving visitors and guests of the laird. Both Derek and I could probably stand upright inside that massive firebox, but I wasn't going to step in there to prove it.

Along both walls were rows of utility tables on which were scattered small weapons of all kinds. Some of the tables were covered in sheets. These must've been the weapons that the staffers had brought up from the basement.

I stood next to Claire. "Do you think these will ever be organized well enough to be displayed in glass cases for the world to see?"

She trailed her hand along the edge of the table. "I don't know if the world will ever see them, but it would be a lovely way to display them."

"Maybe if we see a staff member we can ask." I followed Claire to another table, where she lifted a sheet to reveal rows and rows of shields and swords, many obviously very rare and valuable.

"Wow," I said for the fortieth time. "These are like beautiful pieces of artwork."

"But it's distressing to see so many items missing."

"How do you know they're missing?" I asked.

She pointed out an elaborately carved and inlaid wooden box. She ran her fingers along the edge. "See the indentation in the velvet lining? This should hold a matching set of Regency-era pistols, but there's only one here."

I frowned because I hadn't noticed it. "Good catch."

"And look here." She held up a small wooden case with inlaid ivory strips. "This should contain a matching set of decorative dirks." She lifted a small knife with a fancy hilt made of mother-of-pearl and a beautifully carved brass pommel. "But there's only one dirk in the case."

"Maybe their matching partners are still somewhere in the basement."

"I hope so."

We wandered over to another table. She stared at the plethora of daggers and knives and smiled. "This is a very impressive collection of daggers and dirks and dubhs."

"Oh my."

She gazed at me in confusion, then grinned. "Oh yes. Lions and tigers and bears. Good one."

"So what's the story with all of these knives?" I counted at least twenty of the smaller knives, scattered about in no particular order. "What's the difference between a dirk and a dubh and a dagger?"

"Good question." She picked up a stubby, single-edged knife. "This is a Sgian-dubh." She pronounced it "skee-en-doo." "It's part of the traditional Highland dress kilt. Highlanders once used these for eating, cutting meat and cheeses, and such. But not so much anymore."

"And the dirk?"

"It's basically a longer dagger. But not always."

"That's helpful."

She smiled. "I know. Sorry." She pointed to two different weapons. "This is a dirk and that is a dagger. There are other differences, but that's good enough for now."

"So what are all these things here?" I pointed to the table.

"It appears that the items on this table are starting to be sorted out. They're all sixteenth- and seventeenth-century Scottish dirks."

"There are some pretty ones," I said.

"Yes." She picked up one of them and held it lovingly. "I envision this in a two-way display, perhaps inside a plexiglass box. You'd want to be able to show off the intricate engravings on both sides of the blades because they're different. See?"

She handed it to me and I turned it over to compare.

"You're right, both sides have interesting details. You should mention that to his lairdship."

She grinned. "Perhaps I will."

We got to the next table and nothing was in order. In fact, this display was worse than the first few tables. Many of the weapons were in a jumbled pile and everything was tarnished.

I wrinkled my nose. "I sort of dread walking into the library after seeing the condition of some of these weapons."

"I don't blame you," Claire said. "And Allen already warned you about the dust."

"He did, but I thought he was exaggerating. Looking at this, I'm not so sure."

In the corner were two life-sized suits of armor. I ventured closer to one of them. "They're badly tarnished, too."

"I suppose that's repairable," Derek mused.

"With a lot of elbow grease," I said, and wondered if the laird would even bother. The room and its furnishings were a study in contrasts between great beauty and sad degradation. But maybe I was being unfair. After all, Harold had warned Derek that the old laird had run the place into the ground. With that in mind, I scanned the room again. The place actually looked pretty good, considering.

Derek gazed at the row of longbows hanging on one wall. On the opposite wall were dozens of long spears displayed in clusters. "Despite some of the disarray, this room is quite impressive," Derek murmured.

"Thank you," a man said behind us.

We all turned and saw him standing in the doorway, casually resting his shoulder against the jamb. It was none other than Cameron MacKinnon, the laird of the castle.

He didn't look quite as intimidating as he had last night in the pub, but he was just as handsome, if not more so, now that he wore an attentive smile.

"We hope you don't mind the intrusion, Laird Mac-Kinnon," Derek said smoothly as he approached Mac-Kinnon with his arm outstretched. "I'm Derek Stone."

They shook hands. "Commander Stone, a pleasure to meet you."

It seemed like a perfectly amiable meeting of the two men. So why was every muscle in my body clenched like a vise? And how did he know that Derek's former title was Commander?

Mrs. Buchanan must've said something to him. And even if she didn't, this guy probably knew every last detail about all of us.

Derek turned to me and Claire. "May I present my wife, Brooklyn Wainwright? And perhaps you already know Claire Quinn."

"How do you do, Ms. Wainwright?" he said to me as we shook hands. "I understand you're a book expert."

"Yes, I am," I said. "Thank you for your kind hospitality."

"I would be happy to show you our library when you have time," he said.

"I would love to see it," I said eagerly, and thought, *Oh yeah, he knew who we were.*

He turned to Claire and gave a slight bow. "We've never met, Ms. Quinn, but I know your aunt and your father."

Claire was about to shake his hand, but jerked back abruptly. "You knew my father?"

He held up both hands. "I should say, I've *met* him. I don't know him well. He and your aunt Gwyneth are lifelong friends of my father."

He extended his hand once again and Claire reluctantly shook it.

Did Claire realize that the laird was speaking of her father in the present tense? Was the man still alive?

I wasn't sure I wanted to say anything to Claire. I would ask Derek about that later.

With her hand still in his, Claire said, "Did you know that my aunt is missing? Have you any idea where I can find her?"

Go, Claire, I thought. *Way to get to the point.* I silently applauded her for asking the question we all wanted to know the answer to.

And now the MacKinnon was scowling at her just as he'd done the night before.

He hesitated, looked as if he might say something important, but then his expression stiffened. "I can't help you." And he turned and strode out the door.

I gaped at the retreating figure, then looked at Derek. "What the heck was that all about?"

Derek continued to stare at the doorway. "He knows something."

"Oh, aye, he does," Claire said, pressing her lips in a tight line.

I gauged her level of anger and distress and finally said, "Does this mean I won't get my library tour?"

"Oh, Brooklyn." Claire laughed, and her muscles seemed to relax again.

I had expected tears so I was happy to see her laughing. Ever since those flowers were delivered the night before, her mood had been lighter and I was glad for it.

"Sorry," I said, tongue in cheek. "My priorities sometimes tend to get skewed."

"Don't be sorry," she said. "I intend to get some answers out of him. And while I'm at it, I'll get you that library tour." She led the way out of the great hall, then looked over her shoulder and grinned. "If I don't get tossed out on my bum first."

Breakfast was served at the big family table in the kitchen instead of the formal dining room. Mrs. Buchanan had offered us a choice and when we saw the sunny alcove off the main kitchen, we were charmed. It was where the staff dined, she explained, but everyone had already eaten and gone off to do their work.

We were served a feast that included every conceivable item in an English breakfast, plus haggis.

"We should eat heartily because who knows when we'll get another meal." I said it as an excuse for having eaten every last morsel on my plate.

"Did the laird find you?" Mrs. B asked as she poured more coffee.

"Aye, he did," Claire said, then glanced up at the housekeeper. "Mrs. B, has the laird ever said anything to you about Aunt Gwyneth's disappearance?"

"No," she said. "And that's odd, don't you think?"

"I do."

"Do you think he might know something?"

Claire took a deep breath. "I think he could."

Mrs. B considered that. "Well, he certainly has connections that none of us has."

Since we were all finished with breakfast, the subject was dropped. Derek stood and turned to Mrs. Buchanan. "Do you know if Jenny MacDougall is available? I had a question to ask her."

"Jenny? I haven't seen her, but she might've gone straight to work." She frowned. "Although she usually stops in the kitchen for a sweet roll and coffee."

"Where would I find her?" he asked.

She checked her wristwatch. "She'll be finished with the front hall and the stairs. She's probably in the blue parlor. If you go past the great hall two more doors, it's on your right. It's quite pretty with a view of the Loch. You might consider having an afternoon aperitif in there when you get back from your rambles."

We all thanked her for a fabulous breakfast, then left the kitchen through the dining room.

When we got to the blue parlor, there was no Jenny.

"It is a pretty room," Claire said, strolling around the room and stopping by the large bay window. "All the views are wonderful, aren't they?"

"Yes." I joined her at the window. But I was acutely aware of Derek's tension and finally looked back at him.

"Shall we check a few more rooms?"

"Yes."

We followed him farther down the main hall, opening doors on either side. We found a pink parlor and a pool room next to a very clubby-looking bar.

"Maybe she's late coming to work," I said.

"Maybe." He checked his watch. "We've spent enough time looking for her. We should go into the village and look at your aunt's apartment."

"Oh yes." Claire clasped her hands together. "I want to check on Heathcliff. And I'd love it if you two would work your magic and discover something that will help us track down Aunt Gwyneth."

"That's exactly what I intend to do," he said.

I slipped my arm through his and gave Claire a bright smile. "Me, too."

Chapter 16

We were able to trek through the woods more quickly in the daylight and within minutes were back on the high street, enjoying the pretty storefronts and friendly faces. Among them, I found Sophie the bartender walking toward us. Today she wore her dark hair flowing down over her shoulders. She wore oversized sunglasses and was dressed from head to toe in black: black turtleneck, short black leather jacket, leggings, and knee-high boots.

Claire waved and Sophie hurried to meet us. "Good morning. I hope you all had a fun time last night."

"We did," I said. "The food was great and the axe throwing was awesome. Thank you so much."

"I heard a rumor that Claire was pure dead brilliant," Sophie said.

"She was," I gushed. "She's fantastic."

"You already heard about it?" Claire asked.

"Of course." Sophie laughed and elbowed Claire. "You know how gossip moves around here. People couldn't wait to come back to the pub and go on about our Claire's prowess. As though you're our village champion."

"She's good enough to qualify for that title," Derek assured her.

Claire's cheeks turned pink. "It was fun."

"So, did the laird find you?" Sophie asked, changing topics.

Claire frowned, then scanned the sidewalks in both directions. "Is he looking for me?"

"Last night, I mean. He came in, asked me if you were in the pub. Said he wanted to say hello since he found out you're staying at his place. I directed him to the axe lanes."

"Did he say anything else?" Derek asked, his tone casual.

Sophie thought for a moment. "He asked me how Heathcliff was doing."

He chuckled dryly. "Does the laird often inquire about the cat?"

Sophie smirked. "As far as I can remember, this was a first."

"What did you tell him?" I asked.

She shook her head. "You all ask the funniest questions, but since I like you, I'll share. The MacKinnon said that it was his housekeeper, Mrs. Buchanan, who was asking about the cat."

My mouth fell open. "Really."

Sophie laughed. "Yeah, I thought it was odd, too."

A nice-looking middle-aged couple walked toward us and Sophie hailed them in her usual buoyant way. "Greetings, Mr. and Mrs. Gordon."

"Hello, Sophie dear," Mrs. Gordon said. Her accent was more English than Scottish and her tone was decidedly haughty.

"I don't know if you've ever met my friend Claire Quinn," Sophie said. "Claire, this is Harriet and Oliver

Gordon. They own the Manor House Hotel and also the antiques shop at the opposite end of the high street from your aunt Gwyn's shop."

"You're in the antiques business as well? It's so nice to meet you." Claire extended her hand to shake theirs.

Mr. Gordon shook her hand, but Harriet Gordon didn't bother. "Oh, I know your aunt." She sniffed. "I noticed she recently nashed out of town so quickly, you'd have thought she'd robbed a bank. I wager she can't stand the competition."

What was she talking about? Whatever it was, I was ready to deck this evil witch, but Sophie ignored the derisive tone and said cheerfully, "And these are our friends from the States. Brooklyn and Derek, meet Mr. and Mrs. Gordon."

"Hello," I managed.

Mrs. Gordon sniffed again. "Haven't we enough riff-raff coming through the village without inviting more?"

"Harriet," her husband began.

"We're late, Oliver." And with that, she pivoted and continued walking down the street.

Mr. Gordon tried to smile, but his embarrassment was painfully obvious. "Good day to ye," he mumbled, and hurried off to join his hideous wife.

I turned to Sophie. "What a despicable woman."

Derek, who was usually better than me at sloughing off offenses, looked ready to kill. "She's insufferable."

"Maybe she should've introduced you as the Commander," I murmured to Derek.

He glowered, but said nothing.

Sophie stared at the couple hurrying down the street. "Insufferable is what she is. Harriet Gordon is known far and wide as a stone-cold harpy, claws and all. But on the bright side, she treats everyone the same way."

"So we're not special?" I asked. "She's an equal opportunity harpy?"

Sophie threw her head back and laughed. "You've the right of it there, Brooklyn."

Sophie's words managed to appease me only slightly. "Do you know why she's so obnoxious?"

"Aye." Sophie grinned. "It's because Oliver is twenty-seventh in line to the throne of England. Harriet is chomping at the bit for her chance to rule Britannia."

That got a laugh out of us and the ugly scene was momentarily forgotten.

"Okay," I said, still shaking my head at the idiocy of Harriet Gordon. "That explains a lot."

"Funny thing, though," Sophie continued. "She let loose a bit of slang just now that tells me her hoity-toity act is a sham."

"What did she say?"

"She said Gwyneth had to *nash* out of town. The word is straight out of working-class Edinburgh." She sneered. "Mrs. Gordon isn't quite the grand lady of the manor she wants us to think she is."

"Very interesting." I studied her. "Can you really pin down a slang word to a specific area of the country?"

"With some words you can, while others are used far and wide. I'm familiar with that one because it came from a movie that got a lot of attention over here."

"Which movie is that?"

"*Trainspotting*," she said, and wiggled her eyebrows. "With Ewan McGregor, such a cutie."

"Aye, he is," Claire said.

I glanced at Derek. He shifted from foot to foot and I imagined he was ready to run up and check out Gwyneth's place, but I wanted to hear more from Sophie.

"So this snooty woman doesn't like us," I said. "And she doesn't like Gwyneth. Does she like you, Sophie?"

"I'm a bartender," she said with a cheeky smile. "Everybody likes me."

"I'll bet she's jealous of Aunt Gwyneth," Claire said. "Her shop is the most popular on the high street."

"Aye, that's true," Sophie said, nodding. "It's because Gwyneth is a lovable character. She's no snob."

"True enough," Claire said fondly.

For a moment I wondered if Mrs. Gordon's antipathy for Claire's aunt could have something to do with Gwyneth's disappearance. Maybe not, but it would be smart of us to check out every hostile actor in the village.

Derek and Claire stepped closer to peer through the windows of Aunt Gwyneth's shop and I could hear them speaking quietly. After a few seconds, Derek looked at me. "We're going to go upstairs."

"Good. I'll be up in a minute."

The two of them took off down the street and I turned to Sophie. "Why did you bother introducing us to that creepy woman?"

She eyed me for a long moment. "Because you need to know the obstacles Claire might be facing here in the village."

I was surprised by her insight, but I probably shouldn't have been. She was, after all, a bartender. A trained observer. "Are there other obstacles we should be aware of?"

She pursed her lips to ponder whether she would open up to me, a virtual stranger. But in the end, my clear connection to Claire won her over. "Right after her aunt disappeared, I noticed that a couple of local men were suddenly taking an interest in Claire's every movement."

"How do you know that?"

"I've eyes, don't I?" She huffed out a breath. "But it's more than that. Claire is my friend. She would come into the pub in the afternoon or the evening, and sure enough, each time the same two men would walk in, trying to act casual, you know. They would sit nearby and nurse a beer. And they would get up to leave right as Claire left. They were a ham-handed twosome to be sure, but I get a sixth sense about such things when a woman is in the pub alone. I keep my eyes and ears tuned. And sure enough, these two never spoke to each other, but I could tell they were hanging onto Claire's every word and watching her a little too closely. And it happened every night she came in. I'm one of her best friends so naturally she would come in to visit me often. So I started to watch."

"Did Claire know you were watching?"

"No, no." Sophie shook her head. "Nobody really notices what I do."

I wanted to argue, but she held up her hand. "No, it's true, and I prefer it that way. And sure enough, when Claire suddenly left for San Francisco, those two men disappeared from my pub. I found out they left town the same day."

"Did you warn Claire?"

She sighed. "She was already gone by then."

"Were those two men the only ones who left town when Claire left?"

She stared at me in surprise. "Good question." She had to think about it. "The answer is no, they weren't the only ones. There were others. In fact, there was a veritable parade of locals leaving town that day. I do keep tabs on such comings and goings." She stared up at the sky, thinking about it, then counted them off on her fingers. "Mr. and Mrs. Gordon went off to London on a spur-of-the-moment buying trip. Allen Brodie left town for the annual livestock auction in Sterling. He goes every year, by the way."

"Okay." I knew I would remember this and write it all down when I had a free minute. I didn't want to take out my phone just now.

"Oh, and the MacKinnon left for a Clan Chiefs Council meeting at the same time."

That was a new one on me. "Clan Chiefs? Where do they meet?"

"They've a big to-do in Edinburgh every year about this time."

"How do you know all this?" I asked.

She raised an eyebrow. "I keep my eyes and ears open."

I smiled. "And you're very smart."

"Aye, there's that." She flashed another grin.

"The two men who were keeping watch on Claire. Do you know them?"

"Sure and I've known them all my life, haven't I? 'Twere Reggie MacDougall and Jerry Smith. They both worked for the old laird when they weren't throwing dice in the back room of Beatty's Garage." She stared out across the street. "They haven't yet returned to town."

And they wouldn't be coming back, I thought, but wasn't about to say so. I assumed that Jerry Smith had to be Jerome Smith, who'd died in the driveway of Derek's parents' home. "Is Reggie MacDougall any relation to Jenny MacDougall at the castle?"

"Aye, he's her father."

"Really? Are they close?"

"Oh, aye. Her mother died when Jenny was a young

lass and Reggie raised her. She still lives with him in the cottage where she was born."

"Does Claire know those men?"

She wrinkled her nose. "She might've seen them around, but I doubt she actually knows them. Claire visits her aunt a lot, but she hasn't lived here since she left for college."

"Any other suspicious characters you can think of?"

Her eyes narrowed. "Any reason why I should be giving you all this information?"

"Because a few people came after Claire in San Francisco and terrorized her. I want to know the names of anyone who could've possibly done that to her."

She nodded slowly. "I'll give you the names, then, and when you learn who those people were, you'll let me know."

"That's a promise."

"Right, then." She leaned against the wall of Gwyneth's shop and closed her eyes for a moment. "Okay. The laird's security team traveled with him to the council meeting, of course. Silas Abernathy and Roy Turnbull."

"Do they actually perform security for him?"

"Silas is in the way of being a bodyguard. He's a big man. Roy takes care of the laird's vehicles."

"I see."

"By the way, my parents left town about the same time. They went to Oban. Wanted to see a performance at Corran Hall and spend a few days on the beach."

"That sounds nice."

"Aye. We own a little beach house there with my cousins. It's more in the way of being a shack, but it's practically on the water, so it's great."

I doubted that Sophie's parents were involved in terrorizing Claire, but they would go on my list anyway.

"How long have you known Claire?" I asked.

"Since she first moved here to live with her aunt."

"A long time ago, then. You were what? Six years old?"

"Almost seven." She smiled. "Little girls that age have a sort of radar, you know. They want girlfriends and they're not afraid to seek them out. So I sat on the bench outside the pub with all my dolls lined up next to me and when Claire walked by, I lured her in with my Pretty Ballerina doll."

The picture she painted made me smile. "I don't remember that doll."

She made a face. "She was a creepy one. Didn't do much of anything, but she had beautiful curly blond hair and she wore a pink tutu and ballet shoes. She stood on her toes if you held her upright."

I laughed and thought of my friend Robin. Radar was probably the best way to explain how we homed in on each other at eight years old. And how odd that there had also been a doll involved with us becoming friends. Robin's bald-headed Barbie had been a big hit with me.

"So you're probably Claire's oldest friend," I said.

"I am. Of course, soon after Claire moved to town, her aunt shipped her off to boarding school. She had work in London, you see."

"I know."

"Right. But whenever Claire was home, we would get together, play games, spend an afternoon on the Loch, or go off to the movies in Inverness." She wagged her finger at me. "So yes, she's my best friend. And let me warn you. I'm protective of my friends."

I met her gaze. "So am I."

She took a deep, slow breath and let it out. Finally

her sharp expression softened and she smiled, for real. "All right, then. You'll keep me in the loop."

"I will."

"Then it's nice chatting with you, Brooklyn Wainwright."

I stepped inside Gwyneth's apartment and was amazed to find the place in good condition. Claire had indicated that there was complete destruction, but Sophie must've found a really good cleaning crew.

I could see the remnants of damage, of course. The cushions were gone from the couch and while the bookshelves had been put back in order, many of the books themselves were still in sad shape. The crew had stacked a lot of them in vertical piles, rather than lining them up next to each other.

But the floor was swept clean and had probably been mopped to assure Sophie that there were no glass or porcelain shards from the broken dishware. She wouldn't have left the cat here if that were the case.

From what Claire had told us, I had no doubt that the person who had wreaked the destruction in Gwyneth's home was the same creep who had also ravaged Claire's home in San Francisco. It was the same level of vicious, nonsensical damage. And it made me sick.

"It looks so much better in here now," Claire said softly, glancing around the apartment. She was standing by the kitchen counter, holding a small bag of kitty treats.

"I'm glad," I said. "Do you know anyone in the village who could've done it?"

She looked bereft. "No."

"I wouldn't think you did," I said quickly. "But I saw your place and it was awful. It felt personal."

"Exactly," she whispered angrily. "It's personal. The men who did it know my aunt."

"Are you sure they're men?"

Her eyes widened at the question and she had to consider it. "I can't imagine a woman toppling a bookcase like this."

"It could've been a woman who gave the orders," I suggested.

I could see that I had upset her. She shook her head but didn't answer my question. Instead she hugged herself, running her hands up and down her arms as if she was freezing.

"I'm just grateful that they didn't hurt Heathcliff," she said at last.

At the sound of his name, the cat peeked out from behind the sofa.

Claire smiled. "There you are, precious." She held out the treat and the cat approached warily.

"So this cat is Heathcliff," I said. "And your cat is Maxim de Winter."

She grinned. "Yes."

"Boy, you and Gwyneth really are gothic fangirls."

"We are indeed." The beautiful cat gave the treat a tentative lick, then took it and began to munch on it. Claire turned and opened a cupboard in the kitchen and pulled out a small can of cat food. She popped open the can and spooned the food into a small bowl, then found a larger bowl and filled it with fresh water. After she set both of the bowls down on a plastic mat at the far end of the kitchen, Heathcliff pounced on his meal.

I took a minute to study the apartment. It was a good size, with a front room that overlooked the high street. The kitchen was open to the living room and separated by a narrow island with two stools. I caught a glimpse of a bedroom down a short hallway and I assumed there was a bathroom attached.

The main entry was off the back stairway and there was a balcony that held two comfortable chairs, a table, and a small barbecue grill. I had caught a glimmer of blue water peeking between the trees, so there was a view of the Loch as well.

Heathcliff continued to attack the cat food as though he hadn't been fed in a month, but we knew that Sophie had been here yesterday.

"He's a handsome boy," I said.

"Isn't he?" Claire gave the cat a quick stroke, then stepped away, as if to allow the animal some privacy to enjoy his meal.

Derek continued his search through the somewhat straightened piles of magazines and knickknacks that had been returned to tabletops. He worked his way through the kitchen cupboards and even opened the refrigerator. He was nothing if not thorough.

I took on the job of going through the books. It was slow work because I wanted to check inside the books while making sure that all the bent and crumpled pages were straightened out before I returned them to the shelves.

I had a real aversion to anyone who would deliberately damage a book. It was a different kind of cruelty and showed a lack of humanity as well as a pitiful deficiency of character.

But that was just me.

I came across a treasure trove of Gwyneth's favorite gothic novels and smiled at some of the titles. She was definitely a fan of the genre. I noticed a copy of *Jane Eyre* sitting by itself on one of the shelves so I picked it up and absently opened it in the middle. And that's where I found a small sealed envelope addressed to Claire.

"Claire," I called.

I heard her walk down the hall from the bedroom. "What is it?"

"I found this." I handed her the small envelope.

She stared at her name on the outside. "It's from Aunt Gwyneth."

"Yes, I thought so. The handwriting matches the first note that came with the flowers."

Her hand was shaking and she had to take a moment.

Derek was watching from the other side of the room. "Can you open it?"

"Yes, of course." She carefully pulled up the sealed flap, slid the small notecard out, and read the words on the inside.

Finally she exhaled heavily and looked from me to Derek. "She says she's safe."

"May I see it?" Derek asked, crossing the room.

She handed it to him and he read the contents out loud.

"'I know you're worried, darling. But I'm safe where I am and Derek will keep you safe until I can return. I love you, Claire. Yours, Gwyneth.'"

"It's as if she's watching me," Claire whispered.

I looked at Derek and wondered if maybe that was exactly what Gwyneth was doing. But that was impossible, wasn't it? It was a mystery no matter how you sliced it.

"I found the book sitting all by itself on this shelf," I said, pointing to the empty space. "She must've put it there for Claire to find."

It took Claire a minute to recover, but then she shook herself and straightened up. "I'm still going to worry about her, but I'm better now. She says she's safe."

I nodded. "And she expects us to keep you safe. And we will."

"You have so far," Claire said with a tremulous smile.

Derek returned to the other side of the room. "I found something else over here. I think it's important."

I crossed the room. "What is it?"

"Look at this."

It was a faded color photograph of two teenaged girls frolicking on the banks of the Loch. I assumed it was Loch Ness, and I also assumed that one of the girls was Gwyneth. The frame was still intact but the glass was shattered.

The photo was inscribed: "To Don, in friendship and in fun. Beatrice and Tanya."

"Who's Don?" I wondered.

"It's me," Derek said, and grinned. "Don Danger. It's what she used to call me."

I started to laugh. "You're kidding. It's so silly, but I like it. But why couldn't you be Derek Danger?"

"Because in our line of work, we tended to use names other than our own."

"Oh, all right." I chuckled. "Just to be clear, though. You never actually used the name Don Danger in your work?"

He was still grinning. "No. Just around the office. And mainly just with Gwyneth."

"You called her Gwyn Quinn before. Was that her special name or did you call her something else?"

He began to laugh and it took him a full minute to get the name out. "She insisted that I call her 'Tanya Roma.'"

"Wow." I chuckled. "Exotic. Sexy."

"Exactly. She insisted that I pronounce it with an accent. Roll the R and all that."

I rubbed his arm affectionately. "You were good friends."

"Yes." His laughter died out and he set his teeth. "We have to find her."

"May I see it?" Claire asked.

"Of course." Derek handed her the photo.

I tapped the frame. "What does this photograph tell you?"

"If I'm not mistaken, this is Aunt Gwyneth and Mrs. Buchanan."

"Ah, Mrs. Buchanan," I said. "So her first name is Beatrice?"

"Yes. Aunt Gwyneth calls her Bea."

"Good to know."

Derek nodded. "And wherever this was taken, wherever it is they're playing, I believe we'll find a clue."

"That has to be right," I said. "She wouldn't have displayed a photo of herself and a girlfriend that was signed off to you."

"No, of course not."

Claire handed it back to Derek. "You should hold on to this."

"I will," he said.

"When we get back to the castle," I said, "we should track down Jenny MacDougall. Sophie confirmed that she's Reggie MacDougall's daughter."

"Is she?" Claire asked, surprised.

"Yes," I said. "She might know something."

"She might know who hired her father to come after Claire." Derek glanced at his watch. "We'll go look for her first thing. And later, you'll tell me everything else that Sophie told you."

I nodded. "Some very interesting stuff."

"I'd love to hear that, too," Claire said.

There was a knock at the back door and the sudden sound gave me a small jolt.

"Who can that be?" Claire wondered aloud.

"I'll find out," Derek said.

"No, it's fine. I'll get it," Claire said, and headed for the back door.

Derek crossed to the kitchen and with a flick of the wrist whacked the inexpensive frame against the edge of the metal trash can. Shards of glass cascaded into the can. Then he tossed the frame in, too, and slipped the photograph into his jacket pocket.

A half minute later, Claire walked back into the room, followed by Cameron MacKinnon. I exchanged a quick look with Derek and Claire. It was clear that the laird was the last person any of us expected to see in Gwyneth's apartment.

The laird scanned the room. "Well, it doesn't look as bad as I thought it would."

"Sophie hired a cleaning crew," Claire snapped, then took a deep breath and exhaled slowly in an apparent attempt to calm herself down. "It looks a lot better now than it did a few days ago."

"Good," he muttered. "Good."

"But it's disturbing anyway," she said. "And the fact that Aunt Gwyneth is still missing makes it even more so."

"I'm sorry," he said.

She clutched her hands together. "We were hoping to uncover some clue in here that would help us find her."

"Did you find anything?"

Claire glanced at Derek. "No. Not so far."

Derek shook his head and said nothing about the photo he'd found. None of us said anything about the note found in the *Jane Eyre*. By unspoken agreement we weren't about to pass any information over to the laird.

The MacKinnon nodded and walked around the room, studying the stacks of books and the various doo-dads here and there.

He picked up another picture frame and I noticed the glass was cracked in this one, too. He studied the photo, then laid the frame on the end table. He stood still for a long moment and seemed to wrestle with what he wanted to say. Finally he spoke. "I'm sorry to interrupt your work here, Ms. Quinn, but it appears that I require your expertise."

"My expertise?"

"You're a weapons expert, are you not?"

She was taken aback. "I am."

"Then I need you," he said. "It's a matter of grave importance."

"Grave importance." She glanced at me, then Derek, and then looked back to the laird. "That's unusual."

"Most definitely. I apologize again for disrupting your work and for distressing you in any way. I wouldn't ask if it weren't urgent, but I'm afraid it is."

She frowned. "You're not distressing me."

"Good." He managed a half smile. "Then you'll come with me?"

"I don't know."

"You're not a coward, Ms. Quinn," he murmured.

Her spine straightened. "I most certainly am not."

"I'm glad to hear it." He nodded his approval. "If you're ready, we need to leave now."

"My friends will come with me."

He narrowed his eyes at Derek and me. "Will they?"

"You bet your boots we're coming," I said, before the

MacKinnon could refuse us. It probably wasn't the most proper way to speak to his lairdship, but it worked for me. I grabbed my backpack and slipped my arms through the straps.

MacKinnon's cheek wavered. Was he biting his tongue? Trying not to laugh? "Yes, of course. Let's be off, then."

"I'll lock up," Claire said. She stopped first to give the cat several long, smooth strokes and some scratches between his ears. "I'll be back to spend more time with you, Heathcliff my love. Yes, I will. I promise. And Sophie will come by to visit you this afternoon."

"Can't Sophie take him home for a few days?" I asked.

"She tried, but Heathcliff wouldn't stop yowling and it turns out that Sophie's mother is terribly allergic. So we keep him here where he's happy and she tries to visit several times a day." She stood up, picked up her small backpack and keys, and we all walked out of the apartment.

The laird drove a large, all-terrain vehicle that was dirty and mud-splattered on the outside but spotless inside. Derek and I climbed into the back seat, where we were able to enjoy the view as he drove north and then east over the hills.

He glanced at Derek and me in the rearview mirror. "We have about twenty miles to drive so you might as well sit back and enjoy the ride."

After a minute, Derek asked, "How do you like the all-terrain?"

"I like it," he said. "It's a good truck for driving around the property, as you might imagine. It's a smooth ride and comfortable enough to carry guests around in. I have a Jaguar for street driving and for long distances, but I get a lot of use out of this one on the back roads."

"How much land do you have here?" Derek asked.

"Seven hundred acres."

"That's a decent size," Derek said. He glanced at me and winked and I wanted to laugh, but I didn't dare interrupt the guy bonding thing.

I knew that Derek wanted to establish a rapport with the MacKinnon, but I doubted that he would be helpful in finding Aunt Gwyneth. Of course, if he was the one responsible for Gwyneth's kidnapping or death, I would be more than happy to take him down.

"Did you bring your golf clubs?" the laird asked.

"Not on this trip," Derek said smoothly. "Perhaps next time."

I gave him a sideways glance. I'd never seen him play golf or even heard him mention the sport. I'd lived in the same house with him for several years now and I could swear there were no golf clubs anywhere.

But since he was playing along, I decided to join in. "I do wish we'd thought to bring our clubs. It's always an adventure to play golf in Scotland. Your courses are so wild and wooly."

"The wilder the better," he said with a smile. "We Scots are justifiably proud of our ancient courses."

After another minute, I asked, "Where are we going?"

"We're going to a place called the Clava Cairns," he said.

Claire perked up. "The ancient burial grounds."

"Yes. You're familiar with it?"

"I've never been there," she said, "but we had talked about visiting while we're here."

"We won't have time for a lengthy visit, but you'll surely get a feeling for the place while we're there."

"Good. I'd like that."

He was silent for a moment, then said, "I understand that you met Allen yesterday."

"Yes," Claire said. "I've met him before, through Sophie."

"Ah," he said.

"He was very nice," I said. "Took us to the pub."

"And you threw axes," the laird said.

I grinned. "It was a lot of fun." I almost added, *We saw you there, looking really hostile*. But this wasn't the time or place to bring it up.

"Was it fun for you, Ms. Quinn?" he asked.

"Oh yes," Claire said. "I love it."

"You're quite good at it."

She nodded. "I learned at a very young age."

"From your father, I imagine."

"He wasn't actually the one who taught me, but he always encouraged me to learn to protect myself."

I had thought that the laird's mere mention of Claire's father would cause waves of anger and resentment to radiate out from her, but she seemed to have calmed down. For the moment, anyway.

Before Claire could utter another word, the laird announced, "We're here."

All conversation was halted as he pulled into a parking lot and brought the car to a stop in front of a thicket of tall, leafy trees. Fog was beginning to gather in hazy wisps across the hillside and I was glad I'd worn a jacket.

"We'll have a bit of a walk," he said as we all climbed down from the SUV.

The number of ancient burial sites in this area was amazing. They were scattered across acres of mostly green lawn and scrub, surrounded by trees and hills.

Each individual cairn had its own peculiarities and patterns. It was fascinating.

The MacKinnon pointed out the types as we walked. There were standing stones, chambered cairns, and a ring cairn. There were smaller rocks layered in circles up to three or four feet high.

"This one here is called a passage cairn. The layered rocks are spread out in a wide pattern with a small walkway—or passageway—leading into the center." He pointed. "Theoretically, the center spot would lead into the crypt."

I stared at the multiple outcroppings of stones laid out in various shapes, from wide, flat circles, to a ten-foot-tall tower of stones, to a narrow, cylindrical cairn at least thirty feet long and only about ten feet wide.

"How old are these stone circles?" I asked.

"Bronze Age," he said automatically.

"That was helpful," I muttered.

He laughed, shocking me. Who knew the laird had a sense of humor?

"Sorry," he said. "Bronze Age begins about three thousand BC."

"Ah," I said. "Thanks."

He chuckled. "We Scots tend to steep ourselves in our history."

"I know for a fact that's true," I said. "I've spent some time in your country and I love the pride that Scotsmen show for their land and its history."

"Where have you visited?" he asked.

"I mostly stick close to Edinburgh because I come for the book fair every year."

"Ah, yes. Books."

I smiled. "They're my thing."

After we had walked for about ten minutes, I stared into the distance and saw two men standing next to a shallow, circular pile of rocks. They appeared to be talking quietly. I didn't see anyone else in the park.

"Isn't that Allen Brodie?" I asked, shielding my eyes from the sun to get a better look at the figure.

"You have good eyesight," the MacKinnon said.

Claire squinted. "Who's the other man?"

"Silas Abernathy. He works for me."

I recalled the name. Mrs. Buchanan had said that he was the laird's head of security.

"I asked them both to stand guard while I drove back to town and picked you up."

"What's he standing guard over?" Claire wondered.

"They're standing next to a cairn," Derek murmured, then slowly added, "But . . . there's . . . something . . . else."

The MacKinnon didn't say what.

Several seconds later Derek muttered, "Christ Almighty." He rarely used profanity, but this situation called for it.

We stepped up the pace until we could see quite clearly that it was the body of a woman, sprawled atop the rocks in the middle of the circle. She was fully dressed and I had to give thanks for that small favor. She wore old blue jeans, a faded T-shirt, and sneakers.

"Oh no," Claire moaned. "Oh my God." She began to step forward.

"Wait." The laird grabbed her arm. "Don't go near the body."

"Why not?" She turned on him. "Why am I here if not to see how she died?"

"It's a crime scene," he said, then shouted to Allen, "Brodie, contact the constabulary now, if you will."

"Aye, sir." He pulled out his phone and made the call.

Despite the horror of the scene, I was distracted by the fact that Allen had called the laird "sir." The night before, as we were walking through the village, he had referred to him casually as Cameron. Maybe it was a matter of showing respect. Or maybe the laird demanded it.

Out of the corner of my eye I noticed Silas Abernathy moving his position in order to block our view.

Derek and I took a few subtle steps farther to our right until we had an unobstructed view of the victim as well as a good eye on Abernathy and Allen Brodie. Something was odd here.

"Who is she?" I asked.

"Jenny MacDougall," Silas Abernathy said, his tone stark.

The downstairs maid, I thought, and my heart ached for her. No wonder she was dressed so simply in old, comfortable clothes. She had probably been snatched on her way to the castle for a day of cleaning and scrubbing. Or was she snatched *inside* the castle? I remembered the pretty girl in the kitchen, whispering to her girlfriend Treena.

Derek was right beside me and he clutched my hand. I took a few steadying breaths and knelt at the edge of the ring closest to the body. And then I heard Claire gasp.

"What is it?" I looked up and saw the color draining from her face. She pointed a shaky finger at the young woman so I turned to study the body. From this angle we could see so much more.

The dagger sticking out of Jenny's neck had a gleaming mother-of-pearl hilt with a decorative brass pommel. We had commented on its twin just that morning in the great hall of Castle MacKinnon.

The laird's own weapon had killed Jenny MacDougall. She had died in the same manner that her father Reggie had been murdered in our parking garage at home.

Chapter 17

My first thought was that our killer had made it back from San Francisco to Oddlochen in record time. My second thought was that he was disturbingly agile with a dagger. Also, the victim and killer had to have known each other pretty well. How else could the killer have gotten close enough to his victim to shove a knife in her throat?

There was another possibility. Maybe the killer had been trained to throw a knife from a distance with such pinpoint accuracy that it could stab a victim in the throat each time.

Either way, the only person I knew who might've been able to accomplish that feat was Claire.

I glanced at Claire and realized she was beginning to shake very badly. I jumped up and grabbed her, pulling her into a tight hug. "It's okay. It's okay."

"Ye should take her back to the car," Abernathy said, scowling. "A girl needn't see such a thing."

Another opinion from a caveman, I thought, and tried to ignore him. But I couldn't. Here was another member of the laird's inner circle who would probably do anything the laird asked of him. That might've included taking a trip to San Francisco with Reggie MacDougall and Jerome Smith.

Sophie said that Abernathy had accompanied the laird to the Clan Chiefs meeting, but that didn't mean anything. He could've gone with the MacKinnon to Edinburgh and easily hopped on a plane to San Francisco.

The man was a decade or two older than the laird, but he was in good shape. Tall and muscular, he was obviously strong and not exactly friendly, I thought.

I wasn't about to take Claire back to the car, but I did help her walk a few yards away from the men.

"I'm sorry, Brooklyn." Claire leaned her forehead against my shoulder, which was easy to do since I was at least six inches taller than her. I could hear her breath heaving as she tried to stop the shakes. "You know how my mind tends to wander into a book when I see something awful?"

"I do." The death of Jerome Smith in my in-laws' driveway had reminded Claire of the penultimate scene in *The Castle of Otranto*, where the father killed his own daughter with a knife. And when she heard from Allen that Cameron MacKinnon might've killed his wife in the Loch, it caused her to recall the scene in *Rebecca* where Maxim de Winter drowned his wife. Oh, yeah. I wouldn't forget those flashes of hers for a long time.

"Well," she said, "this time I fell right into an old Phyllis Whitney story."

Despite the horror surrounding us, I smiled. "I read her books when I was a teenager." I figured this was as good a time as any to be distracted by an old gothic novel plot. "Which story was it?"

She sniffled again, then said, "I honestly can't remember the title. Aunt Gwyneth and I went on a marathon binge one summer and read every one of Miss Whitney's books that we could get our hands on."

"You called her Miss Whitney?"

"Oh yes. To show our respect, my aunt said."

"That's nice."

She sighed, a little wobbly still. "This particular story featured a woman whose friend had disappeared two years before. I think the woman's name was Hallie and her friend's grandfather asked her to come to their seaside home to look into the disappearance of his granddaughter. He thought that because Hallie had known her so well, she might be able to help. So Hallie goes to the grandfather's home and naturally becomes entangled in the usual web of deceit and dark betrayal."

"Malice around every corner," I said.

She managed a wan smile. "Oh, aye. And all of it was done by the grandfather's family, none of whom want the granddaughter to be found. They were simply waiting for grandpapa to die and leave his money to them."

"A typical gothic mystery, in other words."

She actually giggled, a good sign, I thought. "It wasn't the best of Phyllis Whitney's works, but back in those days, I considered her worst book to be far superior to a lot of other authors' best efforts."

I asked, "What about this scene reminds you of that story?"

She sniffed. "It was the fact that someone had disappeared and that's what set everything in motion. The betrayal, the bitter feelings, the danger, the awful secrets."

I nodded. "And Gwyneth's disappearance has set all of these awful things in motion."

She turned and stared at Jenny's body, draped so casually across the rocks. "And now I look at the body of this poor young woman. She must've been so frightened. Why did she have to die?" She gazed at me, her eyes glistening with tears. "It hurts my heart to look at her."

"I know." I had just thought the same thing. It was a blow to one's heart and mind.

"What is going on here?" she whispered. "Where is my aunt Gwyneth? Is she even alive?"

I gripped her arms and leaned back to meet her cloudy gaze. "Listen to me. Your aunt is alive and we will find her. I don't know why she's in hiding, but we'll find out. That's what we do. That's why we're here."

She cocked her head. "You think she's hiding?"

"Yes." I took a look over her shoulder to see where the men were, then whispered, "Let's talk about this with Derek when we get back to the castle." I glanced over her shoulder. "You know, when the laird and Allen aren't watching our every move."

"Oh God." She rolled her eyes. "They're right behind me, aren't they?"

"No, but they're nearby," I hedged, "walking around the area, looking for clues. They can't hear us talking."

It was one thing for Claire to share her gothic fever dreams with a fellow booklover like me, but something altogether different to reveal her fanciful thoughts to three men she barely knew and hardly trusted. Derek, of course, was completely trustworthy. But the laird? And Allen Brodie and Silas? Who knew if they could be trusted?

We heard the first siren approach and knew that it was only a matter of time before the cairns would be crawling with police.

"I'm pulling it together," she muttered, and after a couple more sniffles and a brisk shake of her head,

Claire turned to find the MacKinnon and Allen nearby. "I beg your pardon. It was the shock of seeing this young woman's body that caused me to . . ."

"Please, Ms. Quinn." The laird took two steps closer and reached for her hand. "I'm the one who should apologize for putting you through this."

"You had your reasons, I believe." She straightened her shoulders and shook her hair back. Her bearing was positively regal now as she spoke. "You wished for me to analyze the weapon used to kill her."

"Yes. I'm anxious to hear your thoughts."

"But, Laird MacKinnon, you—"

He scowled. "I beg of you, Ms. Quinn, and all of you." He turned to include Derek and me. "Please call me Cameron. It's the twenty-first century, after all, and we lairds no longer run off to fight feudal battles and rescue fair maidens."

"Maybe not," Claire said, "but you're still the laird."

"By accident of birth," he insisted.

Claire stared at him, then nodded. "All right, then, Cameron. Please call me Claire."

In spite of poor Jenny lying dead nearby, he managed a warm smile. "With pleasure."

Claire had to clear her throat and I couldn't blame her. The man did have a devastating smile.

"The weapon is a dirk," she began, "with a tapered double blade approximately eight inches long. Made of English steel, circa 1800. The cross-guard is engraved brass and the hilt is mother-of-pearl with a lion's head pommel carved out of brass. It is part of a pair of ceremonial dirks presented in a wooden box inlaid with mother-of-pearl and lined in velvet."

The laird just stared at her. "You're good at this."

Despite her diminutive stature, she spoke with such authority that Cameron and his men appeared captivated. "I am, as you say, an expert."

"I'm impressed."

"Yes. Still, I don't understand why you've asked me here today, my laird . . . I mean, Cameron. The weapon is part of your own collection."

He frowned. "That's impossible."

"It's true," she insisted. "I saw its twin this morning in your great hall."

"We saw it, too," Derek said. "It was part of a box set. Do you have no recollection of it?"

"None at all."

Derek and I exchanged a look. Did we believe him? It was hard to say whether he was lying or not, but against my better judgment, I was starting to like him and therefore wanted to believe him. I already liked Allen, too. He was funny and a charming host who'd taken good care of us the night before. But if these two good-looking, charismatic men weren't killers, then who was? My gaze drifted toward Silas Abernathy and I wondered.

"We'll show you its twin when we return to the castle," I said.

"I insist that you do," Cameron said, then his lips twisted into a frown. "Granted, I don't know every item in my collection because apparently half of it was pilfered by my father and the other half has been rotting in the castle cellar for generations."

"But if it's true," Allen said, "then whoever killed Jenny must've stolen the dagger from your collection."

Derek asked, "Who in the village has access to the castle?"

Allen chuckled. "There's a good question."

"He's laughing," Cameron explained, "because even

though I've closed off the castle to the public, it is open to virtually anyone who wants to visit. Everyone in the village is aware that they can come to the kitchen door and Mrs. Buchanan will let them in. I believe she knows the entire population of Oddlochen, along with plenty of folks who live farther afield."

"Police are here," Allen murmured.

Cameron glanced over his shoulder, then turned back to Claire. "I'd like you to show me the weapon you're referring to before we involve the constabulary."

"Perfectly understood," Claire said quietly, and Derek and I both nodded our agreement.

"Thank you. I appreciate your discretion."

His words gave me a chill. Even though we had given him a temporary pass, I reminded myself that Cameron MacKinnon might have been responsible for his first wife's death. What was the story there? Was it a mistake to trust him? I supposed we would be free to call the cops once we'd proven that the weapon came from his own cache. I was very interested to see what his reaction would be when confronted with the evidence.

The police had turned off their sirens and drove right into the park, carefully avoiding the cairns. They didn't stop until they reached the edge of the ring of stones where Jenny's body lay.

Two constables stepped out of the car and Cameron walked over to greet them. They all shook hands and spoke together for a few minutes, then one of the officers stepped gingerly onto the rocks to check out the body of Jenny MacDougall. The other turned and approached us.

"Good afternoon," he said, and we all murmured our greetings.

"I'll need to collect information from each of you and

then you'll be free to go. We'll likely follow up tomorrow with additional queries. I understand you're all staying at Castle MacKinnon in Oddlochen."

There were obedient murmurings from Derek, Claire, and me. None of us wanted to spend more time with the police than we had to.

He glanced up from his notes and stared at Derek. "Commander Stone?"

"Yes," Derek said, and once again I was pleased that his military rank had been included in the introduction. It seemed to smooth the way in every situation.

"Thank you for your service, sir."

Derek nodded, but said nothing.

"You're visiting from San Francisco, I understand?"

"Yes. My wife Brooklyn and I are visiting with our friend Claire Quinn."

He scribbled down his notes, then looked at Claire. "And you, miss? You're visiting?"

"Aye," she said. "I used to live in Oddlochen with my aunt, but now I live in San Francisco. So yes, just visiting."

He asked several more innocuous questions, but I had stopped listening. Instead, I was riveted by the sight of the other constable, who reached for Jenny's wrist in order to lift her arm. That was when I noticed the ligature marks around her wrists and it turned my stomach. I felt a wave of anger, revulsion, and deep sadness at the sight. I had to breathe in and out a few times before I could harness my emotions.

Had someone managed to trap Jenny and tie her up in order to drive her out here? She must've been scared to death, poor girl.

And despite what I'd told Claire a few minutes ago, the thought of Jenny being tormented so badly led me to wonder if we would actually find Gwyneth alive. If the same person who killed Jenny was also responsible for Gwyneth's disappearance, what would be the reason to keep her alive? I had no idea, but I knew that we were running out of time. We had to search the west tower tonight.

Derek and I were quiet on the drive home. We leaned into each other, content to listen to Cameron and Claire bantering in the front seat. I was surprised and pleased to hear her going head-to-head with him, at one point teasing him when he tried to silence her by pulling his laird-of-the-manor routine.

I had seen people react in all different ways in the aftermath of violent death. I realized now that Claire and the MacKinnon were clearly blowing off steam and that made it all right.

Finally he glanced in the rearview mirror and said, "Help me out here."

Derek and I realized at the same time that he was talking to us.

"How may we help, your lordship?" I asked.

Claire giggled, and I had to appreciate the MacKinnon's ability to cheer her up.

Cameron grumbled, "'Tis a shame we did away with the dungeon in the last century." But I saw his smile and knew he was enjoying the playful interchange between Claire and himself.

"That would take care of a world of problems," Derek agreed.

Less than a minute later, I saw Cameron wince and check the clock on the dash. "I completely forgot I've got an engagement this evening."

"Murder can make you forget most things," I said.

He sighed heavily. "Indeed. I should cancel the entire affair, but I've got several guests visiting from out of town who are only available tonight."

"Another reason to bring back the dungeon," Claire said, and caught the MacKinnon by surprise.

He laughed for a full minute, then finally managed to speak. "They're coming to dinner, at any rate, and I would be most grateful if you all would attend as well."

"Who are your other guests?" Claire asked politely. "Perhaps I know them."

He waved away her question. "Just an older couple from the village and a few friends I've known for years. And Allen will be there, thank God."

Derek and I exchanged a look and I nodded. He said, "We'll be happy to join you."

"Good," he said briskly. "Thanks. Always nice to have some friends in the room."

"But you'll have your friends," I said. "And Allen."

He hesitated, then explained, "Allen's loyalties will be split, unfortunately. The older couple happen to be his aunt and uncle."

"Ah." Derek nodded sagely. "They could tip the scales against you."

"Exactly."

I chuckled, meeting his gaze in the rearview mirror. "We promise to take your side on every issue."

He smiled back at me. "The perfect guests."

We drove for a few minutes in silence. Finally I asked, "How well did you know Jenny?"

"Not as well as I should have." His voice was shadowed in regret. "She was always there, you see. She grew up around the castle and worked in the kitchen, but she was a decade younger than I, so while we were friendly, we were never actually friends. Her father Reggie worked for my father. And he still does the occasional odd job around the property."

Her father, I thought. Reggie MacDougall.

"Are you close to her father?" I asked.

"I know Reggie well enough," he said, "because he was always around, working on something or other for my father. But we were never mates, if that's what you meant."

I noticed he was talking about Reggie in the present tense. Was that deliberate? Or did he honestly not know that Reggie MacDougall was dead?

He raked his fingers through his hair. "Jesus. I'll have to break the news to Reggie about Jenny."

"That's never easy," I said quietly.

"No, but it's got to be done." He flexed his neck and his shoulders and sat a bit straighter in the driver's seat. And I could see him mentally cloaking himself in the armor of the laird.

"The twin daggers were originally meant to be housed in this box." Claire held up the wooden box with the inlaid mother-of-pearl design. She opened the case and showed him the one remaining dagger still set on the velvet lining.

We had come straight to the great hall as soon as Cameron brought the all-terrain vehicle to a stop outside the kitchen door.

He took the open box from Claire and weighed it in his hand. He stared at the lone dagger, picked it up, and held it up to the light. "Mother-of-pearl," he murmured. "Carved brass lion. Double-edged steel." With a sigh, he set it back in the box. "Damn it."

"I'm sorry," Claire said.

"It's not your fault. You were right."

"I'm sorry to see you suffer."

He stared at her for a long moment. "I thank you for that."

He walked along the utility tables, gazing at the dozens of weapons haphazardly displayed, many of them tarnished or broken. He found the other box Claire had mentioned that morning, that contained only the one pistol. "Another one missing?"

"It's probably somewhere in the cellar. Your people will find it and it'll be a matched set again."

"My people are all from the village. They don't know anything about weaponry or . . . much of anything, really. But they're good workers. That's all I wanted in order to start this inventory."

"Why did you decide to do an inventory?" I asked.

He took a deep breath and I wasn't sure if he would tell us or not. But then he said, "When I moved back to the castle, I began to have my suspicions that something was wrong. Things were missing. A piece of priceless artwork had vanished. Some cherished family heirlooms had disappeared."

"So you decided to catalog everything," I said.

"Exactly." He looked abashed now, but he continued. "My father was deeply in debt to some local gamblers and had sold off some of our land when I got word of what was happening. I warned him to stop. But as long as he was in charge of the estate, I had no control over much of anything. The land or the castle itself, or the family money."

"What did you do?"

"I moved to London for five years, but I would come back every few months, just to keep an eye on things." He idly picked up a sword and swooshed it back and forth, then put it back on the table.

"And then he up and left one day," he said. "Allen called me out of the blue to let me know. I came rushing back and took over everything. Allen's been a tremendous help in getting things back on track."

"You're lucky to have someone you can trust," Derek said.

"Aye. That I am." He glanced at the hodgepodge of weapons and artifacts scattered across the tables. "But I see I'll need someone better at organizing and cataloging this mess than my young friends from the village." He shook his head. "If it even matters."

"It certainly does matter," Claire insisted. "The history of your people and your land is important. You said yourself that we Scots take pride in our history. So yes, it matters."

He was staring at her again, and he continued to do it until I saw Claire beginning to twitch. She flipped her hair back and straightened her jacket, then fiddled with the buttons.

"Stop looking at me," she finally said. "What's wrong?"

His eyes were focused on her. "You can do it."

"Do what?" she demanded, then backed away, shaking her head. "No."

He snorted a laugh. "Yes. You can organize my collection."

Claire was so horrified that I quickly came up with a way to change the subject. "I would love to see your library."

He stared at me for a long moment, then smiled. "It would be my pleasure to show you the library. You'll have to forgive me if it's not in the best condition. I had planned to begin the cleanup as soon as we finished with the weaponry."

We followed him as he walked out of the great hall
and turned toward the main stairway, veering off to the
right toward the foyer before coming to a heavy wooden
door I hadn't noticed before. "It's in here. Brace your-
selves."

"It's that bad?" I said.

"It's not . . . pretty."

He opened the door and walked inside and I could
smell the musty odor before I entered the room.

I looked around and marveled at how he could've
kept this room hidden from view. It was spectacular,
with high ceilings and wall-to-wall bookshelves. A
beautiful library ladder was suspended from a track that
ran all the way around the room.

But the musty smell was disturbing. "Did you have
water damage in here?"

"No. It's just been closed off for the last year."

"I see." I frowned.

He rushed on. "It smelled so stuffy that I told Mrs.
Buchanan to keep the door closed."

"It would be better to keep it open and let the smell
and the stuffiness dissipate."

"That makes sense, but . . ."

"But then you smell it all over the place."

"Yes."

"I have a few suggestions. I can give them to Mrs.
Buchanan later."

"That's marvelous," he said, with the slightest nod.
"Thank you."

"Books are my thing," I said with a smile. "Do you
mind if I meander for a few minutes?"

"Meander away," he said with a wave of his hand. "I
must go and prepare for my guests."

At the library door, Cameron turned and said, "We'll

serve cocktails at eight o'clock in the blue parlor and dinner at nine. I look forward to seeing you."

"We'll see you then," Claire said.

"And, Claire," he added. "Do think about what I said."

Claire was frowning as he left, but said nothing.

I walked straight to the closest bookshelf and began studying the titles. With a smile, I said, "There are a lot of Scottish authors."

"That makes sense," Derek said, and stared up at the impressive vaulted ceiling.

I pulled a book out at random. "*Treasure Island.*" Then I noticed it was perched between *Kidnapped* and *The Strange Case of Dr. Jekyll and Mr. Hyde.*

I pulled the other two from the shelf. They were beautifully bound in matching brown leather and appeared to be in excellent condition. I grinned at Derek. "I think I'll take these to our room and just, you know, savor them."

Derek laughed. "You do know how to have fun."

Claire joined in the laughter. "It does sound fun, but I'm going to run upstairs and take a bath."

"That's a good idea," I said. "We'll go up with you."

"Yes, let's all go together," Derek agreed.

Claire was glowering again as we climbed the stairs and didn't speak until we reached the door to her room.

"Do you know what you're going to do, Claire?"

"I'm certainly not going to help him! His men follow his orders without question." She gave me a beseeching look. "What if he arranged my aunt's kidnapping?"

"We have to find out," I insisted. "We'll go to the west tower tonight after everyone has gone to bed."

"Yes," she said. "The sooner the better. Aunt Gwyneth may only have a short time left. If it's not too late already."

"It's four o'clock now," Derek said, checking his watch. "Shall we meet right here at seven forty-five and go down together?"

"Yes," Claire said. "I'm fair exhausted so I'm all for taking a nap and then a bath."

"Sounds wonderful," I said. "I may take a quick nap. Then I'll probably do some work and then jump in the shower."

"Will you sweep my room again?" she whispered to Derek.

He considered. "I'll do it just before we go downstairs for cocktails. You're not planning on phoning anyone before then, are you?"

"No. And I'm not planning on giving up any state secrets in the meantime."

I smiled. "Good. We don't want any international incidents."

Derek and I waited until she was in her room and heard the door lock before we walked down to our room.

Back in our room, Derek said, "Are you planning to take a nap, darling?"

"No."

He smiled. "I didn't think so."

"I have to find some time to finish reading the *Rebecca*. I ran out of time on the plane and I'm wondering if Gwyneth might've left more messages."

"All right. I'm going to check in with my office and see if my company is still functioning."

"Oh, I hope it is."

"Thank you." He leaned down and kissed me. "You were very good with Claire this afternoon."

"She was suffering. And I get it." I pulled the *Rebecca* out of my backpack and set it on the table with the three Robert Louis Stevenson books.

"I didn't see you freak out over the blood."

I stared at him, taken aback. "I didn't even realize it. And there was a lot of blood."

"Yes, there was."

"Wow." Now I shivered at the realization and held out my arms for him to see. "Look, I've got goose bumps."

He grinned. "Delayed reaction."

"Weird."

"You were more concerned with Claire than your own phobia," he said. "She needed you so you couldn't let down your guard."

"You're right," I said, a little awestruck at the realization. "She's become a good friend in a very short period of time."

"I like her, too," he said. "She's a unique character."

"We sort of meet on the same plane."

"Is that the astral plane?" he asked, tongue in cheek.

"It's close. Speaking of which, have you noticed her aunt sounds a bit like my mother?"

My mother was the original earth mother, a volatile combination of Wiccan power and Deadhead coolness. And speaking of astral planes, my mother had her very own astral travel guide, Ramlar X, and boy, had she traveled. She was the queen of the local shamanic drum circle and could cast a protection spell "faster than a coffee enema could clear your Muladhara," as Mom would say.

Muladhara was the first chakra, or the root chakra. Anyway, Mom said stuff like that all the time.

"Gwyneth is a special person," Derek said. "But even she could never compare to your mother for uniqueness."

"Aw." I kissed him. "Sweet."

He ran his hand down my hair and then tugged me

close for a hot, thorough, and utterly tender kiss. "I love you, darling."

I reached up and wrapped my arms around his neck. "I love you back."

He touched my cheek and brushed a strand of hair away from my face, then kissed me once more. "I'll let you get to the book." In less than a minute, Derek was already sending out a flurry of texts as he crossed the room.

"What did we do before we could text?" I asked, as I sat down at the table to study the book.

"I believe there was something called the telephone," he said. "It plugged into a wall. Strange, archaic instrument."

I laughed, and soon settled into *Rebecca*. I took it one page at a time, but I was quickly able to get into a rhythm, turning the page, scanning, then moving to the next page. It was a little like speed reading, but I didn't have to comprehend the meaning of the words, just skim the pages for anything unusual.

It took twenty minutes, but on pages 314 and 315, I finally found a slew of additional markings. I almost missed them because they were noted in a different way from the earlier pencil marks. Each letter selected on these pages had a tiny dot at the lower corner of the letter that could only be seen if you paid attention to the font style.

Being a book nerd, I recognized the font as Caledonia. I took my tablet from my backpack and after a little online research I discovered that it was brought to the market in 1938, the year that *Rebecca* was published in England. As a side note, Caledonia was the ancient name for Scotland. So go figure. I had to smile at that connection, however fragile it was.

The reason why the font style was important in this case was that certain fonts have a very specific style and if you alter it, it's almost like scratching a black mark across the page. It was very noticeable and not in a good way. This particular font had what was called a sweep, which was why Dalton didn't notice the tiny markings when he thumbed through the book.

I was tickled at the thought that I, the amateur sleuth, had for once bested Dalton, the master sleuth.

I would keep that news to myself.

I pulled my magnifying glass from my tool case to make sure I got each letter, and jotted them down in order on a blank page. Then just to be safe, I continued scanning the rest of the book.

When I was finished, I closed the book and said, "I found more letters."

Derek immediately set down his phone, jumped up from the wingback chair, and came over to the table. "Let's see."

I showed him the pages of letters, then opened Google. "I'll type while you read off the letters."

"Fine," he said. "Ready?"

"Yes, go ahead."

"F-A-I-G-H-N-I-C-H-D-O-B-H-E-A-T-R-I-C-E-M-U-N-T-R-A-N-N-S-A-D-I-O-M-H-A-I-R-D-O-N-L-O-C-H."

As he said them, I typed the letters into Google Translate. It still felt a bit like cheating, but I was okay with it. When he finished, I stared at the results. "I think I screwed up."

He leaned over to look at the screen. "What have you got?"

"Well, the first two words are *ask Beatrice*. That's Mrs. Buchanan. So that makes sense because she's

Gwyneth's good friend. But then all the rest of the letters are piled into one long, nonsensical word."

He scowled. "How did Dalton do it?"

"We had to figure out some of the Gaelic words first. Then Dalton typed them into the translator."

"You're right."

We both stared for a long moment at the words in the Google Translate box.

"The last word is definitely *Loch*," Derek said.

"Okay, I'll separate that from the rest and we'll take it one little bit at a time."

"Good." He looked at the screen. "And you should separate Beatrice from the previous word."

"Of course." I did that, and suddenly the mishmash started to look like a sentence.

"*Ask Beatrice* . . . hmm."

"Right," he said. "We still need to separate more of the letters into words."

"I'll just start experimenting."

"Might as well."

I played with the letters, adding and deleting spaces until it suddenly transformed into *Ask Beatrice about the secret passage to the lake*.

I looked at Derek, wide-eyed.

He shook his head. "Now I realize why we needed that photograph *and* the markings in the book."

"The photo of Gwyneth and Mrs. B frolicking on the shore?"

"Yes." He smiled. "That was a good clue, but we never would've understood that there was a secret passage nearby if we didn't also have the clues in the book."

"It's the secret passage that means the most."

Derek paced back and forth in front of the fireplace.

"And we know there's a secret passage in the castle because of what Sophie told us the other night."

"That's right." I closed down my computer. "So first we've got to go to the west tower and find whatever's hidden under the wooden plank."

Derek turned. "And then we must ask Beatrice, Mrs. Buchanan, about the secret passage to the Loch."

I slid my tablet back into its case. Then I checked my wristwatch. "It's five o'clock."

He grinned. "We can make it to the west tower and be back down in time for cocktails."

Chapter 18

We debated whether to tell Claire that we'd worked out the clues.

"If we find something or not, I don't think we can put her through any more stress today," I said.

"Then let's find the tower and see what's up there," Derek said.

I thought about it a bit more. I wouldn't want to be left out of the loop if I were in her position. But then, Derek and I were used to tracking down suspects, looking for clues, searching out the answers, and, well, finding dead bodies. She wasn't. Finding Jenny's body, worrying about her missing aunt, and dealing with the MacKinnon had done her in.

"All right," I decided. "We'll let her sleep."

"We can report on what we found before we go to dinner with Cameron and his people."

We slipped soundlessly out of the room and got to the top of the stairs before I turned to Derek. "I'm all turned around. Which way is west?"

"Our rooms are in the east wing, so it's that way." He pointed in the opposite direction of our rooms. "Let's keep walking until we hit a wall or find a stairway that goes up into a tower."

"Makes sense," I said.

We walked down a hallway I hadn't seen before. It looked similar to our hallway in the east wing so I figured we'd made it to the west wing. When we reached the end of the hall, we stopped.

"Now what?" I asked.

"Let's check these doors and see what they lead to."

"I hope nobody's living in any of these rooms."

He chuckled. "I haven't seen anyone else in the house but the staff and us." He began opening doors, starting with the one at the end. There was a staircase, but it was only going down.

"That won't work," he said, closing the door. "We want to go up."

He opened another door. "Now, this looks promising."

It was a narrow spiral staircase going up. "Oh yeah, this is a good sign."

Derek began to climb and I followed him, naturally. The stairwell itself grew narrower the farther up we went, which I took as another good sign that we were ascending into a tower. It was most likely the narrow western tower I'd first seen when the helicopter dropped us off.

"Maybe we should've gone outside and looked at all of them before we started climbing. I can't tell if we're in the right tower."

"There are quite a lot of towers," he said. "Let's see what we find at the top of this one."

"I just don't have a good sense of where we are."

"North is toward Inverness," Derek said easily. "Which means that west is toward the Loch."

But the farther we climbed, the more disoriented I got with what was north, south, east, or west. "I'm usually pretty good with directions, but . . ."

"We're in a different country so it gets confusing."

"Not for you," I muttered, making him laugh. "And the spiral staircase doesn't help."

"This is almost definitely the west tower." He continued to climb. "And if we're wrong, we can always study all the towers from the outside later."

But we weren't wrong and we realized it when the stairs opened up to a small, square room with a floor made of wide wooden planks and a low-hanging cathedral ceiling. There was one arched window lined in brick, and hanging from the top of the arch was an old bell, about two feet tall by two feet wide.

"We found it," I whispered, amazed. "The western bell tower."

It had grown dark outside so Derek pulled the mini-flashlight out of his pocket and shone it around. "Now we simply have to find the right plank."

How hard could that be? I thought. The room was barely fifteen feet long by fifteen feet wide.

"This is where it would help to have a third person with us," he said, taking note of the floor plan. "We could cut down the workload."

He walked over to the bell and tapped on it. "I believe this is bronze. Very thick. And old."

"Does it work?" I asked, then quickly added, "Don't try it."

He laughed. "And give away our position? Don't worry, darling." He continued to aim the beam along every plank in the floor. "Do you see any oddities? Any worn edges?"

"I haven't seen anything yet. And it's getting pretty dark."

"Yes, too dark to accomplish much of anything. But

now we know where it is and we'll come back tomorrow morning with Claire."

"We still have two hours," I said. "Do you want to find Mrs. B and ask her about the photograph and the secret passage?"

Derek thought about it for a moment. "I would love to get to the bottom of this, but I fear that with the Mac-Kinnon's dinner party tonight, she might be frazzled."

I scowled. "Of course, you're right." I hated to give up, but it couldn't be helped. We would come back in the morning prepared to go to work. I sighed. "In that case, we'd better go get ready for dinner with the laird."

At seven forty-five we knocked on Claire's door. She opened it right away and silently waved us in. I turned off my phone and we both watched as Derek went through his routine of checking everywhere. Finally he turned off the detector. "You're clean."

She clapped her hands together and powered up her cell phone. "Thank you."

"So let's quickly tell you our news," I said.

Derek and I proceeded to tell her about the bell tower.

"It was too dark to start searching," Derek explained, "but now we know where we're going."

"So we can go up there first thing tomorrow and start pulling up planks."

"Wonderful," she said, taking the news perfectly well that we'd gone off without her.

Her afternoon nap and the long soak in the bathtub had perked her right up. She looked relaxed and wide awake, with her hair pulled back in a chic French twist and chunky earrings that sparkled in the light. She wore a short blue, black, and white plaid skirt with a black sweater and black boots. She grabbed a black wool scarf dotted with shiny beads and wrapped it around her neck.

"You look beautiful," I said. "You ready to go?"

"I am. And you look lovely as always." We both grinned.

I had packed one semi-dressy outfit that consisted of black silk pants, slim white tunic, and black heels, and a simple necklace of multiple strands of black beads. I wore my hair down.

"I forgot to pack earrings," I said, wincing. "You can never tell my friend Robin. She would smack me for that fashion faux pas."

"She sounds like Sophie," Claire said as she led us out the door. "I used to call her up whenever I needed to know what I should wear." She sighed happily. "It's nice to have a friend like that."

I frowned. "Except when they harangue you for wearing Birkenstocks around the house."

Claire's mouth gaped in horror. "Brooklyn, you don't."

I stared at her. "*Et tu, Brute?*"

Derek laughed and pulled me close. "Your Birkenstocks are a major turn-on for me."

I gazed into his gorgeous blue eyes. "I've never loved you more."

We were joking and laughing all the way until we reached the doorway to the blue parlor—and stopped cold.

The room had a gentleman's club vibe, thanks to the handsome bar in one corner where the bartender was shaking a martini. Everyone looked elegant. The dark velvet drapes were pulled open to reveal a stunning view of the moon shining on the Loch. The music was low and jazzy. The lighting struck the perfect mood for spending the evening with familiar friends.

The only fly in the ointment was the presence of horrible Harriet Gordon. I felt my stomach drop as my appetite fluttered away in the breeze.

Derek squeezed my hand and whispered, "We can do this."

"Life's too short," I groused quietly.

My dismay was complete when she turned and glared at me, then turned to Allen and Cameron. "You didn't mention we were dining with foreigners."

"They're guests," Cameron said easily. "And I'll take that to mean that you've all met."

Derek gave an obligatory nod for Cameron's sake. "We met them on the high street earlier today. Good evening, Mr. and Mrs. Gordon."

I could detect a steely resolve beneath his words. The fact that Harriet Gordon would display her boorishness right in front of the MacKinnon made me realize how foolhardy and insubstantial she was—*despite* being twenty-seventh in line to the throne.

I wanted to laugh in her face, but my mother had raised me to be polite to everyone. Thinking of my mother right now, though, I knew she would've found some polite way to stick it to Harriet Gordon.

I would simply do my best to ignore the shrew.

Cameron introduced us to his old friends visiting from London, Eloise and Marcus Thompson. "Marcus grew up in the village. He and Allen and I were young hooligans together."

Marcus grinned. "I grew out of that stage, but these two are still causing mischief wherever they go."

Allen protested. "I am an angel."

Eloise guffawed. "A *fallen* angel, perhaps."

Glancing around the room, I quickly noted that most of us were of a similar age—except the Gordons. By process of elimination, I deduced that they had to be Allen's aunt and uncle. *Ugh*, I thought. Poor Allen. I liked him, which meant that I'd have to be nice to his aunt.

Since that was going to be impossible, I decided to stick with my original plan and just ignore her.

"Shall we go to the bar?" Derek suggested.

"Why aren't we there already?" Claire murmured.

I laughed and the three of us moved eagerly across the room. Derek ordered a dry martini while Claire and I both opted for champagne.

Cameron soon joined us and offered a quiet apology for Harriet's rudeness.

"Don't worry," I said blithely. "We experienced her special brand of hospitality this morning." I lifted my champagne glass in a mock toast.

"I've just spoken to Mrs. Buchanan," Cameron said. "She's assured me that none of you will be sitting near her at the dinner table."

"That's kind of you," Derek said, although I could hear the subtext in his voice. Something along the lines of *Throw the witch out!*

I was projecting, of course. That was my internal dialogue, not Derek's.

"I really am sorry," Cameron continued, keeping his voice low. "She is capable of holding her tongue on most occasions, but I believe Ms. Quinn's presence has virtually caused her head to explode."

"Me?" Claire asked.

"You've done nothing on your own," he quickly

assured her. "But your connection to your aunt is a thorn in Harriet's side."

"She can't stand the competition," Claire grumbled under her breath. "Maybe she's the reason why Gwyneth disappeared."

Cameron stared at her. Claire suddenly realized what she'd said out loud and her cheeks turned pink. "Sorry. I haven't a clue what I'm talking about. That woman just set me off." She took a big gulp of champagne.

"I am well aware that your aunt is missing," Cameron whispered, "but I believe it's by her own choice."

"I agree with you," Derek said quietly.

"Oh, do you know Gwyneth?" Cameron asked.

"Our paths crossed a few years ago in London," Derek explained smoothly. "Charming woman."

I gazed at Cameron. "I understand your father grew up with Gwyneth and her brother."

"Her brother was my father," Claire clarified sharply.

"Yes, and they were all good friends," Cameron said with a laugh. "If you thought we were hooligans, you should've seen them. They ran this town and everyone in it. In a good way, of course. Including Allen's father George," he added, "who was my father's estate manager for many years."

"Did I just hear my name besmirched?" Allen said with a grin as he approached the bar.

"Yes," Cameron said dryly. "We're secretly ridiculing you unmercifully."

Allen pressed his hand to his heart. "We were friends once," he lamented, and we all laughed.

"Hey, we want in on the joke," Cameron's friend Marcus said, as he joined the circle we'd made around the bar. His wife Eloise squeezed in at the far end.

They spent a few minutes goofing on one another until Oliver Gordon walked up to the bar. He asked for a vodka martini and a Gibson, then joined in the merriment until his cocktails were ready.

"Oliver," Harriet barked. "My Gibson is getting warm."

"Yes, my dear." He picked up the two cocktails and walked back to join his wife.

A few seconds later, I heard her hiss in disgust, "My drink only has two onions. You know I insist on three."

Oh my God, I thought. Why hasn't he killed her yet?

The thought of killing anyone made my mind flash back to the horrible discovery of Jenny MacDougall's body on the cairn that afternoon. I took a deep breath and tried to return to the bantering around the bar.

With the exception of Harriet Gordon's presence, the cocktail hour was delightful.

When Mrs. Buchanan came to the door to announce that dinner was served, I was more than ready to eat.

Everyone cheered the news and we followed her out of the room. I was halfway down the hall when I realized I'd forgotten my backpack. It was a little embarrassing to carry it around as a purse, but I wasn't willing to let the *Rebecca* out of my sight.

As I approached the door to the blue parlor, I heard someone talking quietly.

"I thought you took care of it," a woman said.

"I did," a man insisted.

"No, you didn't," she ranted. "And now these meddlers have arrived."

"Stop pushing me," he said, his tone menacing. "I can push you back a lot harder."

"If I don't push you, nothing gets done," she griped.

"You've got to take care of it once and for all. Immediately."

"Or what? You have no power over me!" His laugh sent a chill through me.

"Your father would take a strap to you if he heard the disrespect in your tone."

"My father never took a strap to me in his life."

"Perhaps he should've."

"Don't talk to me about my father," he said, his low voice becoming more threatening.

"Your father is the reason we're here," she shot back, then added quietly, "You must avenge him."

"I know what I must do."

I could tell without looking that the snooty female voice belonged to Harriet Gordon, but the man's voice was so hushed that I couldn't make it out.

Was it Cameron? And if so, what had happened to his father that Cameron now had to make right?

All I knew about Cameron's father was that he was the laird until he suddenly up and left the castle. I wasn't sure if he'd died or had just given up the title for some reason.

I couldn't think of another reason why Cameron had invited Harriet Gordon to this dinner party, unless they had business of some kind. Did he have a relationship with Harriet? If so, did that mean he was also related to Allen?

And if not, why would Harriet Gordon care about Cameron's father?

It made more sense if the man talking to Harriet was Allen Brodie. She was his aunt and would have more of a familial stake in his conduct.

But then, it could've been any man in the village. It

could be Silas Abernathy or the chauffeur. What was his name?

And I was suddenly starting to put the pieces together.

"Don't you ever forget," the woman snarled. "I'm the only thing standing between you and the hangman's noose."

"That's a charming but archaic phrase," he said cynically. "You need some new material."

"And you need a course in manners," she snapped. "We won't speak of this again. Just take care of it."

Sensing the conversation was over, I rushed back to the great hall and dashed behind one of the open double doors. When I heard both sets of footsteps pass by the doorway, I thought the coast was clear. But I waited another minute before poking my head out and looking both ways to make sure.

Only then did I skedaddle back to the blue parlor, where I found my backpack tucked under an end table near one of the couches.

I checked inside to make sure that the *Rebecca,* a book that several people had been killed for, was still safe.

Dinner was a marathon affair. Everything was cooked and baked to perfection and the wine flowed from start to finish. The guests were charming and interesting and there was plenty of gaiety. Even Harriet had her moments, I was shocked to see. Maybe her little rant in the blue parlor had perked her up.

I was exhausted by the time Derek, Claire, and I found our way back to our rooms. It hadn't been easy pretending to be sociable after overhearing that ominous conversation earlier.

We stood in the hall and spoke quietly. I told them what I'd heard in the blue parlor when I returned for my backpack.

"It can't be Allen," Claire said. "I like him."

"I do, too," I said. "And to be honest, I'm not sure it was him."

"It can't be Cameron, either," she insisted.

I almost smiled. We only had a few suspects to choose from. "Maybe it was Marcus. He grew up in the village, too."

"Perhaps," Derek said quietly.

"Did you notice anyone entering the dining room after you got there, but before me? Or did you see one of the men come in with Harriet?"

"The problem is," Derek said, "we all stopped off at the library. The door was still open and none of the other guests had seen that room in a long time, if ever. So we spent a few minutes in there, and we all reached the dining room about the same time."

"Well, that's not helpful," I muttered.

"I'd much prefer if it were Marcus talking to Harriet," Claire said. "Oh. Could it have been her husband, Oliver?"

I stared at her for a moment. "I suppose it could've."

"That possibility appeals to me," she said, nodding.

"He doesn't seem aggressive enough to have carried on that way, but maybe his passive behavior is just an act." I sighed. "I wish I'd had enough courage to peek inside the room."

"No," Derek said instantly. "These people aren't fooling around. I'm afraid they might've killed you if they knew you'd overheard them."

"That may have been why they killed Jenny," I mused. "She could've known what her father was up to."

Derek's eyes turned cold. "I believe killing Jenny was a wrong step. It brings death into the castle."

"I have a feeling this is where it all started," I said.

"And it will end here," Derek said.

Claire's hands were bunched into fists. "Let's please find my aunt before anyone else has to die."

"That is a good plan," Derek said.

I nodded in agreement, stifling a yawn. "For now, let's get to sleep so we can wake up early and search the western bell tower."

"I know you're both exhausted," Claire said, unlocking her door. "But would you mind doing one last sweep of the room? I'm feeling quite paranoid again."

"Paranoia is the proper response," I said.

We all turned off our cell phones and Derek went around the room with the device. When he got to Claire's fireplace, we all heard a low-level beeping sound.

"Oh, crap," I whispered.

Claire's eyes grew wide with fear. She stared at me, but didn't dare say a word. I knew exactly how she felt.

Derek held his finger to his lips. He glanced around the mantel, lifted up several books, and moved the vase of flowers. He picked something up and showed us. It was a tiny black object that bore a strange resemblance to a bug.

Just to be safe, he continued around the room in case there were any other bugs. We didn't hear another beeping sound, so he walked into the bathroom and Claire and I raced over to watch. Setting the bug down on the tile floor, he lifted his foot and smashed it, squashing it . . . like a bug.

He took the dead thing, dropped it in the toilet, and flushed.

"Probably not good for the pipes," he said. "But it's the best way to get it out of your room."

Derek found our very own bug in a similar place on the mantel in our room. It was perched cleverly on the branch of a decorative spring foliage arrangement. Now it was floating somewhere in the bowels of the castle plumbing system.

The fact that we were debugged did little to lull me to sleep. I tossed and turned for two hours before finally grabbing my earbuds and listening to a bookbinding podcast on the merits of laminated book cloth. I was asleep in minutes.

Early the next morning, Claire joined us in our room for a quick cup of coffee before we went downstairs for breakfast.

"I still can't be sure who was talking to Harriet last night," I said. "But whoever it was must be the same person who killed Jenny and the two men in San Francisco and Dharma."

Claire looked at me. "What do you think Harriet meant when she told him to 'take care of it'?"

"I'm afraid she might've been talking about your aunt," Derek admitted.

"The good news," I said, "is that apparently he hasn't taken care of it yet."

"That gives me a little hope."

I frowned. "There might be something else going on here. I started thinking about it yesterday when we were at the Clava Cairns."

"Let's hear it," Derek said, knowing this was the best way to suss out our theories.

"Okay. We've been concentrating our efforts on

finding your aunt," I said to Claire. "But what if there's something more sinister going on? Something that goes deeper than one woman disappearing from her home. Something that maybe goes back a generation or two."

"Good heavens," Claire said. "What are you thinking?"

"Whichever man was having that conversation with Harriet, it all centered on his father." I quoted her words again. "'Your father is the reason we're here,' Harriet said. 'You must avenge him.'"

Claire rubbed her arms. "Her words give me chills."

"Me, too," I confessed.

"So that's going back at least a generation," Derek agreed.

"I looked at those three men yesterday," I said. "Allen Brodie, Cameron MacKinnon, and Silas Abernathy. Allen and Cameron have been friends all their lives, just as Allen's father and Cameron's father, the old laird, were friends. Silas worked for the old laird, too. They all worked together and they were friends."

"Right," she said. "I'm following you. Sort of."

"And Silas Abernathy still works here, for Cameron now," Derek said.

"And then there's your father and your aunt," I said.

"They grew up here, as well," Claire acknowledged. "They were all friends."

"That's right," I said. "I'm not sure of the timing, but at some point your father left for the States about the same time as your aunt went to work in London."

She thought about it. "That's close enough."

"And then your father got into some trouble and took you back to Oddlochen to live with your aunt."

"And then he disappeared." She scowled and took a sip of coffee.

"I wonder why your father would take you all the way to Scotland and then disappear. Why didn't he stay here with you?"

"I have no idea." She huffed out a breath. "I've spent my entire life trying to figure that out."

"It was too dangerous for him to stay," Derek said.

I pointed at him. "Right. Do you think he sold whatever he'd found in that bundle and ran off to Scotland with the money?"

Claire frowned. "I'm beginning to think he must have."

Derek leaned forward. "Bill and the other men he was working with might've followed him here. Which was why he couldn't stay."

I nodded. "They're all Scottish, you said."

"Yes." She rubbed her eyes, clearly upset by the conversation. But she continued. "He came all this way to protect me and then he had to keep running. It makes me sad."

"Did you ever ask him who that other man was? The one who saw you in the hallway?"

"The same one who spoke to him from the car," she said.

"Yes. Your father clearly realized you were in danger."

"We packed up and left the next day." She shook her head. "I never found out who he was."

"It's good to know that your father was worried about you," I mused.

"Then why did he leave me?" She waved her hands in the air. "Never mind. We've been over this before. It wasn't safe for him to stay."

"So follow me on this," I said after a moment. "Your father got here, then realized he was being followed, and maybe hid a stash of weapons or money, or something, somewhere around the castle. Your aunt may have had a vague notion of what he'd done."

"She never said anything."

"No, she wouldn't have," Derek murmured. He had known her well.

"Didn't you say that your father gave your aunt the book?" I asked. "The *Rebecca*."

"Yes."

"So what if part of the message in the book is from your father," I theorized, "and the rest of it is from your aunt?"

"That's kind of . . . crazy," Claire said. "But then, everything we've been through this past week has been crazy."

"It's just a theory, of course," I began, "but what if the first half of the message was from your father. This came from the part of the book where the letters were marked off."

"You think the message about the western bell tower and the wooden plank is from my father?" Claire said.

"Exactly," I said.

Derek jumped in. "And the second part is from your aunt."

"Right. That's the one where the letters have tiny dots next to them. In Gaelic it says to ask Beatrice about the secret passage to the Loch."

Claire glanced from Derek to me, all the while shaking her head. "Do you actually think my father left me something in the bell tower?"

"It's a theory," I said.

"And you also believe my aunt left something in a secret passage that leads to the Loch?"

"That is what the message says."

Claire sucked in a deep breath and slowly exhaled. Rubbing her stomach, she said, "I'm not sure my digestive system will ever be the same."

After we had our fill of another spectacular breakfast— even Claire managed a second helping, despite her topsy-turvy stomach—we rushed back to our rooms to gather supplies for our quest.

I wrote out the messages from the book for reference and folded the piece of paper into my jeans pocket. Then I packed my thick roll of bookbinding tools into my backpack alongside the *Rebecca* just in case. You just never knew when you'd need a bookbinder's hammer or a bonefolder.

Derek tucked his mini-flashlight into his pants pocket. Then I saw him slide his very scary gun into the inside pocket of his jacket. I tried to remain calm about the gun. After all, whoever had killed Jenny and those two men was not kidding around. We would need to protect ourselves.

There was no doubt that Claire would have a knife or two—or three—concealed somewhere on her person.

Which meant that I was the only one who wasn't carrying a weapon—until I remembered that I had a bookbinder's hammer with me. So look out, bad guys!

We reached the door in the west hallway. I watched Derek consider the old-fashioned keyhole for a long moment.

"We have no way of locking it," he said. "We'll just have to take our chances that nobody's following us."

"There's nobody around," Claire said. "We'll be fine."

"Besides," I added. "We'll hear them climb the stairs. It's like an echo chamber in that narrow passageway."

"True enough," Derek said.

He didn't add that even if we heard someone approaching, we'd be stuck. No way out. I wouldn't think about that, I decided.

We climbed the narrow spiral staircase and a few minutes later, we stood in the bell tower. After dividing the room in three sections, we each took our one-third and began examining each plank, starting from the north side of the room and moving south. The hardwood planks were fairly uniform in size and they were screwed into the subflooring at each of the four corners. We had to get down on our hands and knees to check out each piece of board in our section, looking for oddities: a wobbly board or some screws that were easily jiggled loose. This would've happened after being tightened and loosened too many times.

After a half hour, my back was starting to cramp up so I stood up and stretched. I was surprised to see that we were already two-thirds of the way through the room.

"We're lucky this space is so small," I said.

"Aye," Claire said. "But my last few feet of flooring will be tough to navigate."

This was because part of the mechanism for ringing the bell and the support beams ran along the far wall, close enough to the floor that we would have to lie down on our stomachs to get a look at the last row of planks.

"Okay, here goes," I said, and lay down on the floor with my elbows supporting me. The rest of my planks were solid. I was certain none of them had been moved or lifted up in the past thirty years, if not longer.

"I hope one of you finds something," I said, crawling out from under the beams. "I'm finished and I had no luck at all."

"I have a few more rows to go," Claire said. "I'll let you know what I find."

"Do you need help?" I asked.

"I'm fine, Brooklyn. You go ahead and rest your weary old muscles."

"Did you just call me *old*?"

She giggled, and it made me happy to hear the sound. I knew she had been bummed out by our theorizing about her father and aunt earlier. But now she seemed back to her old self. Well, not *old* old, I thought with a grin.

"I'm on the last row," Derek said, "and I don't believe I've got anything."

"Oh crap," I said. "What if this is all a big bust?"

Claire choked and began to cough.

"You okay?"

"I'm fine. It's just so dusty under this old machinery."

"Well, come out, then."

"No, no," she said, and coughed again. "I actually think I've found it. I got so excited that I took a deep breath and must've swallowed some dust."

"You found it," I said. "Oh my God. Do you need help?"

"It's right up against the wall and I can barely budge it, but it moves. The screws are loose." She let out another giggle. "Loose screws. Oh my God."

"Do you want me to pull the plank up?" Derek asked.

"You might have to," she admitted. "But you'll have to get into a very awkward position under these beams."

"I'll handle it. You come out."

She lifted her head and hit the beam. "Ouch. That hurt."

"Be careful," I warned, too late.

"Okay," she said. "I'll have to wiggle out backward."

I laughed. I couldn't help it. We were all getting silly after working for over an hour without a break. And trying not to think about the fact that any minute now, someone might want to kill us.

Claire wiggled out of the tight space, rolled over, and rested her back against the wall.

Derek said, "I'll open the plank and whatever is inside, I'll pass it straight on to you. You need to see it all first." Then he slid into the space.

I watched her eyes tear up, but she quickly quashed the waterworks. "Thank you," she said, then stood and stretched her entire body, bending over to touch her toes, then reaching up to work out all the kinks.

She folded her arms across her chest and paced around the small space.

I reached out and rubbed her arm as she passed by me.

She shook her head. "I never would've found this if you guys hadn't helped me figure out that code." She managed a weak laugh. "Even if I had somehow figured out the code, that plank is so completely hidden under those old beams that keep the bell working. I'm not sure I ever would've found it."

"Gwyneth would've found it," Derek said from beneath the wood beams.

"Of course she would've," Claire said. "She's brilliant with things like this."

"And she's a fairly excellent code breaker, as well," Derek said.

"Is she? That's so good to know."

I bent down to check out Derek's progress. "How's it going?"

"Almost there," he reported. "I'm using the universal tool you gave me for Christmas."

"I'm glad it came in handy."

"Yes, it's quite handy. I'm almost there."

"Okay." I grinned. "We're sending good vibes your way."

"That helps," he said, chuckling, "in fact." He paused and I heard the soft groan of old wood being moved. "Got it."

"Yay!"

Claire raised her fists in victory. "Now we'll see just how big of a wild-goose chase this was."

"There are definitely some items stuffed in this space," Derek said. "Here's the first one." He reached back and passed something out to me.

I handed it off to Claire. I could tell it was a book, but didn't look at the front cover.

She stared at it, then really did burst into tears. "It's a book. My favorite when I was a wee lass."

"What's the title?"

"It's a Katie Morag book," she murmured, clutching the book to her chest. "This one is *Katie Morag Delivers the Mail*. There was a whole series of books featuring this young lass, Katie, who lives on an island off the coast of Scotland and has adventures. She was funny and feisty and rather independent, and I loved her."

"I don't think we had those books in the States when I was growing up."

"My dad must've read it to me a hundred times." She laughed despite her tears. "He must've been so sick of it." She stared at the book and sniffled. "I don't need any money. This is enough to show he cared. He thought of me." She held the book out. "This is real."

I took the book and studied the cover. "It looks really cute."

The tears kept coming and I had to admit I was shedding a few myself in sympathy.

"I don't know what this means," she whispered.

"It means he was thinking about you and wanted you to know it."

"Something else," Derek said, and passed me a wool scarf. Before I handed it to Claire, I shook it out. It was shorter and narrower than a typical wool scarf so I assumed it was made for a young girl. "It's a pretty one."

She ran the scarf through her fingers. It was predominantly green-and-blue plaid with black stripes running through it. "On our way to Aunt Gwyneth's, we stopped in Edinburgh for the day. The weather was so much colder than we were used to, so he bought me this scarf and a beautiful blue coat. I felt like a princess."

"That's a lovely memory."

"And here's something else, if you're ready," Derek said.

"We're ready."

He passed a foot-long wooden box to me and I handed it to Claire. She unlatched it and opened the top. "Oh, this is definitely from my father."

I moved in close to see what was in the box. It was a matched pair of knives. "Wow."

"Yes." She let out a breath. "These were his pride and joy."

They were daggers, or dirks. I still wasn't sure what the difference was. But they were in pristine condition and looked very sharp.

"So you recognize them as your father's," I said.

"Yes. I can tell by the engraving in the quillon."

"Where is it?" I asked.

She pointed it out to me. "Right here. It's also called a crossguard."

I saw the fancy initials: SIQ.

"SIQ? I don't think you've ever mentioned your father's name before. What do the initials stand for?"

"I never said?" She smiled. "His name is Stewart. Stewart Ian Quinn."

"That's a nice name," I said. "Sounds very Scottish."

"Aye, it is," she murmured, staring at the matched set.

"The name may be nice," a voice drawled from the stairway. "But the man himself is a thief and a liar."

Chapter 19

Claire and I turned at the sound and Derek came sliding out from under the beams.

The man wore a blue baseball cap low on his forehead, but it couldn't disguise his height, his muscles, even the short strands of blond hair peeking from the cap. There was something familiar about the look.

"You were in San Francisco," I said, putting it together.

Allen Brodie sneered. "How would you know?"

"It's the baseball cap. You were wearing it on the street the same day Derek ran after your buddy Jerome Smith."

"You're daft."

"No, Allen. But *you* are for wearing a Los Angeles Dodgers cap in San Francisco. Who does that?"

Allen's nostrils began to flare. He didn't like being ridiculed. "You need to shut up."

I laughed sharply, but I was seriously scared to death. He didn't have a weapon but he was big and strong and now he was mean and angry. Derek could take him, but Claire and I were closer to him. "What are you doing up here?"

"Looking for thieves."

"Everything here belongs to Claire."

"Claire." He looked straight at her. "Your father destroyed my father. And I'm going to destroy you."

He sounded like Inigo Montoya in *The Princess Bride*. *You killed my father. Prepare to die.* I wondered if maybe he'd try to start a swordfight.

Instead, he reached behind his back and pulled out a gun.

"Put it down, Brodie," Derek said, holding his own gun pointed right at Allen's chest. "You don't want to die this way."

But maybe he did because he aimed the gun at Claire and looked ready to pull the trigger.

Without thinking, I flung the Katie Morag book at him. It barely grazed his ear, but he flinched and then ducked to avoid getting hit by the flying object. It was enough of a distraction that Claire was able to grab one of the daggers from the wooden box and throw it, instantly hitting her target.

He dropped the gun and let out an ear-shattering scream as blood soaked through his pale blue dress shirt. The knife was embedded in Allen's upper arm.

"You bitch!" he squawked. "You hit me!"

"Oh my God." I had to take some deep breaths and step back a few inches at the sight of all that blood. But I managed to reach over and squeeze Claire's shoulder. "You're awesome."

Allen leaned over awkwardly to try and grab the gun. But before he could reach it, Derek was across the room in an instant. He kicked the gun away and immobilized Allen's good arm in one sweeping action. It was an amazing move!

He yanked the dagger out of his arm and Allen

groaned. I thought he might faint, but Derek held him upright.

"Oh, stop moaning," Claire said. "It's barely a flesh wound."

"Claire," Derek said, holding up the knife. "Can you take this?"

Claire rushed over and took the dagger, gingerly holding it by the pommel as blood dripped onto the floor.

"Brooklyn, will you pick up the gun, please?"

"You bet." Avoiding the drops of blood on the wood floor, I moved in and picked the gun up, then handed it to Derek, who engaged the safety and shoved it into his other pocket. Then he yanked Allen's arms behind him, causing the man to shriek with pain.

Derek was unruffled. "Darling, did you bring tape with you?"

"Sure did." I found my backpack and rolled out the leather tool case. Bookbinder's tape was a bookbinder's emergency tool. Nearly invisible and acid-free, it was my go-to fixer in many situations. But this was a first.

I pulled several long strips from the roll, cut them with my X-Acto knife, and handed them to Derek. The tape was strong enough to fix a torn endpaper but for this job, Derek doubled the tape and twisted it as he wrapped the strips around and around Allen's wrists to give it ropelike strength that would secure him for the short time it would take to get him downstairs.

I thought of Jenny MacDougall's body and couldn't help but confront him. "You killed Jenny. She was an innocent young woman and you killed her. Why?"

"She knew too much."

"Like what?"

"She knew her dad went to San Francisco with me."

"So Reggie told her where he was going."

He shrugged. "She could've blackmailed me."

"Did she try?"

"No, but she could've. And I had to stop her."

Damn it, this guy was a murdering creep.

I looked at Claire. "Do you have your phone? Can you contact Cameron or Mrs. B and ask them to call the police?"

"Yes."

"Good shot, by the way," I said with a grin. "Did you mean to hit him in the arm?"

"Yes," she said simply. "I wanted him taken alive. This way, he'll spend the rest of his life in a cage."

"Good thinking."

As Claire spoke on the phone to Mrs. Buchanan, Derek finished taping Allen's wrists.

"Hurry, please, Mrs. B," Claire said. "We've caught Jenny's killer."

Derek shoved Allen Brodie face-first against the wall and held him there while we waited for help.

Allen was completely unrepentant. I hoped I could get him to talk some more, for Claire's sake.

"Where is Gwyneth Quinn?" I asked.

That surprised him. "How the bloody hell should I know?"

I glared at him, but said nothing.

Derek asked, "Did you threaten Gwyneth?"

He snorted. "What do I care about a dotty old woman?"

For some strange reason, I was starting to believe him. But if he had nothing to do with Gwyneth's disappearance, who did? Why was she missing? Did she know too much, like Jenny did? Did someone kill her because of it?

"Why did you kill Reggie and Jerome?" Derek asked.

"They were too chatty," he said in an offhand way. "They were loose ends."

"They were your friends. They did the dirty jobs for you."

He bared his teeth. "How could I trust that they wouldn't betray me like my father was betrayed by his mates? Besides, they couldn't even take care of one mere woman." He nudged his chin toward Claire and snorted in disgust. "I couldn't let them live."

Derek was getting responses from him so I didn't want to interrupt. But the man was so blasé, I wanted to kick him. After watching Claire's dagger fly across the room and into Allen's arm, I had suddenly realized that the two murders in California hadn't been stabbings at all, but something that required a great deal more skill. "Where did you learn to throw a knife?"

"My old man taught me." His voice was filled with arrogance and I realized he was proud of his accomplishments. Apparently, that was why he had deigned to answer my question.

I'd bet Claire could beat him hands down any day.

"Why did you come after Claire?" I asked.

"I wanted the book. Her father told mine that he'd hidden a secret code in the old book. Before my father died, he told me to find the book and break the code. Said it would lead me right to Quinn's cache of weapons."

So now I was confused, which was not all that unusual. I couldn't figure out who had left which secret message in the black book. I hoped that when we found Gwyneth, we would find the answers.

Something else occurred to me and I tried to phrase it as innocently as I could. "Cameron said that someone's been stealing from the castle for years. Who do you think was doing that?"

His expression was almost snotty. "Boo-hoo. Too bad. They've been stealing from my family for generations."

"Really?"

He bared his teeth again. "Didn't I just say so?"

"What were they stealing from you?"

He screwed up his mouth like an obstinate child. "Our honor. Our name. Now I want mine back."

"I don't understand."

He rolled his eyes as though I was a complete fool. I waited, and finally, his temper flashed. "He took my birthright."

"Birthright?" Had we teleported back to medieval times?

"The old laird was my real father." He stared out the bell tower and turned in every direction. "All of this should've been mine."

I watched him. "Were you born before Cameron?"

"Yes!"

"So you're claiming primogeniture?"

"That's right."

"Did the old laird recognize you as his legitimate son?"

He made a sound that resembled a growl.

I took that as a "no." Which meant that Allen was never going to be allowed to take over the lairdship.

"Were you ready to take over when the old laird disappeared?"

"I was born ready."

"But then Cameron MacKinnon showed up and took over."

"Now you've the right of it."

"He was the golden child," I said.

He looked over his shoulder at me and his anger was palpable. His lips were a tight, flat line. "So he thinks."

"Did the old laird tell you he was your father?"

Allen refused to answer me.

"Did your mother tell you?" I asked.

He blew out a breath. "No. But before she died, she told my aunt the real story."

"Ah. Aunt Harriet told you." It was beginning to make sense. I wouldn't be surprised to find out Harriet had made up the whole story just to rile Allen enough to go after Cameron. Wretched old woman!

"That's right. Cameron MacKinnon took what was mine and he deserves to die."

"Did you take a DNA test? Or did you just believe whatever your aunt told you? She seems a bit dodgy to me. Maybe she told you a big fat lie."

"You're the one who's lying!"

Claire stepped up and said, "When you said that your father taught you how to throw a knife, which father were you talking about? Mr. Brodie or the old laird?"

But he wouldn't even look at Claire.

She tried again. "You said my father destroyed your father. What did he do?"

"He promised my father a fortune. My father relied on his word and it destroyed him. I blame Stewart Quinn for my father's death."

"What kind of fortune was he promised?" I asked.

Allen shrugged. "He dealt in weaponry. He promised an arsenal of weapons for us to fight the MacKinnon. And he promised him money. A lot of money."

"I don't believe you," Claire shouted. "The MacKinnon was his friend. My father didn't betray his friends. That's a lie."

"It's the truth," he bellowed. "My father even traveled to Florida to make sure the deal was set in stone."

"Wait," I said. "Your father was in Florida? Meeting with Claire's father?"

"He had kept in touch with Quinn over the years," Allen explained. "During one phone call, Quinn bragged about a big payoff coming up. He owed my father some money, so Dad decided to go to Florida himself to make sure Quinn knew he expected a piece of it. Dad threatened Quinn, just to keep him in line. But instead of paying what he owed my father, Quinn skipped town. It was easy enough for Dad to follow him back to Oddlochen, but then he really disappeared. And we were left with nothing. He was a thief and a liar, just as I said. My father spent the rest of his life trying to track him down. He was obsessed with finding him and getting the money he was owed, but he never found him. It killed him."

That was heavy, I thought. I could tell that Claire was stunned and angry. And I knew without a doubt that Allen's father was the man she had stared down in the hallway that night. He was the man who had threatened her father on their way to school the next day. What a creep!

I had to wonder if Allen's father had lied about Claire's dad owing him money. Knowing how the son operated, I wouldn't put it past Allen's father to lie about such a thing.

And then I remembered Claire saying that her dad's friend Bill had told him "he was going to be very angry" to find out there was nothing in the bale. Was "he" Allen's father? And how did Bill know him? Maybe Quinn had introduced them. Oh, this was getting way too complicated.

While Claire caught her breath, I thought of another question to ask. "Does Harriet Gordon want you to kill Cameron MacKinnon?"

He looked at me and for the first time, I saw real hate in his eyes. I didn't take it personally. I knew it was aimed toward Cameron.

Footsteps thundered on the steps and echoed in the narrow chamber of the stairwell. Derek had his gun in hand, ready for anything.

Seconds later, Cameron appeared out of breath at the top of the stairs. "What the hell is going on?" he demanded, and stepped into the room.

The tower room was getting smaller by the minute with all these big men in here.

"Mrs. Buchanan said that Allen . . ." Cameron began, but then he saw Allen standing there and his expression clouded. "What's going on, Brodie?"

"He tried to kill us," Claire said, not giving Allen a chance to make his case. "He had a gun. He killed Jenny and Reggie MacDougall and Jerome Smith."

Cameron stared at his old friend. "You're bleeding."

"Piss off," Allen snapped.

"Claire took care of him," I said. "You thought she was good with an axe? You should see her with a dagger. She nailed him in the arm from across the room."

"I'm glad you didn't kill him," Cameron said, his eyes narrowed in fury. "I want him to pay for a long time."

I took a quick look at Claire and saw her smiling at the laird's comment. It echoed her own.

"What do you have to say, Brodie?" Cameron asked.

I gazed at Allen. "Do you want to tell him or shall I?"

He jerked his chin. "Bugger off."

I turned to Cameron. "He thinks he's the real laird, not you."

Cameron stared at me for a long moment, then turned and looked at Allen. "You always were a pathetic wanker."

Derek gazed at the MacKinnon. "I'll be happy to get him downstairs if you'd like."

"I'll do it," he said, taking responsibility for his own problems.

"The tape isn't too secure," Derek warned. "But it should hold until you get him downstairs."

Grabbing Allen's good arm, Cameron yanked him toward the stairway. "Shift yer hurdies."

Puzzled, I looked at Claire.

She smiled and translated, "Move your ass."

I thought about it. "I like it."

Claire and I quickly picked up the treasures her father had left her and fitted them into her bag and mine. Then we followed Derek downstairs.

When we got to the foyer, Derek suggested they find a more secure way than the bookbinder's tape to keep Allen from bolting. Cameron pulled out his phone and called Silas. "I need you in the foyer immediately. And bring a strong rope."

Silas was there in less than five minutes and Cameron pulled him aside. They spoke in hushed tones and then Silas grabbed Allen, hog-tied him, and dragged him outside.

"Now, that's secure," I said with a smile.

When they were gone, Cameron turned and faced us. "I'm sorry you had to deal with him. I've always suspected he was jealous of me. It feels stupid to say it, but

I had a sense that something was off about him. He always showed me a smiling face, but I could sense a simmering rage underneath."

"You might want to check on his aunt," I said, and told Cameron about the conversation I'd overheard the night before.

"Good God," he murmured. "What is wrong with that family?"

"You have everything they want," I said simply.

Derek pulled Allen's gun from his pocket, slid the chamber open to empty it of bullets, and then handed it to the constable. A minute later, the constables drove off with their prisoner in the back seat.

Cameron turned to Silas. "Thanks, mate."

"No problem, boss." Silas gave us a little salute and walked away toward the garage.

Cameron looked at the three of us. "Thank you."

"No problem," Derek said.

"What were you doing in the west tower?" he asked.

"It's a long story," I said.

Claire laughed. "We'll tell you later, but right now we've got something to do."

"Where are you off to?" Cameron asked.

I glanced from Derek to Claire, then gazed at Cameron. "Before we tell you, I want to know something."

"What is it?"

"Did you kill your first wife?" I asked.

He blinked once, then his eyes narrowed in on me. "What in the bloody hell are you talking about? I've never been married before."

I stared at him for a long moment. "Okay. Just checking." So Allen had lied about that, too. What a plonker!

I glanced back at Derek, who nodded in silent agreement. We would trust Cameron.

"We're going to look for my aunt Gwyneth," Claire said. "Would you care to come along?"

"I would."

I glanced at Derek. "Should we ask Mrs. Buchanan about that photo?"

"Rather than involve her," Derek said, "I think we should first find the spot on the shore and go from there."

"Do you think we'll run into trouble?" I asked, considering the gun he was carrying in his side pocket.

He smiled. "What do you think?"

"We always seem to, so might as well be prepared."

"I've got a knife on me," Claire said.

"Only one?" I asked, grinning.

She batted her eyelashes. "Perhaps an extra, just for good measure."

"I really need to learn how to throw like you."

"You did pretty well with the weapon you had."

"The children's book?" I laughed. "Yeah, I'm a black belt in book throwing."

"It certainly got the job done," she said. Turning to Cameron, she said, "Brooklyn was able to distract Allen by throwing a book at him."

He gazed at me. "You really do know your books."

I smiled. "I do."

We followed Derek to the south end of the castle, where we found a wide path that led to the front lawn.

"Do you know where you're going?" Cameron asked.

"We're trying to get down to the shore," I said.

"You think we'll find Gwyneth by the Loch?"

"Yes," Claire said. "We have some insider information."

"Who's the insider?"

She smiled. "My aunt."

That stopped him. He thought for a moment, and then gave a swift nod. "Let's go this way," he suggested, and led the way to a stone path on the far side of the lawn that widened as we headed for the sand.

"Tide is out," he said.

"That's probably a good thing."

"Do you know about a secret passage under the castle that leads to the Loch?" Derek asked. As long as we'd decided to trust Cameron, we might as well go all the way in.

"It's not really a secret. It used to be part of the ghost tour, so every adult in town has probably been inside it. But it was boarded up and bricked over years ago because my father suspected that smugglers were using it to store contraband that they planned to ship south by way of the Loch."

"So, not so secret," Derek mused. "Well, let's give it a shot."

We stepped onto the sand and walked along the shore for a few dozen yards. The water was slowly creeping up onto the sand, indicating that the tide was coming in.

"According to our source, there's an opening along here somewhere." Derek pulled out the photograph of Gwyneth and Beatrice and held it up. He glanced at the photograph, then looked around at the brush along the edge of the sand.

"Not absolutely sure," Derek said. "But this could be the spot."

"May I see that?" Cameron asked.

"Sure." Derek handed him the photo and he stared at it for a long moment.

He studied the bushes, too. Then held up the photo

and studied it for another minute. "It's been a few years and the trees have grown in, but I recognize this stump here. We used to stand on top of it and jump into the water when it was high tide."

The stump was barely two feet tall where someone had sawed off the rest of the tree. He looked around, walked a little farther, and then doubled back. Then he stared into the bushes. Suddenly he pointed. "There." And he stepped into the brush again and wandered around, staring down at the ground.

Claire followed him and did the same, occasionally reaching down to push away the growth to see what was underneath.

"Found it," Cameron said triumphantly.

Claire grinned. "There it is."

I gazed at Derek, who said, "Let's go."

It was a circular grate, about eighteen inches in diameter, with a hinge on one side. Cameron grabbed the small handle on the opposite side and lifted it. There were stone steps leading down under the ground.

"It's a little creepy," I muttered.

"Yes," Derek whispered. "So be careful."

"Right."

"I'll go first," Cameron said. "I don't want any of you to be injured."

Derek offered his tactical flashlight and he accepted.

He stepped down and quickly disappeared.

"Claire, you go next," Derek said. "Then Brooklyn. I'll bring up the rear."

We followed in single file until we were all underground. The passageway had stone walls and a dirt floor. It was wide and airy and not too claustrophobic, unless I thought about where we were.

We walked for about forty feet before I began to hear something.

I stopped. "What was that?"

"Sounds like static," Claire said.

"Static and voices." Derek frowned. "It's a police scanner."

We walked a few more yards and the sound stopped abruptly.

"Do you know where it's coming from?" I asked. "Is the house above us?"

"No," Cameron said. "The house is another hundred yards inland."

"It's coming from somewhere down here," Derek said.

It was another thirty or forty feet before we saw the boarded-up entrance to some room or passageway. Cameron stopped and waited for us to catch up to him.

"What is this place?" Claire asked.

"It's the old dungeon. I boarded it up six months ago after I found some kids playing in here."

The static came back and it was louder.

"Weird," I muttered.

"I think it's coming from the other side of this plywood barrier," Derek said. "Is that possible?"

Cameron shook his head. "I have no idea. I haven't been down here in months." He stared at the plywood. "Maybe it's a short from the electrical wiring running through here."

Derek pushed against the heavy plywood and felt it give a little. He felt along the edges all the way around, then grinned. "There are hinges on this side."

"That's crazy," I whispered. This had to be a good sign. I was getting excited.

Claire suddenly spun around and gasped.

"What is it?" I asked.

"This is familiar to me."

"Have you been down here before?" I asked.

"I . . . I'm not sure." Frowning, she gazed around at the walls and up and down the passageway. "How odd."

"Maybe you came on the tour with Sophie," I suggested.

She shook her head and waved away our concerns. "Don't mind me."

"Maybe when you were little? Maybe you came down here with your father," I said.

She had to take a deep breath and let it out slowly. "Yes. Maybe."

Derek gave her one last look, then glanced at Cameron. "Was this really the dungeon?"

"Yes," Cameron said.

He held out his hands. "Let's open it."

But pulling the plywood away from the wall wasn't as easy as lifting the grate. "It feels like it's locked from the inside."

"There's only one thing to do," Claire said, and started to pound on the wood. "Hello!"

I looked at Derek, who glanced back with eyebrows raised. I shrugged. This was her show, I thought. Hers and Cameron's.

Claire was not holding back anymore. "Aunt Gwyneth! Open the door!"

"Claire? Is that you?" the voice said in a hush.

"Yes. Let us in!"

"Who's with you?"

"Some friends. We've been looking for you. We followed your clues."

"Thank goodness."

We heard locks click and chains slide back. Thirty

seconds later, the plywood door was slowly pushed away from the wall.

And Gwyneth Quinn stood before us.

"Claire," she whispered, sounding awestruck.

"Auntie." Claire stepped inside and grabbed her aunt in a tight hug.

"You found me," Gwyneth said.

Claire was laughing and crying. "We followed the clues."

"Good girl." She rubbed Claire's back, then stopped. "Is that Don? Don Danger?"

I laughed out loud.

"Hello, Tanya Roma," Derek said in a suave accent, then chuckled as Gwyneth wrapped her thin arms around him in a ferocious hug.

"I knew I could count on you, Don," she said.

Derek reached for me and pulled me forward. "Gwyn, this is my wife, Brooklyn. She helped unravel the code."

"The bookbinder," Gwyneth said, and reached out to take my hand. "I thought you might find the clues intriguing."

"I did. Thank you for leaving them for us to follow."

"You know I didn't leave all of them," she whispered confidentially.

"Your brother left some of them," I said.

"Oh, you are a smartie," she said, beaming at me. Then she clapped her hands together like a school-teacher. "Let me show you my home away from home." She spread her arms to indicate the space. "My dungeon, as it were."

"Pretty nice," I said, trying to ignore the total implausibility of this moment.

It was one big room divided into a living space, a bedroom, a small kitchen, and what I would call a command center. A long table covered with three computers, tracking devices, and a full security squad's worth of monitors that showed two different views of the shoreline, one of the woods, and one screen showed the large double doors leading into the castle.

And good grief, she even had a camera showing the back door of her apartment above her antiques shop.

"You have closed-circuit cameras set up in all these places?" I asked.

"Yes, of course. I had to keep an eye on things. I knew my enemies would be looking for me."

I frowned. "Did you see Allen kidnap Jenny?"

"No," she said softly. "I'm sorry. I wish I had. I would've taken action immediately. But I didn't think anyone else was in danger but me. I realize now that it was shortsighted of me. But I had to see who would show up at the castle. And I wanted to keep an eye on my place. If the men who ransacked it came back, I'd be able to report them."

"How long were you going to stay out here?" Derek asked.

"Until you kids figured out the secret code."

Derek shook his head and laughed.

"Did you sneak into your apartment two nights ago?" I asked, remembering the lights I thought I'd seen inside her place.

"Yes. I wanted to leave another note for Claire."

"In the *Jane Eyre*."

"That's right." She beamed. "You're very smart."

"If there's a book involved, I'm your girl."

Cameron took in Gwyneth's cozy room and state-of-the-art electronics. "Who set this up for you?"

"I did," she said matter-of-factly. "What do you think I was doing all that time I worked at MI6?"

Derek laughed again. "Tanya, you haven't changed." He glanced at the rest of us. "Among her other duties, Gwyneth was an electronics genius."

She nodded coyly. "Thank you, Don."

I giggled. I never giggled, but the way she said it cracked me up.

"Aunt Gwyneth?" Claire said. "What about my father? Is it true that he left those clues for me?"

Her aunt wrapped her arm around Claire's waist. "Yes, love."

"But where did he go? Why couldn't he stay?" she demanded. "Did he tell you why?"

"Staying here would've put you in danger," she explained softly. "There were men after him who thought he had betrayed them. He didn't, of course. But they were desperate. And they knew that you had seen them stealing from your father, so he had to find a way to keep you safe."

"But I didn't see anything."

"You did," Gwyneth said, stroking her hair. "You just don't remember. You were only five years old."

"So they chased him all the way here?" I asked.

"They did."

"Is he still . . ."

"Alive?" Gwyneth finished the sentence. "Yes. But don't ask me where he is. He almost got you killed, so he wasn't about to take another chance on that happening."

"But he was safe here, wasn't he?"

"He was for a while. He took the precaution of hiding a few of his weapons and cash where he could find them quickly if he needed them. But someone saw him and the trouble began all over again."

"We found some things in the bell tower," I said.

"Yes," Gwyneth said, "but that was just a small treasure that he put away for Claire."

"He left a bigger treasure?"

"Oh my, yes."

"Do you know where?" I asked.

She sighed. "No. He knew it would put us all in danger."

"But—"

"That's enough," someone shouted from the passageway.

Claire let out a little scream and we all turned to see the woman pointing a gun directly at Gwyneth.

I sniffed haughtily, imitating her. "Hello, Harriet."

"Mrs. Gordon," Cameron said. "How did you find this place?"

She sniffed. "You weren't exactly subtle. I just followed a distance behind you." She jerked the gun. "And now I want those weapons your brother stashed away."

"You think you have a right to them?" Gwyneth said.

"Why shouldn't they be mine?"

She sounded like her nephew, I thought, but kept my mouth shut. Something told me Harriet was much more ruthless with a gun than Allen had been.

"Your brother stole them from my family," Harriet claimed.

Gwyneth snorted. "No, he didn't."

"He did," she insisted. "And my brother chased him and saw where he hid everything."

"Your brother is Allen's father?" I asked.

"That's right."

I frowned. "So why didn't he just take them when he saw where they were hidden?"

Harriet scowled. "He was suffering from a rare type

of dementia. Apparently he told his wife where the weapons were, but she thought he was delusional. And then she died shortly after he did."

"All this is tragic indeed," Cameron said, "but it doesn't mean the weapons belong to you."

"I don't care!" Harriet shrieked, clearly on her last nerve. "You people have been stealing from the Brodie family since time immemorial. You owe me!"

"That's a ridiculous lie," Cameron said, his tone carrying the full force of the lairdship. "Besides, I haven't the foggiest idea where the damned weapons are hidden. And if I did, I wouldn't tell you anyway. So you'll just have to shoot me."

Harriet's eyes grew wide and she raised the gun and aimed. Before she could pull the trigger, a dagger flew across the space and landed deep in her right thigh, stunning her.

Harriet took a step on her good leg and without warning, another dagger zipped through the air and skimmed her left thigh.

Harriet gaped at Claire, then stared down at her legs. "You stabbed me twice! I'm bleeding!"

The gun clattered to the ground.

I looked at Claire. "Two knives?"

"She would've run if I'd stopped at one."

"Good point."

"I'm dying!"

"You'll live," Claire said drolly. "I was careful not to hit the femoral artery."

I blinked in shock. "Damn, you're good."

"You certainly are," Cameron said, gazing at Claire with admiration.

Claire met his gaze. "She would've killed you."

He took in a deep breath and let it go. "Thank you."

Then he pulled out his phone to contact the police and the EMTs.

Derek rushed over and grabbed Harriet. Gwyneth followed him, carrying several thin bungee cords. Together, they secured Harriet's hands behind her back despite her moans and cries.

I picked up the gun. I was getting good at that.

When they were finished securing her, I walked over and handed the gun to Derek, then wrapped my arms around his waist. "Wow, this team is good." I glanced from Derek to Gwyneth to Claire to Cameron and laughed. "We all work pretty well together."

"It's always a thrill with Don Danger on the team," Gwyneth said.

Derek laughed out loud. "Nice working with you again, Tanya."

EPILOGUE

Harriet was carted off to join her nephew in jail.

Two hours later, we all regrouped in the blue parlor to discuss everything that had happened since the three of us arrived in Scotland. I watched Robbie the cat wander into the room and jump up to nestle in Claire's lap. I couldn't help but wonder if the cute black-and-white cat was a distant relative of Claire's Mr. D.

Watching the MacKinnon, I realized that he scowled on a regular basis, even when he was happy. Maybe it had been a happy scowl that night in the pub when he couldn't keep his eyes off Claire.

"I believe I remember the dungeon," she said suddenly.

"I was wondering if the memory would come back to you," I said.

"I spent some time hiding in there with my father because there were bad men coming after him. I just remember the tunnel and the memories are coming back in bits and pieces."

Aunt Gwyneth patted her leg. "I can try to fill in more blanks in your memory. For one thing, he was going to put you into witness protection in Florida, but you were such a wee little girl and he decided you would be better off here with your old auntie, until he could come back for you."

Tears sprang to Claire's eyes and I could feel my own wanting to join in.

"You know," Aunt Gwyneth said, "I'm beginning to have an idea where Claire's father hid his weapons cache. And by the way, they're mostly antique weapons and worth millions of dollars. But I'm hoping he'll return someday, so I'm going to keep it a secret."

"Good thing Harriet didn't hear you say that," Claire groused. "That woman is evil."

"From day one," I said. "And she spread her evil to her nephew."

"Speaking of the return of missing people, where is your father?" Claire asked Cameron. "Did he really abscond with a fortune in family artwork?"

"Not that I know of," Cameron said.

"Were there really gambling debts?" I asked.

"Oh yes. Not only was he a terrible gambler, but he couldn't stop. Always a bad combination."

"Do you think he'll come back someday?"

"I doubt it," Cameron said philosophically. "He's probably somewhere on the French Riviera, living off a good-hearted woman."

"Well, good for him," Gwyneth said. "Although he's a rogue and a rascal, I always had a soft spot in my heart for him."

Two days later, the helicopter landed on the castle grounds to take us back to Inverness.

I had Aunt Gwyneth's *Rebecca* packed in my bag. I was taking it home to refurbish and rebind in a beautiful black leather with a gilded title on the front. It would be a fresher, newer, more sparkling version of the old cover.

Cameron had given me five books to fix for him for his library, which he planned to reopen as part of his castle museum. I would have to mail the books back this time, but someday soon we would return to Oddlochen to see all the changes that were being made.

As we approached the helicopter, Cameron gave Derek a manly smack on the back. "Next time you visit, bring your golf clubs with you."

"Absolutely, mate," Derek said with complete sincerity.

I could barely keep from rolling my eyes.

Then I overheard Cameron make an official offer to Claire to come work for him as master curator and director of antiquities at Castle MacKinnon.

"And if you don't like that title, you can make up your own," he said. He also promised she would live in the castle in a suite of rooms overlooking the Loch. "If you want to, that is. And to sweeten the deal, I'll add an axe-throwing lane in the castle."

She didn't say yes, but she didn't say no, either. She had to think about it.

"What's to think about?" I asked on the helicopter. I didn't mention that I thought she was already halfway in love with the guy, because that would've squelched the deal. But I did point out all the benefits.

"I'll think about it," she murmured, and I left it at that.

In Inverness, we hopped on board another luxury private jet back to San Francisco. I knew I could definitely get used to that lifestyle.

By the time we arrived home, we were well and truly exhausted. It took all of us a full week to recover, but it was wonderful to be home with Charlie at last.

Claire stayed with us for a few days while her home was cleaned up and fumigated. I had remembered to recommend my friend Tom, who ran a specialty crime scene cleanup company. He took care of everything, and she was thrilled with her nice, clean home and vowed to forget what had happened there only a few weeks earlier.

Two weeks later, we picked up Claire and drove to Dharma for Robin's belated baby shower hosted by my mother. When she opened my book-baby-mobile, she began to cry. "It's so beautiful. I love it."

"I'm glad. Because I know how everyone feels when I give you books for presents."

"But, Brooklyn, this is so clever. The book is so pretty and it floats on air. And the creatures sway in the air as if they're floating right out of the story."

I gave her a hug. "That's the idea. I hope you and Jamie love it forever."

After the shower, we returned to Derek's parents' home. Claire was ready for a nap, but Derek wanted to take a drive.

"Come with me," he said.

"Of course."

We left Claire to take a nice, relaxing nap. We got back into the car and Derek drove down the hill and past the winery toward Robin's house. I knew where we were going, of course. Halfway up Red Mountain Road, he turned onto the narrow lane that led to our new property. At the end of the road, he stopped the car.

"Oh," I said. "Oh. Is it really finished?"

"It's really finished," Derek said. "Let's go see it."

We both climbed out of the car and stared at the house. "It's gorgeous," I whispered.

"It had to be," he said simply. "It's for you."

I felt those tear ducts twinging again and told myself I wouldn't cry. But the moment was so lovely.

"I love you so much," I said.

He wrapped his arms around me. "And I love you back."

"I can't wait to start filling our Dharma home with wonderful new memories."

"Then let's not wait," he said with a laugh, and we ran to the front door to get started.

Recipes

Brooklyn wanted to share four soup recipes to celebrate the places her adventures took her in this book. We threw in a fabulous recipe for savory scones to serve with any of the soups. Enjoy!

COCKALEEKIE SOUP

A traditional Scottish favorite, this recipe was created in honor of the Scotland setting of *Little Black Book*.

2 tbsp vegetable oil
1 whole chicken, cut up
3 carrots, divided
4 celery stalks, divided
3 cloves garlic, minced
2 cups white wine
6 cups water
1½ tsp salt
6 leeks
10 prunes
¾ cup barley

Heat oil in soup pot over medium-high heat. Brown chicken in three batches. You're aiming for some burnt bits to be stuck to the bottom of the pan. Remove chicken to a bowl and set aside.

Cut one carrot and two celery sticks into three-inch pieces. Add to pot with the garlic and saute for a minute. Then deglaze the pan with a little white wine, scraping up the burnt bits. When the bottom of the pan is clean, add the rest of the wine, the water, the salt, the chicken, and the accumulated juices in the bowl. Heat to a boil. Lower heat, cover, and simmer for 45 minutes.

While chicken is simmering, clean leeks thoroughly, careful to wash all of the dirt out from between the layers. Slice leeks ½-inch thick, and then quarter. Slice two stalks of celery. Dice two carrots and all of the prunes.

After 45 minutes, remove chicken and vegetables from the liquid and set in a colander in the sink to cool. Add the leeks, carrots, celery, prunes, and barley to the liquid in the soup pot. Heat to a rolling boil. Lower heat, cover, and simmer for 45 minutes. When the chicken is cool enough to handle, discard skin and bones and cut meat into bite-sized pieces. Add back to the soup for the final 10 minutes to heat through. Taste and add more salt if desired.

> Shortcut: If you don't feel like spending four hours in the kitchen, here's a shortcut that tastes AL- MOST as good: Skip the initial chicken-cooking time and substitute four cups of cooked chicken. Instead of using water, use chicken broth. Start with the step of adding the vegetables and barley to the chicken broth and wine.

COCONUT CURRY
LOBSTER BISQUE

This is a variation of one of the delicious meals Brooklyn and Derek eat on the private jet that whisks them to Scotland in *Little Black Book*.

2½ cups chicken broth
¼ cup red curry paste
2 cans coconut milk
¼ cup lime juice
2 tbsp rice, pureed
1 tsp fish sauce
2 cups cooked lobster, crab, or shrimp
Cilantro for garnish

Heat chicken broth to boiling. Lower heat and stir in curry paste, coconut milk, lime juice, rice, and fish sauce. Simmer for 15 minutes, stirring frequently. If rice is still in lumps, puree the mixture in a blender or with an immersion blender. Add cooked lobster, crab, or shrimp and continue to cook for five minutes, until the meat is heated through. Garnish with cilantro.

DHARMA LENTIL SOUP

This hearty lentil soup is vegan—unless you add the optional Italian sausage. This recipe is to honor Dharma, one of the four settings in *Little Black Book*.

¼ cup olive oil
1 onion, diced
3 carrots, sliced
2 celery stalks, sliced
1 potato, diced
1 lb dried lentils, rinsed and picked over
6 cups vegetable broth
1 lb Italian sausage, browned (optional)
5 cups greens, such as arugula or spinach
Salt and pepper to taste

Saute the vegetables in oil until onions are soft. Add vegetables through broth. Stir. Raise to a boil, then lower heat and simmer for 25 minutes. If using Italian sausage, add for the last five minutes to heat through. (The sausage should already be browned/cooked.) Stir in greens, then season with salt and pepper. Serve warm.

HOT AND SOUR SOUP

This recipe is to honor one of the four settings in *Little Black Book*—San Francisco, with a loving nod to its Chinese heritage.

½ lb pork (about two chops)
½ cup + 1 tbsp soy sauce, divided
2 tbsp chili garlic sauce, divided
1 tsp brown sugar
¼ cup Worcestershire sauce
2 tbsp rice vinegar
1 tsp sesame oil, plus more for drizzling

2 tsp corn starch
2 tbsp vegetable oil
4 green onions with tops, sliced
4 oz mushrooms, halved and sliced
1 tbsp grated fresh ginger
4 cups chicken broth

Slice the pork into about ¼-inch by 1-inch strips. Mix together 1 tbsp soy sauce, 1 tbsp chili garlic sauce, and brown sugar. Add pork strips to this mixture and allow to marinate while you continue prepping the soup.

Mix together ½ cup soy sauce, 1 tbsp chili garlic sauce, Worcestershire sauce, vinegar, 1 tsp sesame oil, and corn starch. Set aside.

Heat soup pot over medium high. When it's hot, add 1 tbsp vegetable oil and heat until shimmering. Add pork and marinade and spread across the bottom of the pan. Without stirring, allow to cook for three minutes. Add white part of onions and mushrooms. Continue to cook for two minutes, stirring occasionally. Add ginger and cook one minute longer, until fragrant. Add broth and soy mixture. Heat to a boil, then simmer for 10 minutes.

To serve, drizzle with sesame oil and top with green parts of onions.

SAVORY CHEESE SCONES

These savory scones are terrific with any of the soup recipes included in *Little Black Book*—or on their own with a lovely cup of tea.

2½ cups all-purpose flour
1 tbsp baking powder
½ tsp baking soda
½ tsp garlic salt
2 tbsp sugar
½ cup Greek yogurt
1 egg
8 tbsp cold butter, cut into small pieces
1–3 tbsp cold milk, divided
½ cup grated Parmesan cheese, divided
2 oz sharp cheddar cheese, cut into 1/8-inch pieces
2 tbsp fresh chives

Whisk or sift together the flour, baking powder, baking soda, salt, and sugar. In a separate bowl, whisk together the Greek yogurt and egg, then put in the fridge until you're ready for it.

Cut the butter pieces into the flour mixture until it resembles wet sand. Stir in the cold yogurt/egg mixture. The dough is meant to be crumbly, but if it won't come together at all, sprinkle with one tablespoon of cold milk and stir again. If it still won't come together, sprinkle with one more tablespoon of cold milk. Fold in half the grated Parmesan, all of the cheddar, and all of the chives. Turn onto a lightly floured surface and form into a ball of dough, and then into a round disk, about ¾-inch thick by 9 inches in diameter. Wrap in plastic and refrigerate for at least two hours.

Preheat oven to 375 degrees and line a cookie sheet with parchment paper. Cut the disk into 12 wedges. Put 1 tbsp cold milk in a small dish and brush top of each scone with milk. Then sprinkle with remaining Parmesan cheese. Bake about two inches apart until golden brown, about 20 minutes.

ACKNOWLEDGMENTS

The character of Claire Quinn has been percolating in my brain for several years now and I am so grateful to my brilliant plot partners, Paige Shelton and Jenn McKinlay, for helping me bring Claire to life—just in time for her to join Brooklyn and Derek in this new adventure. Jenn and Paige, thank you for being my besties. No memory is sweeter than the laughs we shared as we swigged what would be our last margaritas together, just as the lockdown was announced and our world turned weird.

We'll do it again. Soon. Can't wait!

I'm happy and grateful every day to work with executive editor Michelle Vega, who always makes my life and my books so much better.

And to the amazingly talented team at Berkley/PRH, thank you for making me and my books shine the brightest!

I am so lucky and thankful that I get to work with the wonderful Christina Hogrebe and everyone at Jane Rotrosen Agency. Thank you!

And to my family, my brothers and sisters-in-law, nephews and nieces and cousins and all y'all, for your love and support throughout this hellish year, thank you! That which doesn't kill us makes us stronger, right? Sure, yeah, blah blah blah. I love you guys!

Keep reading for a sneak peek of

The Paper Caper

The next Bibliophile Mystery by Kate Carlisle!

> "San Francisco is a city of startling events. Happy is the man whose destiny it is to gather them up and record them in a daily newspaper!"
>
> —Mark Twain's letter to the *Territorial Enterprise*,
> December 23, 1865

Joseph Cabot was a multibillionaire, an entrepreneur, a technological genius, and a social media superstar. He had his creative fingers in dozens of the most lucrative pots, as well as a few that weren't so lucrative—but they made him happy, so he didn't care. Real estate development, aeronautics, restaurants, manufacturing, computer design, you name the industry and Joseph's name was invariably connected to all the top performers.

He was a gregarious man who loved people. He was a sportsman, too, and enjoyed everything from basketball to fly fishing.

When something intrigued him, he would immerse himself in the subject. His latest obsession was windmills.

And he was a voracious reader. He loved books. He had amassed an impressive library of hundreds of rare antiquarian volumes, as well as thousands of bestsellers in every genre known to man. It was Joseph's love of books that made him a superstar in my book.

But more than anything else he'd accomplished, Joseph considered himself a newspaperman. It was an old-fashioned term, but that was why it appealed to him. He loved being the owner and publisher of the *San Francisco Clarion Press*, along with its affiliated nationwide network of television and radio stations that specialized in news, weather, and sports. He loved the idea of keeping people informed.

The ladies of San Francisco high society adored Joseph, for obvious reasons. He was in his late forties, tall and strong and video-star handsome, with thick, graying hair and a twinkle in his bright blue eyes.

And he just happened to be one of my husband Derek's best friends.

The two men had met fifteen years ago when Derek and his Stone Security team carried out a daring operation to rescue Joseph from a group of militant kidnappers who had stormed an elegant conference room in Mindanao and forced him at gunpoint off the stage and into a van. They had transported him blindfolded to their lair in the middle of some jungle where they threw him into a cage and then began the negotiations for his release.

Joseph refused to allow his company to pay a ransom to these hooligans, deciding instead to take his chances on escaping on his own. Joseph's business partners had balked at this plan and instead contacted Derek Stone to aid in liberating the stubborn man.

With negotiations falling through and the militants threatening to kill Joseph, Derek decided that their only choice was to overwhelm the captors, storm the lair, and rescue the prisoner themselves. And that was what he did. He led the raid himself and the operation was successful.

Once Joseph was back home and safe, he contacted Derek to say thanks. The two men began a friendship that has lasted to the present day.

Soon after Derek and I started dating, he insisted on introducing me to his friend Joseph. The three of us met for dinner and I found the older man to be smart and kind, with a good sense of humor. I liked him. When I learned that he was a booklover, as well as a major contributor to the Covington Library, I liked him even more. I knew we would be great friends for life.

My name is Brooklyn Wainwright and I'm a bookbinder specializing in rare book restoration. Anyone who loved books as much as I did was destined to be my new best friend.

"Almost ready, Brooklyn darling? We don't want to keep Joseph and the Covington crew waiting."

I jolted slightly, surprised to see Derek leaning against the doorway of my workshop, smiling at me. I couldn't help but smile back. We'd been married almost a year now, and every day spent with him was even better than the day before.

"You're home," I said lamely.

"Yes. And you're still working."

"This book is so badly damaged," I began to explain, then stopped. "Don't worry. I'll have it all cleaned up in no time." As I organized my work space, I wondered if my heart would always give a little jolt when I heard Derek's voice. His tone was deep and masculine with a whisper of the Oxfordshire countryside, along with a twinge of wry humor that always brought me instant pleasure. Added to that were his ruggedly handsome face and rock-hard body. The man had bewitched me from the first moment we met, despite the fact that he had used that first tender moment to accuse me of murder.

Ah, those were good times.

Derek studied the bedraggled pieces of book that I'd

placed on top of a white cloth. "This is the book that Lisa Chung found?"

"Yes. She found it in the gutter."

Lisa and Henry Chung lived down the hall with their three adorable young children. I had been repairing the children's books ever since they moved into the building a few years back.

He frowned. "It's quite a mess."

"Yes, it is. I wish I knew how it happened." I sighed. "I just need another minute, then I'll change my shoes and we can go."

He glanced down at my feet and I watched his eyebrow quirk, but he said nothing.

"Unless," I began, "you're thinking my Birkenstocks would be the perfect party shoes?"

"They would . . . make a statement," Derek declared after pondering for a moment. "They're really quite fetching, but . . ."

I had to laugh. His British accent, along with his choice of words, tickled me sometimes. "Fetching? Really?" My friends and family members were always giving me grief about my personal choice of work shoes, but what could I say? They were ridiculously comfortable. However, I would've never called them *fetching*—unless maybe I were a cave woman. The thick, clunky sandals definitely gave off a "Fred Flintstone" vibe.

"Don't worry," I assured Derek. "I plan to wear a pair of glittery yet painful stilettos for the occasion."

"That's my brave girl," he said with a smirk.

I snorted politely, then watched Charlie the cat slink out from under my worktable and saunter over to weave around Derek's ankles as her way of welcoming him home.

"And here's our Charlie." Derek leaned down and scooped her up, much to the cat's delight. As Charlie purred in his arms, I had to wonder if there was anything in the world more appealing than a big strong man cuddling a sweet little cat. I didn't think so.

Dragging myself back to my task, I finished arranging the pieces of the book on the white cloth. When my neighbor first brought it to me, the book had been dirty and wet. It had dried off now, but there were skid marks on the cover, plenty of torn pages, and the spine was dragging badly. Despite its haggard condition, I was determined to bring it back to its' former luster, because that's what I did. I'm a bookbinder and I fix books.

I spread a second protective white cloth over everything, then pushed away from the table.

Still clutching Charlie in one arm, Derek wrapped his other arm around my shoulders and kissed me warmly. Together we walked out of my workshop and into the living room.

"Give me two minutes," I said, "and I'll be ready to go."

We drove across town to the top of Pacific Heights where the magnificent Covington Library stood in all its elegantly Italianate glory overlooking the Golden Gate Bridge and the dark blue water of the Bay. At the front entrance, I stopped and took a deep breath of anticipation. The outside of the building was impressive, but walking inside was like stepping into another world. The foyer was dramatic with its gorgeous Tiffany chandeliers, black-and-white checkerboard pattern on the marble floor, and wide, sweeping stairways that led up to the second and third floors.

But then you stepped into the massive main hall and simply had to stare. I can still picture my little eight-year-old apprentice-bookbinder self, walking into this space for the first time. I had been mesmerized by the walls that were covered from floor to ceiling in gorgeous leather-bound books. At intervals across the room, glass display cases were filled with gorgeous antiquarian books and historically significant ephemera: a letter from Walt Whitman; symphony notes from Mozart; a baseball card signed by Babe Ruth.

Looking up, I was impressed as always by the coffered ceiling three floors above me. The top two floors of the library open onto the main hall and decorative wrought-iron railings lined the narrow aisles.

On occasions like tonight, there would be musicians playing up on the third floor. Guests could gaze up at the players and be treated to the performance itself as well as the amazing acoustics of the room. Usually it was a string quartet or trio playing a classical concerto or sonata, but tonight, because of the nature of this all-American event, there was a fiddler and a ragtime piano player. The tunes were what I would call old-fashioned, down-home Americana.

Standing behind the musicians tonight were four men in matching striped jackets and handlebar mustaches. I smiled at the thought that a barbershop quartet would be singing the most popular songs of the 1860s and '70s. It wasn't the usual type of musical offerings, but the crowd seemed ready for it. It would set the tone for the gala opening night of the first annual Mark Twain Festival.

Underwriting this entire five-day event was none other than our good friend Joseph Cabot, whose literary hero was another American newspaperman, Mark Twain.

To organize the five-day event, Joseph had called upon the *Clarion*'s own very talented events coordinator, Ashley Sharp. The young woman had gone into overdrive planning the numerous Twain-centered activities that would take place at the Covington and various sites all over the city for five days. It was shaping up to be one of the most ambitious, wide-ranging festivals the Covington had ever presented.

Just reading the schedule of events had sent shivers up and down my arms. If I attended every activity, I wouldn't have a free minute to call my own until the day the festival ended. But that was okay, right? It would be fun. And it was only for five days. I mentally waved away my concerns because it promised to be a total blast. Or utter chaos. Either way, it would be memorable. And I would play a role in it.

A month ago, Ian McCullough had called and asked me to come by his office. Ian was president and head curator for the Covington Library and one of my oldest and dearest friends. He wanted to talk about the two workshops I would conduct as part of the event's activities. Naturally, one of the workshops was all about bookbinding. The other was connected to my fledgling interest in paper arts. I was to give a workshop in the Children's Museum on newspaper art. I agreed to that one immediately. It sounded like pure fun, especially since kids were involved.

"Your bookbinding workshop will be a little more complicated," he said, then told me that I was to refurbish, rebind, and regild a vintage edition of *The Prince and the Pauper*, one of Mark Twain's many great novels.

Then he handed me the book. It was a mess, to say the least. "I can barely read the title. The gilding is gone. These pages aren't bad, but the whole thing is catawampus." I held it up and we watched the entire book tilt dangerously. "And you're only giving me four days to finish it?"

"Come on, you can do it in your sleep," Ian had enthused. "First of all, the book is fabulous—or it will be when you're finished with it. And here's the best part. We're going to set you up in the main hall with a live audience. You'll be holding court while you turn a *pauper* of a book into a *prince*."

I'd rolled my eyes, but I had to admit it was kind of a clever play on words.

"You're going to be on public display," Ian had continued. "You won't mind, will you? It's going to be a very popular event. We're setting up a few rows of bleacher seats for people to watch you work."

"Good thing I'm not shy," I had muttered. But seriously? Bleacher seats? In the main hall? This would be a first.

"You're talking to yourself," Derek murmured as we wound our way through the opening night crowd to find one of the three cocktail bars before the lines grew too long. "It's a sure sign you're nervous. What is bothering you?"

I frowned, a little annoyed to realize that I had an obvious "tell," while I couldn't read him at all. "You need to stop being so perceptive."

"I beg your pardon, love." He laughed, but quickly sobered. "Come now, darling. Are you nervous about this evening or about your bookbinding work this week?"

"Nervous? Me?" I thought about it. "Yes, I am. But it's not about either of those things. And I'm too embarrassed to talk about it."

He stopped me, holding my arms so he could study my expression. "Surely you can tell me."

He was right again. I could tell him anything, even if it was humiliating. "I was just thinking about the book-binding job I've been assigned to for the festival. It's not exactly glamorous."

"Glamorous?" Puzzled, he frowned at me. "But it's what you do, darling. Your work is fascinating. And despite your choice of footware, you do it better than anyone else in the world."

I smiled and squeezed his arm. "I love you, Derek."

"I love you, too, but it's simply the truth."

He gave me a quick glance. "So what are you really bothered about?"

My shoulders sagged. It was useless to try and hide my feelings from him. "Okay, here's the deal. You know I really like Joseph and I'm totally psyched that I'm going to be working the festival with him. Even if I'm not doing anything very glamorous."

"So what is it?" Derek ordered our wine and after leaving a nice tip, he handed me my wineglass. "Now, spill. Not the wine. Tell me what's bothering you."

I smiled again at that. "It's just that, well, lately, wherever Joseph is, there's Ella." Which only made sense since Ella was Joseph Cabot's wife. I winced. "I know that was a dumb thing to say."

The couple had only been married for six months so yes, they were always together. I was being ridiculous, but really, did the woman have to be six feet tall and blond and gorgeous? Did she have to speak with that sexy Swedish accent? And her wardrobe was to die for, seriously. Tonight and every night of the festival she would sashay around the Covington in some slinky designer dress while I would be stuck in a corner wearing blue jeans and my Birkenstocks. If I really thought about it, I knew I would be happier in blue jeans than in some slinky designer dress. But that wasn't the point.

Finally, I admitted, "It's demoralizing, but I can't help it. I'm completely intimidated by her."

He glanced at me sideways and nodded sagely. "So am I."

"Oh, please." I rolled my eyes. "I appreciate you trying to make me feel better, but come on. You're tall, dark, and dangerous. The original international man of mystery. You carry a gun. Nobody intimidates you."

He laughed. "She does."

I stared at him for a long moment, realized he wasn't kidding, and shook my head. "What is it about her? I mean, I can't think of the word. It's almost indefinable. Besides the looks and the hair and the attitude and . . . everything else. What is it?"

"First of all, darling, you are the most beautiful woman I have ever known."

I almost choked on my Cabernet, and that would've been a real waste because the wine was really good. He eased my glass away from me while I took a minute to catch my breath.

"And you're fun and you're funny and smart, and simply adorable," Derek said. "I love being with you."

He had said lovely things like this to me before and they never failed to thrill me. "Um, likewise," I murmured, embarrassed now.

He chuckled at my words, but then glowered. "Ella is not fun."

That stopped me. "What are you talking about?"

"The woman has no sense of humor."

I stared at him until realization dawned. He was right. "Why do you think that is?"

"Among other things, there's a language barrier."

"But she speaks perfect English," I said. "With a Swedish accent, of course, but still, perfect."

"Yes, she speaks our language and even understands it," he continued, "but she doesn't always comprehend the feelings and the meanings behind the words. She doesn't understand nuance, so our humor goes over her head and confuses her. That's why she comes across as so serious."

"I've never thought about it that way." I frowned. "What must Joseph think? He has a great sense of humor."

He pressed his lips together. "Yes, he does."

"But she wouldn't think so because she doesn't get his humor." I crooked my neck, looking up at him as I thought about it. "Wow. Now that you've said it, I'm trying to remember if she's ever laughed at anything we've said."

Derek glanced over his shoulder to make sure nobody was listening in. "Joseph and I have actually had this conversation."

"Really?"

"Yes. He says he didn't marry her for her sense of humor."

I grinned. "Okay, I can guess what he *did* marry her for." But then I winced. "I shouldn't have said that. It's not fair. I'm sure she has many lovely qualities."

Derek nodded and handed my wineglass back to me. "Joseph made it clear that she does in fact have many attributes that he finds appealing."

I shook my head in amazement. "So you guys really have had this conversation?"

"Just so we're clear," Derek said, holding up his hand. "Joseph brought up the topic."

I nodded. "I wouldn't think you'd bring it up."

"Absolutely not." He sipped his wine. "We talked about it the week before he married her. He asked for my opinion, but before I could give it to him, he forged ahead and gave me all the reasons why it was a good idea and why she was perfect for him. What could I do but agree?"

"Of course you had to agree." I took a sip of the Cabernet. "You're a good friend."

"Perhaps a better friend would've told him what I really thought. But then we wouldn't be friends anymore."

"And that would be a shame."

He looked over his shoulder. "We should change the subject before we're caught out."

"Good idea." I thought of one more thing. "But I just want to add, before we change the subject, that the worst part about my feelings for Ella is that she is at heart, I think, a nice person. She always has something kind to say."

"That is true," Derek murmured.

"If she were a witch, I would feel a lot better about my own feelings," I said, frowning.

He laughed. "I actually understand that. And now, seriously, let's switch topics."

"Yes, please."

We both glanced around the room, watching people enter the main hall and mingle with others. Everyone was looking glittery tonight, which added to the overall good feeling about this unusual festival.

A few years ago, many members of San Francisco's book-loving society would show up to these events wearing unrelieved black from head to toe. The women dressed like beatniks from the fifties with their skinny turtlenecks, black tights, and miniskirts. All that was missing was a jaunty beret. These days, though, there were delightful bursts of color throughout the crowd and they brightened up the whole room.

Derek turned and gazed at me. "Tell me, what part of the evening are you most looking forward to?"

I smiled up at him. "The part where we go home."

He lifted my hand to his lips and kissed my wrist. "Coming home to you is always the best part of any day."

I leaned against him and laid my head on his shoulder.

"Darling," he murmured, "have I mentioned lately how much I love you?"

I eased back, checked my wristwatch. "It's been a few minutes."

"Then it's well past time I told you again." He gave me a brief but meaningful kiss. "I love you."

"There you are," Ian said, rushing over to join us.

"Here we are," I said, and supposed it was just as well that we'd been interrupted. I lifted my glass in a toast. "Good party, Ian."

"Thanks, kiddo." He glanced around anxiously.

"May I get you a glass of wine, Ian?" Derek asked. "You look like you could use one."

"I totally could, but I'd better stay alert."

"Why?" I wondered. "You've got everything wired down to the last little detail. What could possibly go wrong?"

"Are you crazy?" he hissed, and slapped my arm lightly. "Don't jinx it."

"Sorry." I grinned, but as he continued to look around the room, I asked, "Who are you looking for?"

"The Swedish Bombshell."

Derek and I exchanges glances. "You must mean Ella."

"No," he whispered. "Her mother, Ingrid. Have you met her?"

"Not yet," Derek said.

"Well, apparently she's put herself in charge of tonight's agenda."

"But why is she in charge of anything?" I asked.

He glared at me. "How should I know? Maybe she used to be a party planner in Stockholm. She wanted something to do."

"Then give her a jigsaw puzzle," I suggested. "Or take her shopping." I pondered the situation, then gave up. "It doesn't make sense. Joseph would never give her that sort of responsibility, would he?"

"Not Joseph," he muttered.

"Then who?"

He was still glaring. "Have you met Ella?"

"Ah." I exchanged a quick glance with Derek. Apparently Ella's ability to intimidate was far-reaching. "Joseph's wife is formidable, to say the least."

"You have no idea."

I stroked his arm. "Just breathe."

"What about Ashley Sharp?" Derek asked. "I was led to believe that Joseph had put her in charge of the festival events."

"Ashley is a complete wonder," Ian agreed, nervously glancing around the room. "She's excellent. Brilliant. But where is she?"

Derek pulled out his cell phone. "I haven't seen Joseph yet, but I'll be happy to call and ask him to straighten things out."

"Would you?" Ian sagged with relief. "Oh, thank you, Derek. You're my hero." But his attention was suddenly diverted by some scuffle going on near the entryway. "Oh God, I've got to go put out another fire." And he darted away.

I watched him scurry off, then turned to see that Derek was still talking on the phone to Joseph.

As soon as he ended the call, I asked, "What's going on? What did he say?"

"He very calmly said that Ashley Sharp is in charge of everything. Ella and her mother have nothing to do with any aspect of the festival."

"So why is Ian so upset?"

"I have no idea. And neither does Joseph."

I frowned. "I hate to say it, but it sounds like Ella and her mother might be gaslighting Ian."

"It's possible." He slipped his arm through mine and we began another stroll around the room. "Let's keep an eye on things, shall we?"